MW01503258

SHADOW SELF

Paula Marais

Product group from well-managed forests and other controlled sources.

For my mother, Marilyn Marais, whose importance in my life cannot be expressed in just one sentence.

It was Hansen who first made me aware of shadow selves. He would lie in bed watching me for whole minutes, and I would look back into his eyes and wonder, What does he see? How can he not see the truth? Where is it hidden? It made me ask, when I looked at other people, what possible selves they were hiding behind the strange rubber masks of their faces. I could nearly always find one, if I watched for long enough. It became the only one I was interested in seeing.

– *Look at Me* by Jennifer Egan

How to plead

I'm sitting on a bench in some small room, a cramped musty space. *They're coming for you*, I hear and I look around. I can't see properly. It's like being asleep and feeling that you need to open your eyes but you can't. The more you try to focus, the more you panic, and the more out of touch you feel. I want to scratch the cataracts from my eyes, but even if I squint it's like the room is moving up and down.

A wave of room. A wave of noise.

Clattering.

Jangling.

I sit still, putting my head down between my knees.

"It's okay, Thea, I said I was here, didn't I?"

Robbie. My heart is bulging with voices, and my brother sounds exactly the same as ever. I feel seasick, leaning in a glass-bottomed boat, with fish floating around below me all dead and bloodied.

A shark dropping below me, its fin cut off, crimson and spinning.

A top, going round and round. And round and round.

Lights on. Lights off.

Lights on. Lights off.

"Ma'am, you've got to come now," and I'm not sure if it's the shark talking, but I feel a grip on my elbow, and I push it away. There's a squealing noise, like a piglet, a kettle whistle. Then I'm being lifted, floating in a balloon.

Weeeeeeeeeeeeeeeeeeeeeeeeeeeeeee . . .

"This is the courthouse, *mevrou*," that voice says. "You need to stand up now. We're going up the stairs."

"Don't want to," I say. "I need to sleep."

"Lady, after what you did, you've got a lifetime to sleep. Not much else to do in Worcester."

Worcester? What are they talking about? I'm not in Worcester – I'm supposed to be asleep with my kids and with Robbie. Didn't he promise?

"Leave me alone," I say. "I don't like you."

"Lady, I don't like you either."

I peer at him, and his face appears as though through mist.

Fat nose. Stubby eyelashes. Coffee eyes. A peaked hat.

"We're going to have to cuff you, ma'am," someone says, but I don't think it's him because his lips don't move.

"As in *hand*cuffs?" I ask Robbie.

"I think so," Robbie says. "What else could he mean? Just go, Thea. Remember how we used to play with handcuffs in the tree house? Cops and robbers?"

But that was fun and this hurts.

"No need to push me," I say, sounding like Mother.

"Listen, lady, just get a move on now. This magistrate don't like to wait."

So I walk. I don't like waiting either. And it irritates me when Clay is late. Clay, my husband. I always check my watch a thousand times and wonder why he can't respect me by arriving on time. Always another emergency at one of his coffee shops.

As I walk, each step is heavy as if my legs are in water. I wade the stairs.

Up, up.

The chains clank behind me where the policemen are standing. They're talking.

"So she told me that my son stole my car when I was attending an accident scene. *Dronk, jy weet.* And only sixteen. I found him at Muizenberg Beach. And he thought he was too old for a klap."

Mother specialised in those. My first husband was more like her than she would ever have admitted.

Violence. Bodies on bodies.

I shiver. What's that saying again? Like someone's walking over my grave.

At the top of the stairs, I walk into a uniform. The man holds me back.

"Steady on, wait until we're ready."

Go. Wait. Walk. Stop. Go. I wish they'd just make up their damn minds. Below me, the other cops chat on.

"And the car? What about it? No problems with the car? A dent in the front, *jong*. He's going to rake leaves for a year to pay for it."

Rake. My Zen garden relaxed me. Patterns in the sand. Swirls. Twirls. Until Joe tipped the sand on the lounge carpet and Clay said, *Enough of this. I don't like the grit under my feet.*

At the top, it's buzzing. Voices up and down. And the lights are so bright.

I blink, blink, blink.

There's a hand coming towards me, and then it goes away. Someone's shouting, "Keep away from the prisoner!"

"That's you," says Robbie.

"I know," I say back. "I can feel my wrists."

My oldest daughter, Sanusha, is there, I think, with her hot olive eyes shouting, *why, why, why?* And I wish Robbie would just explain it to her. It's better. For Joe. For baby Caitie. For me. Even for Sanusha.

She has her father and he'll care for her. She doesn't need *me* to save her.

The policeman's pushing me; I could feel his fingers in my ribs.

"Ouch," I say, massaging my side.

"There," he says. "Stand over there."

I'm in front of a microphone with the sound turned off. The judge – is that what he is? – is whispering to me. And I look at him, concentrating, trying hard to hear.

"Madam," he says to me.

There's my defence attorney, Tom Harper. I know *him*, have for a long time. He's smiling at me, nodding gently. But Tom's not gentle and he's confusing me. He says something to the judge and comes closer.

"Just answer the questions, Thea," he says.

"What questions? I can't hear him."

"He asked you for your full name."

"Doesn't he know it? He needs to speak up."

"Your Worship, the prisoner says she can't hear you properly."

Then the judge booms at me and he sounds like God, like Ganesha: "Madam, please state your full name for the court."

"Just do it," says Robbie. "Do what he says, and say 'sir'. Show him some respect."

"Thea June Middleton . . . sir."

"And your full address, please?"

"28c Jamieson Road, Rondebosch." (Currently incarcerated elsewhere.)

"Now I do this for the purpose of confirming you are the correct accused, and from the records in front of me, you are."

I realise Tom is standing still in front of me, facing the judge. He has his hands folded at his waist, like a contrite schoolboy. But he turns once or twice to look at me, as though I'm supposed to understand him. As I watch the judge, his mouth opens like someone blowing smoke rings at the bar.

I sniff. The room smells of hate and despair. The judge shrugs and I want to step away, step back and float on a cloud, catch a smoke ring like a Bentley Belt.

"Does the accused speak English? Why isn't she answering me?" calls the red man, man in red piping.

"Yes, Your Worship. She understands you."

"Plead, Mom!" I hear a voice and it sounds like Sanusha. Sanusha under the water I'm drowning in.

"Not guilty," I say. I think I sound firm, solid, but then the big man, Mr Law, says, "Can you repeat that please."

"Louder," says Sanusha.

"Silence, miss, this is a court. We can't have interjections from the observers."

So I clamp my mouth, like Joe used to when he didn't want to lie but didn't want to tell the truth either.

"Not you," says Tom, and now I recognise his voice.

"Oh, there you are, Tom," I say.

"Yes," he says, flint-eyed. "The plea, please, Thea."

"Not guilty," I say again.

The lawyers and prosecutors and policemen and judge all jump. They heard me this time and I laugh.

Panty boys.

Before long, the cops are escorting me down the stairs and I see Clay.

Lovely Clay looking grey.

He shakes his head at me, but all the time his eyes don't leave me, as though he can't believe it's me in front of him. I wave. Kiss-kiss.

Now I can finally go back to sleep.

Part One

Preconceptions

Sanusha (aged 5): Important family facts

I am 5 and I know 3 things about Mom:
1. Her eyes don't match.
2. Being happy is hard for her.
3. She doesn't like Asmita Ayaa. (Mom says she does but I'm not stupid.)

I know 3 things about Appa, my father:
1. He's not always at the university when he says he is.
2. He shaves 2 times a day, so he must be super-hairy.
3. He has friends who are ladies who are our little secret.

I know 3 things about me:
1. I'm not beautiful like my mother.
2. I like numbers the best.
3. I hate secrets.

3 + 3 + 3 = 9 important family facts.

    If you take 9 and make 3 groups, there are 3 in each group.

    Also, a polygon with 9 sides and 9 angles is called a nonagon. See?

    There are 9 planets in the solar system: Mercury, Venus, Earth, Mars, Jupiter, Saturn, Uranus, Neptune and Pluto, plus the sun, which is actually a burning ball of gas. Pluto is the furthest away from the sun. Mercury is the closest.

    Cats have 9 lives. (But our cat, Marmite, has only got 7 left. Appa rode over him once, and once he landed in the swimming pool and got his head caught under the pool net.) Beethoven wrote 9 symphonies, but I don't care. I hate classical music, but I love Abba, especially "Money, Money, Money" because it's about counting.

Also, 9 sounds a bit like "new". And Mom taught me 9 is *neuf* in French, *nueve* and *nuevo* in Spanish and *neun* in German.

I like the number 9.

It takes 9 months to grow a baby. So this means that when I count to 9, I can make a new start.

I would like a new start.

Mom cries a lot. We're still in this godforsaken garden flat with not enough room to swing a cat (but Mom says don't swing Marmite).

Oh, there's another thing I also know about Mom.

$3 + 1 = 4$

She's smoking in the garden under the blue gum that Appa wants to pull out because it's Australian. Appa doesn't like Australians. Also smoking. He says Mom smells like an ashtray. She carries Stimorols in her handbag to make her breath sweet but they're burny and they make my tummy growl. Appa says she'd better give up the cigarettes, or else. I'm not sure what else, but I think Mom knows. She still smokes sometimes, but she tries not to. That's another secret I have to keep.

Mom's lungs are going black inside her body, but she told me it helps her relax. Relaxing is good, but smoking is not good.

I think I should rub her feet, but she doesn't sit down long enough. Mom walks up and down the cottage like a trapped animal, peeking out the window. I don't know what she is waiting for. Sometimes Annie comes down the path, and Mom's eyes shine. When Annie leaves, Mom's eyes are dull like my shoes after a long day in the dust.

I have another granny, but she and Mom aren't friends any more so she doesn't want to meet me. Mom says I'm not missing anything, but it feels like she is lying. There are 5 things I think I am missing:

1. The other granny's beautiful house, which Mom talks about sometimes.

2. The other granny's cooking. When Appa isn't around, Mom sometimes makes food from recipes. I love oxtail, which is meat, but Appa doesn't ever eat meat.

3. Mom's old toys. She says when she was little she kept them carefully in a big wooden box at the bottom of her bed. Mom says this granny probably chucked them out, but I don't think so. Why would someone throw away toys?

4. Other photos of Mom's brother whose name was Robbie. He died when she was small. Mom only has one photo, which she took the night she left that granny. (Appa says Mom got kicked out.) So Robbie only looks like Robbie in that one photo. I don't think anyone looks the same always, even if they're dead.

5. The tree house Mom's dad made for her and Robbie. Mom says that granny chopped it out of the tree, but I saw it. One day, Mom thought I was sleeping in the car, and she drove to this big-enormous-gigantic house and then she stopped and looked at the tree for a long time. She drove away quickly when the gates started to open. When she got home, she gave me to Asmita Ayaa, and got into the bath to cry.

When I cry, and I don't cry nearly as much as I did a long time ago when I was 4, Mom holds me tight. She tells me she is filling me with love from her skin to mine. Sometimes she holds me too tight so I can't breathe nicely, but I like the way her body feels, so I turn my face to gulp some air. Appa taught me that word "gulp". He also taught me "polygon" and "nonagon". Fishes gulp in the water. Snakes gulp down whole frogs. I saw that on TV. I like TV but my grandmother, Asmita Ayaa, says I must only watch for 1 hour total a day, and because it is her TV, I have to listen to her for my obedience star on my chart. I've been thinking about it. 1 hour is 60 minutes, and there are 60 seconds in 1 minute, so 60 x 60 = 360 seconds in 1 hour.

So it's 360 seconds of TV a day. That sounds like more than 1 hour.

That's why numbers are better than words, but there are a few words I really like:

1. Smile

2. Kangaroo

3. Aeroplane

They make me feel like hot chocolate in my tummy.

*

Mom has been acting a bit funny. She is sad all the time. She wakes up sad. Even sunshine doesn't make her happy. I love sunshine – it's better than rain. When I go to see Mom, I open the curtains to let in the sunrays to make her feel happy, but it doesn't work. Sunshine always works for me. And chocolate, and bubble baths, and making biscuits in Asmita Ayaa's kitchen, because Mom's kitchen is too tiny.

I heard Appa talking to Asmita Ayaa. He was very angry with Mom; really, really furious – like when I spilt paint on his computer when I was supposed to be helping Mom hang up the washing. Why is he angry that Mom is sad? Why doesn't he hug her and make her better? Asmita Ayaa found me behind the door and told Appa he must calm down. He pinched his mouth together and picked me up, but he didn't send me love through his skin.

Appa doesn't enjoy cuddling me, but he likes cuddling my teacher at Humpty Dumpty's. He thinks I don't know. When she looks at him, her eyes are all gooey like in the cartoons. Appa doesn't get all gooey. He's got lots of ladies who like him. Once he saw some ladies on the side of the road and he stopped to say hello. Their boobs were popping out, and they had long silky legs and very high shoes. They looked in the window. One of them was chewing gum. Mom says chewing gum is not for children because they can choke. The ladies had shiny bits of gold in their smiles. I liked their make-up. It was pretty, like in the movies.

I also said hello.

One of the pretty ladies' faces changed.

"What kind of a jerk are you?" she said. "With kids in the […] car?"

She said a bad word, and I wasn't "kids". There's just one of me.

"Calm down, love. I forgot she was here."

So that hurt my feelings. I was driving with him all afternoon telling him my news about the plastic containers we need for collecting buttons, and Melanie's new doll that has hair that really grows. Also, I was telling him that "dog" begins with "d" and rhymes with "frog". I know all about rhyming, you know. 1 = fun.

"Well, I have kids and I don't bring them out here, mister. Go home to your wife."

Appa drove away and then he looked at me.

"Your mother can't even fetch you from school," he said. "Doesn't she know how busy I am? Now, don't tell Mom about this. It's just our little secret, okay?"

Years ago, when I was actually 3, I slept in the same room as Mom and Appa in the cottage. But then I heard Mom saying, "No, no, no." They were playing wrestling. Appa was on top of Mom and she pushed him back so he hit his head on the wall and then he said a naughty word and smacked Mom on the face. She cried very quietly but then I got out of my bed to hug her and tell her I was awake.

"I love you, Mom," I said. "Do you know how much I love you?"

Mom wiped her tears and smiled for me, but it didn't look like a real smile because there was blood coming from her lip. She said, "I love you too, poppet."

Appa said nothing. He lay back on the bed and switched off the light. He grunted like a piggy pig. Mom took me outside and we looked at the moon. She smoked a cigarette, but I didn't tell Appa. When we got back to the cottage, he was snoring. I don't like that because he sounds like a train going through a long tunnel.

I didn't fall asleep the whole night. Seriously. Children can do that, you know. I got up in the morning and I wasn't even a tiny bit tired. I don't know why I always have to go to bed so early.

I'm not allowed to sleep in the cottage any more. Asmita Ayaa made up a pink room for me in the house. Mom and Appa said I needed my own space.

These are the things in my bedroom:
1. Bookshelf with 5 shelves
2. Bed
3. Cupboard
4. Fairy lamp
5. Bedside table
6. Toy box
7. Art table
8. Blackboard with photos stuck on
9. Kiddies chair (purple)
10. 13 stars on the ceiling

I like my room, but Mom can't understand why we can't get our own flat where we can all be together in the same building. She doesn't actually mean *all* of us, because she wants to leave Asmita Ayaa and my grandfather Kandasamy Ajah behind, and be just 3:
1 = Mom
2 = Appa
3 = me

Appa gets cross when she says this, because why waste money when we have a perfectly good place to live and we're all very comfortable? Money doesn't grow on trees, and why doesn't she bring in some cash of her own and stop lying in bed feeling sorry for herself? Then Mom says she's 24 and married 5 years and we can't be tied to Appa's parents forever. Then Appa says he knew what he was like when she married him, and after 5 years she still doesn't make a decent curry.

I like Mom's curry.

Some days are very bad. Every day when I wake up, I always run to the cottage to say good morning, but sometimes Mom doesn't even open her eyes. I know she's not dead, because I can see her breathing with her lungs. Her lungs are inside her body getting rid of the bad air and giving her blood beautiful fresh oxygen.

Appa is normally gone when I wake up, but sometimes he has breakfast with my grandparents and me. When I don't have Humpty Dumpty's on Saturdays and Sundays and holiday time, I like to crawl into bed with Mom. She moves over without waking, but I can hear her sigh. Moving over for me is good. I can hug Mom as much as I want to, even if she doesn't hug me back.

Thea: A mother's sense

In jail I have a lot of time to think, and I don't always have control over where my mind wanders. A lot of the time, and despite myself, I think about Clay: how much I loved him, the mistakes I made.

So many mistakes! My daughters. My little boy, Joe.

But my thoughts aren't always completely clear. I think through gauze, through filters. Being locked away minute after minute, second after second (for that's how slowly time passes) has made me realise that I've spent my whole life in a fog. Some days it's like parting a thick black curtain in front of me, and just when I manage to open it and see a little light, the curtain falls closed again and I'm left in the dark.

Most people want to know where this all started, and I sometimes wonder that too. Perhaps it began the day I was conceived. I wasn't planned, nor even a wanted baby. My birth mother came from Glencairn, near Fish Hoek. Mother said I inherited my high cheekbones from her, and my breasts. The beauty spot on the right side of my face just above my top lip, the one Mother said I would tempt a man with, and my eyes – one hazel, one a blue-grey – are apparently mine alone.

But how would Mother know really? She used to tell me she only ever saw my birth mother once.

My parents adopted me when I was six weeks old. I swear I can remember my time in the womb. A hostile place, churning with bitterness and fear. At the age of sixteen, my birth mother didn't want me. A therapist once told me that even as a foetus I must have felt the intensity of her rejection. I've spent a lifetime seeking approval, and after what I've done, I'll never get it.

Once my dad told me that my birth mother called me Sofia. When I was adopted, our maid's name was Sophie, so that had to change – quickly. I'm not sure if I'll grow into Thea. Sofia seems so soft and pliant, with just the right bit of haughtiness and disdain. I wish I was Sofia. I'm not Thea, not Sofia, but something vague and impossibly in between.

I had a brother once. Robbie. He was three years older than me. He was my parents' genuine flesh and blood: my mother's blue eyes, my dad's blonde hair, my paternal grandfather's mannerisms. I remember how Robbie used to stick his tongue out the side of his mouth as he cut paper shapes at the kitchen table. Same as Gramps. Robbie was kind, and protective. Once he hid me under the stairs while we waited for Mother to calm down because I'd thrown wet toilet paper onto the ceilings down the passage – huge globules of loo roll stuck fast. When Mother started breathing again, Robbie told her that he'd done it as an experiment. And in Mother's eyes, Robbie could do no wrong.

Whenever we needed to escape, we used the tree house in the beech tree at the bottom of our garden. Dad built it for Robbie – *every boy should have a tree house* – but it was my special place more than Robbie's, especially after he got sick. I didn't know what to do then, so most of the time I tried to make myself invisible. So my parents would forget that the wrong child was dying.

Perfect, kind, beautiful Robbie throwing up in the bathroom and leaving clumps of hair all over the house until he was bald as a baby squirrel.

Home was like a mining town after the gold had ran out. I learnt to feed myself – make Bovril or peanut-butter-and-jam sandwiches, and giant cups of rooibos with milk and spooned heaps of sugar. When my parents were asleep, I'd patter down the passage, ruffling my big brother's duvet with a tentative hand.

"Thea?" I'd hear him smiling at me in the dark.

"Yes."

"Bad dreams?"

"Yes."

He'd roll over to make space for me and I'd slip into bed next to him

25

as though somehow if I held him tight enough, he wouldn't be able to leave.

When my mother found us cuddled together under Robbie's duvet, she didn't like it. Not at all.

"Get out! Robbie needs his sleep, Thea. How many times do I have to tell you?" she'd yell.

"Relax, Veronica – don't overreact," my dad would counter.

"It's inappropriate, Stuart. You know that."

"Don't be ridiculous. They're just kids. He's her *brother*."

It was only much, much later that I realised what she'd feared.

*

My mother always had a sense of what was *seemly*, and what wasn't. It was *seemly* to wear skirts to church. It was *seemly* to wear a full costume, not a bikini. Girls didn't go to discos with boys until they were sixteen. Holding hands in public, even between husbands and wives, was outrageously exhibitionistic. Tattoos were too horrendous to contemplate. Skirts without pantyhose? Never. And crying? Well, it just wasn't something you did – unless completely silently behind closed doors.

As Robbie faded away, she bit her lip, and I hated her seemliness with every inch of my unseemly body and mind.

But Robbie was a fighter, and dying didn't come naturally to him. I remember him sitting in the hospital in blue pyjamas with great white sharks all over them, entertaining the medical staff.

"Knock, knock," he said to the nurse.

"Who's there?"

"Isabel."

"Isabel who?"

"Isabel out of order? I had to knock."

I thought he was absolutely hilarious.

Dad didn't want to expose me to it all – the retching, the chemicals, the IV units and beep-beeps of heart-rate monitors. Mother said it would be good for me to understand what Robbie was going through. So I'd sit at his bedside, drawing stick-like dinosaurs that he put up around his bed with Prestik.

When Robbie was at his worst, Mother forgot to fetch me from school.

I was in Sub B by then, and I sat near the gate on my satchel, watching the sun go down and wondering what Robbie would do if he were me. I imagined he would try to walk home: pick himself up and find his way back.

I knew the landmarks but it was raining, hard.

I missed a turn, got lost. A man with no front teeth and a Pick 'n Pay trolley piled high with his belongings found me crying next to a dumpster overflowing with shattered glass bottles. He smelt of beer and sweat and I was frightened of him, but he lifted me gently onto his trolley and took me to the local cop shop.

Who are you and where do you come from?

I didn't know then that this question would plague me my whole life.

My mother apologised, truly horrified by her forgetfulness. She bought me my own world globe to cheer me up and pointed out countries she'd been to: France, Germany, New Zealand.

But she wasn't really present. Her eyes were misted over, and her conversation was confused and garbled, as though she couldn't straighten out her thoughts in her own mind.

What if it was me? I wanted to ask, but was too scared to hear the answer.

*

Robbie hung on, tough as steel-capped boots. When his immune system was weak, I wasn't allowed near him. Not with my snotty nose, and tendency to pick up stomach bugs at school. I spent my afternoons with Dad, riding around the neighbourhood in his bakkie as he supervised his team installing taps and toilets, and unblocking putrid, smelly drains.

My mother seemed ashamed of what my father did. If asked, she said he was an entrepreneur.

"I'm a *plumber*, Veronica. It pays the bills."

"Well, Stuart, there's just no reason to go on about it. Anyway, you own a successful business."

"Yes. A *plumbing* business, which gets you your twice-a-year holidays and expensive private schools for the kids."

On days when Dad had meetings I stayed at home with the maid. Not Sophie – she'd already left. Dad would leave me plastic elbow joints and plumbing pipes to fit together. I liked it. I concocted intricate symmetrical designs all over the bedroom floor, and they seemed too beautiful to break.

"It's not ladylike, Stu. I bought her dolls to play with."

"They're plastic tubes, for crying out loud. It's not like they've been used."

I was the baby in the family but I didn't like baby dolls. Children didn't fascinate me as a child the way they did Joe when he was a toddler. In fact, I ignored them completely. I longed for a pet – a dog, a hamster. Or silkworms even.

"Unhygienic," said Mother. "It won't be good for Robbie."

Never mind that when Robbie was up to it, we'd go for walks in Kirstenbosch, and Robbie and I would disappear under the oak trees to dig for earthworms. Once, we found a rotting sugarbird, all maggoty and bloodied, and he picked it up.

"So this is what will happen to me," my big brother said. "Unless they cremate me." He meant our parents. Mother would have told him to stop talking like that, but I didn't. "I want to have a bench," Robbie said, "with my name on it. Right here under the trees."

Of course Robbie wasn't allowed to raise the subject. Not ever. And when the time came, the bench never happened because my mother bit down on her already grooved lips and looked away.

But I realise that understanding a mother's sense of helplessness with a sick child is almost impossible unless you've experienced it yourself. The closest I got was chicken pox, with Sanusha scratching raw wounds into her perfect, unblemished skin but it wasn't as if *that* was life-threatening.

It takes a mother like me to achieve that.

Holidays happened less often after Robbie got sick. He couldn't face the long journeys, and the airlessness of the back seats of the car or the humming air-conditioning on planes. The stares of strangers didn't really bother him. Little children would walk past and point. *Look Mommy, he has no hair.* Robbie didn't hide under caps or bandanas, though of course Mother wanted him to. *Darling, there's no reason not to wear this one, it's very smart.* Both Robbie and I knew it was nothing to do with "smartness". She hated our family to stand out. One move into the Spur (which was already a step down for her) and we instantly had extra balloons and colouring pages. We all knew why. On the playground, kids studied Robbie curiously.

"Wanna feel it?" Robbie offered.

And one child after the next would touch his head, tentative fingers over the bumps and grooves of his skull.

"What's wrong with you?" a child asked once.

"Cancer."

"Oh." His forehead crumpled, then: "I've got Fizzers. Want one?"

Even though I was only five, I remember a particular holiday Robbie did manage, in the earlier years, when our family had its closest stab at normalcy: 1970 somewhere near Knysna. Rising early every day, Robbie, who was nine, and I would walk to the beach, our reluctant dad in tow. He never was a morning person, and Mother needed time to titivate, as he called it. She'd join us later, her make-up perfect, her face protected under a huge sun hat, giant sunglasses shading her eyes.

It was only on holiday that Mother relaxed enough not to criticise our every move. In fact, on some days she was quite transformed, picking up the Frisbee and tossing it with practised strokes that had us ducking, diving and exhausted within half an hour. She even dived after the Frisbee into the water once, sending Robbie and me into peals of laughter when her fancy pink hat flopped over her face. The hat dried all wonky, so after that Mother only wore it in the garden when she was killing those yellow-and-black rose beetles by dropping them into methylated spirits.

Those beetles came back every year, and Robbie always refused to have anything to do with the extermination. So I'd go get the tightly closed meths bottle and the jars from the garage, and Mother and I bonded in our killing fields with our own brand of Agent Orange – except ours was purple.

Robbie adored teasing Mother, and sometimes he had her giggling like a girl. She would ruffle her hands across his head, and comment on how well he was catching a ball or writing or building his LEGO. But I liked being at the beach with her more than anything else. She was very concerned about my skin, and would rub sun cream over the parts of my body not covered by my swimming costume. I loved the touch of her hands on those days; gentle, yet thorough. It made me feel cared for, loved.

Dad would sit on his towel with the day's paper – he was a bit of a news addict. "Not sure what that Ringo Starr is going to do now the Beatles have disbanded," he'd say, or, "Does Vorster seriously think this Bantustan thing is going to work?"

He wouldn't expect an answer, but sometimes Mother would smile at him and say something surprising like, "Ringo was a star drummer before he even became part of the Beatles. He wrote 'Octopus's Garden', you know." Where Mother got titbits like that I never knew, but she *was* an avid reader, something she passed on to Robbie but not to me.

I could never sit still long enough to bother. Besides, I just liked the sound of her voice as we sat on either side of her for our bedtime story. She could make her voice boom like she was talking down an amplifier, or go soft and silky like a snake. Robbie, always more affectionate, would throw his arms around Mother and kiss her on the cheek.

"I love you overcountable to infinity," he would tell her.

"You too, kiddo," she said back.

Every afternoon on our holiday, Mother would disappear for a few hours. At first we looked forward to it, because we knew Dad would sneak us an ice cream, despite the fact that we were supposed to be on a special diet that Mother's cancer support group had recommended for Robbie.

When it came to being ill, Robbie wasn't like me. He submitted to Mother's care with a patience I longed for. He seemed able to do things for the simple reason that it made others happy. And Robbie made me happy like nobody else ever would or could.

The holiday seemed to make Robbie stronger. He didn't tan as easily as I did, but within a week his body was browner and less ghostly. He made enough friends for both of us. I trailed behind him like a spoilt pet, joining in volleyball and Frisbee games with the big kids, when Robbie could manage them.

At night we shared a room in the self-catering unit our parents had rented, and Robbie would read to me by torchlight or scare me with ghost stories, setting my imagination racing with images of blood, guts and gore. Together we created a fantasy world entirely obscure to my parents, which delighted us all the more.

Yet despite these pockets of joy, there remained a tension we couldn't escape. My mother couldn't keep her eyes off Robbie, so concerned that he would tire or hurt himself. And when my dad eventually lugged a deck chair down to the beach for her, she couldn't relax, was constantly reaching for the sunscreen, and sipping obsessively from a large bottle of water. In the afternoons, she ordered us off the beach to rest.

And she prayed. A lot. Perhaps even on the beach. We said grace before every meal: *Thank you for the delicious food. May it bring good health to Robbie and help him through his recovery. Amen.* I didn't resent the lack of a mention for the rest of the family: it seemed right that God's attention should be on my brother. But it also seemed that Mother was spending a great deal more time with God than with Robbie. She would walk or drive to the nearest Catholic church for confession every afternoon, returning hours later – cheeks red, eyes bloodshot – to help herself to a whiskey. Dad would open a bottle of wine for dinner and she'd drink a lot more of it than he did. Thinking about it now – and I have enough time to do that – I wonder if those copious amounts of water and the lie-ins on that holiday were the after-effects of an almost constant hangover. Ironically, this only continued while Robbie was alive and it didn't seem to affect her management of our household.

It took my dad's heart attack to change that.

*

At school I had one special friend.

Annie was the purest sunshine. She was blonde, and pale, with sparkling white teeth, and thick glasses that perched on her nose so she looked constantly curious. Though she wasn't beautiful, she drew people to her like gravity. For reasons I never understood, she locked onto me. She didn't care about my constant need to impress every-body: the best Barbie, the most books, the prettiest clothes. At thirteen, I would be the first person in our class to lose her virginity – and to a boy three years older than me, who went to Bishops, and whose parents had three BMWs and a palace just next to Kirstenbosch.

Annie was captain of the netball team and a provincial swimmer. Most of the time she had a salmon-pink slice off the skin of her nose, and freckles from spending too much time in the sun. She wore her socks rolled into sausages over her ankles, and sewed up the hem of her skirt so it just covered her bum. Annie organised sleepovers and could cook the meanest Thai curry – with prawns!

She is also the person who introduced me to my first husband, Rajit – perhaps one of the only things about our friendship I truly regret. Of course, Sanusha would resent my saying that, for obvious reasons. Sanusha can bristle even at the slightest comment; she's always been so *touchy*.

As far as I recall, Rajit and Annie knew each other from some inter-schools debate on whether the British Royal Family were entitled to privacy since the recent birth of Prince William. They were on opposing teams. Annie's team won (of course), but he took the beating so well that she invited him to a party that weekend at her house in Rondebosch. It went without saying that I would be there. One look at Rajit and I thought I was in love. He was a delicious boy, even then – dense eyelashes, almond-pool eyes, and taller than me, which in those days was unusual. His skin didn't have a trace of acne, and he already had wide shoulders, a perfect narrow waist and a voice for radio. Later, when we were first married, we would lie in bed and I would listen to the rumbling of his deep baritone. Just that voice alone could make my stomach twist tighter than a French braid.

That night, Rajit noticed me immediately, just as Annie had expected him to. Annie liked to matchmake and the fact that he was Indian attending a party in the less-than-liberal Southern Suburbs made it even more exciting. My parents hated the very idea of him immediately; my friends thought I was daring as hell.

"It's not that I'm racist, darling," Mother said, "but just think of the *cultural differences*! What about *Christmas*?"

My dad said less, which meant more. It wasn't like him to be so silent on this sort of issue, especially when it was clear he agreed with Mother. Actually, it wasn't so long afterwards that he dropped down dead on the contour path near Rhodes Memorial. He'd been training for the Argus with his mate Denzel, who then told me I was the death of my dad, with my wild ways, terrible marks, and cavorting with that "curry muncher".

I guess that makes me guilty of patricide, too.

It wasn't as if Rajit was the only boy I'd *cavorted* with. Boys lusted after me and didn't have to wait long either. After a day on the beach we'd go to parties disguised as sleepovers (I told Dad I was staying at Annie's house while she told her parents she was at mine). I'd stand around with my smokes and my new BIC lighter bought on the sly from the Spar. Lighting up, I'd adjust my boob tube and return a precise glance to the boys who interested me.

In those starlit evenings, everybody would be getting drunk on rum and Coke or boxed wine. I usually chose the wine, sipping it quickly until my head spun. Greg-Dave-Fabio-Adriaan-Grant-Costa would soon have his arm around me, making me feel special. He'd say things like, "Isn't she gorgeous?", "Look who I found, isn't she something?", "God, you're hot", and for those few hours of fondling and casual, unprotected sex, I didn't doubt myself. It isn't easy to feel confident when your mother always tells you not to be full of yourself.

But it was after all those boys that I married Rajit, at the age of eighteen, in a red sari encrusted with turquoise beads and embroidered with thick gold thread. His mother, Asmita, bought it for me on a trip to Jaipur.

And what else could I do? My matric was so poor there was no way I was going to university, not that I was interested. In class at school I had dreamt about travelling – about Galápagos, Antarctica and Route 66. And when I wasn't doing that, I was thinking about Rajit and his naked body against mine in the back of his father's Honda Ballade. (It's amazing what you can get up to right under your parents' noses.) I'd had no inclination at all to read my set works, and no patience with studying. History was dull, maths was incomprehensible, Afrikaans was tedious and I enjoyed the biology I was learning with Rajit a lot more than fungal spores and the life cycles of amphibians. Geography was my only saving grace.

But I was map reading my way out of there when I hit a dead end.

*

Sanusha.

Though half of her DNA is mine, after she was born she looked and acted nothing like I did. For one thing, she's incredibly clever, like her father, whose brilliance was one of his main attractions until he started belittling me with it. Sanusha was a bit on the chubby side, so the combination of striking intelligence and, well, porkiness meant that she was often bullied by the little bitches she went to school with. Unlike me, Sanusha was lucky enough not to care what anybody thought, or at least she put a lot of effort into pretending that she didn't.

Rajit chose Sanusha's name, which we didn't know the meaning of, though he told her it meant "Princess". Physically, she resembled his mother in every way – a more exact version of Asmita would have been difficult to create.

I didn't like it; I wanted my daughter to be a younger, better version of me.

My pregnancy was the final straw for Mother. She was standing next to the kitchen sink chopping onions when I came home to tell her. Raj and I had decided I should do it alone – since my parents hated the very sight of him, his presence on Upper Torquay Avenue was scarce.

The one and only family supper we'd ever had – a year earlier, when we'd started going out – had been something of a disaster. I remember how my dad had put out his hand to shake Rajit's and how he'd then wiped his palm on the back of his jeans, his nose flaring ever so slightly the moment they separated. Dad liked bone-crushing handshakes, shows of strength and manliness; Rajit was the kind of guy who filed his nails. That was one of the things I liked about him, his long gentle fingers, his manicured cuticles.

"Wet fish," I heard Dad tell Mother in the kitchen.

Then we sat down at the dinner table. Because of Rajit, for the first time in my life, I noticed the room from somebody else's point of view. My mother was very into lineage, even if it wasn't all her own. On the sideboard, rather than the usual bowl of fruit and odd condiments, my mother had endless family portraits. Lined up in silver and gilt frames were my – well, Robbie's – ancestors, all stiff collars, tight hair, unsmiling poses for the camera. In amongst them was the odd grin, one or two spontaneous shots, people caught off guard, their emotions captured for all eternity (and I was sure I hadn't imagined the look of under-standing between my much younger grandmother and a man who was apparently my grandfather's older cousin). But even more noticeable was how *white and similar* they all looked. It was probably for that reason that my favourite photo had always been the one of my mother's grandfather at a hunting lodge in Rajasthan: Indian men with their tur-bans and elegant moustaches, handling shotguns while hunting dogs yapped at their feet. I liked to imagine myself in that exotic scene.

On the table, Mother had laid out her best china, her silverware that our maid spent hours cleaning – usually with a cross face and a longing look out the window where the sun was shining and the gardener was mowing the lawn. Mother had put out a bowl of flowers and candles, but the whole combination seemed intimidating rather than welcoming, even to me. Like she was trying to chase away this unwelcome boyfriend with drapery, Czech crystal and sparkling cutlery. She'd dressed for dinner so that Rajit, wearing jeans and a T-shirt, looked ridiculous.

Imperious, my mother stared across at Raj, as though daring him to pick up the wrong knife, while my dad, doing his uncomfortable best in a smart jacket and trousers, offered his only insight into the Indian population: "I do love a good curry."

Silence.

"I'm glad," Rajit smiled eventually, his beautiful teeth white against his dark skin. "I always enjoy a vindaloo. The hotter the better."

Recognising the mockery in Raj's voice, I kicked him under the table. He smiled at me and winked.

Silence.

"Rajit's going to study actuarial science," I tried.

Dad's face was blank. "What the hell is that?"

"Darling," Mother patted his giant paw.

"I want to work with numbers," Rajit said.

"What, like in a bank?"

"Not necessarily," Rajit said.

"Can I serve you?" Mother said, indicating the perfectly matched tableware piled high with potatoes, and broccoli, salad and meat. Lots of meat.

"Raj is a vegetarian," I piped up.

My dad blanched and my mother pushed back her chair. It was a definite movement, but the chair didn't make a noise on the wooden floor.

"Dear me," she said with a look I knew well. "Thea, please come help me in the kitchen – I seem to have forgotten the gravy."

I followed her meekly.

"You don't think you could have mentioned the fact he doesn't eat meat?" she hissed, cornering me near the pantry.

"He didn't want me to make a fuss."

"Well, now *I'm* making a fuss. What do I feed him?" she said, as she swung open the fridge door. It thudded loudly. She bent down, pulling out a packet of brown mushrooms.

"Don't bother, Mother. He'll just not eat the meat."

"Are you trying to bring shame to this household? Do you absolutely *insist* on embarrassing me? Is that what you want?"

"You didn't even want him here, Mother. I didn't want to make more work for you."

"Everything about you involves work," Mother shoved a pan onto the stove, turning on the gas. She poured in olive oil, chopped in onions and garlic. The mushrooms. Lemon juice. Mixed herbs. I could see the tension in her shoulders. She was stiff as a shop-window mannequin, her face plastic. Then turning abruptly, she shoved me forward, bumping my arm against the counter. "Go to the dining room and help your father. I'll come in a moment."

"Right."

In the dining room, neither man was speaking. I caught Rajit's eye as I walked in and shrugged. Dad leant forward, elbows on the table, and glugged down his wine in a single gulp.

"So, why are you here, exactly?" Dad said, pushing the bottle towards Raj, who shook his head almost imperceptibly.

"I like your daughter," Raj said softly.

"So do I," Dad said, "but I'm not sure I like you."

"Dad!" I said.

"Quiet, Thea – this is between me and this young man."

"I wouldn't say that, exactly," Raj countered. "Thea has a right to an opinion."

My father rammed his fist onto the table and porcelain clinked. "I know what's best for my daughter!"

"Maybe I'm what's best for her," Raj said.

"I wouldn't exactly say you have the life experience to know that."

Rajit lifted his chin, and looked my father squarely in the eyes. It was like watching two rhinos squaring off. Dad glared at Rajit and Rajit didn't flinch. In fact, I think he may have moved slightly forward, which seemed to confuse Dad, who blinked and then immediately sat back.

"You have siblings?" he attempted mildly.

"Two younger sisters," Raj said as he relaxed into his chair. "Layla is fifteen and Kesiree is sixteen."

"And what do your parents do?"

"My dad's a teacher. My mom's in litigation."

"A lawyer?" Dad said, as he bit hard on his fork. He sloshed some more wine into his glass, gulped it down.

"Yes." Rajit sipped his Coke.

My mother scuttled back in the room carrying her best platter and brown mushrooms piled on a bed of couscous.

"Rajit," she said, "you eat mushrooms?"

"Thank you, Mrs Malan. That's great."

Of course, nothing Rajit did could impress my parents – including eating mushrooms, which he'd always told me tasted slimy and reminded him of black slugs. If he'd hovered cross-legged above the table and juggled fire, Dad would have just glared at him, and Mother would have said it was getting late.

Not that it got late. The Cape's summer sun was still shining by the time dinner was over, the atmosphere was so tense that I'd developed the beginnings of a migraine. I rubbed my palms against my temples, wishing, not for the first or last time in my life, that Robbie was there. Even charming Rajit seemed to be taking strain. Beneath the tablecloth I gripped his hand tightly.

"Well," Mother said, after another pained silence. "How about some coffee?"

Rajit tried one of his winning smiles. "No, thank you, Mrs Malan."

"You're going to tell me you don't drink coffee either?" Dad asked. "What the hell is wrong with a cup of coffee? You should have a cup. Put some hair on your chest."

Rajit's eyebrows rose. "That really is a wonderful offer, sir, but I've got an assignment I need to do still. I should probably get home before it gets too dark."

"Your parents let you ride your bike at night?" Mother said.

"Sometimes they work late."

"Ahhh," said Mother, as if that explained everything. "Busy parents."

"Yes, I guess so."

"I'll walk you to the door," I said, hoping for a kiss away from my parents' disapproval.

My dad stood up, not offering his hand this time. He nodded briskly. "Rajit."

"Sir. Mrs Malan, thank you for a delicious meal."

Outside the front door, Raj took me in his arms.

"That went well," he said, starting to laugh.

"I'm glad you still have your sense of humour," I said.

"I see I'm going to need it." And then his body was against mine, his lips opening to envelop me. "I've got something to give you before I go," he whispered. "Something to remember me by." He placed a little package in my hand.

It was his serviette, neatly folded, containing his remaining mushrooms.

*

And then, just a few months later it seemed, it was just Mother and me in the kitchen, different mushrooms waiting uncooked in a polystyrene tub next to the sink.

If my mother blamed me for Dad's death, she didn't say, but her experience of loss made her increasingly distant: two deaths in her nuclear family. Both people more important than me.

"Can I help with something?" I asked.

She looked at me, a tight smile crossing her lips. "What about a salad?"

I nodded, took lettuce, cucumber and tomatoes out the fridge.

I noticed a glass of whiskey, no ice. Drinking alone because there was no one else to drink with.

"What are we having?" I asked.

"Risotto."

"Great."

Mother had let a lot slip, but her culinary talents were still sharp. Glassy onions sizzled in the pan; in a bubbling pot asparagus became a brighter, deeper green. We worked systematically, silently. Cooking was the one thing we could do together without arguing.

Mother had her "wireless" in the kitchen. She listened to Springbok Radio from first thing in the morning when we could hear Eric Egan calling out his favourite catch phrase "I looooveee yoouuu", until well into the evening after the news bulletin at seven sharp. The radio was a relief. It eased the tense silence, but not completely. I cut the cucumber skin in alternating stripes of dark and light, as Mother insisted, then sliced it up.

"You're home early," Mother commented as she measured cups of Arborio rice into the pot.

I knew that was a dig. I'd become one of those clichéd teenagers using the house like a hotel. In for meals and dropping off my washing, then out, out, out. At home, I couldn't stand the intensity of my mother's stare, or the memory of the past we shared that she seemed to have conveniently forgotten. I was trying forgive her for the way she'd treated me, but I wasn't like her – I wasn't blessed with a walk-in confessional and the knowledge that a few Hail Marys would sort out anything.

"I wanted to see you," I told her.

"Really?" Mother looked up at me, her plucked eyebrows arched. "Why?"

"Well, we haven't spent much time together."

"I should never have given you your father's car. I should have sold it. Every time you roar up the drive I think it's him."

She didn't need to say any more. Even the act of coming home pained her.

"Maybe we should sell it then," I suggested. "Get something else."

"It's not every eighteen-year-old that has a car. When I was your age, I caught a bus. Or I walked. When your father and I were courting I used to walk from Bishopscourt to Mowbray with a book just to see him. I could read two chapters en route."

I'd heard that before. My lack of interest in reading was another of her disappointments. We didn't swap books like other mothers and daughters, or visit the library together filling baskets with hardbacks.

"You must miss him terribly," I told her.

"He was my soulmate," she said simply, "which is something you'll need to be a little older to understand."

"I love Rajit, Mother," I said.

"Love!" she replied, pouring a cup of Chenin Blanc into the pot, then slowly adding the water from the asparagus. "What do you understand about love?"

"You weren't much older than me when you met Dad."

Mother stirred, turning down the temperature on the hob. I sliced through a tomato, just pricking my finger. Blood pumped to the surface and I licked it off. Why did conversations with Mother always taste so rusty and metallic?

"I was a woman when I met your dad. You're just a girl."

My face burned, a red-hot flush coming to the surface. "I'm pregnant, Mother, so I guess I'm going to have to grow up."

She switched off the stove, pushed the pot to one side. Then she turned, her pinched face just under control, and slapped me across the face.

"You little slut," she said. "Every day I pray you'll turn into a better person. And now this."

I touched my cheek, uncertain if there would be more violence, instinctively moving away from the knife still lying on the chopping board.

"I'm not a slut. Rajit's the dad. I love him. He loves me."

"He's not the first guy you've slept with, Thea – I'm not a fool. I know your reputation. It follows me every time I go to church. I've prayed for you so many times."

"I've changed."

"Really? You think you know that boy. You don't, Thea. You know nothing about him."

"I can learn."

"You're going to learn the hard way."

Mother brought her face so close to mine that I could see the blood vessels in her eyes. Then she grabbed my wrists, banging me hard against the cupboard, my back against the door handle, a shock of pain down my spine. Letting my wrists go, she grabbed a handful of my primped-up hair, and slammed my head against the cherry-wood cabinet.

Once.

Twice.

Three times.

Dizzily, I tried to push her away, but felt the crushing weight of her stiletto through my foot. I winced, tried not to cry out.

I knew these moods. Play dead. Be limp. But this time I couldn't do that. What if she hurt my baby? With all the force I could muster, I pushed her away. Mother's face registered shock and she stepped back for only a moment before pushing her face into mine.

"You're a filthy whore, Thea. Just like your mother." Mother tucked her hand under my chin and her fumes filled my face. "Get rid of it," she hissed. "Get rid of that baby or I will never forgive you."

I longed for Dad then, the soft-spoken reason he offered when he dared disagree with Mother. I was crying and I tried to stop, but the sobs rose in my throat, almost choking me.

I gasped. "What are you saying?"

"You know damn well what I'm telling you. Abort it. I won't have a crossbreed bastard in this family."

"I thought Catholics don't believe in abortion."

"That's not a baby – it's a mistake."

"I'm going to marry Rajit, Mother. We've already decided."

"Over my dead body. You think raising a baby is easy? Marriage? Your father would be turning in his grave. God only knows how ashamed I am of you. I plucked you off the streets, raised you like my own and this is what you do to me?"

"I won't kill my own child. I won't."

And I need someone to love me.

My mother straightened her skirt, ran her fingers through her hair.

"You've got twenty-four hours to think about it. If you do what I say, I'll pay for it and all will be forgotten. But if you marry Rajit and keep that spawn, then pack your bags, my girl. I do not want you in my life."

Sanusha (aged 5 ½): Some top things to know

One day, Auntie Annie took Mom to the doctor and he gave her some happy pills. They're like magic, because some days Mom smiles a real smile even more than once. She even laughs. When Mom smiles she is really, really pretty. When she doesn't smile she is still pretty, but not quite as good. I'm not pretty even if I smile. My mom is tall and skinny – she has the longest legs. I am short and round. I look like Asmita Ayaa and even though I love Asmita Ayaa around the world 10 times, I'm not happy that I look like her.

Here are the 5 top things I know about my grandmother:

1. When we rent a video, Asmita Ayaa sits next to Appa on the couch with Kandasamy Ajah on the other side. Mom sits on her own or sometimes with me.

2. Asmita Ayaa plays with Appa's hair and calls him "my boy" even though he is a grown-up. Then Mom gets irritated and bites her nails.

3. There is more of Asmita Ayaa to cuddle than there is of Mom.

4. Asmita Ayaa was a lawyer once. Now she is the boss of us. Mom wants her own house so she can be the boss of us instead.

5. Ayaa's skin bumps up and down like the moon, and make-up doesn't help it look better. I'm not allowed to talk about that.

Asmita Ayaa and Mom get on better when Appa is away at the university. When Appa comes home, it feels like a running race of who's going to get to Appa first. Mom kisses him (on the mouth) and Asmita Ayaa hugs him. He smiles and picks me up and tells me I am his princess. Then he goes to the cottage for a shower and a shave. When he is finished, the dinner is on the table. (We hardly ever eat in the cottage.) Appa eats fast and smacks his lips so it sounds like girlfriend-and-boyfriend smooching on TV. He has food dripping on his chin, but he doesn't clear it off like he's supposed to. We all eat with our hands, except Mom, who uses a knife and fork. At the end of dinner, Appa is tired and doesn't help clear, because that's women's work.

I don't understand about Appa's job. Mom says he's studying and working to pay the bills.

Since the happy pills, Mom has also been studying. She's a tour guide and now she is going to use her French that my other granny made her learn at school.

In the mornings Mom goes to a place in town where she says "*bonjer*" and "*ohrevwor*". Sometimes she brings back children's books from the library and reads to me in French. I like the pictures. Mom says she is going to make something of herself, but I don't know what you can make when you are already something. And when will she spend time with me if she's so busy *making it in this world*?

Now that Mom smiles sometimes, she takes me to the park after Humpty Dumpty's. This means I get to slide and swing for an extra hour every day unless it's raining. I like the ladder that goes right into the branches of a tree the best, but because I'm so short, it's difficult for me to get back down. Mom has to catch me and she doesn't even care if I get mud on her clothes. We get home all dirty and we jump in the bath together. Mom's skin is lighter than mine, but it isn't perfect under her clothes. She has bruises. They change colour: red, blue, green. One of her newest ones is the shape of Africa, and Mom showed me Egypt and tells me about the pyramids where there are stacks of dead bodies wrapped up in white cloth. They're kings and queens, so they don't go into the ground or get burnt like Amoy Ayaa, although I'm too young to remember her. Mom says she is very clumsy because she bumps herself when she tries to go to the toilet at night without switching on the light. I wish she would be more careful.

"You could turn on the light," I say, touching the bruises on her tummy.

"What?"

"Turn on the light, when you go for a wee."

She looks at me, but she's only pretending to smile.

"Good idea," she says. "I'll try that."

With Mom, both of us pretend a lot, because she pretends to listen and I pretend to believe her.

When we get out the bath, we choose clothes that match. We like to wear the same colours, and my favourite colour is pink. Mom's favourite colour is also pink, so that's good. We wear pink all the time, and yesterday Mom bought a new jersey, which is soft as a bunny rabbit. She looks extra beautiful in it and she touches it like she loves it as much as I do.

Here are some other favourite colours:

1. Appa's favourite colour is black, but I don't think that's a good colour. Black is dark and scary and night.

2. Asmita Ayaa loves red like a fire engine.

3. Kandasamy Ajah says why am I bothering him, a colour is a colour. So I think that even grown-ups can be wrong. A colour is not any colour, or why would we choose different paints at Humpty Dumpty's?

Mom is not studying all the time. Some mornings, when she isn't learning "*bonjer*", she takes tourists around Cape Town. A tourist is a visitor who doesn't live there. If I was in Durban, on a sight-seeing boat that's what I'd be. In Cape Town I am not a tourist so I am not allowed to go with Mom on her special bus rides. I don't think that's fair because buses have lots of seats and I am only little. But Mom says these strangers like to be private and don't want other people's children on the bus. Meanies. Asmita Ayaa said it's good manners to share but maybe they have different manners where these people come from.

Appa drops Mom off at the bus so she doesn't have to leave her car where the buses park. He always says hello to all the tourists and tells them he is Mom's husband. Sometimes I wait in the car.

I have another word for bus: coach. Appa and I read it off the side of the bus. *Coach tours.* That means going round Cape Town with Mom.

These are the 7 top things to do in Cape Town:

1. Table Mountain. You can go up in a cable car, which is like a train hanging from a rope that goes up to the top and down again.

2. Greenmarket Square. You can buy things there and there are lots of people, so you mustn't let your mom's hand go. You might get lost or stolen by baddies.

3. 2 seas meeting. You drive a long way to see 2 seas mixing. It's the tip of Africa, but not really because Mom says there's another tip somewhere else. You can watch divers swimming in the water with seaweed and baboons can steal your picnic because one baboon ate my bread roll and it was cheese and jam, my favourite.

4. Kirstenbosch. This is a big garden with proteas and bushes, and mountains in the back. There is a bath we are not supposed to climb in. (Once Appa let me put in my toes.)

5. Grape farms – if you drive for like 2 years you get to this place where people drink wine in little glasses you get to keep. Children don't drink wine, of course. We drink grape juice. Red is the best. I already said colour is super-important.

6. Company Gardens. The man built a castle and he also planted fruit trees to feed the sailors so they wouldn't get not-enough-vitamins disease. There are lots of old-fashioned buildings there. My best place has all those paintings. We go there sometimes when it is raining. Mom tells me stories and makes me laugh.

7. Seal Island. You can visit it on a boat that leaves from Hout Bay. I went once and the seals are cute but *very* smelly. I saw a dead one floating.

When Mom comes home from her work, Appa always asks her lots of questions because he is very curious. Appa likes numbers like me, so he asks things like: How long did you spend at Kirstenbosch? How many people arrived? How long did it take to get back? He also likes to know a lot of things about them: Where do they come from? Were they a family? Will Mom be meeting them again?

Mom answers all the questions, but she looks bored. When Appa can't drop Mom off, we go to the coach (new word!) with Asmita Ayaa. Mom says thanks quickly, and jumps out. Sometimes she forgets to kiss me she's in such a hurry.

Sometimes Mom takes a small group with a driver, who is a friend of Appa's, called Lankesh. Mom takes the tourists and Lankesh waits in the car. If they have lunch in a fancy restaurant, he eats takeaways in the car. Mom doesn't like Lankesh. He's not handsome like Appa, and she says he smells funny. Appa laughs and says she's a fussy little thing. No one knows the back streets like Lankesh. I wonder where the back streets are, and if they are the back ones, where do you find the ones at the front?

Thea: Learning to be a good wife

When I married Clay, we had enough between us to start life independently. But with my first marriage we had nothing, so Rajit and I moved into his parents' house. Asmita and Kandasamy renovated the little granny cottage in the garden. It had its own little kitchen, with a microwave – a bit of a novelty, then – a two-plate hob and tiny oven. The double bed was moved from the main house, but always seemed too short for me. When I woke up in the morning I'd feel my feet peeping over the end of the mattress. When I mentioned it to Rajit, he tucked the duvet under my feet after kissing me gently on each toe, though he probably had the same problem.

"Best I can manage," he said.

It wasn't going to improve my sleep anyway. The baby woke up the moment I lay down, jumping on my bladder until I couldn't last an hour without a pee.

Although my mother hadn't taught me much about love, I really thought that watching her had taught me how to cook. I'd seen her often enough, a wisp of hair tucked behind her ears, an apron tied over her twinsets and pearls. What I hadn't discovered yet, and would soon, was that nothing I cooked could satisfy Rajit. Consulting a vegetarian cookbook I'd found at a second-hand bookshop, I set to work winning over his palate. Butternut risotto was "too sweet', asparagus quiche "had a weird texture". Aubergines – in any form – were "meaty", "too rich" and "actually rather disgusting". Sweet corn soup was "insipid". I made bread, which "made his stomach blow up" and pasta that was "overdone".

On her way back from campus, Annie put her feet up on our bed and ate the leftovers.

"Delish!" she would exclaim about almost everything.

"You're a poor student – not very fussy."

"Have you ever thought Raj might just be *too* fussy?"

Rajit didn't like Annie to be there when he came home from the days he spent at UCT.

"I want to spend time with *you*, not Annie," he told me.

"I get lonely," I said.

"Do something with my sisters," Rajit said. "Kesiree adores you." He dug in his pocket and extracted some cash he'd earned tutoring. "Go to the movies, the two of you. I've got an evening lecture tomorrow. I'll get Amma to lend you the car."

When we got back in the early evening, Rajit was already waiting for us in his mother's lounge.

"What did you see? How was it? Can I see the ticket?"

I didn't understand this ticket obsession, but early in my marriage I learnt to keep evidence. Squirrel it away, just in case.

"Amma's made dinner," Rajit said. "We're eating here tonight."

And after the inquisition I watched him wolf down Asmita's lentil curry like he hadn't eaten for months. Licking his lips, he smacked and sighed, his single hand moving like a darter. Before Asmita had even sat down, his plate was empty. Asmita smiled, heaping another giant spoon of rice onto his plate, then the curry.

I didn't know how to eat with my hands. I tried, but my chin ended up slimy with sauce, the tablecloth in my corner a turmeric yellow. I spooned the curry, trying to get used to a taste that was too spicy for me, though I didn't say anything.

"Isn't Amma a brilliant cook?" Raj said.

"Wonderful," I agreed.

Kesiree smiled at me across the table. She had a secret boyfriend that only I knew about: a Muslim, the son of an imam no less. Waafiq was even more unsuitable than I was, and Raj's parents would have been beyond furious if they'd known. I hadn't even told Rajit. It turns out the movie was the perfect subterfuge: Waafiq had met us at the cinema, and I'd watched the two of them saunter off, hand in hand, to watch *The*

Karate Kid, which I didn't want to see. Waafiq reminded me of a wild boar, his black hair bristled stiff like a spine on the top of his head and his nostrils too big for his face. I wasn't actually sure what Kesiree saw in him.

"Please, Thea," she'd begged me. "You know what it's like to be in love."

I couldn't resist. I reasoned that at least if I kept my eye on them there'd be no chance of the shag-fests Rajit and I used to have in the car at Signal Hill. No more unplanned babies like the one inside me.

The problem was that the movie outing hadn't solved my loneliness. I'd watched *Romancing the Stone* alone, picking at my popcorn. By the time Kesiree and Waafiq emerged fifteen minutes after I did, my sister-in-law's heart-shaped face was alight, her dark eyes glistening and her hand still firmly clamped in his.

It had been ages since Raj held my hand that way.

And hanging out with Kesiree wasn't the same as seeing Annie. Though I did catch up with her now and then, she was slipping away from me. She spent her time partying in Observatory, going to the odd lecture and sunning herself on Llandudno Beach. I'm not saying she wasn't supportive. She'd even secured me a cot from a neighbour she used to babysit for; it was wedged firmly between our bed and the cupboard. But things weren't the same. Our lives were taking diffe-rent paths, and though I swore to myself I wouldn't regret it – regret my husband and my baby – I wondered sometimes what would have happened if things had been different.

If I hadn't been sitting here in this foreign place, spooning dhal over my rice to neutralise the spices.

I gulped down water and thought longingly about the strawberry yoghurt in our little fridge.

"So, how was today?" I asked Rajit.

"Lectures," he said dismissively. "Ma," he said looking at Asmita, "can you teach Thea how to cook?"

I just about spat out my dhal as Asmita beamed at me.

"I *can* cook," I said.

"Not *our* way," Rajit replied.

"Amoy Ayaa taught me. It could be fun to cook together," Asmita said, looking at her mother hunched on the other side of the table. Rajit's grandmother wafted in and out of reality so I wasn't sure if she'd even heard she'd been mentioned.

I looked at Asmita hugging Raj, who crumpled into her like a custom-made glove.

"Could you?" Rajit said in a little-boy voice I suspected would some-day be used on me. "I can't eat anything she makes."

I felt the heat racing up my cheeks.

"You need to give Thea a chance," his father said. Just when I was giving him a grateful smile, Kandasamy continued: "She's young. She can't help it if she doesn't yet know how to be a proper wife." Kandasamy dipped his hand in his dinner, the food disappearing between his greased-up lips.

"And you're getting thin, Rajit." Amoy Ayaa looked up from her meal. "Eat. Eat."

It was like everyone ganging up against you on the playground; even Kesiree, my new best friend, whose secrets I was guarding so closely, didn't defend me. Mentioning Waafiq would have changed the conversation, and I was sorely tempted.

"You need to start by buying some proper ingredients," Asmita told me.

Proper ingredients, as she termed it, required money, which we rather lacked.

"I'll get a job then, shall I?" I said.

"Every wife needs to add value," Kandasamy said. "That's the first lesson."

"No one's going to hire you with that belly," Asmita commented. "And no qualifications. We'll shop together."

"And then cook together," said Raj.

"Great." My voice said otherwise.

"Eat, Raju, eat," said Amoy Ayaa. "You're wasting away. Asmita, why aren't you cooking for your son?"

I leant forward to say something, but Rajit shook his head. Nevertheless the movement must have caught Amoy Ayaa's attention.

"Now who are you, dear? I don't think we've met," she said to me. "Asmita, you should have mentioned that we have a visitor. And look, Asmita, our guest is having a baby!"

And that's actually how I felt, like a guest. Just then I was missing the aromas of basil and garlic wafting from Mother's kitchen. Nothing about living in this house, with this family, was familiar to me. Here the overwhelming scents were of coriander, garam masala, onions and frying fat. My mother's home had an understated elegance, everything placed exactly so; Asmita's home was all overstuffed pillows, loud fabrics and religious statues and images everywhere, the meanings of which I hadn't yet untangled. And no privacy. At Asmita's, neighbours were constantly arriving – and then leaving with food parcels of sugar beans curry and basmati rice.

"I don't understand it," I said to Rajit. "Surely just feeding us is enough?"

"It's our way," Raj said. "We'll go down the road for a meal if you like. Selvie Ayaa makes a delicious potato curry and roti."

Great. More strangers. More curry.

I'd liked the feeling at first; it was a bit like living in another country. But after a few weeks I wanted *someone* to speak my language.

Back in our little room outside, Raj transformed into the man I thought I'd married. We played gin rummy, lay on the bed and read to each other, and Raj gave me foot rubs as my feet started swelling. We debated names for our child, though it wasn't much of a debate since Raj had already decided.

And I liked the name Sanusha for a girl. It sounded like music. Boys' names would follow Rajit's family tradition. If it was a boy, our son would be named for his grandfather – not my dad, Stuart, but Rajit's dad, Kandasamy.

I didn't mind. I loved Rajit and what he wanted mattered to me more than what I wanted. I guess I wasn't much of a feminist, and my ambitions were limited. I wanted a happy home, a new foundation for my dreams.

But as the pregnancy advanced, and I began to nest, Rajit grew restless. He was on a fully paid sponsorship but he earned extra cash tutoring statistics. I didn't resent those after-hour activities, but I began to suspect he wasn't always telling me the truth.

"But why do you have to tutor so late?" I would ask.

"That's the time she asked for," Rajit would answer. "Don't you want me to go? How are we going to pay for the car seat?"

When he rocked up near midnight, he was usually in a good mood. A bit too good.

"You've been drinking," I said.

"One glass of wine, Thea. Do you want me to look like a wuss?"

But it wasn't just the wine. It was the way, when he took me to Pick 'n Pay, he'd have one arm around me and his eyes on any beautiful woman that passed him. He didn't try to hide it either.

"So what?" he said. "Looking is free."

"I'm pregnant, Raj. I'm not feeling my best."

"Well, Thea, you're not exactly *looking* your best either. It's a phase. Get over it."

I tried to look better. I spent hours blow drying my hair and touching up my face with make-up I bought on special at Clicks. I exercised religiously and ate very little, especially in front Rajit.

"You're ballooning," he said watching me climb out of the shower.

Fighting back tears, I wrapped myself in a towel and tried not to hate the little being who was taking over my body.

I tried to find pretty Punjabis to wear – I always thought Indian women looked so elegant pregnant. Asmita came with me, even nodding at my colour choice.

"Turquoise looks good on you," she said.

But I never felt that I ever looked good enough, even when Annie bounced in for a quick visit while Raj was out.

"T, you look gorgeous. You can't even tell you're preggers from the back."

"Raj doesn't think so."

"Raj is a fool. If I look even half as good as you when I have a baby, I'll celebrate."

I wanted to believe her, but my thoughts kept returning to Raj and what I could do to make him happy. The night before, I'd dressed in a lacy number before bed and padded into our little room in bare feet. Looking up from his textbook, Raj had smiled at me with the old smile from our courting days, and a wave of relief had washed over me. He put the book on the bedside table and sat up.

"That must feel a little tight," he said. "Remember how sexy you used to look in it?"

My reaction must have registered in my face.

"Oh, let's have a cuddle, anyway." Raj gestured for me to sit next to him, then kissed me on the forehead, his hand wandering to my moving belly.

"I need you to be nice to me," I told him. "I'm doing my best here."

There was silence, then Raj pulled me onto him, his lips caressing my neck. "And I need to go out later when we're done," he said. "I promised the boys a game of poker. You can buy a new nightie with my winnings. Just think how that will cheer you up."

Sanusha (aged 6): Going for it

My mom has lines on her wrists. They're pale white, like spider webs. I've counted them. On the arm with the watch on, she has 7. On the right (the one she writes with) she has 5.

7 + 5 = 12

There are 12 months in the year. 12 in a dozen, which is how Mom buys eggs. But you want to hear something funny? A baker's dozen is not 12, it's 13! That's because bakers in England a long time ago, maybe even when there were dinosaurs, used to give away extra bread in case they got into trouble for being mean. So if Mom had 13 lines on her wrists, she'd have a baker's dozen. Numbers are so cool!

When I ask my mom where her lines come from, she says they are scars from getting hurt.

"How?" I say.

"What?"

"How did you get hurt?"

"It was an accident," she tells me. "Like when you fell off your bike and broke your tooth."

"My tooth is going to grow back," I say, putting my finger in the hole.

"Lucky you," she says with a smile.

"But if I break it again, no more chances," I tell her.

"Who told you that?" she asks.

"Asmita Ayaa. She says I must act like a lady, and not go too fast."

"Mmphhh," Mom says. "I used to go on my bike down our driveway with Robbie. We had races. I won sometimes, but mostly only after he got sick."

"Maybe that's where you got your lines," I offer.

"No," Mom says, very clearly. "That wasn't it at all."

Then she starts tickling me on the grass and I giggle.

Today we are at Kirstenbosch. Mom doesn't have any tourists, so she has lots of time for me. We already packed a picnic, with real junk food! Viennas. Chips. Jelly worms. And Melrose cheesies. Also apples and naartjies, and a big bottle of passion fruit juice. We put a big blanket on the lawn and we watch the view. It's a sunny day, and we look for animals in the clouds. I find a lion and lizard, but the lizard has wings. Mom sees a unicorn, which is a horse with a horn like a rhino.

It's nice, just us. And then this man comes running along, and stops. He's very sweaty. He's dripping like a tap when you forget to turn it off properly.

"Thea?" he says.

And Mom answers. "Hi Clay! You look thirsty."

"I am," he says. "Been along the contour path."

"Keep running," I say, very, very softly, because I want him to go away.

"Sanusha!" Mom says with her scary voice. "Would you like some juice, Clay?"

"Sure," he says, but I didn't like the look of his big eyes that stare at Mom.

"This is my daughter, Sanusha," she says.

"Hello, Sanusha. You look just like your granny."

Boring! I stuck my tongue out the corner of my mouth. Who is this guy?

"Clay manages the coffee shop where I have my coffee in the morning," Mom tells me. "He makes pictures in my cappuccinos. It's a new type of art!"

"So what?" I say, and Mom's face goes hard like a piece of rock.

"Please just ignore her," she says to the sweaty man, and holds out a cup of juice.

"A quick sip," he says, "thanks."

He sits down next to Mom. His hair is going grey at the edges, and he has very big muscles on his arms and legs. So I'm a bit confused. His face looks quite young but his hair is old.

He has to drink from Mom's cup because we only brought 2, which is a pair. You get lots of things in pairs – socks, shoes, trousers (because there are 2 legs), stockings. Even a knife and fork make a pair because there are 2.

"How old are you?" I ask.

"Twenty-seven," he says. "How old are you?"

"I'm 6."

"Wow, six," he says. "You're so old, you're almost a teenager."

"That's rubbish," I say. "Teenagers are 13. That's, like, only in 7 years. There are 7 days in the week. And 7 colours in the rainbow. They are red, orange, yellow –"

"Sanusha," Mom says, which is her way of telling me to keep quiet.

I get up and go to a tree to hang myself upside down, close enough to hear what they are saying.

"You haven't come in for a few days," the man says.

"Lots of groups, and I've been busy with the family."

"How is Rajit?"

Mom doesn't say anything, so I shout from the tree: "Appa's fine! He's got this big fancy job in the city and I went to his office and I photocopied my hand and it looked exactly the same as the real thing except it was black and white."

"Cool," says the man. "Maybe you could show me some time."

"Why?" I say. "You're not even invited to our house."

"Sanusha!" Mom says and she gets up and pulls me down from the tree and gives me a paddywhack on the bum. It isn't even sore, but she never gives me hidings so I start to cry and I make it go really, really loud with real tears. Then she puts me on the grass, and tells me to keep quiet right now or so help her, she will not take me to the park for 2 weeks. That is 14 days, which is a lot, so I shut my mouth and reach for a jelly worm and Mom smacks my hand and says enough of that – I can have an apple and say sorry to Clay for being such a rude little girl.

"Sorry," I say.

"It's okay," he says, but I can see I've hurt his feelings so I am glad.

But by then Mom's scarf has untwisted and I can see the man looking at the ugly blue mark on her neck. She quickly rolls it up again.

"Mom is very clumsy," I tell him. "She, like, bumps herself all the time. I told her she should switch on the light."

"So I see," the man says.

"It really is nothing," Mom says.

"If you say so," Clay says.

"I do."

That man slurps his drink and he doesn't even say pardon and then he stands up and says he must go because he's meeting his friend for a braai and he's already late. I can see he thinks Mom is pretty, but he also looks sad.

"Come in for a drink at the coffee shop, Sanusha," he says. "I can make you a number 6 in a cup of hot chocolate, just like how old you are."

"You can?" I say, because actually that sounds quite awesome.

He doesn't touch Mom or touch me, but waves at us and says enjoy your picnic and don't eat too many worms, Sanusha, but didn't he hear Mom say I have to eat apples now?

Mom waves a little and then looks miserable, like Mr Miserable who hasn't learnt to turn that frown upside down.

"I think we should go, baby," she says. "Asmita Ayaa asked me to get some carrots."

"That man shouldn't have had our passion fruit," I say to Mom. "And it was supposed to be just us at the picnic. That's why we left Asmita Ayaa behind."

"It's kind to share, Sanusha. And you don't need to mention this to Appa. He'd be a bit upset if he knew we went on a picnic without him."

"Appa hates picnics. They make his pants dirty."

"That's right, darling, he does."

*

At the house Asmita Ayaa and Mom peel the carrots. Sometimes they talk while they're working and sometimes they don't – today is a quiet day. Mom turns on the radio and Asmita Ayaa hums softly. Asmita Ayaa can peel 10 carrots in 3 minutes – I timed her with the clock on the wall. You have to watch the second hand, the fast one, and each time it goes past the 12 then that counts as 1 minute. The peels shoot in all directions, even on the floor. She doesn't pick them up till afterwards and sometimes I step in them and pretend to fall down like I've skidded on a *vrot* banana.

Mom peels neatly and slowly. She holds each vegetable like a fragile little baby (fragile means it can break easily – just like Mom) and then curls the peels off, one by one. She makes neat stacks on the newspaper, and when she lifts the paper up, you can't even see where she was working.

Then they chop the onions. I don't like onions. They make me cry, and not because I'm sad. They make Mom and Asmita Ayaa cry too, and soon we are all there, the Moonsamy women, crying in the kitchen while the sunflower oil gets hot, hot, hot. The fan above the stove goes hummmmmmm, so we can't even hear the radio. That's why we don't hear when Appa drives into the carport because he doesn't have a garage for his car, which is quite new. He got it for his fancy job in town. Mom got his old car, which smells of off milk when it gets sunny, because I spilt my bottle once when I was a baby.

Appa walks into the house, and we only see him when he puts down his keys on the kitchen counter.

I wait for Mom to run to him like she used to, so she can beat Asmita Ayaa to say hello, but she doesn't look up from her onions. Asmita Ayaa puts down her knife, wipes her hands on her apron, and hugs Appa.

"Hello, my son. You're home early."

From behind his back he pulls out a bunch of flowers. Pink ones. Mom's favourite.

"I came home to see my family, and to give my wife some flowers," he says.

Mom turns the pot, tipping in the last of the onions. They sizzle. (A good word. It sounds like what it means.) She stirs.

"You can put them in a vase, Rajit," Mom says.

"Now, now," says Asmita Ayaa, "is that the way to thank your husband?"

Mom looks at my grandmother. "What do you want me to do? Screw him?"

I don't know what that is, but Asmita Ayaa's face drops like Mom spat at her. It's very bad to spit even though it is really cool to see how long it gets before it breaks.

Mom switches off the stove and holds out her hand to me. "Come, Sanusha – I want to go for a drive."

I don't know what to do because Appa looks like he needs a hug.

"Go on your own, Thea," Appa says. "The kid needs a bath."

I'm not *the kid*. I'm Sanusha.

Mom just ignores him and marches us through the front entrance. She straps me in, and I wave at Appa, who's followed us out to the car, his face scary like a big storm.

"You watch how you drive with my daughter," he shouts at her.

Mom slams her door and makes the engine go grrrrrrrrrrrrrrrrrrrrrr. We drive down the street and I can see Mom is crying.

"Are you hungry, angel?" she asks.

"Yes."

"How about a big, meaty burger and then a movie?"

"In the middle of the week?"

"Sure. Why not?"

Mom lights a cigarette and opens her window, blowing smoke out in big clouds. It's already getting dark so I can see the red tip of her cigarette glowing as she moves her hand. Appa would shout if he knew she was smoking with me in the car. Mom reaches over to turn on the radio. She makes it so loud that my ears hurt and I can't even ask her to turn it down.

"You're having us followed?" she shouts, all of a sudden, and she swings her head so she can look behind our car. She turns down the music, and flick-flick, she moves sideways across the road.

"Okay there, darling?"

"Yes."

Then she shouts a really dirty word over and over again, and changes to the left. "Leave me alone!" she says. "Leave me alone!"

But Mom isn't alone – she's with me, and we're going for a burger and a movie in the middle of the week. Mom leans over. She's looking in her handbag.

"Where is it? Where is it?" she says.

"Where is what?" But she doesn't hear me, because she has to swing the car around a bus filled with faces with mouths like big O's.

"Jesus," she says, and I'm very confused because she doesn't talk about him except at Christmas, which is his birthday, 25 December. This is a good day because 5 can go into 25 exactly 5 times.

Mom throws her cigarette out the car, which I know for sure is a naughty thing to do. She's a litter bug damaging the environment. Then the world will end and we will have nowhere to live.

Mom's car is going grrrrrr, grrrr, grrrr. My seatbelt squeezes my shoulder when we turn a corner.

"It's too fast, Mom," I say. This is true. I saw a big sign and it said 60, which means 60 kilometres an hour. She's going to get a speed fine! Maybe she doesn't hear me because she doesn't slow down, and she turns another corner so fast I think I'm going to fall out the car. I push down my door lock button.

"Go away," she says. "Piss off." (That's another word for wee, so I think this is also a dirty word.)

"Where are we going, Mom?" I shout.

"I need to get to Annie."

I like Auntie Annie. She once bought me a book about a guy called Newton who had an apple fall on his head and he worked out why it fell. I had an acorn hit me on the head once, but I didn't think up anything clever after that.

"Don't worry, Sanusha – we're going to be fine."

I just want Mom to slow down.

"Slow down, Mom!" I say.

"We've got to lose him," she replies.

I don't know who she's talking about.

"Lose who?"

"The man who's following us. We need to get to Annie."

My stomach goes grumble, grumble like Winnie-the-Pooh when he needs honey.

"What about our burger?" I ask. "You promised me a burger and a movie in the middle of the week!"

"We'll get to that once we're safe. I'll keep us safe," Mom says, but her voice sounds weird.

Grumble, grumble, goes my tummy.

"He's there!" Mom shrieks, and the car jerks forward like flicking an elastic band. "Hold on, Sanusha – the next turn I see, I'm going for it!"

Going for what?

I hold on to my car seat. Tyres squeaaaaaaaaaallllllllllllllll. Mom's screaming. I'm screaming.

The car goes round and round.

Then we hit something. Hard. Glass falls over Mom in a big shower. She's covered in blood. Bright red like my jersey.

I'm not in my car seat. I'm lying near Mom, but I don't know how I got here. My arm hurts – it's hanging funny like a sleeve.

Mom's eyes look strange, but she's breathing so she's not dead.

"Mom? Mom?"

She doesn't say anything.

1, 2, 3, 4 . . .

"Mom?"

Shouts and some lights and some people running. They open up the door at the front.

. . . 31, 32, 33, 34, 35 . . ."

"You okay, little girl? We've called an ambulance."

I point at Mom with my good hand. "She's not dead," I say. "But she was going for it."

Thea: Not dying easily

The first time I was in hospital, Mother told me to "be polite" and "not say anything about how it happened". So this is what actually happened. (I did not knock a kettle of boiling water over my legs as my dad told the nurses.)

They'd put Robbie in the ground that day. He didn't get the bench he wanted and I was forced to wear a frilly dress I hated. I'd wanted to wear jeans and a T-shirt that said "Little Sister" because Robbie liked it. Used to like it.

"Don't give me any uphill *today* of all days, young lady," Mother said, ripping off my jeans so hard she scraped the skin of my bottom with her nails.

I held my arms across my chest, guarding the T-shirt, but Mother was much stronger. I thought she was going to hit me and that was the end of it because when I put my hands up to my face, I lost my grip. Mother took my scissors from the pencil box on my desk, and she made me watch as she sliced my favourite T-shirt into shreds. Piece by piece dropped into the dustbin as I howled.

"You're not a little sister any more, Thea. Now wear the damn dress. And shut up."

Dad came into the room, saw what was going on and walked out again like he always did.

Mother pushed a vest over my head while I stood still, wanting her to get away from me. The skirt of the dress was a horrible green, the colour of baby poop. It had white buttons all the way down the top to the waist, and white lace ruffles in circles all round the skirt. I looked like those crocheted dolls to cover toilet-paper rolls Nana had at the farm. But the farm was Robbie's favourite place, so I tried to reassure myself by thinking about that.

After he got sick, Robbie used to sleep for most of the long drive to get there, his head on a fat pillow, his mouth half open. I'd watch the lights over Cape Town as we left home in the early hours of the morning, yellow puddles flicking and trees waving spooky hands in the wind. Further on, the mountains were like giant dinosaurs with spikes, their heads lifted in our direction. When the road straightened out, it rolled out to the horizon, like it went on forever. Finally, the car would slow, then bump over railroad tracks and along the fence I could see the heads of Gramps's ostriches painted pink and orange by the dawn. Like they were welcoming us.

I'd shake Robbie awake, gently, gently. He wouldn't want to miss this – he loved birds and he even kept a list. Like Dad, he knew how to recognise birds by the way they flew, or the shape of their tails, or the colour of their beaks. I couldn't tell the difference, but I was quite happy to follow him around, gathering feathers for his jewelled collection box from India. He even had a vulture feather, which was almost as long as my arm, and certainly wider. Mother used to comment about the germs.

When he got even sicker, he couldn't have that box in his room, and I wasn't allowed to visit either, in case I brought in bugs from school. Robbie gave me the box for safekeeping, and I recognised this as the honour he'd intended.

One of our favourite things to do at the farm was to visit the ostriches, although we were never allowed near the adult birds without the grown-ups being near. Ostriches are very protective parents, sharing time at the nest as their eggs incubate; if you looked like you might come close, a kick from one of them could kill you. Of course, Uncle Ray and Gramps didn't let the ostriches keep all their eggs. They had a special shed at just the right temperature, so that the babies had the best chance. Like Robbie, ostriches are sensitive and prone to catching all sorts of diseases. But they die easily, which is how they differed from Robbie, who had taken all this time before he had finally given up.

And today we were going to say goodbye for good.

The funeral was in Mother's church, with big stained-glass windows reflecting coloured lighting on the pews. It was completely full, because Mother and Dad had a lot of friends and Robbie had been dying for years. These were the same people who, for the previous eight weeks as things were nearing a close and a nurse had moved in, had left our kitchen counter at home piled with dishes of food: lasagnes, boboties, stews and cottage pies; Tupperwares of cakes, biscuits, cupcakes and fudge; and pies, lemon meringue and apple cobbler in CorningWare dishes we'd have to return.

Robbie had been expected to lie on the couch and receive people. His skin was mustard and his body thin, but he had a huge belly from all the water his system couldn't get rid of. Robbie's hair, however, had grown back thick, curly and dark brown. Each visitor had been allotted five minutes.

The whole process had exhausted Robbie, and when I asked why he didn't just tell Mother, he said, smiling, "Oh, Thea – it gives her something to do."

I think perhaps I hated it more than he did – all those do-gooders stealing my last weeks with my brother.

As the service went on, I looked at Mother and Dad. They were holding hands tightly, a rare display of affection. Gramps had slid in next to me, and I felt the pressure of his suit leg next to my skirt – still a comfort. He touched me lightly on the hand, then looked ahead, trying to stop himself from crying.

Afterwards, grown-ups I didn't know and some I did patted me on the head and glanced at me with big, sad eyes, but when they looked away they talked about ordinary things – how the weather was so perfect for winter, and have you heard that Sandra and Freddy finally got married, after all these years.

I was standing on my own when the reality began to hit me.

I'd got used to Robbie not playing outside with me, but even from his bed he used to look at me and say, "Hey, Thea? Why're you looking so miserable? I'm not dead yet." He read me stories and, when he was too sick, I'd sit next to him and tell him about school and Annie and his friend Tony, who was still the school marble champion – even though we knew for a fact he stuck Prestik on his shoes to steal marbles when people weren't looking. "My idea," Robbie once told me, and I thought he was super-clever.

When we were finally back home I tried to break away from the guests, even Annie, who'd come with her parents. When Gramps coaxed me to eat something, I shook my head and walked to the bottom of the garden, where the tree house was, shimmying up the trunk in my baby-poo dress. In the corner of the tree house, I traced my fingers over the initials Robbie had carved. The T was better formed than the R – he'd battled to get his pocketknife to do the curves as the blade kept snapping back in. This was our equivalent of Robbie's bench – a view over the mountain and a quiet place to think. Through the window, I watched the people milling about. I knew that they'd all go home and forget about us. The food deliveries would stop and I would be stuck in this silent house with no Robbie, and just Mother and Dad for company.

I wanted to be sad for a long, long time, thinking about my brother. Then a head peeped up into the tree house.

"I knew you'd be here," said Annie. After clambering in she offered me a bit of her cake. "Want some? It's like caramel or something."

I bit into her cake and it didn't taste of anything – just powder dissolving on my tongue. Robbie had left his special feather box in the corner of the tree house and I leant over and opened it, noting the new guinea fowl feather I'd found in Kirstenbosch a few weeks back, when Dad had taken me "to get out the house for a bit".

"What do you think you'll do tonight?" Annie asked, crumbs in her mouth.

"I don't know. We're supposed to be praying with Father Patrick."

"What for?" Annie said, her pale face all squashed up. "It's a bit late isn't it?"

I looked at Annie and started to giggle. Soon I was laughing so much I could feel the tree house shaking. Then Annie started to laugh with me, until tears were pouring down our faces.

It felt good.

"I wish you could come to my house. It's not so sad there," Annie said as we hugged each other.

"Mother wouldn't let me."

"Right," Annie said. "When you gotta pray, you gotta pray."

This sent us into another torrent of giggles.

We heard Annie's dad calling from the veranda.

"You okay?" she said, holding her hand against mine to form a steeple.

"I guess."

And then I was alone again in the tree house.

I don't know how long I sat there; I got cold when the sun started setting. Here, in our special place, the loneliness began to overwhelm me and I began to sob from a part of me I didn't even know existed. This wasn't sadness: it was deeper, wider, higher, longer and I didn't think I'd be able to move until I put my hand over my heart, where Robbie had told me he'd be when his body had left. But I couldn't feel him there – all I could feel was how I hurt, and I knew that he'd lied.

He was never going to be with me again. And now who could I trust?

Without thinking about it, I grabbed Robbie's feather box, and I climbed through the tree house window onto the outstretched branch where we'd once seen a sugarbird. With one hand to steady myself, my thighs gripping the rough bark, I opened the box and grabbed a handful of feathers, sending them drifting into the wind. Angrily, I grabbed another palmful, and another and another, until all that was left was the vulture feather, too big to fling.

Suddenly, my heart burning, unable to see through my tears, I realised that all that was left of Robbie was flying away from me, getting stuck in the leaves, and I tried to get some of the feathers back. I couldn't reach,

so I stretched, and the branch under my weight, was bending, bending –
CRACK!

I screamed as the branch snapped, sending me flying into the shrubbery and mud. My fall was broken slightly as my skirt caught and ripped on another branch. The landing wasn't too sore, but I was wet through, a puddle of old rainwater soaking into my dress. I sat a moment, too dazed to move. But then I heard some footsteps.

"Thea? Thea?" my dad called. "What are you doing out there?"

I stood up quickly, patted myself down, then sprinted towards the house, the grown-ups still inside. As I burst into the lounge, everybody turned to look at me.

"Thea?" Mother said, her voice tight.

"I fell out the tree house," I said. "I'm sorry."

"Go upstairs *immediately*," Mother said. "I'm coming in a minute. And don't dirty anything else."

Dad nodded, having followed me quietly into the room, his eyes on my funeral dress. "Do what your mother says."

I shuffled my way to the stairs, feeling big adult eyes judging me when they didn't know anything about being a kid, a lonely child like me.

I waited in my bedroom, listening to people saying goodbye. Then the heavy thud of the front door closing. The latch on, the key in the lock. Shivering through my wet clothes, I desperately dabbed at my dress with a sponge, trying to wipe away some of the mud.

Mother's footsteps sounded on the staircase, my dad's mild voice following. "I'm sure it was just a mistake."

The footsteps stopped. "She's deliberately spiteful, Stuart. Why today? Why would she embarrass me like this?"

"Let's just bath her and move on, darling. It's been a rough day."

"I'll deal with her. Just bring in the plates from outside."

"Can't we leave them for tonight, just this once, Veronica?"

"Darn it, Stuart, I can't wake up tomorrow in a pigsty!"

"Okay. But be gentle – she's also grieving."

My mother walking again. "That's no excuse." And then she was in my bedroom looking at me.

"I'm sorry! I'm sorry. It was a mistake."

"Don't lie to me, Thea. You didn't like the dress. You did it on purpose."

"I wouldn't, Mother. I didn't mean it!"

She moved forward. "Look at you! Father Patrick will be here in an hour and I've got enough to worry about without your filth. Strip!"

I tried to unbutton my wet dress, but my fingers shook.

"Are you making fun of me, young lady?"

"The buttons are stuck."

With one swooping movement, she ripped off the buttons all the way down the front of the dress. It dropped to the floor.

"It's ruined. You ruined it!" she said.

I held my arms to my chest, shaking.

"Take off your knickers." She stalked out.

From the bathroom, I could hear water battering the tub.

"Thea!" she barked.

Steam rose in giant swirls around the room.

In one movement, Mother lifted me up and threw me hard into the bath. With my whole body in the scalding water, I felt as though my skin was being peeled off. I screamed and screamed.

It was Dad who took me to the hospital for second-degree burns over my legs and bottom.

Mother stayed with Father Patrick to pray.

*

All those years later, in another hospital, I woke up with Clay standing next to my bed. It wasn't possible, was it, that the manager from the coffee shop was there, and Rajit didn't even know?

"Your brother's a good man," the nurse said to me as she waddled her broad bulk next to me.

How does she know about Robbie?

"He's just a boy," I said. "He's never really grown up."

The woman blinked, then scratched her head.

Why do people always look at me like that?

While I was there, I tried to remember the nurses' names, but I couldn't. There were just too many of them, and because they were in uniform I couldn't tell which one worked for Raj. But I was watching, analysing them just as they were analysing me. This one stuck a thermometer under my arm, connected me to a blood-pressure monitor like I was the subject of a scientific experiment. When would they have enough temperatures, enough blood pressures, enough urine, enough *blood*?

"I'm going to have to go now," Clay said. "I've got to be at work."

I nodded as he kissed me on the forehead.

"Get better, Thea." He slipped away so silently that I began to wonder if he'd been there at all.

Raj's visits, however were upbeat and chirpy, as he bounced around the room like a cicada. Maybe the hospital made him nervous. I could see the patients in the other beds looking at him, wanting him to sit down.

"I'm sorry I hurt you," he said. "I've learnt my lesson. I won't do it again." He put a picture of the three of us on the bedside table. "See how happy we once were?"

"You keep *them* away," I said, flicking the frame over, cracking the glass. "You keep away too. I want to see my daughter. Only my daughter."

"Now don't be like that . . ."

"I need to think."

"You're not in a state to think," Raj said. "You're imagining things. I'm your husband. I need to think for you."

Idiot. As if I want him *to think for me.*

I fixed him with the gaze I was perfecting. It certainly made the nurse's squirm.

"I want to see Sanusha."

Raj nodded. I could see he was angry but for once he kept it all in. "I'll bring her tonight."

"Thank you. Now go and tell that head shrinker the hospital keeps on sending round not to bother. I won't talk to him."

That night Sanusha sat on the edge of my bed reading to me. She looked away from the story for a moment and asked, "Why won't you let Appa come?"

"Appa and I are having a little disagreement."

"A fight?"

"If you want to call it that."

"He's sad. He told me to tell you he was very sorry."

So, Rajit's emissary. Without the aid of any monitors, I knew my blood pressure was rising.

Is she watching me too? What did she tell Rajit?

An uncomfortable knot was forming in my stomach. I bit down hard on my lip and fell back into the sheets.

"You're bleeding, Mom."

"What?"

"Your mouth is bleeding."

I wiped the scarlet onto my palm. "It's nothing."

"Blood has platelets and plasma," Sanusha said. "If your body runs out of blood, you die."

"I'm not running out of blood."

"An adult body has five litres of blood."

Yes, and if I can slit my wrists properly this time, I might get rid of enough of it. Get her out of here – she's driving me nuts.

"Mom's tired," I said forcing a smile. "I think you need to run back to Appa."

"But I want to sleep with you tonight," Sanusha whined.

"This is a hospital, for God's sake, not a slumber party. Go home with Appa. Mom's exhausted."

"Thea?" A voice at the door.

Annie. Thank God.

"Can I come in?"

Sanusha ran over to my friend. "Mom's very cross, Auntie Annie."

"Mom's sick, darling."

"She won't talk to Appa and she wants me to go home."

Annie looked at me. Her face was flushed – she'd been in the sun. Normally, Annie looked like a paler version of the lead singer of Roxette – her hair was cropped short because she was still playing so much sport. But she had no curves whatsoever. Flat as a diving board – no hips, no breasts, no bum.

"What are you staring at?" Annie asked after a pause. "Do I have spinach in my teeth?"

"I don't like spinach," Sanusha informed her. "It tastes like grass."

"And when was the last time you ate grass?" Annie said, picking her up. "Are you a cow?"

Sanusha giggled. "Cows have four stomachs," she told her.

"Well, I have an extra stomach just for pudding. Even if I eat all my food, I always have space for lemon meringue."

They were making my head buzz.

What are they talking about? Why don't they just go away?

Annie cuddled Sanusha. How could she be so angular and still give my daughter these hugs she could sink into?

"Did you check?" I murmured.

Annie put Sanusha down. "Listen, darling girl. Go and ask your dad to get Mom a cup of coffee. Okay?"

"Did you check?" I said a little louder as soon as Sanusha was out the room.

Annie moved closer, sat on the bed and patted my hand. "There was no one, T. I walked up and down. I even checked the bathrooms."

At least someone is listening.

I nodded. "Visiting times are the worst. They masquerade as family."

"I can imagine. But think about it, T. They don't need to be here if Raj is already in the hospital."

I beckoned Annie closer, and put my mouth to her ear. "I think he's got to Sanusha. She's asking me all these questions. Telling me stuff," I said to her. "Do you think I'm right?"

Annie looked at me, an unreadable expression on her face, then she picked up my brush. With long, sweeping strokes she tidied up the matted nest about my face. "No, Thea. I don't think so. She seems just the same to me."

"She's not his spy?"

"Sanusha is your daughter. She loves you. She wants you home so you can make pancakes and take her to the park." Annie turned my head slightly, clipping some strands behind my ear. "Listen to me, T. You trust me, don't you?"

"Of course."

She cupped my chin in her hand. "Repeat after me: 'I do not have to worry about Sanusha.'"

It felt weird, but I said it.

"Sanusha is my beautiful daughter, and she will always care for me," said Annie

"Sanusha is my beautiful daughter, and she will always care for me."

"I am just having a hard time and she is worried about me."

"I am just having a hard time and she is worried about me," I repeated.

Annie smiled. She'd had corrective surgery and no longer wore her glasses. They used to hide the colour of her turquoise eyes, but now they were her best feature. They twinkled, and I felt the tension begin to ease out of me. But then I remembered.

"And what about Clay? Did he get to *him*?" I said.

"Who the hell is Clay?"

"The guy from the coffee shop. He's visited a few times."

"Really?" Annie's eyes glinted.

"He brings me muffins. He bought me a jersey once. I like him."

Annie looked at me and I could see she didn't think this was a good idea at all. "Listen, Thea, I don't know the guy. But what I can say is that your life is complex enough at the moment."

"I like the way he looks. He has this silver hair. He smiles in his eyes. Like you."

Annie linked her hand through mine and changed the subject. "Have you read that mag yet? D'you need another one? What about some more hand cream?"

"I'm not feeling good, Annie. I have these headaches –"

"You'll get better, sweetie. It's just a matter of time."

"I can't go home with *him*," I told her. "I don't trust Rajit. Asmita's probably putting something in my food. It's bitter sometimes. She doesn't cook like Mother, that's for sure."

"Well, your mom certainly made a fabulous paella."

I missed Mother. My heart ached and I wanted her there. The number of times I'd driven up to her gate with Sanusha to show her what she was missing, but driven away again. A mother is a mother, even if she is the worst one on earth.

"She's not here for me, Annie."

"No," Annie replied holding my hand in hers. "But I am. If you want to, come and stay with me for a while, T. With or without Sanusha. Until you decide what you want to do next."

Sanusha (aged 6): Cracking eggs with 1 hand

Appa isn't happy having Mom at Auntie Annie's. I can see the way he crosses his arms when he parks the car.

"Auntie Annie's house is ginormous," I tell him as I try to unclip myself. "It has big trees, a swing, a jungle gym, a trampoline *and* a sandpit."

"I know, Sanusha," he says in his grumpy voice. "I've been there."

"So why don't you come with me, and have tea with Mom?"

"Your mother is ill. She needs to rest."

"She doesn't rest when *I'm* there. We walk in the garden and play Ludo and Snap, and drink Oros out of fancy cups. We pour it from a teapot with roses on it. They're yellow."

"So just the two of you drink tea?" he asks.

"It's not tea, Appa. It's Oros. I told you that already," I say, as I jiggle the door. Sometimes Appa doesn't listen.

"So, you drink Oros with Mom on your own?" Appa asks.

"No," I answer. "Last time I brought Big Bear and Matthew also came. Matthew was messy. Are all boys messy, Appa?"

"Nobody else?" He doesn't answer my question.

"Appa! I said are all boys messy?"

"Most of them, I guess. Sanusha –"

"Can I go now? We're going to bake today."

Appa doesn't even get out the car to walk me to the gate. My satchel is really heavy and I have to stand on my tippy-toes to reach the door-bell. Auntie Annie's doorbell is cool. Every time you ring it, it makes a different tune. I ring it again to hear what song comes next (*Walking on Sunshine*). The door opens and when I turn to wave at Appa, he's already gone.

Mom's face still has scratches on it from the glass. She looks over my shoulder, checking the street.

"Who dropped you?" she asks.

"Appa."

"Anyone else in the street?"

"No. Can I come in now? I want to bake."

Mom leads me in through the front door like I don't know where I'm going. Auntie Annie isn't always here, which is a pity. I wish Mom would hug me hard, like Auntie Annie. Like she used to before the accident. I know she's sore inside, but I have a sore arm and I still love to cuddle.

Mom moves like she's old. She crosses her arms over her body and shuffles like she's wearing Asmita Ayaa's winter slippers.

"We're baking, hey Mom?" I remind Mom.

She nods. In the kitchen, we pull out the flour, the eggs, the butter, the sugar. In baking, it is really, really important to get the measurements right. Here are some important things to remember:

1 teaspoon is 5ml

1 tablespoon is 15ml

1 cup is 250ml

With that you can bake anything. But today we are making *soetkoekies*. We line up all the spices on the table: cinnamon, ginger, nutmeg, cloves. Then the chopped nuts, and baking powder and some other white stuff that helps the biscuits rise. This recipe even has wine in it – it is the colour of a plum that's ready to eat.

Once all the dried ingredients are together, we cut in the butter. My arm isn't working so well, but I manage because Mom does the hard stuff with the knife. I hold the mixer with my other arm and Mom keeps the bowl still. Mom has this trick with eggs – she can crack them with 1 hand like a real chef.

"How come you can do that?" I ask.

"My mother," she says, but that's all.

"Like I'm learning with you!" I say.

"Exactly."

We make a lovely dough, and then we roll it out onto the counter and choose some cookie-cutter shapes. I like the squares and the stars, but Mom likes to cut circles with a glass. She dips the edges of the glass into the flour, and then pushes it down hard in the dough. I can't roll dough, so my job is to put the biscuits onto the tray with butter on it. We don't talk much. As soon as the little light goes off outside the oven, we know it's hot enough. Mom pushes the first trays in.

We hear Auntie Annie's keys but I don't look up.

"Look who I found on the doorstep!" Auntie Annie says.

I see that man from the coffee shop standing right behind her.

"Clay!" Mom says, and I think of mud.

What a funny name.

"Hello, Thea," Clay says. I can see he likes Mom quite a lot, because he stares at her. "And Sanusha!" he says to me. "I've brought your number 6. I heard you might be here today."

I want to be grumpy with him but then he hands me a cup, and he has made a 6 right in the middle of my hot chocolate.

"Cool," I say.

"Sanusha," Mom says in *that* voice.

"Thanks," I say quickly.

"Thank you, *Clay*."

"I said thanks already."

Clay shrugs, then smiles. "I brought you something else as well, Sanusha, but I'm not sure your mom will let me give it to you. It'll have to be our secret." In his hand, he has a little cupcake with fairy dust and a ballerina on top. (I would have liked a jet more, or maybe a rocket.)

I look at him. Is he stupid? Doesn't he know you tell secrets in private? I lean closer to him, and whisper: "Not now. Mom can hear you."

"Right," he whispers and steps back, placing his treasure in a little pink box. He puts it behind the fruit bowl and winks.

"What are you talking about over there?" Mom says with a smile. I like it when Mom is happy.

Clay walks over to Mom. "Your cappuccino, *madame*," he says with a stupid accent.

"Thank you, sir," she says. "You do the best deliveries."

"Well, only for our most important customers. How are you feeling?"

"I'm getting there."

Auntie Annie swings Matthew off her hip and puts him on the floor. "Why don't we all go sit in the garden? It's such a beautiful day."

I like *that* idea until Matthew pads after us. He's not even 2 yet, but after I taught him to spit he started following me around, and it's so irritating. I don't know why Mom doesn't just come home so I don't have to have him around all the time.

"Go away," I say, but not loud enough for Mom to hear.

In the garden under the trees, Auntie Annie puts out a big striped blanket and a smaller one with grass stains on it. Auntie Annie sits down next Clay. I prefer the jungle gym. I can already hang from the monkey bars with just my legs and feet. No hands.

Mom is holding her coffee, and has already lit a cigarette, as she always does when we're outside. I already drank my 6, and it didn't taste any different from normal hot chocolate. I thought that 6 would taste like something! Mom lowers herself onto the blanket, and Clay reaches over to help her.

"I'm okay," she says. "Sanusha, just be careful if you're going to climb on those bars. They're still slippery from the sprinkler."

"I'm not a baby," I say. She's told me that, like, 1000 times.

"Oh my God!" Mom suddenly says, which Teacher Candy says is a very bad thing to say. "I forgot the biscuits in the oven. They'll probably be cremated by now." Mom tries to stand up, but Auntie Annie pats her arm. "Don't worry about it, sweetie – I'll do it."

"You'd better hurry! Your kitchen may be on fire."

Now that would be cool. I'm hanging upside down, wondering if I should follow Auntie Annie, when I hear a big noise like Kandasamy

Ajah's toolbox. The big garden gate that goes onto the road swings open, banging against the wall.

Mom tries to stand up as Appa crosses the grass with his long legs.

"Get down from there now, Sanusha," Appa says, no nonsense. "Go inside, and take Matthew with you."

Appa looks scary so I heave Matthew up round his tummy, and flee into the house. Auntie Annie's in the kitchen opening the windows to let the smoke out.

"Auntie Annie," I yell, "I think you'd better go outside right now. Appa's really angry and he's come into the garden the wrong way!"

Part Two

Clay

Elephants in the foam

I first met Thea at my coffee shop through my best mate, Tom. Strictly speaking, it wasn't actually *my* coffee shop, though it felt like it. It had huge windows overlooking Devil's Peak. The mountain changed so often the view was never the same. My favourite time of the day was at sunset. The staff had left and I'd be cashing up on my own with my last cappuccino for the day. I liked watching the clouds scud. Yellow and pink. Some summer days the sky would be completely clear and I would think about a quick run on Camps Bay beach. On days like those, I would hurry the accounting, leave quickly. On other days, I could feel the air go thick and the chandeliers over the bar counter would look like UFOs hanging above the coffee mugs. I'd stick around, check that the floor was clean, mopped; the blackboard with daily specials wiped; the mosaics behind the bar shiny.

That day we were right in the thick of things. It was a Friday morning and the whole place buzzed with voices anticipating the weekend. People were even prepared to queue for a table: our baked goods were always worth waiting for, and the coffee, well, it was something else. This isn't an exaggeration. After I left varsity I travelled to Seattle where my grandparents had emigrated. I discovered latte art there: crema and microfoam balanced to make pictures in coffee. Though later this became commonplace, when I brought my skills back to Cape Town, every place in town wanted to snap me up. Back then, most people had only ever heard of a cappuccino. And God! they were shit. Coffee with cream plopped on top. My coffee was nothing like that. My coffee was special. So was Thea.

I don't even remember now how Tom actually knew her but he'd set up a meeting between her and his wife at the coffee shop. I was twenty-six and unmarried, and rather tired of the constant setups. I detested blind dates or being the lone male allocated to the lone female around some dinner table; I couldn't escape quickly enough. Single men are rare in Cape Town. Single women, not so much. I got a shag when I needed one, but no strings.

Tom, on the other hand, had a kid already. His wife, Françoise, was French – he'd met her in London. Exotic, great tits, but nothing to say for herself. The best times Tom and I spent were when she took the daughter and we had a beer on our own at my pad.

Anyway, Françoise had her parents and sister coming to stay from Bourgogne. She wanted a special tour for them: Cape Point, Franschhoek, Table Mountain. Thea was a tour guide apparently. Freelance, and she spoke French fluently, which is why they were meeting her. Françoise was already sitting at a table near the window when Thea walked in. I noticed her immediately, despite the crowd. God, she was gorgeous. Tall. Slim, gorgeous legs. Hair so long she could sit on it. She was wearing a pink sundress with tiny little straps and ankle boots that on anyone else might have just looked silly. Her nose was pierced, glinting as she turned her face. Her hands were hennaed. I know now they call that mehndi. I found out later she'd been at a wedding on the weekend. Her husband's sister. She stopped a moment as she came in; for someone so spectacular she didn't seem completely confident.

"Can I help you, ma'am?" I asked her, sidling past the people in the queue. (Ma'am? What the hell was I thinking?)

"I'm meeting somebody," she said.

It was then that I noticed her eyes. They weren't the same colour and that disconcerted me. A lot.

"Françoise?" I asked.

"You know Françoise?"

"You could say that." And then, fearing that might have come out wrong: "Yes, yes, I do."

Thea ran her fingers through her hair and I realised the move was from nerves. I was so caught up with staring at her that I probably looked a bit blank.

"Françoise?" she prompted.

'Over there," I said, reining myself in. Just being near her sent a jolt through me. I felt like I'd been hit by lightning.

She hesitated, then nodded, walking towards Françoise. They were both beautiful women, but Thea, jeez …

One of my waiters moved to take their orders, but my hand was out before I could contain myself. I blocked him. "I've got it," I said, taking the menus away from him.

After I'd explained some of the new vocab – espresso, flat white, macchiato – Thea ordered a latte and I made her the most beautiful elephant in the foam. When she saw it, she gasped, clapping her hands like a delighted toddler.

"It's wonderful? Isn't it wonderful, Françoise?" Her smile was solar.

That was the moment I fell in love with her.

Later, when Françoise had left the coffee shop, Thea sat on, staring into the distance. She seemed impenetrable. Unapproachable. Later, she told me she was shy. Yet her delight at the elephant encouraged me.

She started coming into the coffee shop every morning she didn't have a group – exactly ten past eight, after she'd dropped off her daughter at school. She'd always find herself the same seat near the window, then pick up her mobile phone (this was long before every Tom, Dick and Harry had one). I wasn't trying to be nosy (alright, I was); I just couldn't help myself from listening.

"Okay, I'm here now, Rajit. Yes. Mmmhmm. I'll give you a call." Once or twice she passed one of the waitresses the phone. "Please tell my husband about this beautiful place where we are now."

Plucked eyebrows raised, Zama obliged.

It didn't take me long to work out that her husband, this guy Rajit, liked control. Bit by bit, over a few stolen conversations, I found out that they lived with her father- and mother-in-law, her daughter and a houseful of servants. Keeping an eye on her every moment, I thought. Rajit's sisters had left home, gone to Durban with their husbands, and

Thea didn't see them often – even the sister called Kesiree, who'd once been Thea's closest ally.

So the truth was that Thea was lonely. Lonesome, is how she described it – that word seemed to carry more weight for her.

Sometimes Thea would arrive at the coffee shop with her mother-in-law, Asmita. I liked to know my customers, and so I got to know her too. Unlike Raj, whom I met later, Asmita was round and fairly squat. She had a double chin that jiggled, and she sweated a lot – she was constantly mopping at her pockmarked forehead and cheeks with a pink handkerchief that she kept in her giant handbag. Big enough for a corpse. She lacked allure, but she was incredibly imposing. I learnt she'd recently retired and she was spending a lot of time around the house – so she just invited herself to join Thea for coffee.

She and Thea hardly spoke. When I arrived with heart-shaped coffee foam, she tilted her head and peered at me through her reading glasses. Next time I made the same coffee pattern for her, she nodded. I was off the hook.

Thea herself always seemed skittish. She was like a newborn giraffe, with limited control of its too-long legs. Her eyes darted around the room, taking everything in. Once she told me that the tables would look better with pottery vases than the tiny glass ones I'd bought.

"You wouldn't see the water going off," she said. "And ceramics would bring a little colour into this room. Sometimes I find it, a bit . . . stark."

Alone, she would express an opinion. With Asmita, Thea retreated into herself, bowing to her mother-in-law's wishes.

"She'll have Eggs Benedict," Asmita would say, when I knew Thea preferred carrot-and-walnut muffins with grated cheddar cheese on the side.

Some weeks Thea didn't come in at all, and then I knew she had a group in from France or somewhere else where they spoke the lingo – Mauritius, the Seychelles, some other African country. She was passionate about her French, often bringing in French magazines to read at her table at the window. There was something incredibly sexy about the way her lips moved as she read. I'd catch myself staring at her full mouth, picturing it doing other things.

But it was as if Asmita could read my mind. She'd frown, pat her sweaty forehead and call for the bill. Thea would startle, pack away her mags, and walk meekly behind Asmita to the stairs. Sometimes she'd turn back to look at me and I'd sense something more than goodbye in her expression.

I became obsessed with Thea. Obsessed with her obvious melancholy, her incredible beauty, her fragility. It seemed to me she was calling out to be rescued.

I started dreaming about her. Dreams so intense I almost expected her to acknowledge them. I walked around with an almost permanent hard-on. Tom said I needed a good poke.

"You're grumpy as an elephant in must. Bone someone already," he said.

But I wasn't all that interested in *someone*. I wanted Thea. I followed his advice for a bit, though, picking up birds at braais and house parties, at clubs, even at the coffee shop.

And then I saw Thea in Sea Point.

She was standing alone watching the sea, her arms crossed over her chest. I could see she was cold. Lost in a reverie. I hesitated, but this was the only chance I was going to get without Asmita the bloodhound on my scent.

"Thea," I said, patting her on the arm.

She jumped as though I'd slapped her.

"I startled you," I said. "Sorry."

Thea's eyes narrowed, trying to place me.

"Clay," I said, "from the coffee shop."

"I know who you are," she said. Her voice was less than welcoming but I persisted.

"You look a little chilly."

She rubbed her arms. "I'm waiting for my group. We're meeting at the bus in half an hour."

There was nothing about her reaction to suggest she was happy to see me.

"Would you like to borrow my jersey?" I suggested. "You can give it to me next time you come in."

Thea shook her head. "My husband wouldn't like that."

"Well, let me buy you a jersey then," I said impulsively. "For my favourite customer!"

"Rajit wouldn't like that either." A hint of a smile.

I put my arm around her, pulling her towards the shops. "Don't tell him then. I won't if you won't."

Thea wasn't at all relaxed with me. She shifted to an arm's length away. I could sense her looking around, and I wondered if I'd made a big mistake. But my heart was soaring: I was alone with Thea. *Thea!*

As we walked into one of the little roadside shops, I can't recall which, her eyes followed me. I'd shopped with girlfriends before, and was used to standing back while they hunter-gathered their way through the merchandise. I knew when to be enthusiastic and say the right things, like *very sexy, nice colour* and *that'll suit you.* (Actually, that was about my repertoire.) But usually the women I dated knew exactly what they wanted – they just needed me to agree.

Thea was completely different.

She stood to one side. She waited for *me* to show her where to go. It was the blind leading the blind, but I wasn't about to be defeated.

"I think blue would be nice, or red or cream," I said. "What do you think?"

"Not cream. Sanusha will dirty it."

"Okay. Not cream."

I filtered through between the stacks of jerseys, pulling out this and that, while Thea watched, a quizzical expression on her face. Maybe I looked a bit desperate, picking out random items, knowing I was working against the clock – half an hour to win her over. That was it. It wasn't like I was used to chasing married women – never mind any with children. In a way I might have been looking for a flaw so I could stop obsessing about her.

It didn't happen. I held jersey after jersey in front of her while she nodded or shook her head or sometimes – which I liked most – laughed as if I'd just said the funniest thing on earth.

She was completely captivating.

"This one!" Thea said.

The one she finally chose wasn't red or blue. It was the softest pink wool, with a draped neck and a diamond pattern. She put it against my face and I held her handbag while she slipped it on.

She was right. It *was* perfect on her.

"Beautiful!" I said, meaning her more than the jersey.

We walked to the cashier together and I took off the tag while she kept her new jersey on.

"Are you sure about this?" she said. "It's a little pricey."

The cashier stopped mid-transaction, awaiting my response, and I smiled. This was an *investment*.

"Of course I'm sure."

I checked my watch surreptitiously to see how much time we had left: five precious minutes.

"I've got to go," Thea said. "I haven't been shopping in ages. This was really fun. Thanks!"

"Glad you enjoyed it." I wanted to hold her back, resisted the urge to pull her hand. Her face. To kiss her.

"Clay –"

I pushed my hands into my jeans pockets. "I'll see you at the coffee shop?"

"I'm coming in on Thursday. My group leaves tomorrow."

I couldn't help myself. "With your mom-in-law?" I asked.

"Probably. She likes your cappuccinos."

"We aim to please," I said mildly.

"Well, I'm pleased," said Thea, touching the cuff of her new jersey against her flawless cheek.

I suddenly I felt like a fool. This little exercise hadn't helped at all: I was even deeper into Thea than before. "You have to go?" I reminded her.

"I do."

She didn't go though, and neither did I. Hesitating slightly, she leant towards me and kissed me softly on the cheek.

Go. Don't go.

Then she walked away, a retreating pale-pink beacon in the distance. It might have been better if we'd left it at that.

Lame duck

That Thursday I woke up feeling the kind of pent-up excitement I recognised from when I played first-team rugby for Rondebosch. I hadn't been this worked up since the Currie Cup final. That was when Carel du Plessis scored that last-minute try giving WP a 16-all draw with the Blue Bulls. And that plonker Riaan Gouws missed the conversion. *That* would have given Province its sixth title in a decade. Watching that match, my knee twitched. Nerves. I noticed it was twitching today too. But this time, I was losing sleep over Thea. I was so worked up I got out of bed early, paced with a cup of coffee warming my fingers. Outside, slivers of streetlight cut the tar road below my flat into shards. A cat howled, searching for a mate. I knew how it felt.

I pulled on my running shorts and tackies and jogged downstairs, out into the drizzle. It was crazy to go out, but I felt crazy. My feet met the pavement – the wet made me unsteady and I slipped, whacked my elbow against the side mirror of a parked car. Bloody alarm went off.

"Shit, shit, shit," I muttered, stopping to rub my arm. Wondered if I should keep going.

Lights turned on in the opposite house. Car was flashing like a disco as the owner unlocked his front door, chain rattling. I thought I should high-tail it out of there, but I was worried the guy might shoot me, thinking I was a thief.

"Sorry, sorry," I said, when he came out wearing only a pair of shorts. "I slipped on a puddle, fell against the car."

"Prick," he said, scratching his head. "Watch where you're going!"

He unlocked and relocked the car door, and went back inside. I kept on running, unnerved. Not a great start to an auspicious day, but I wasn't going to let the incident ruin my mood: It was Thursday. Thea Thursday.

By the time I opened up the coffee shop, I'd shaved, put on a light cologne. With adrenaline from the run pumping, I felt strong. I'd bought new vases just as Thea had suggested. I'd even had my hair chopped. I'd prepared for this day like a lovelorn teenager, but when Tom asked me what I was up to, I shrugged and said, "The usual, you know."

"And the fancy haircut?"

"Wednesday special." (I didn't mention the fact that I'd even been conned into some fancy gel that cost more than the haircut.)

I went through the motions. Order checks. Accounts updates. Staff briefing. Cosmo was off sick so I called Prins, asked if he could cover. I checked my watch. It was only seven thirty. A while before Thea's normal time. The time snailed past. I looked at my fingernails. My thumbnail was bitten down and I hadn't even noticed I was biting it.

8:10 a.m.

No Thea.

8:20 a.m.

No Thea.

By eight thirty, I began to think she wasn't coming. I walked into the kitchen to check the cakes. I won't go into the sales spiel but we baked everything ourselves – no premixes.

When I came back out again, Thea was halfway across the room.

I couldn't help it. My face lit up like a bloody headlamp, and then her head moved slightly.

No.

He was walking close behind her, a hand at the small of her back. I moved to the piles of forks and knives folded in paper serviettes. I'm not in the habit of studying other men, but this guy was different: this man was keeping me from Thea. Even with the slight glance I had before I could study him properly, I could tell he was the kind of guy women swoon over. Jet-black, straight hair, cut so just the right amount of fringe fell across his face. Hugo Boss stubble. A strong aquiline nose. Iodine skin. Wide shoulders. Narrow waist. And at least a head taller than Thea.

I was staring.

Breathing in quickly, I picked up some forks and moved to the kitchen, not sure how I was going to come out again. Moments later, Prins handed me the order, grinning:

Was I that obvious?

1 carrot & walnut muffin w. ched. cheese (side)

2 poached e & toast (brown)

2 capps (1 dbl shot)

"Thanks."

He nodded and turned away. I gave the food order to our chef, Wallingford.

"I'll take this one out," I said.

"I know, boss."

But how to do this. Casually? Professionally? Distanced? Hurried? Not eager or excited, which is how I'd felt until I saw that husband of hers. Now I was just nervous. Hanging out in the kitchen like a lovesick schoolboy wasn't going to solve my problem.

I decided to make the coffees myself. Nothing fancy. No hearts and twirls. But then what if she'd mentioned the coffee pictures, and he didn't get one? I settled on a duck for both of them, wondering if any special message could be read into that. Lame duck? Sitting duck? Out for a duck? Get your ducks in a row? Rubber duck? The duck stops here, ha, ha!

"Morning," I said as I put down a tray on their table. "Two cappuccinos?"

Thea smiled at me, but not the way she had the last time we met. "Thanks."

"Nice place you've got here," the husband said. "My wife loves it. Talks about it all the time. Thought I'd come see it for myself. Keep her company."

"Welcome," I answered, hoping my voice didn't betray me.

"I'm Rajit," he said, extending his hand, which I shook. It was soft and smooth. Like a girl's.

"Clay."

"Must be hard work managing a place like this," Rajit said, pouring sugar into his coffee. He stirred vigorously and didn't even look into the cup. So much for my bird.

"The hours are good," I said.

"And free coffee all day," said Rajit, smiling broadly.

"That too. I drink tea at home just for a change."

"I'm not surprised."

Thea looked different today. For one thing, her hair was tied back, demure. Her shirt was loose-fitting, hanging on her a little. Her eyes didn't meet mine. Not even for a moment. Her gaze was fixated on Rajit, and I could see why – this was a man who was used to being centre stage, but not in an unpleasant way. I found myself liking him, despite myself. His smile was warm, reaching his eyes. His conversation not in the least patronising. We moved from talk of the coffee shop to sport, to gentle ragging about schools: 1990 and who won the Bishops-Rondebosch match.

"You do look familiar," said Rajit. "When did you matriculate?"

"1982. You?"

So he was a year older than me. Better looking. Charming.

"I remember you now," he said. "You kicked for goal five times in a gale-force wind and got the ball over every time."

All these years later and I could still relive that game. I felt myself preening but I shrugged. "Long time ago now."

"We talked about it for weeks. You still play?"

"Not really. I run, cycle."

Wallingford rang the bell. I nodded at Prins, who brought over their food.

I stepped back, looking briefly at Thea. She was twirling a tendril that had escaped from her ponytail. She didn't look back at me, and the message was very clear. Our little shopping trip had been a mistake, apart from her scoring a pretty jersey. And me having a few sleepless nights.

"Well, nice to meet you, Rajit," I said. "Both of you enjoy your breakfast." That was the closest I came to addressing Thea directly.

"Thanks," she said, finally acknowledging me with a proper look.

God, she was beautiful. I gulped. "Right," I said, "duty calls."

For once I wished I had an office to retreat to, where I could pretend they weren't in my space, eating a cosy breakfast together. I picked up my menus and headed to my corner. We were doing a private function in two weeks' time: a twenty-first. The mother (mutton-dressed-as-lamb, keen to impress, flirtatious to the point of embarrassment) couldn't make up her mind about the pastries. She wanted something unusual. Sophisticated. Her poor daughter was being steamrolled.

A while later I risked a glance at Thea. She was playing with her fork, the muffin half eaten. Rajit leant slightly forward, patted her lightly on the shoulder. Her reaction was difficult to describe. She pulled away, but seemed magnetised back into her previous position. Were those tears? Rajit was stroking her face, his soft, girly hand tracing her cheek. She looked at him. A half-smile. Whatever he was saying seemed to be working.

I stood up, moved to the bookshelf behind the desk where I kept the recipe books. I needed to focus on something else. I paged through my books, trying to find inspiration. But my mind couldn't settle. Thea was wiping her mouth with a serviette. Rajit was speaking to her, and I wondered if she was listening. She smiled slightly, in that vague way she sometimes did, and I knew that she was.

The phone rang.

"Is she there?" Tom asked as soon as he heard my voice.

"Yes. With her *husband*."

"Ouch. Don't say I didn't warn you."

"You didn't, actually. You said something about poking someone."

"I think I said 'bone'."

"Whatever. I'm feeling crap enough as it is, without you rubbing it in. What do you want?"

"I want a game of squash tonight, so I can clobber you and make you feel even less of a man than you do already."

"Awesome."

"Is that a yes, or are you going to wallow at home and play with yourself?"

"Fuck off, Tom."

"'Great, I'll see you at six at the courts. Bring a better game than last time. I hate having to humiliate you."

If anything my squash would be better tonight. I always played better when Tom pissed me off, but I actually wasn't sure what I was feeling. Disappointed: yes. Sad: yes. Humiliated: a little. Okay, *a lot*. Nothing like finding out your rival is likeable, better looking than you, and that the woman of your dreams may be a figment of your imagination.

When Thea picked up her handbag and walked to the toilets, Rajit called me over.

"That was great, man, really great," he said. "Totally up Thea's alley. So, how often does my wife come in?"

"Most mornings, I guess," I said. "I'm not always here." I needed to change the subject. "So what do you do, then?"

"Finance. Pays the bills." The answer was as vague as it was probably meant to sound. "You married?" Rajit asked.

"Yes," I said. "To the coffee shop."

He laughed. "I hear you. We're watching the game on Saturday at my mate's house. Maybe you'd like to join us?"

"I would have loved to," I said, a little confused that I actually meant it. "But work calls."

"You work on Saturday afternoons too?"

"This Saturday, yes. Rain cheque, maybe?"

"Sure." Rajit fell silent, and his eyes lifted as Thea approached. "You ready, darling?" he said. "Nice to meet you, Clay."

"You too."

"Thea," I said.

She nodded, adjusted the strap of her handbag. "Let's go, Raj," she said. "You're going to be late."

Rajit glanced at me. I knew that look. Women! I shrugged, smiling briefly. Rajit picked up his briefcase, put the cash down on top of the bill. Without even a backward glance, Thea was already walking towards the door. Rajit followed her. He nodded to me as he left.

So much for the anticipation – I'd exchanged more words with her husband than I had with her. As Tom would have said, I felt like she'd taken my balls in her hand and squeezed. Hard.

"Coffee, boss?" Wallingford said, putting down a cup and saucer.

I nodded. "We need to talk about the pastries for the Carlson twenty-first."

"I'm coming," he said. "I must check the muffins. You can read this while you wait."

"Read what?" I said blankly as he handed me a piece of toilet paper folded into a small square. My name was written on top, ink leaking into the paper making the writing seem spidery.

"From the *lady*," he said.

My fingers were trembling as I sat down on the corner sofa.

I'm sorry, the note said. *It isn't what you think.*

How did she know what I thought? How did she know any damn thing about me? Passing me secret messages she didn't want her husband to see?

What the hell was going on?

That berry place

And then I bumped into her at Kirstenbosch with Sanusha, who clearly thought I was the biggest prat since the beginning of time. I didn't have Thea's number, and I didn't try get it, though I could have asked Tom.

Despite this, I couldn't stop thinking about her. And that mark on her neck worried me – Sanusha's story about it was so rehearsed, I realised she was trying to convince herself. A smart little girl like that wasn't going to be fooled too long by make-believe. And neither was I.

I didn't see Thea for weeks after that. I tried to tell myself it wasn't really my problem, that life goes on. Truth is, I was in love. The twenty-first passed uneventfully, although the mother chose *nattes*, which are complicated plaits with four lengths of brioche dough and took ages to do. A real pain in the ass. But she was obviously happy with the results and stuck a fat tip on the bill. She mentioned that her husband was away for a week, and did I want to come round and see a new painting she'd bought? I took the money, and refused.

Once we'd split the cash between the staff, I spent mine on expensive brandy. I drank it with Tom, my feet on my coffee table watching *V* miniseries reruns non-stop for the rest of the weekend.

"You should have taken her up on it," Tom said, when he heard about my client's offer.

"Where *is* Françoise anyway?" I ignored him.

"I told you, visiting her sister in Bourgogne. New baby. You know how it goes."

"Isn't it about time you guys popped another one?"

Tom threw a shoe at me, hitting me solidly on the forehead.

"Ow."

"I've only just begun to catch up on the sleep we lost with Martine. And anyway, I'm working so many cases at the moment; I barely have time to cope. I should be there right now – at the office grafting."

I didn't ask him which cases he was talking about. I saw Tom Harper's name often enough on the radio and in the papers: *It doesn't take much to know that my client is innocent of this tragic death/ murder/ terrible tragedy and the facts will show this. Mr Henries/ Miss Botha/ Mr Shivangu is looking forward to his/her day in court.*

"I heard you on the radio again," I said.

Tom shrugged. "Just paying my bills." A hesitation. "How did I sound?"

"Like the arrogant son of a bitch I know and love."

"Now don't get all homo on me."

"Ah, come on, Tommy, give me a kiss," I said, making smooching noises. "Tommy-Boy, just the one?"

*

"We're out of cheddar cheese." Wallingford's head was down and he barely nodded at me.

"For God's sake, Wallingford. How the hell are we out of cheddar? You're supposed to watch the stocks."

"Sorry, boss," he said, not sounding at all sorry.

I picked up my car keys and headed back out again, muttering under my breath. At the nearest Pick 'n Pay store, I parked quickly, then dashed inside with my list (we were also out of flour, sugar sachets and bicarb). I had half a mind to make Wallingford walk the next time and get the stuff himself. That would teach him to fall behind and land me in it. I grabbed a basket, checked my watch. Almost nine. Shit. *So much still to do today.*

I stepped back from the shelf and barely missed walking straight into Thea's mother-in-law. Sanusha was sitting in the trolley, between rice, a bag of potatoes and some vegetables. I moved back quickly. But not before I registered Sanusha's arm in a sling. Her left cheek a faded yellow-green.

"Hello there," I said, and I could see Asmita looking at me, caught off guard. "Clay, from the coffee shop," I offered.

"You're the man who drank my juice," Sanusha said accusingly.

"What are you talking about?" Asmita said to her granddaughter. Then she nodded at me, as if to continue moving past.

I wasn't going to be deterred from this tenuous link with Thea. I grabbed the side of their trolley and Asmita stopped sharply. Her coal-black eyes faltered. I'd once said that Sanusha looked like her grandmother, but now I noticed the differences: Sanusha's clear skin enhanced by Thea's cheekbones (and the bruise, of course); straight black hair down her back that was so much more beautiful than Asmita's hennaed perm, cropped around her head.

"Shame, what happened to you, Sanusha?" I directed my question at the little girl.

"We crashed the car," she said. "Someone was chasing us!"

"We?" My stomach sank into my toes.

"Me and Mom."

"Mom and I," Asmita said.

"We still crashed." Her voice expressed her irritation. "Mom's back in hospital and I have to come to Pick 'n Pay with Asmita Ayaa. I hate shopping."

Asmita glared at Sanusha as though she thought she deserved a good clout. But who could hit a kid with a broken arm?

"What's wrong with your mom?" I tried to sound casual.

"She's fine," Asmita said. "Just some infection."

"Which hospital is she in?" I asked.

"Oh, she'll be home any day now."

"No, she won't," said Sanusha. "Mom said three more days in that berry place, and then we're going to make gingerbread men with Jelly Tots for buttons."

Asmita began to move the trolley. "Nice to see you, but we've got to get going. We've got a lunch date with Rajit in the city."

"Yes . . . well," I said, "please give her my regards. The coffee's waiting for her when she's ready."

But Asmita had already started walking away. I'm not sure she even heard me.

My drive back to the coffee shop took exactly six minutes – and that included giving the car guard a tip so that he could get out my damn way while I was trying to reverse. In my head I ran through all the possible hospitals: Vincent Pallotti, Constantiaberg, Tygerberg, Groote Schuur . . . I'd once been knocked out during a school rugby match, but other than that I tended to avoid hospitals. Like most people, I guess. I'd never even done a newborn baby visit – Tom's daughter was born in France.

Wallingford looked at me dismissively when I walked into the kitchen.

"No 'thanks'?" I said, gritting my teeth.

"Thanks, boss," he repeated woodenly and I wondered what was up with him.

"You okay, today?"

But Wallingford just cleared his throat and shook his head. He turned to the cheese, removing a slab from its wrapper. He didn't want to talk and I could respect that I wasn't the only one with problems. I just doubted he was on some weird treasure hunt in which the prize was a married woman with an infection in an unknown hospital.

Prins walked past me carrying the remains of a cheesecake and a plate of slightly burnt toast that hadn't been touched. Wallingford! I wanted to say, but I didn't bother. I had other worries on my mind today, as did he, clearly.

Prins tapped me on the shoulder. "You have a call."

I went back to the desk and picked up the phone.

Tom said. "I'm out of court for half an hour. Thought we could do squash later. You keen?"

"Thea's in hospital. That's why I haven't seen her."

"And?"

"And I don't know which hospital it is."

"Christ, Clay. You really are a mess. How the fuck do you even know she's in hospital?"

"I saw her mother-in-law and daughter. Her daughter has a broken arm and bruises."

I heard him sigh heavily. "So how can *I* help?"

"Sanusha said she was in 'that berry place.'"

"As in strawberry?"

"I think so."

"Hang on," Tom said, then his voice became muffled as he directed his attention elsewhere: "I told you the pathologist hasn't got back to me. Yes, yes. Suicide watch . . . Pollsmoor. Now *you* try find a place to sit with a client during visiting hours at Pollsmoor. And they said in seeing not in hearing distance, what a joke!"

'Tom?" I said.

"Hang on, Clay," he said. Muted: "You tell his mother that miracles don't just happen overnight. The wheels of justice grind slowly . . . Of course it's a bloody cliché – that's where they come from. Now sort it out."

"Tom?"

"It's Kingsbury," he said. "That's the only thing I can think of. Now don't come crying to me when this all blows up in your face, Middleton."

"You're a genius, even if you are a prick."

"And you owe me a beer and that squash game. Later, say seven?"

"I'll call you." I put the phone down, my heart speeding up as I prepared a coffee, a takeaway muffin, serviettes and some extra grated cheddar cheese, which luckily I now had.

"I need to go out, Prins," I said as he walked by. "Back later. And don't let Wallingford let another piece of burnt toast leave the kitchen, okay?"

*

104

It took a bit of engineering and a few white lies, but I finally found her. Thea was lying in a room with four beds, a curtain drawn halfway around hers. Against the white pillow, the cuts on her face looked raw. Her hair, normally shining and brushed, fell about her face in oily strings. On her lap lay an unopened magazine. From her wrist a tube travelled across the sheets rising to a drip bag attached to a metal wire on the left of the bed. Her eyes were open and she was staring in front of her – even as I sat down next to her, I sensed she hadn't noticed me.

"Thea," I said.

Her face flickered before it lit up.

"Did they see you come in?" she asked immediately, her voice just above a whisper so I had to strain closer to hear her.

"Who?" I asked a bit bewildered. I knew Asmita was having lunch with Rajit, so there was no chance of me being seen.

"'Them. The people following me."

I remembered Sanusha's comment about being chased. Who would have been chasing them? I thought about the corridors – empty except for doctors and nurses and a cleaner who'd been mopping the ward.

"There wasn't anybody," I reassured her.

Her body relaxed into the sheets. "They think I haven't noticed them," she said. "But I'm not an idiot. Make sure you look out for them when you leave."

"I will," I said, but I was a little unnerved. Remembering the coffee and the muffin, I produced them for Thea. "Extra cheddar cheese," I said. "Just how you like them."

When she smiled at me, her beauty emerged from beyond the cuts and bruises. She took my gifts but didn't move to sip or eat them.

Having dispensed of that part of the visit, I didn't know how to proceed. We sat without speaking, the sounds of a bed being pushed from a nearby room echoing down the corridor.

"How long have you been here?" I asked eventually.

105

Thea looked at me. "Since yesterday. I was admitted yesterday. Septicaemia." She looked at my present. "I'm sorry. I'm not sure I can eat that yet. I'll have to ask a doctor . . . my intestines . . ."

"It's fine," I said quickly. "It doesn't matter. I just wanted you to know I was thinking of you. I haven't seen you for three weeks."

"You were counting?" Thea said, almost smiling.

My face burnt.

"The accident happened the same day I saw you at Kirstenbosch. I had an operation. Sanusha –"

"I saw Sanusha today. That's how I found out. She's doing just fine."

"They were chasing us," Thea explained, "and I was trying to get away. To Annie's. I hit a wall."

"You've been in the wars, I think," I said, sounding like my mother.

"The *wars*?" she said. "God, I haven't heard that expression in years." Thea looked towards the doorway, her face clouding. "Just check again, Clay. Check they haven't come back. If Rajit hears you've been here . . ."

"Should I leave?" I said as I stood up.

"Just check."

From the door I peered down the corridor. An old woman on a walker pushed her way towards me.

"What do they look like?" I said.

"They could be anybody. I always know them. Rajit sends them out. They always wear the same colour as my knickers."

Did I ask her now what colour her knickers were? Did I get to find that out? This conversation was getting stranger and stranger.

"It's a code," she said. "Rajit tells them. Who's there now?"

Surely an old duck trundling down the passage wasn't a threat. I pictured her lifting up her Zimmer frame and shooting a spray of bullets from the end like in an action movie.

"There's an old woman," I said, then: "She's wearing purple."

"Not her," Thea said, a little grumpily. "Anyone else?"

"A young man. Tallish. Moustache. Narrow shoulders. A little slumped. He's in black. Blue jeans."

"Oh my God." Thea turned her face away and then looked back at me. "You didn't sign in, did you? He'll check the register."

So much for subterfuge.

"No," I lied, thinking I'd have to sort out that problem when I left. I sat back down next to Thea, wanting to take her hand in mine. "I'm worried about you," I said.

"He's got Sanusha. You'll need to check she's okay. He fucks prostitutes, you know."

The sentence didn't fit her pretty face and it shocked me. "I didn't know," I said, trying not to show my reaction.

"Well, he does. Actually, he fucks anything, anyone. He even tried to fuck Annie once. But it wasn't her fault and she said no."

I didn't know who Annie was, so that meant little to me.

"Is Sanusha okay?" I said.

"Oh, yes. Even Rajit has his limits. Annie was drunk when she told me about his little offer. I only found out last year. She's married now. Anyway, that thing with Rajit, that was long ago, when we were dating. I was pregnant already. Annie's rich now. Really rich. She sold some sort of IT business – I don't understand it at all. She could retire already she's so loaded."

I hated to admit it, but I wasn't following. Whatever meds Thea was on were seriously messing with her. I thought about Tom and what he would be telling me right now: *Get out of there, you wally.* I considered it, but then Thea reached out her hand and grasped mine tightly.

"You came," she said. "You came for me."

I didn't know what to say, so I didn't say anything. I stroked her hand, looking at the beautiful shape of her fingernails, the piano-playing fingers. Thea closed her eyes. A trapped sigh rose from her.

"I need to sleep. I'm exhausted. Will you watch out for me, Clay?"

"Sure," I said, knowing I should be at work.

"Thank you, thanks so much." She smiled. "Don't let them see you. They'll tell him and then he'll hurt me again." Her voice faded. ". . . And, Clay? I don't want to be hurt any more."

Coffee to froth

Sitting in Annie's garden, I heard the noise first. Rattling and metal.

Then Rajit was in the garden, furious, his bolt cutter moving from one hand to the other. This time, he looked nothing like the affable guy with the ready smile that I'd met in the coffee shop. Instinctively, I felt my palms to either sides of my hips. I stood up.

"Raj!" Thea flinched. "What the hell do you think you are doing?"

"Me? What am *I* doing? Are you out of your mind, woman? You're the one on a blanket with a man who isn't your husband!"

"I'm drinking coffee and chatting to a friend, *not* that I have to defend myself to you."

"You think I'm an imbecile? I've been outside the house. This isn't a random visit."

"Watching the house?" Thea said, her voice rising, but then she nodded, unsurprised, and her shoulders sagged. The fight was already out of her.

"Not watching, Thea, sweetheart. Just passing through."

"I just brought Thea and Sanusha some coffee," I said, trying to sound calm. Despite my attempts to look unaffected, my heart was pounding.

Rajit glared at me, and although he wasn't yet close to me, he seemed taller than the last time we'd met. His nostrils flared like a charging bull.

"You think she can't drink Nescafé? Or isn't that good enough for you, my lady, now you're living in a mansion?"

"It's just a treat," she said, hiding her half-smoked cigarette in the palm of her hand. "A taste of my old life, before the accident."

"If you really wanted your old life, Thea, you'd be at home – not hanging out with Annie and the coffee guy!" Rajit was still walking towards us. With the gate onto the road wide open, I saw a passing domestic worker peer in curiously. *Move along,* I thought. *You don't want to be involved in this.*

I wanted to help Thea up, but I wasn't going to risk Rajit's fury. Maybe I was a coward, or maybe just sensible; my presence here wasn't helping things. "Listen, Thea, I just wanted to say hello. Why don't I just go now?"

Just then Annie came running through the lounge door.

"Rajit," she said, "I don't think this is a very good idea. You could have just rung the doorbell like an ordinary visitor. I would have let you in."

"I'm sorry about the damage – of course I'll pay for it – but I'm not an ordinary visitor, as you well know, Annie. I'm Thea's husband, and you've been keeping her trapped in here like some fairy-tale princess."

"She's not Rapunzel – she can leave whenever she wants to!" Annie moved swiftly to help Thea up. "And she certainly doesn't need you to break her out of here." Then Annie did what I hadn't been brave enough to do: she put her arm around Thea, shielding her from Rajit. He would have to get past Annie before reaching his wife. *His wife.*

Rajit looked at me. "Shouldn't you be *managing*?" he said. "Isn't that what you do, *manage*?"

Prick.

"This was a brief visit, a delivery if you will," I said, and what a pompous ass I sounded.

"Ah," Rajit said, throwing down the bolt cutter. "A *delivery boy*."

I dug my nails into my palm, concentrating on remaining composed. "Sure," I said. "It's an honest-enough living."

Rajit lost interest in me for a moment. "I've been sitting in the car down the road, Annie. I was going to go back to the house, but I miss my wife. I want her to come home. I want my family back."

Annie held on to Thea. "It's not me you need to convince, Raj. What I think doesn't matter."

Rajit grinned broadly, and I recognised that charm from our first meeting. I'd fallen for it, and if I hadn't seen his angry entrance, or Thea's violet bruises, I might have fallen for it again.

"It seems I'm required to speak through you," Rajit said. "I don't mind. What I have to say isn't a big secret: I love my wife." He looked pointedly at me.

I wanted to sweep Thea up, carry her off, but I didn't even know where I stood with her. It wasn't a risk I could, or would take – God, I was weak. I wasn't used to this sort of situation, or that was my excuse anyway.

Rajit moved forward, and Thea's mismatched eyes did not leave him. His hands were open in front of him as though he was offering her something. "My flowers didn't work last time," he said, "so it's just me today." He was smiling. "I miss you, Thea. Sanusha and I want you to be with us. We want you home."

"Are you okay, Thea?" Annie said. "Do you want me and Clay to leave?"

Thea's hand gripped Annie's tightly. "He's been watching me, Annie," she said. "He knows everything I do. Everything I think."

"That's not true, Thea. But I want to know you again. Know what you think. We could start from scratch," Rajit said. "I could court you. Win you over, like I did once. You still love me, you know you do."

Thea hadn't looked at me once in this whole exchange. It was as if she was in a trance, completely hypnotised by Rajit.

I couldn't contain myself. "You hurt her!" I spat out, jealous of his hold on her. "You beat her and you hurt her."

"Delivery boy," Rajit said to me. "Don't you have some coffee to froth?"

"Don't dismiss me," I said, anger building. "I may not be Thea's husband, but I *am* her friend. And I want her safe."

"Delivery boy," Rajit said. "Why don't you go and deliver something?"

"Can't you see Thea is frightened of you? She's cowering against her friend as though Annie can defend her from you."

Raj clicked his tongue as though he was calming a child. "Thea, darling, tell this man to go away. I'm not going to hurt you again. Sanusha needs both of us. We'll even find ourselves a little flat of our own like you've always wanted."

"I want my own home," Thea said, her voice like a robot's. "I want to paint accent walls and sew my own curtains."

Fuck. I'd give her my flat in a second if that would win her over. I'd even help her sew the bloody curtains. By hand.

"Don't listen to him," I said to Thea. "He's making promises he's not going to keep."

Rajit looked at me. "As far as I know, coffee-shop guy, we've met only once. With respect, chap, how on earth would you even presume to guess what promises I will or won't keep?"

It was unnerving. There I was facing off with a man who'd forcibly entered the garden, but who hadn't used one bit of bad language in the whole time and who'd first made sure the kids were inside. He hadn't even commented on Thea's cigarette, which I knew from her, he'd normally go ballistic about. Rajit hadn't touched Thea, he hadn't touched me, and yet I knew without question that he was entirely in charge. Even worse, with just one look and a few well-chosen words, he'd identified my insecurities and had homed in on them.

"Maybe you're right," I said, trying to pull back some power. "But I have seen what you've done to her. And in my book, that makes you untrustworthy."

"Luckily, I don't read your books," Rajit said. "Thea, go upstairs and pack your bags, darling. Get Sanusha and Annie to help you."

Annie's arm was still around her friend. "I'll do whatever you want, T," she said. "You decide."

Thea nodded, then dropped her *stompie* onto the grass. "Let's go," she said. And to my chagrin, she didn't even look at me.

Rajit and I stood there, watching her slow shuffle back to the house.

"You have your answer, Clay," Rajit said, his face a picture of triumph. "Now I probably don't need to tell you this, but I'm going to anyway: Stop sniffing around my wife. She's mine, not yours. And that's never going to change. If you were a man, you would've done something right here, right now. But you're nothing. A snail. The trail of a snail. Mere slime. Thea doesn't need the likes of you in her life. So for the last time, I'm warning you: *Keep away* from my wife."

I turned to leave; Rajit's eyes tunnelling into me, the smirk on his face doubling my humiliation.

And how that humiliation cost me.

Heavy feet

I did what Tom suggested. I joined his water-polo team, often training at the tidal pool at St James, burning away my frustration. I was a good swimmer and I liked the sea, even when it was so cold my nuts froze.

It was at least a year later before I heard or saw anything of Thea or her family, but the mortification I'd felt that day changed me in a fundamental way. I didn't laugh as easily. I didn't want to connect with anyone and I avoided hook-ups, despite my married friends trying to set me up. My ego, frankly, was shattered. I threw myself into my work. I arrived early and left late. And I began a business plan to open up a coffee shop of my own. I was going to call it Au Lait Au Lait, and had found a great site on Kloof Street that would work. Tom was going to loan me some of the money. As the year passed, I thought of Thea less. Then I only dreamt about her. She didn't return for coffee, and I was grateful. I couldn't have stood being near her, knowing that she'd turned away without even saying goodbye. And that I couldn't have her.

Then one Thursday evening, I was walking towards my car when I heard these heavy footsteps coming up behind me. Before, I'd always wondered how I'd respond to a hijacking, but I was strangely calm. Gripping my car keys between my fingers, I turned abruptly, hoping to surprise the person before he struck. It was only then that I recognised my attacker.

Rajit was carrying a cricket bat, but it wasn't raised in my direction – yet. Instead he was holding it as though he was about to throw it in the car boot. I was too far to jump in my car and drive away, but close enough to think about it.

Our eyes met. What did I feel? Fear? Nerves? Resolve? My adrenaline surged; I could hear the thud of my heart. I was broader than Rajit, but he was taller. After all the training I was fit and strong. In those precious few moments I realised that he'd put on weight in the last year. Traces of a paunch, I thought with satisfaction.

I could take him, I realised, as long as I could get the bat.

Then Rajit stopped. Without any greeting, he lifted the cricket bat, holding it against his chest.

"What have you done with my wife?" he demanded.

"Your wife?" I was flabbergasted. *Was this some sort of joke?*

"Don't give me that dumb look; I know she's with you."

For a moment I felt sorry for Rajit. His anger was bubbling to the surface, but he also seemed bereft. Under his eyes, his skin was almost black, so his face looked like a skull.

"You can put that down, right now," I said, "or I'll call the security guard. I'll speak to you, but not like this."

"Fine," he said, tossing the bat onto the tar. It clattered loudly and I had to stop myself from jumping. "Do you want to come inside and have a drink? I can open up again, if you like."

Rajit nodded, and I noticed how his shoulders sagged. He followed me to the door as I disarmed the alarm. I thought for a moment of allowing the security guard to leave; he was usually only on duty during the day. But with the fire and ice that was Rajit's mood, I might still need backup.

We walked up the stairs, him first. I wasn't going to have him stand behind me.

"Have you eaten?" I asked, and he shook his head. I pulled out some leftovers, put them on a board. If he thought I was actually going to serve him, he was mistaken. This was my limit. Come to mention it, I wasn't going to give him a knife either.

I cut the cheese. He took a slice, biting into it like he hadn't eaten in weeks.

"So ... Thea," I said.

"Where the hell have you put her?" he said, a dollop of spit landing on the table between us. He picked up a serviette and wiped absentmindedly. It was completely weird, as though he'd forgotten his original intention was to beat her whereabouts out of me.

"I haven't seen her since she left with you that day at Annie's. Why? Has she mentioned me?" I asked trying not to sound too hopeful.

"No," Rajit said. "She's been living mostly in her head. She follows the usual routines, but it's been by rote. She's medicated."

"Is it helping?"

"How would I know? She's a woman. Who can understand them?"

He was wrong though: I understood Thea. What she needed more than anything was to feel safe. I could have done that for her.

We let the silence slide between us, except for the chomp-chomp of a carrot he'd picked from the salad. As he ate, I went to the fridge again and pulled out two Cokes.

"No beer, I'm afraid. This will have to do," I said.

He nodded and watched me pour two glasses, splashing a bit of Coke onto the table. Automatically, he wiped it up with his serviette, picked up a glass and gulped loudly.

"She's been gone two nights," he said. "She didn't pick up Sanusha from my mother's."

"No note?"

"Nothing. But her overnight bag is gone, and her toothbrush. She made dinner. Left it in the fridge. Sanusha's lunchbox was all packed for the next day." He peered at me as though analysing my thoughts.

I wondered if he knew what I was thinking: that if Thea had been with me, she would never have left. I would have made her happy. She wouldn't have needed pills to do that.

"I know what you're thinking," he said. "I didn't touch her. Not like that. We bought a flat. She made those stupid curtains."

"So if she isn't with me, where is she?" I asked, not wanting to think how he *had* touched her. God, it made me ill.

"I have no idea. I've called everybody I can think of. Even tried her mother, if you can believe that."

"I thought her mother was dead."

"That what she told you?"

I tried to think back. I thought I'd remembered every word Thea had ever told me, every movement she'd made, but I couldn't recall anything about her family, other than Rajit, Sanusha and Asmita.

"I don't know," I said. "I think I just assumed –"

"That was your first mistake. You can't assume anything about Thea. Anyway her mother tried to put the phone down, and when I explained her daughter was missing, I could hear a slight hesitation."

"And then?"

"Then she said her daughter died the moment she left the house with me, and I mustn't contact her ever again."

"Jeez," I said. I picked at a piece of rubbery quiche – should've heated it.

This whole thing was warped. In the year I hadn't seen Thea, I'd tried to forget her. I'd delayed opening Au Lait Au Lait for several reasons. But as I sat opposite her husband, I realised there'd only been one reason, really: if I left the coffee shop, how would Thea find me?

And now I felt ridiculous. My life on hold, and Thea hadn't even come to *me* when she needed help.

"What about Annie?" I said.

"Annie's in Thailand. I tried the house and her maid said she'd only be back in three weeks. I went there even, and nobody answered the door."

I looked at Rajit and almost felt sorry for him. He looked lost, but I had this nagging feeling that he didn't look desperate. Was this all a charade? Had he done something to Thea? My skin prickled.

Suddenly I felt like the space between us was too small. I pushed my chair back. The bile rose in my throat.

"What?" Rajit said.

I could feel my face going hot. Beads of sweat on my neck and forehead.

"Now don't go there, chap," he said. "I told you I didn't touch her, and it's the truth."

"I think you should leave now," I said, not sure what to believe, except that he was in my face now and I didn't like it.

"I'm telling you, Clay, I'm looking for my wife."

"Well, she's not here, and I haven't seen her. I need you to leave now." I stood up so violently, the chair hit the floor. He started. Then he stood up too. His face was inches from mine. I could smell the cheese on his breath.

"Don't think this is some sort of pissing contest," I said. "You don't intimidate me, and I don't give a fuck about you. If you've hurt Thea, I swear I'll hunt you down and kill you."

"You think I'd come to you if I wasn't frantic? You're the last person on earth I want to see. I'm looking for my *wife*."

"Well, as you can see, she isn't here."

"You've got me all wrong," Rajit said. "I made mistakes before, but not now."

"Have you contacted the police?"

"No. It's obvious she left of her own accord." *Unless, of course, she hadn't.*

"Well, maybe that's *your* first mistake; you need to go to the cops."

"And say what? My wife packed a bag and abandoned me and our kid?"

"That would certainly be a start." I cleared the plates quickly, shoved the remaining food back in the fridge. Then I began to walk towards the stairs, at an angle so I could still see him.

He followed and I realised I was in control.

"You don't get me, do you?" Rajit asked as he descended the stairs in front of me.

"What's there to get? If you were a better husband, you wouldn't be here looking for Thea."

"And if you were the big attraction you think you are, she'd be with you."

118

That stung, but I tried not to let it register on my face. He smiled slightly. *Bull's eye.*

"I'm going to lock up."

Rajit nodded. "Thanks for the grub."

We appraised each other. Then he looked away dismissively.

"Let me know when you find her," I said.

"Sure."

We both knew he wouldn't. But as he walked to his car, my mind was racing. *What had happened to Thea?*

And as I headed to Tom's, I couldn't stop thinking about her.

*

Tom and I were about to cycle from Rondebosch up to Signal Hill – it was far and steep. I knew my legs would be cramping by the time I reached the top. Actually I wasn't sure why I'd agreed to it in the first place. Outside Tom's house, I lifted my racing bike out of the boot.

"You're late, Middleton." Tom was there before I'd even rung the bell. "I'd begun to think you were chickening out on me."

"Thea's missing," I said.

Tom's eyebrows rose. I'd always found them rather expressive. Like giant hairy caterpillars. "I thought you were done with her."

"She was done with me."

"So leave it there, Clay. She's not your responsibility," he said as he patted my shoulder.

"I know that, but she left her daughter without saying goodbye. Maybe that husband of hers has done something to her."

Tom leant over to check his tyres, then hooked in his water bottle as though he hadn't heard me. "Water?" he asked.

"I've got."

"You're going to need it. Let's go." Tom swung himself onto his bike and didn't wait for me. He did not have a biker's body; he was too bulky.

But if you looked at his calves, you could see the muscles popping. Despite his frantic job in criminal law, he was fitter than I was. And I was pretty fit.

I clicked my shoes into the cleats and followed his luminous green stripes down the road. By the time we finished this ride it would be dark, and I hoped he'd convinced Françoise to fetch us again. Otherwise we'd be cycling back in the dark.

The whoosh of the tyres on the tar. The rhythm of my legs.

I began to calm down.

We followed Main Road and the parallel side roads to keep away from speeding taxis and other traffic. In Woodstock some of the furniture shops were still open; saws grinding. Two men carried a door with peeling white paint back inside from the pavement. The material shops were closed, but in one window a woman in a headscarf adjusted a mannequin. Further down, a little takeaway joint selling fried fish blinked "Open" in neon red and blue lights. The quiche that I'd eaten with Rajit ground in my stomach making me nauseous.

That and the thought that Thea was missing. Really missing this time.

Ahead of me, Tom's legs spun. He hadn't slowed his pace once; certainly hadn't bothered to check if I was behind him. Sometimes he really pissed me off. I pedalled faster. We were still on a downward slope, but we'd level off soon. After that it would be uphill all the way through Vredehoek.

Once we were into the City Bowl, I could feel the beginnings of a hot wind blowing. As we began to climb, we cycled past a group of mates having a braai and I eyed their beers enviously. That's what I really needed after Rajit. Not *this*.

Boerewors smells. My legs burning like liquid nitrogen. But still Tom didn't slow down.

"Fuck," I said to myself. "Fucker."

Up ahead, Tom turned as if he had heard me.

"Fucker," I said again, hoping he could read my lips.

He grinned; rose off his seat and pushed hard on his pedals. "Keep up, Clay!" he shouted. "Long way still!"

My calves screamed. My ass hurt. I needed to drink some of my water, but I couldn't keep my balance and drink at the same time, not at that pace. Tom was a machine.

A tourist bus overtook us, leaving behind lungfuls of carbon monoxide.

I began to lose my temper. This was not the afternoon escape I'd imagined when I agreed to it.

Finally, I reached the car park. Tom had already dismounted and was standing gazing at Robben Island, balancing his bike with one hand.

"You're a knob, you know that?" I said, the moment I pulled off my helmet. My hair was slick with sweat.

"Good ride?" Tom took a gulp from his bottle. "Court was packed this morning. Every regional magistrate except one was away on some course, so we were stuck in one court while they postponed case after case."

I gathered we were not going to be discussing his poor qualities, so I said nothing.

Tom glanced at me. "She's not your problem, Clay."

"And if he's hurt her?"

"Oh, come on. You wouldn't even have known she was missing if he hadn't dropped in."

"He dropped in, as you put it, with a cricket bat."

"Well good."

"Good?" I said.

"At least that meant he was worried about her. Thought you'd stolen her from him. Just forget about it. You don't have her. He doesn't have her."

"Neither does her daughter."

"Like I said before; it's not your problem."

"Okay," I said. "So drop it."

Tom shrugged. "You want to cycle back or are you catching a lift with Françoise?"

"Is this boot camp now, Mein Führer?"

"You're awfully touchy this evening." We squared off, and for a moment we were both quiet. Then Tom said in his snooty court voice: "You're going to have to pull yourself towards yourself."

"Seriously?" I said. "Is that your esteemed conclusion?"

Tom waved at his wife as she pulled up. "No. Actually, Clay, this is my esteemed conclusion, as you put it. That woman is taking over your life. Get over her, for fuck's sake."

Part Three

Gestation

Thea: Those black clouds

Things were fine for just over a year after the accident, but I started having the most terrible dreams the moment I tried to adjust my anti-anxiety meds.

In my first dream, we were in our garden. I knew this was our garden, even though in real life we only had a tiny balcony where my herbs went to die. Rajit was standing there with an enormous rusty shovel, digging a deep hole. The hole was large enough to transplant a fully grown palm tree, and the soil was rich and red, not like most Cape Town soil. As Rajit dug, he dislodged creamy-beige earthworms that pulsated and writhed, their saddles engorged and repulsive. Moving the soil, the earthworms began to grow, crowning the soil now as fat, white maggots. I couldn't keep my eyes off them, especially as they began to sprout limbs and fur. Rajit hadn't noticed anything, and was busily beating the soil trying to force the maggots back underground. Yet now they were life-size lambs, bleating and crying, their legs pushing up as they tried to avoid the slicing movements of the spade. I shouted at Rajit to stop, but he didn't. Instead he carried on hitting the mass of bodies and soil until it began to turn crimson. Rajit was like an automaton, beating, beating at the pile, but then the lambs rose through the ground and, phantom-like, hovered above the lawn. One lamb had only three legs, the fourth a bloody horrifying stump. All the time, the lambs were shrieking, and I wanted to reach out to comfort them. But the moment I did, they popped like detergent bubbles, leaving traces of blood on my hands. Rajit, who had stood aside to let the lambs ascend, picked up his shovel from where he'd leant it against the palisade fence, wiped his sweaty forehead with a hanky and continued digging as though nothing had happened.

The second dream was more vividly real, more horrifying. Nana, my father's mother, had just died. My mother was in the kitchen, her face tired, and she was making sandwiches. Ham. Slap. Mayonnaise. Slap. Cheese. Slap. A thermos stood open next to the kettle. Coffee boiled on the stove in a metal jug. I think we were in the farm kitchen at Fish River, because I could see the pantry behind her, preserved lemons and pickles and jams piled high in sealed glass bottles. My dad came into the room, and unlike the way I remembered him, he was arguing with my mother.

It will be good for her. She needs to understand, Mother said.

She's five, Veronica. I began to realise they were talking about me.

Then somehow we were in a wide passage and my brother was flicking stones from a catty. He didn't seem to be aiming at anything in particular but I wanted to be with him. To be safe. As I tried to pull away from Mother, I felt her strong hold on my arm, her fingerprints indenting my skin. She bent down, half-sitting, her face to mine. She hissed something, but I couldn't remember what it was; I only knew I was frightened. Then I felt her shove me forward, into the dark room, so hard I almost fell. All the heavy curtains were tightly shut, and there was a rotten smell. Her disdain soaked into the room and in the dream, I shivered.

Say goodbye. Don't be a ninny. Go. Go. Go, she said.

I walked towards the bed, thinking if I did this quickly, Mother would let me go back outside, to the passage where Robbie stood with his catty.

Bye, Nana, I said, not really close enough to see her.

Then the room was a tunnel of light and Mother was hovering over me, her hair like bat wings at the side of her head. She shook me by the collar like a cat might hold its kitten.

Say goodbye properly, she said. *Kiss her. Go on, Thea. Say goodbye.*

And much as I resisted, I was unable to; I could feel the bristles of a ferrule, beating me about the head. "Kiss her now!" The pain was unbearable, but all I could focus on was my grandmother's teeth floating in a jar, her mouth twisted in a grimace. And when Mother forced me over to her, she smelt of excrement and chemicals. She was Nana, but she wasn't. No twinkly eyes; they were closed.

Her cheek, cold, like a doll's, when I kissed it. Thin as toilet paper.

On the mouth! Mother said.

In my dream, my hesitation felt almost visceral, but my mother squeezed me hard. I kissed Nana again, this time on the lips.

The time sped up and I seemed to be rooted to a chair in the same cold room. My mother was not there, but she was there, because I knew I couldn't leave my seat. I needed to pee. I was supposed to be talking to God, and all I could think to say was: *I don't like it here, God*, then, *Why did you kill Nana?*

Sitting alone with this dead body with the crooked mouth I cried and cried, but quietly because I was terrified of being found out.

When I jolted awake, I was covered in sweat, my eyes sore. I felt my way to the bathroom to relieve myself, realising that this particular dream seemed bigger, more important than being just a response to a bodily urge.

On other nights, the same dreams came in parts or in their entirety and even though I was sleeping I had this feeling of déjà vu. But I found it impossible to wake myself up. When I finally did, I was left with a churning stomach and an uncomfortable feeling of betrayal, as though I'd been privy to wicked acts and intentions and had done nothing to avert them.

Something nagged at me. I couldn't escape the feeling that I was meant to be fixing something. All the more confusing because Rajit had been true to his word: he'd let me choose a little flat in Kenilworth (bought, not rented) and had taken me to Access Park, Fabric World and other material shops to buy material for curtains. And he wasn't even just *pretending* to be interested. As we held up chiffon, suede, velvet, I could see the way his eyes half closed as he felt them with just his fingertips.

And unlike my mother, he wasn't afraid of bright colours. When I eschewed the endless neutrals that had dominated my childhood home – the tan, beige, off-white, snow-white, ice-white, cream and ivory of my memories – he didn't complain, and picked up the rich burgundies, deep avocados, aquamarines or teals without hesitation.

He came home earlier every day, and helped me with Sanusha (although he was uncomfortable with bathing her, claiming she was too old now for him to "wash her cookie", even though she'd been washing herself perfectly since she was four). Rajit tasted my meals, and didn't complain too much, though he didn't exactly enthuse about them. His highest praise was still reserved for the Tupperwares that made their way to our home from the Moonsamy household, where I swore Asmita cooked triple just so her son didn't have to starve while he lived "so far", only three kilometres away.

Asmita and Kandasamy were asked to stop in only if they phoned first, because Rajit could see how their unexpected visits (sometimes twice or three times a day at the beginning) were starting to unnerve me. And, of course, I was already "unstable", as I overheard him saying to someone over the telephone. "Fragile" was another word I heard him use, but I didn't mind that nearly as much since it sounded like petals, or fairy wings, a soufflé or a breath of wind.

Besides, I think he rather liked me this way. I didn't challenge him. But I didn't challenge myself either. I was bored to the very centre of my being.

Rajit stopped pressurising me about the smoking but I knew how it bothered him. With all the effort he was making, I tried to stop twice, and the longest I lasted was seventeen days – 408 hours, Sanusha pointed out. Clearly I didn't have enough will power and determination, since I didn't reach that magic number again.

I was still depressed despite the medication, and I didn't like the way those meds made me feel. The nausea was the worst part. When I woke in the morning, I felt like I was reliving morning sickness, my stomach bloated like a helium balloon. I wasn't drinking any coffee, but that was partly because I hadn't been back to Clay's coffee shop; I knew this would rock the newfound closeness between Raj and me, and I didn't want to expose Sanusha to more of that uneasiness.

Perhaps it was actually less about Sanusha and more about me. What would I do if I actually saw Clay again? Saw the recrimination in his eyes. Would I cope? Besides, I was secretly afraid that this relative calm in our home was a mirage, and that if I studied it closely it would disappear and I'd be back to my old life of purple bruises.

I admit it, though. I thought about him and I dreamt about him. Not Rajit. Clay.

Hot dreams which left me with a sense of longing for something. Something tangible. Something . . . I couldn't quite put my finger on it, but it was something to do with being happy for happiness's sake.

*

It was Annie, though, who made me accept the fact that I needed help. She found a wonderful woman in Tokai who had a little practice dealing with "emotional health". It was all very PC – the very idea of mental health sent most people, including Rajit, spinning, so we all talked in euphemisms. My depressions were "those black clouds", the panic attacks were "those little spells" and the days I couldn't get myself to move were simply "bad days".

The woman listened when I told her that if I closed my eyes, I could see the shapes of brightly lit cabbage leaves behind my lids. I mentioned that I felt as though I could crawl under a rock and disappear, and that I secretly fantasised about being tranquillised for a few days just so I could escape from myself.

I had another fantasy, one I acted upon, and later Rajit would use this against me.

Not that I blame him. I can blame him for lots of other things, but not for that.

It was a Tuesday morning when I felt my world shift ever so slightly. My husband left for work with Sanusha in the car, and without really questioning why I was doing this, I called Asmita. Her voice on the phone was bright, cheerful, but not put on. Since Rajit had claimed me a home, we'd been getting on well. Doped up, I was less stressful to be around, and I was good at faking smiles until they registered finally in the corner of my eyes. I was beginning to appreciate her, in a way that perhaps I should have done before: Asmita was predictable to the point of boredom, which could never be said about my mother. Asmita's heartiness, which I'd distrusted at first, was actually genuine and though I resented her attachment to Rajit, I could see it would be nice for my own mother to have felt that way about me.

"Of course I can fetch Sanusha, Thea," she said. "The same time as usual? Two thirty?"

"Yes, please," I answered.

"Okay. I'll keep her until you collect her later. All right if she has an ice cream?"

I packed my bag. I did it on auto-pilot, so that later I'd wonder why I'd included a suede jacket that didn't fit me, and a pair of socks I never wore because they scratched my ankles. I filled the car with petrol. The back seat was stinking again, that sour milk smell rising up in a fog, so I bought a bottle of spray and doused the interior so it stank of lavender instead. I drew money, shoving the wads of cash into my jeans pocket. Later I searched for the money in a panic, because I couldn't remember where I'd put it.

I drove.

I might have had music on. It's all a bit of a blur. I didn't really know what direction I wanted to go in, so I let the car lead me. I drove through Somerset West. It wasn't far enough. I drove further. All the time lighting one cigarette after the other. I threw the butts out the window because it was too much effort to find anywhere else to put them. And I liked the feeling of the air in my face.

Eventually I went over this pass through the mountains, and it was beautiful, and windy, and it was like I was driving away from myself. Then, I saw a turnoff to Greyton. I'd never been there before, but I'd heard of it. The name sounded like I felt and so I followed the road away from the coast. I passed some little town to the left and it wasn't long before I pulled into Greyton's main street, and realised that this would be fine.

I checked into a hotel on a street corner. I think it was called the Post House, but I'm not sure if I knew that then or later. I asked for a room with a bath.

"That's more of a deluxe room," the receptionist said, but a man who looked managerial came in from the garden and appraised me.

"Mid-week special," he told the woman. "Give her the room. Can I get your bags for you, show you around?"

"I'll manage," I said. "I just want to sleep. No noise."

I pulled out my cigarettes, shook out another.

"No smoking in the rooms, please, ma'am," the receptionist said. "Or here, unfortunately."

I looked at her, shook my head. "Last puff then, right?"

When we got to the room the manager studied me as I kicked off my shoes. I lifted my jersey above my head, and all I was wearing beneath was a vest-top, no bra. I threw the jersey on the floor. His eyes didn't move but I could hear his breath quicken.

"You need anything?" he asked.

"Wine?"

"Sure."

"Merlot, then, and just leave it outside." I started to unbutton my jeans. "I'm tired," I said. "I'm just exhausted." I stepped out of my jeans and moved to the bed. I threw the cushions on the floor, lifted the duvet up at the corner, folded it back.

"You should lock the door," the manager said, his eyes on stalks as he backed away.

"Please lock it for me. Throw the key through the window. I'm too tired to move, too tired."

When I woke it was dark, and I wondered for a brief moment if Rajit was home yet. Asmita would have called him, told him I hadn't arrived for Sanusha. I wouldn't have expressed it aloud to anyone, but frankly, I didn't really care. I went onto my balcony, retrieved the bottle of wine, and sat there at the wrought-iron table to drink it.

I could see lights on already in the main building of the hotel. Cars passed up and down the road, their headlights already on. Dusk. The wine tasted like vinegar and in my skimpy outfit I was cold. I went back inside and lifted the duvet, wrapping it around me. A drop of wine soaked through the cotton cover.

Sitting back outside, I wondered about joy. It didn't come from the bottle of wine, nor from the pills, not even in the endless hours of talk, talk, talk with a stranger who was paid to listen to me. It could have come from my husband, but it didn't. And my daughter knew too much, knew me too well. With her I was putting on a show, but she saw straight through it, and that frightened me. When I was with Sanusha I felt transparent, and how can one feel like that with a seven year old?

The manager-person came out from where I'd signed some check-in documentation. He raised his hand in greeting and began to walk across the grass towards me. Though his steps seemed self-assured, I somehow knew he was hesitating.

"Good sleep?" he asked.

"Fine."

"Can I get you anything? Something to eat? We don't normally do room service, but perhaps for you –"

"Why me?" I asked. "What makes me so special?"

His gaze flickered like a candle blown by a breeze. He paused. "I suppose . . . you seem, you seem like you need special attention."

I leant forward, the duvet falling slightly off my shoulders.

"And where do you get that from? Is it the way I look? I've always been told I'm gorgeous. Am I gorgeous?"

He considered me, moved slightly away, like a horse about to buck.

"I'm not supposed to ask questions like that, hey," I said. "It's not idle conversation, really, is it?"

He smiled slightly. "You are beautiful, if that's what you're really asking. But are you hungry?"

"Steak," I said. "I'd like a steak with a baked potato and creamed spinach. And mushroom sauce."

"Done," he said.

"You can join me if you want," I said, wondering what the hell I was doing. "I thought I wanted to be alone, but maybe I don't."

"I'm off duty at seven."

"I'll eat at seven, then," I said. "And bring another bottle."

Sanusha (aged 7): Private investigations

This is what it feels like to be left behind by your mom when you thought she loved you: it feels like having your skin ripped off, your heart cut out, your breath pushed right out of you.

If she'd left a note, I would have felt better. I would have had something to remind me that she'd thought about me the day she stepped out of our lives. But that was the strangest thing. She didn't give me an extra kiss, put a chocolate in my lunchbox, leave me a present on my bed. It was like she'd gone for a walk and just kept on walking. Except that she took the car.

"She must have been kidnapped," I tell Appa. "We must go to the police."

"She packed a bag," he says. "Maybe she just needed to go away for a bit."

That was the first day. The second day, I say, "I think she's been kidnapped, Appa. Maybe even hijacked. I think we need to call the police."

"I checked the bank accounts, my love. She drew some money and filled the car with petrol with our petrol card. I think she just needed a holiday."

"From us? A holiday without me? Appa, she didn't call me to say goodnight."

"I know you're a big, clever girl, Sanusha, but I don't want you to worry. I'm going to sort this all out."

But, like he says, I'm not dumb. I saw how he phoned Auntie Annie 10 times a day even though she'd come round to say goodbye before she went to Thailand and promised me a silk dressing gown. I heard him on the telephone talking to Asmita Ayaa, and he said, *why, why, why,* like I was saying to him, but he said don't worry. I know he went to that coffee shop guy to ask if he had Mom, but he came back with red eyes and an empty face.

When I'm supposed to be asleep, I hear him going through Mom's cupboards, and I think he's trying to be a private investigator like Magnum P.I., looking for clues. He doesn't sleep very much, because even when I fall asleep myself and wake up much, much later when I need a pee, I can hear boxes scraping and some bad words. I'm not sure but I think maybe he's crying.

On the third day, I say to Appa, "I won't go to bed tonight if you don't go tell the police that Mom has disappeared."

So we drive to Lansdowne Road, and we sit on rocky chairs in front of a counter. The policeman yawns a lot and asks if we mind waiting while he gets himself some lunch, because it's already almost 3 and he's *moerse* hungry.

Appa looks at him, and says in a black voice, "Does it *look* like I want to wait for you to stuff your face? If you're that hungry, give this case to someone who can actually handle it."

The policeman blinks a lot and says, "There's no need to get like that, sir. I can see you're upset."

And Appa says, "Damn right. My wife has been missing for almost three days and you're worried about your lunch."

So the police asks Appa what happened and why we've waited to come in. Appa frowns and says he doesn't know, and that he'd thought she'd be back by now. Then I hear the policeman's stomach rumble, so he wasn't lying about being hungry. I give him a leftover sandwich from my lunchbox (peanut butter and jam), and he smiles and says I'm a *goeie kind*, and should he and Appa be speaking in front of me? So Appa nods at this other police lady, who takes me to another room and says I can draw here with some crayons from her desk. I don't like drawing so much any more, so I ask if she has a police car and can I look inside so I can see which button she pushes for the siren?

So she smiles a little and we walk outside where there is a big car park and she unlocks 1 car and I ask what its maximum top speed is and then I climb on the seat and pretend I am chasing robbers. After that I am driving to find my mom, who has just got a bit lost and needs me to show her the way back home.

Appa and the policeman take forever and when I ask if they've found her yet, Appa says, "They're looking right now, and the cops are even going to come to our house."

"To look for clues?" I say and then he says yes and I say, "But you've been looking all night."

Then he says, "How did you work that out?" and I say I'm not stupid, so he says, "I know that."

But I don't get to see them searching the house, because I have to stay with Asmita Ayaa in my old pink bedroom, and I tell her I don't like pink any more, and I want the room to be camouflaged like an army tank. So she says since when, and I say since today, and she says we'll see about that. Then we eat butter beans and rice in the kitchen and she tells me it will be Diwali soon, and we should start baking sweetmeats tomorrow.

*

Today we have rolled and we have fried and we have cut and we have decorated. This is what we have made:

1. Jalebi
2. Barfi
3. Gul gulay
4. Laddu
5. Murruku

We used:

1. Oil
2. Saffron
3. Cardamom
4. Food colouring (I like the orange)
5. Milk

6. Nuts

7. Coconut

8. Lemon

9. Flour

10. Lots and lots of sugar

When we are finished, I divide the sweetmeats between the different boxes so there are exactly 12 in each box. But all the time I'm looking at the clock above the kitchen counter, and the minute hand goes round and round, and Appa doesn't call. So he hasn't found Mom.

Asmita Ayaa chats nicely and tells me about Diwali when she was a little girl when once she went with her parents to India. I try to concentrate on what she's saying about the temples and markets being lit up and decorated a few days before the new moon. She tells me her auntie had *diyas* and candles all over the courtyard and the outside walls and the garden, chasing away the darkness. Oh so pretty, she says. Outside in the streets the children were playing and there were *phirki*, and sparklers and rockets, twinkling like stars. The streets smelt of cooking food, and oil from the lamps, a bit like the kitchen after the sweetmeats.

Maybe this year, she tells me, we could decorate her house like her auntie's in green, red and yellow, like she remembers. And we'll pray to Lakshmi to bring us good luck. So I say we'll need to pray a lot to bring Mom back. And maybe also to Ganesha. (Even though Mom doesn't believe in them.) And my grandmother nods and doesn't say anything else.

At the end of the day, Appa comes to fetch me. He looks upset, not upset like when he was looking for Mom and phoning Auntie Annie, but a different upset. Actually, he doesn't even say hello to me, because he's talking to Asmita Ayaa, so I listen hard.

"So they asked me if we'd had a fight, and had I hurt her. They said what mother would leave her child unless she was really desperate – maybe I'd done something and was trying to cover it up. They asked me who her friends were, and Annie's just come back from Thailand," (Oh, good) "so they questioned her, and she told them about the car crash and how she thought I'd had her followed, and she didn't think that Thea was very happy with me. Then she told them about that coffee shop guy, Clay, and he told them I'd hurt her and once he'd seen it himself, even if Thea denied it." (I didn't want to think about that, because Mom said she'd bumped herself and I didn't want to believe anything else.) "I told them things were better now between us, and we weren't fighting, but she was depressed and I was worried about her. So worried. And they looked at me, this one guy was huge and looked me in the face with his steel-grey eyes, and he said he didn't believe me and he thought I was making it up. He said we had to go to the station so we could chat a little more and I could give a statement. And who do you think was there when I walked in? That Clay person. He'd come in and reported it the day before I had, so they asked why I'd taken so long. Was I really worried, or was I playing a little game, buying time? Then they said straight out, maybe I'd k–"

The whole time, Asmita Ayaa is nodding and trying to force him to eat some *murruko*, but he keeps pushing her hand away, so it just lands on the floor and the cat licks it. Then she points at me and Appa says, "Oh," and then he says, "hello, little princess. How was your day?"

I tell him I helped make the *murruko* and actually it's delicious. So he picks it up off the floor, brushes it off, pops it in his mouth and says it's the best *murruko* he's ever eaten in the history of *murruko*. (I don't tell him about the cat spit.) And then he tells me to go and get my stuff, because we're going home soon, but Asmita Ayaa says we should stay for supper so he says okay and we do.

*

Every day after that I go to my big school and my friends are very kind to me, you know, sharing and stuff. This 1 boy who isn't really my friend gives me a Chomp and says he hopes they'll find my mom. So how does everyone know about that, I wonder, until the same boy pulls out a newspaper and it has a beautiful picture of Mom and it says,

Mother Disappears without Trace.

2 weeks later, we get a letter. It's in Mom's handwriting, and it says:
I saw the paper. I'm sorry. I'm fine but I'm not coming back. Take care of Sanusha and don't come looking for me – I've made up my mind.
Thea.
P.S. Someone has posted this letter for me far away from where I am.

The stamp is from Wellington and Appa sits at the kitchen table with his head in his hands. And he says, "Well, that's it then."

The policemen take the letter away and check something about the handwriting and tell us case closed.

"She didn't even say she loves me," I tell Appa.

"Of course she loves you. She's just mixed up."

So I am 7 when my mom walks out my life. 2 months later we move back into the house with Asmita Ayaa and Kandasamy Ajah. Appa sells the flat and he either gives away or sells everything that reminds me of my mom. But he doesn't know I've kept a photograph, and it's next to my bed inside a book about how cars work and pictures of engines and stuff.

Sometimes I look at the photo, and sometimes I want to tear it up. But I don't. I'm not sure how long my mother will be gone, but I think she'll come back one day, and I don't want to forget what she looks like.

Thea: When motherhood was invented

When I first had Sanusha, I thought she would be an extension of me: she would want the same things, sleep when I wanted to sleep, eat what I cooked.

But I hadn't realised that the life I'd chosen with Rajit meant something else: I was eating what his mother made – even when my stomach churned from too much curry and not enough muesli – and doing what my daughter wanted of me. *Again, again, again* – endless repetitions of games that were fun at first, then bored me senseless. Sanusha didn't want to play dress up, or go shopping. She trailed after her grandfather with his hammers and screwdrivers, and often ignored me flat. That was one of the biggest reasons I wanted to get away from Raj's parents in the early days of our marriage, when I could still find a voice. Can you imagine what it is like to have borne a child so young, given up everything for her, only to discover that though she loved you, she didn't find you all that entertaining?

And it wasn't like she didn't know what she was doing.

Children are treacherous beasts; they can play you like a piano and be very creative doing it. They work out your secret button long before you do – the one that makes you screech and shout and say "Go to your room!" Sanusha knew that soon enough Asmita would come in and cuddle her and ask in that annoyingly concerned way of hers why I was being "so hard on the child". Sanusha, as bright as Raj, could pitch her grandmother and me against each other, and before long we'd be fighting over her.

I'm not saying Sanusha and I didn't connect, but after she turned five these times were rarer than I wanted them to be. I tried. I took her to the movies and prepared picnics and when we were on our own, our "dates" were joyous and something to be celebrated. The connections we made in those little moments were crucial, because when I went away, I would recall them and remember motherhood as the construct invented for us.

Happiness. Bliss. Instant bonding.

And to hell with the monumental disappointments it offered.

Thea: Don't forget, nobody's perfect

So I thought when I returned to my life in Cape Town, when Sanusha and I saw each other again, it would be like a rebirth. Sanusha would fall into my arms, and I'd fall head over heels with her, like lovers on a starlit beach. But all the time, at the back of my mind, I thought: *She doesn't like me, she doesn't like me.* And, as Annie said, why would she like me? I'd left her high and dry with Rajit, and hadn't contacted her bar a birthday card when she turned eight and a present at Christmas, which, according to Rajit, she tossed in the garbage without opening. (In retrospect, this was probably a good thing, as buying presents for Sanusha is not my forte and I'd chosen something completely unsuitable. A, silver-clasped handbag. I would have done better with a nice hammer.)

I decided that, on my return, instead of controlling her I would work on controlling my environment. This was the cottage, which I bought with some help from Annie.

I hadn't factored Clay in as part of this equation, but he soon became indispensable. I'd phone him and say, "Can you hang a door?" and he'd be right over. So I made the cottage homely, but I certainly wouldn't have managed to do it on my own. I was always phoning Clay to come change a light bulb, fix a tap. He'd pop in after work – he owned the first two of a soon-to-be chain of coffee shops in Cape Town, called Au Lait Au Lait, and was often out of contact during the day. I'd adopted the Eastern practice of shoe removal at the front door, so he would ring the bell, slip off his shoes, match them neatly toe to toe on a little shelf, then pad inside in his socks.

Generally I wasn't too good on wine. I found it interrupted my sleep. A glass too many and I'd wake up at one o'clock and not fall asleep for hours. But I would have one glass, sitting on the kitchen counter, while Clay fixed stuff. As I watched him, I found we could talk. I wasn't the same person he'd known before I disappeared, but just a version of it. When I wore the pink jumper he'd bought me, he beamed. The truth is, I'd forgotten he'd bought it for me in the first place. I mean, a lot had happened since then.

Though not as much as would happen later.

But Clay always trod very carefully with me. Not once at that early stage of whatever our relationship was did he make a move first. I called. He answered. And when I didn't call for a few days, I half-suspected he drove by my cottage to check my lights were on. I'm making him sound like a stalker, but he wasn't. In fact, he'd changed quite a lot too. For one thing, he was doing incredibly well financially; although I didn't know him all that well before, I had known that he was managing the coffee shop previously, and that he didn't own it. His venture was keeping him busy, and he didn't seem to be out on a limb the way he was when we first met.

If I were a bit more like my daughter, I would have made a list, something like: these are the *ten* things I like about Clay. But after we finally became a couple ("finally" is his word not mine, as I hadn't really been counting on it), there wasn't much I didn't like. I loved the way his eyes sparkled when he saw me, how he ran me a bath and brought me tea in the morning, letting me wake up slowly. I loved his way with Sanusha, which was much better than mine, since he was building new trust, not panel-beating something dented. Clay anticipated my moods, understood my retreats when I felt black and panicked, often for no reason at all. I loved his naked body, especially the smooth skin on his back, the colour of perfect fudge. His energy energised me, and his calm calmed me. His voice was the first thing I listened for when I came home, or when I woke up.

I can admit, with a touch of guilt, that I loved him more than my own daughter.

Engaged in a passionate affair that was more than just groping in the back seats of cars, I didn't really want her around. And to his credit,

Clay didn't allow that sentiment in me. Thinking back, he was by far the better parent than I was, even to a child who wasn't his.

Ever perceptive, I think Sanusha worked this out soon enough. When she'd been dropped off for a weekend visit, she'd curl herself into Clay's lap like a cat. He would tickle her, and show her the latest *Car* magazine, which she'd explore with such fascination I even tried to read one to see what the attraction was. I didn't get it. Some weekends, Clay and Sanusha would sit on the patio and play with a set of cards, competing on the engine capacity, top speed, and torque of cars. Clay introduced Sanusha to Formula One, and she started a scrapbook of clippings about the world's top racing-car drivers – and, of course, their cars. So if Sanusha looked forward to her visits, it had nothing to do with me, and everything to do with the man I was falling in love with.

Despite his perceptiveness, I don't think Clay quite grasped my difficulties with motherhood. We didn't talk about it much, and I didn't admit that I was floundering. I had poor role models: my mother, hard as nails and image perfect; Asmita, smothering and a walkover; and Annie, who outsourced so much that I never saw her in full throttle. When I was out shopping, or taking out tour groups, I watched other mothers with a sense of envy. How was it possible that they could divide sandwiches between their broods, negotiating peanut butter versus Bovril with such ease? How did they get their children to listen, to not talk back to absolutely everything they said? And how, most of all, did they arrive at the airport in Cape Town after a twelve-hour-long journey, and still have the energy to deal with whining and tears? I wanted to slap those kids in the first ten minutes.

Thankfully, Clay was my primary focus, not motherhood. We slid into our relationship so smoothly, that it was hard for me at first to differentiate where I left off and he began. After only a month he rented out his Sea Point flat and placed his toothbrush next to mine in the cup in the bathroom. It made my skin tingle. Clay was mine and I was his;

we were part of a new team, making our own rules, choosing our future and sharing a toothbrush holder.

"Look," I said to Annie as I lead her into my bedroom – our bedroom – and swung open the cupboard to reveal Clay's clothes stacked neatly on the shelves.

"My goodness, T," she responded with a twinkle. "You really have it bad."

I smiled. "I don't care. He's perfect, you know."

And that's when Annie looked at me, then hugged me hard. "I'm sorry to tell you this, my friend. But nobody's perfect, and don't you ever forget it."

*

But it didn't matter to me what Annie said; marrying Clay was the happiest day of my life.

I'd done the wedding thing before. Previously, my scarlet sari had covered my rounded stomach, and I'd still felt the raw pain of my missing parents – one dead, one absent. Yes, I even missed Mother, who once might have checked my hair and made sure my make-up was perfect.

This time, I didn't long for a white wedding – that was Clay's choice.

"I'm only getting married once," he told me, "and I'm going to show you off to the whole world."

Rajit, surprisingly, let Sanusha be my flower girl. She was nine, and still resembled Asmita in many ways, except that she'd shot up, no longer had Asmita's rounded features, and wasn't beset with scarring acne – not yet anyway. Sanusha didn't like dresses and spent most of her time curled up in trees or constructing train tracks around the house. For birthdays she asked for Meccano and various connections, and once she and Clay had built a train village from her bedroom into the lounge. But she didn't live with us. I was allowed to have her on weekends, only with Rajit's permission, which was not always forth-coming.

He seemed pleased to be rid of me.

"You're welcome to her. Good luck, mate," I think were his exact words to Clay. But he laid claim to his daughter and wasn't about to relinquish her to me. After all, I was not to be trusted.

Disappearing had been surprisingly easy. I had enough money to last me a few months and I knew not to use my credit card. And actually, I suspected that Raj wasn't exactly going out of his way to find me, not until he thought he might be fingered for my supposed murder. Clay, I discovered later, was a little more concerned. But let's be honest – everybody, at some point in their lives, dreams of walking out of their existence and starting again as somebody completely different. I had the chance, and I took it. So what? People thought I was selfish. I didn't deny it. But isn't selfishness a part of growing up – knowing when to draw the lines? Making a decision and taking responsibility for it? I wasn't the greatest mother to Sanusha, although God knows I tried. I wanted her to be a girly girl, who liked ribbons, and skirts and Hello Kitty. But she liked mud, and camping and, most of all, peering into the bonnet of her grandfather's various motoring projects. She could change a plug (and I mean a spark plug) by six years old – under supervision, of course, though not mine.

I learnt over time that little children are more malleable. Still pre-pared to listen to you. Toddlers can be cajoled into doing what you want with a little bribery and corruption, but the moment Sanusha turned five she didn't seem so amenable. She wouldn't humour me by letting me paint her fingernails and I remember when she broke off her Barbie's head two hours after I gave it to her because she wanted to see what made the doll's arms move and thought she'd look down her neck.

All of this meant that Sanusha walked down the aisle (a petal path-way in Clay's father's garden) dressed in a suit that matched Clay's – a bowtie, hankie in the top right pocket, and everything. Mother would have apoplexy, but maybe that's why I allowed it.

"Too cute," Annie said. "Good thing she likes her new stepdad."

To be honest, I thought she liked the suit rather a lot more.

*

When I'd been in the cottage for about three months, Clay went to Costa Rica to buy coffee beans. He was there for two weeks and it was then that I realised I'd been picking up the phone to talk to *him*, not just to ask him for help. What had started as a practicality had turned into a way of getting him over. And Clay had proven himself to be a gentleman, a saviour. He'd never ignored a cry for help.

But how could I get hold of him while he was overseas? So I phoned Tom, whose number Clay had left me with "in case of emergency". From our casual get togethers over the past few weeks, I knew Tom was now married to Robyn, a fit-looking Pilates instructor whom, I assumed, he'd not married for her brain. His daughter now lived in France with her mother, visiting rarely.

"I need to get hold of Clay," I said.

"You know what, Thea? Maybe you should just leave him in peace. When I set up that meeting with Françoise, I wasn't exactly expecting to hook him up. I mean, you *were* married."

"Something like being married to Françoise and shagging Robyn on the side?"

"Oh, come on, Thea, she's much more flexible than that."

I couldn't help myself. I started to laugh. "I want to see him," I said. "I think I'm missing him."

"You think? You've got his number. Why not just leave a message on his machine? He'll answer when he's back."

"But *you* are fetching him from the airport."

"Ah."

"It'll save you the trip."

A hesitation. "Sure, all right. Why not? I've got work to do. He's coming in on SAA, seven thirty. Don't be late. You know how he hates that."

But when I actually parked my car in the short-stay, I began to ask myself what I was doing. Maybe I was more of a girl for quick fixes than permanent attachments. In Greyton I'd lived for a year drifting from one-night stands to casual sex with a few guys I liked enough to take my clothes off for. But I hadn't really thought about them the next morning, and the moment I picked up any sort of feelings on their side, I just didn't return their calls.

I didn't want to be worried about anyone else; I just didn't have the capacity for that. Reconnecting with Clay may have changed my viewpoint, but I didn't even know how he would react. And that made me nervous.

I sat in my Citi Golf (or the Shitty Shuttle, as Annie had nicknamed it, since it broke down often and rattled more than a kid's toy). Then I opened the windows, lit a cigarette and puffed in the calm.

What's the worst that can happen? He gets in the car, I take him home. Or, he doesn't see me. I don't see him. He finds his own way home.

After a few minutes, I stubbed out the half-smoked fag in my ashtray and took out a Stimorol from my handbag. I checked my face in the rear-view mirror. My lips looked naked and I reapplied some heather-shimmer lipstick.

I fingered my keys, trying to force myself to open the door with my other hand. No response, so I spat out the chewing gum and lit another Stuyvesant.

My hand was shaking, but I sucked in hard, feeling the nicotine being drawn into my lungs. By the time that smoke was all done, the flight had probably already landed. In fact, I guessed it had been on the ground for at least twenty minutes. But I was still rooted in my seat, unable to get out.

I could just let things be. It's not like Clay can't catch a taxi or something.

My palms were clammy, and I rubbed them on my skirt. Another fifteen minutes of indecision, and then I started the car.

I was out of there. And Clay would be none the wiser.

I'd forgotten, of course, about Tom.

That night I finally picked up the phone. It had rung three times, and each time I'd ignored it, ashamed of myself. But I couldn't quite get the nerve to yank the cord from the socket; I deserved a bit of punishment.

He didn't even say hello.

"You choked, Thea. Thanks for making me look like a prick."

"You *are* a prick, Tom. Everybody says so."

I heard him chuckle on the other side of the line.

"And that's why I don't need help from you in that department. I'm not taking the fall. I told Clay all about your little stunt."

"Thanks," I said. "I guess I deserve it."

"I really don't know what's wrong with you. You don't face anything that really matters."

"You have no idea what I do or don't face, Tom."

A pause. "So, did you decide you don't miss him after all? Got that wrong, did you?"

"I do miss him," I said, with a firmness I hardly recognised.

'Well, you have a funny way of showing it." Tom disconnected without even saying goodbye.

I wanted to be angry with him, but I wasn't. Because he was right.

After a few seconds, I realised the dial tone was still reverberating in my ear. I carefully replaced the phone, then flung open the door to the patio. A moon was rising on the horizon. It had rained the day before and the sky was completely clear. It made me remember how Sanusha had first discovered stars at eighteen months. "*Lights,*" she'd told me, pointing. And I remembered laughing. "*Sky lights,*" I agreed.

As the moon became clearer, I paced up and down the tiny patio like a bee in a jar. Back and forth. Back and forth. Then, finally, without letting myself think any further, I retreated inside, locking the door behind me.

When I got to Sea Point, I could feel my heart thumping in my lungs. There was a light on in his window, so I knew he was there. No turning back. This time, I was not going to run. I checked in with the security guard, whom I asked not to call up.

"It's a surprise!" I said, showing him my bottle of wine.

He grinned, nodding. "Second floor, *sisi*."

Knock. Knock.

My fist against his door sounded very loud to me, but there was no response. I could hear Clay's voice inside: "Hang on a bit, Carrie-Anne, someone's at the door. Well . . . okay then, next week, same time?" Then he must have put the phone down.

A key in the lock.

"Thea?" He was just as I remembered him: his shock of silver hair, his smiley eyes.

Nervously, I thrust the bottle of wine in front of me and said, "Welcome back. Sorry about earlier."

Without even the slightest hesitation, he took the Sauvignon Blanc, placing it gently on the table next to the door. Then he put his arms around me and kissed me passionately. As we drew away for breath, I started to laugh.

"God, I missed you," he said, plaiting his fingers through mine. "I'm so glad you're here."

He pulled me inside, his lips at my neck, my shoulders. I kissed him back, and it felt wonderful.

"You're sure now, Thea? You're not going to change your mind, are you?"

So, I took his hand, placed it over my heart. "No," I said, "I'm not." Then I could feel his soft firm hands cupping my chin, his lips on mine again, and I breathed him in. Coffee beans and sandalwood.

"Some wine?" he said, breaking away from me.

Emboldened by his welcome, I smiled and said, "Later, maybe. But right now I'd rather have some of you." And I was suddenly unbuttoning, unlacing myself to nothing but my skin; helping him slip off his T-shirt, his shorts . . .

And then I pulled him by the hand to the passage. "Where do we go now?" I said.

He picked me up and carried me into his bedroom.

Later, when I was less distracted, I noticed that it was surprisingly less masculine than I had expected. A white duvet with silver diamonds at the foot of the bed. Cushions in a light grey. Bedside tables with chrome-based lamps and soft purple shades. A view of the Atlantic.

But right then all I knew was that Clay was sweeping the cushions off the bed and placing me gently down. Then there was the weight of him, the hard muscles of his arms as he lifted himself over me. Tongues exploring, and no need to say the words I'd practised on my journey to his flat. And as he smiled at me, over and over, I felt his joy bubbling up, his expression affirming me, filling the gaps and healing all the doubts I'd ever had about myself.

Clay's touch that night liberated me.

I didn't need to run away to be myself.

Sanusha (aged 8): As good as this mother gets

I am 8, almost 9, when my mom comes back. But she doesn't come looking for me first. First, she goes to Annie's. (I dropped the Auntie part a year ago when Mom's friend said I was making her feel old, calling her Auntie when I was grown up enough to look her in the eye.) Annie then calls me and asks me if I'll come over after school because she has a surprise for me.

I think surprises can only be good things, but I learn my lesson pretty quickly.

Asmita Ayaa has been acting like my real mother – she's been the one fetching me from school, taking me places, making me feel better when I don't get an A+ in a maths test when I know I could have. Anyway, she drops me off and Annie says she'll bring me home later and is it okay if I stay for dinner?

So I walk inside with my satchel, and I ask where Matt is, and Annie says he's at a movie with his granny today.

So I say, "What's up? What's the surprise?" and then my mother steps into the lounge from the kitchen.

"Hello, Sanusha. Look how you've grown."

I find myself running to her, flinging my arms around her neck. "You're back!" I shout. "I knew you'd come!"

But her hug doesn't feel like it used to and that should be my first clue: my mother hugging me as stiff as a dead body. I let her go and I look at her in her skinny jeans, and a cherry-red halterneck, her hair cut to her shoulders.

"Where've you been?" I ask.

"Does it matter?" she replies. "I'm back."

"For good?"

"As good as it gets." We stare at each other. If she isn't going to tell me where she's been, I don't really know what else to ask.

"So, how's school?" she asks. "How's your father?"

I wonder if Annie has told her that he has a new girlfriend, an Indian girl this time, working as a skin specialist at Constantiaberg.

"You're going to have to tell him that you're here," I offer. "He sold the flat, but we're living at Asmita Ayaa's. She let me change the bedroom. I hope you like it."

"I'm sure I will," she says softly.

"You can live in the cottage again, until we find a new house," I say. "But don't get a fright, 'cos Appa moved the furniture around."

"How did he do that?" Mom answers vaguely. "You could barely open the cupboard without standing on the bed."

"Don't worry," I say. "He'll let you have it any way you like."

"I'm sorry, Sanusha, but I'm not coming to live with you," Mom says then. "Appa and I are going to get a divorce."

My mouth drops open. "You can't get a divorce without Appa saying you can."

"Sanusha," Mom says, "that's why I'm here – to sign the papers. Appa got a man to come and find me so I could."

"You're not here for me?" I ask.

"What?"

"You're not here for me?"

She sighs. "Well, it's certainly nice to see you. Of course it is."

"That's why I called you," Annie says. "You're the first person Mom asked me to call."

Somehow that doesn't make me feel any better. "Are you going away again?"

My mother pats my head and it makes me feel more like a pet than a person. "Not for the moment. I've got a job," she says brightly. "I'm going to work for the tourist board. Isn't that great?"

"You've already got a job?" I say. "But how long have you been here?"

But she brushes my question away. "Tell me about school. Have you got any nice friends? What are your teachers like?"

"Why are you asking me all these questions?" I am shouting. "You don't care about me anyway."

She touches my shoulders like she is trying to calm me, but I push her hands away.

"Don't touch me. I hate you! I hate you! I *hate* you!" I run to Annie's front door and yank it open. Behind me, I can hear Annie say, "Let her go. Let her go. I'll check on her, okay?" And then I run into the front garden, where the gate is tall, spiked and totally locked. There is no way I can escape my horrible mother.

I'm sobbing on the step when Annie comes outside and sits next to me.

"You're very angry," she says, and it's such a stupid thing to say that I don't bother answering. "I thought you'd be glad to see Mom."

"She's a bitch." I know I'm not supposed to use that word, so I'm really surprised when Annie doesn't even get cross with me.

"You know," she says, "I think you're right. Sometimes she is."

This makes me look up. Annie is smiling at me. She lifts her hand to wipe the tears from my cheeks. "Nobody's perfect, you know. Even mothers."

"She could have called me."

"Yes," she says, "she could have."

"Then she would have known about my teachers and my school and about Appa's girlfriend, and she would have chased her away so she didn't take Mom's place."

"Moms and dads don't stop loving their kids just because they stop loving each other."

"Well, I *don't* love her."

"Okay."

"And she doesn't love me, or she would have stayed."

"I can see why you'd think that, but maybe your mom loves you in a different kind of way. Maybe, for instance, she thought you would be happier without her, and that's why she left."

"'Now that's just dumb."

"'It may be, but it may also be true."

I pull my legs up against my chest and hug my arms around my knees. "So where's she been all this time anyway?"

"Maybe you can let her tell you that."

"I don't want to talk to her. She can't just come back and think I'm not busy." Annie laughs and I can see she thinks I'm being ridiculous. "Why are you laughing? This isn't funny. Does Appa even know I'm here with *her*?"

So then Annie looks away.

"He doesn't, does he? I bet you asked him and he just said no."

"Well, we didn't exactly mention it to him."

"I want to go home now."

Annie cocks her head like a puppy trying to win me over. "No dinner? I've roasted a chicken, exactly the way you like it."

"I'm not hungry," I say, although I actually am.

"Oh come, Sanusha, sweetie. Stay for *me*. I'll take you home straight after."

I sigh loud and hard. "Okay. But I'm not saying one word to her."

"Deal," she says, and we shake on it.

And even though I have 1000 questions, when we go back into the house I stick to my word. My mother sits opposite me and I don't even look at her. Instead, I pour gravy on my plate so the potatoes and chicken float in it like cream-coloured boats, and the peas are lifeboats at sea. I will my mother to tell me she's sorry or at least to explain. But like me, she is silent.

It feels like the longest dinner in my life.

Clay: Splitting at our seams

We'd talked about it. At least I *thought* we had. What man doesn't address the standard subject before getting hitched? Sex. Dosh. Kids. I loved Sanusha, but she wasn't mine genetically. I wanted my *own* family. Everyone says women get broody, but they don't talk about men getting the urge. I was into my thirties and I was ready. Au Lait Au Lait was growing by the day. Two new branches (one in Claremont and one in Hout Bay). Another scheduled for the Johannesburg airport. I had good managers in place, a system, and more free time than a lot of other guys I knew.

"I want us to try for a baby," I told Thea. "I want a mini you or a little me."

Thea eyed me over the newspaper. Her mismatched eyes caught the light through the stained-glass window. She sipped her tea, then smiled at me.

"What do we need a baby for?" she said. "This place isn't big enough for four."

"Four?"

"Sanusha?" she said, looking at me a little quizzically.

I recovered quickly. "We'll buy a bigger house then," I said. "Let's find ourselves a nice family home, with a driveway and a swimming pool and a garden."

"I don't know, Clay. That sounds nice, but I'm happy here. This is where you courted me. This is where we fell in love."

"Actually," I said, "I fell in love with you at the coffee shop the first moment I saw you. I just didn't tell you then."

Thea came round the table, put her arms around me. I could feel her breasts against me, snuggling, soft lips at my neck.

"Let's have each other for breakfast," she said, effectively ending the conversation. So much for my resolve. I gave in to her.

What hot-blooded male wouldn't?

Yet once the thought had logged into my brain, it grew exponentially. For the first time in my life, I walked past babies and actually wanted to pick them up. I eyed fathers as they charged after toddlers in Au Lait Au Lait. I even realised I was jealous of them, however stressed out they looked. Not long after that I ordered a jungle gym for the patio in the Hout Bay branch, just so I could watch the little tykes play.

Thea stayed oblivious. When Sanusha visited, my wife sipped her coffee and paged through the newspaper while Sanusha tried to get her attention by climbing up the lounge burglar bars.

"Mom! Mom! Look at me."

I nudged my wife.

"Oh," she said, "be careful. Get down from there." Then she disappeared back into the news: Rabin and Arafat shake on peace deal.

I realised that my approach was going to have to change.

"I've been thinking, Thea," I tried, watching Thea eat the omelette I'd cooked. I loved the way she ate like a real person, like she was hungry, though she still had the figure of a supermodel.

"Yes?"

"This cottage is getting too small for us, my darling. If my mom comes from Joburg, where's she going to sleep?"

"In Sanusha's room, of course."

"Not if Nusha's here. We can't kick her out of her room for my mom. It wouldn't be right."

"Sanusha's adaptable. She doesn't mind."

"I want to do some carpentry. I'd like my own workshop. And you need an office for all your files and things. The cottage is splitting at the seams. Let's go house-hunting tomorrow."

"Oh, I don't know."

"Come on, love – it'll be fun. We can nose around other people's houses and see how they live."

Thea loved to eavesdrop, loved listening to other people's conversations when she sat in a restaurant. She had this knack of imitating people's expressions and accents – probably from her language skills. She had a real curiosity for other people's lives.

This, of course, was the deciding factor.

*

House number 1: Plumstead.

The house was no bigger than the cottage, but we saw it advertised from the road, so we didn't know that. It smelt of Jik, reminding me of Thea's time in hospital. But it did have a lovely splash pool in the garden. Thea liked the double oven but she hated the retro avocado bathroom. There was a palm in a pot so huge you could barely get to the toilet, so they were probably hiding damp or a leak or something.

House number 3: Absolutely gorgeous Hansel-and-Gretel-style.

Upstairs was an open-plan pad with a view of the mountain. An easel under the skylight with giant canvases of savannah landscapes – not a crag or cliff to be seen. The top floor reeked of turps and oils, but still smelt of happiness. Downstairs, however, it was sombre. Heavy antiques blocking the windows and cluttering up the passages. So … claustrophobic. And way beyond our price range, though I wouldn't have minded selling the Sea Point flat if Thea loved it. She didn't.

House number 6: White on white.

I remember it for the ornate silver balustrade going up the granite staircase. I could picture a child falling from upstairs and cracking his (yes, his) head open on the stone floor.

House number 7: Lie in bed and watch your partner taking a dump.

Thea said there were just some things she didn't want to share with me. She wanted a bathroom with *walls*. And *doors*.

"It's no use," Thea said. "The cottage is lovely. It's pretty and sweet, and it's *home*. My feet are sore and I'd like a G&T."

158

"One more," I said, "then I'll take you to Blues. Come on." I pulled her over and kissed her.

"You and your lost-puppy eyes," she said, laughing. "That's it then. Promise?"

*

I knew it as soon as I saw it.

What I didn't know was that in a few years I would drive past that house and feel my heart thudding, my stomach heaving, and I'd be forced to stop the car so I could vomit on the side of the road. I didn't know that I would avoid that neighbourhood and move to another country so I didn't have to remember. But right on that day, I was captivated.

We parked on the road, and walked up the driveway. Unlike so many Cape Town houses, which in our budget are usually on a smaller stand, this one was not double storey and was still spacious. An old Victorian in Rondebosch – high studded ceilings, wooden floors. Thick walls so solid you couldn't hear any noise from the rooms next door. The layout was quaint. Characterful. A bathroom off the country kitchen on the one side, the garage accessed through a door next to the scullery.

"An actual garage!" Thea said, though she didn't say much more. But it was the first time she'd shown some interest. Her old car had already been sideswiped in the night – bugger didn't bother to leave a note.

Down the passageway, five bedrooms. All big enough for double beds. The main bedroom had a fireplace, with an iron grate and a marble mantelpiece. The lounge led to the garden, with a pool. The dining room on the other side of the kitchen was long enough to fit a ten-seater table. I was already imagining the parties we'd have.

But it was the outside workshop that clinched it. The walls were lined with saws, lathes, hammers, wrenches. Some organised bloke had marked each tool's place in black paint. I liked the order of it. Even then I could picture building furniture. The smell of sawdust. The feel of wood under my fingertips. And so what if anyone could see the house needed a rescue? So what about the ceilings bubbling with damp, the odd section of scuffed floor, the paint peeling outside? I wanted *us* to be the ones to fix it.

The estate agent was hovering. When the doorbell rang, I was thrilled she had to detach her limpet-grip. Clearly she sensed a sale. Later we realised that she'd had us the moment she rushed back and told us that the guy at the door wanted to put in an offer. *If you like it enough, you'd better move fast!* We eyed him skulking round *our* house, an intruder with his hands calmly positioned behind his back. His receding hairline and giraffe-like neck. I watched him poking into *our* bedroom. *Our* kitchen. And where we'd probably split the enormous lounge into two rooms to make a space for Thea's office. He retreated into the garden, ambling towards the workshop.

"It's his third time here today!" the estate agent whispered to us conspiratorially. "But he's on his own, no kids. This is a house for a family. Your daughter would love it."

"Can you leave us alone for a bit?" Thea said, and I wondered at the sharpness in her voice.

"Of course."

"I don't like bullies," Thea told me as the woman retreated. "She's bullying us."

"I don't care!" I said with a passion I hadn't expected. "This is *it*. It's perfect. It's close to schools. It's near the motorway to get into town. You can see Devil's Peak from the stoep!"

"I can see Devil's Peak from the cottage."

"Not like this. *And* you can do the kitchen exactly how you want. We can rip the whole thing out and start again. You can decorate, and Nusha can choose her own paint. She can choose a *room*, damn it. We can have more than three people round for dinner without having to breathe in!"

"It's a lot of money."

"We have the money. We do, Thea – it would be amazing."

She began to smile. "Clay, angel, I think you may love this house more than you love me."

Even then, I knew that was completely impossible.

Thea: The choice

After we moved into our new house, I had no more excuses. The house was renovated, Clay's Au Lait Au Lait branch in Joburg was open, Sanusha was settled at Herschel. (She moved from Rustenburg because Raj preferred the shorter drive and could afford the fees. Who was I to object – I'm just her mother).

I wanted to *want* Clay's children, but all I could think about was the sleep and time I would lose, precious time alone with my husband. I started to fear, though, that I wasn't quite enough for him. I didn't *complete* him in the way he completed me. He wanted more – the nappies, the toddling and the tantrums. He wanted school cricket matches, family dinners and camping holidays on the banks of the Breede River.

I wanted Clay. Period.

So I went with it. When I woke up one morning from a nightmare in which Clay was standing in the garage loading up his suitcases, his back stiff and his face stony, I realised I couldn't live without him. That, I believed, was my choice: Clay and babies, or no Clay. Thinking about it, I realised that not all children would be like Sanusha. Not every child would have this way of deliberately hurting your feelings or blocking you out to punish you for your betrayal. I wasn't going to let this family down, and maybe in time I would repair what I had damaged with my first-born.

I could be a better mother with Clay by my side. And not only to Sanusha.

So, on the night of our anniversary, I dressed myself up, packed the last of my contraceptive pills in a little box, and wrapped it extravagantly in black paper with foiled gold hearts. I think by the size of the box Clay might have been expecting a pair of cufflinks; he gave me a pretty necklace with an amethyst pendant (my birthstone). But when he tore off the paper at the restaurant and saw what was inside, he got the message immediately.

"Really?" He got up from his side of the table and drew me into a kiss.

Other people looked at us curiously, but I was thrilled to delight him, so I kissed him back.

"Absolutely," I said.

"You're not going to change your mind?"

"I love you, Clay, and this is what you want."

I guess at the time neither of us really noticed how I'd phrased it, but both of us remembered it later. When Clay had returned to his seat, he reached out his hands and clasped mine over the table.

"This is the best present you could ever have given me," he said, adopting a goofy grin.

"I haven't given it to you yet," I said, batting my eyelashes at him, to which his smile widened even more.

"I'm liking the sound of that!"

A waiter passed by, his eyes on the strewn papers. "Are we celebrating something?" he said.

"We are," said Clay. "We really are."

And when the Graham Beck Brut Rosé arrived, and we toasted our unborn children, Clay looked like the happiest man alive.

Sanusha (aged 11): Critters and punishment

There's something kind of gross about knowing your mom's been doing *it*.

It's not like I don't know about the birds and the bees – and isn't *that* a stupid way of putting it? I've looked up sex in the Encyclopaedia Britannica and there are pictures and everything. Not that I couldn't have worked it out on my own. Appa brings all sorts of women home and the noises they make at night aren't exactly soothing. But Clay's always seemed like a nice guy and I can't imagine him and, well, all that stuff. But there's my mom, her tummy getting bigger and looking completely green as she eats whole pineapples to stop herself from puking.

And boy, is she grumpy. I'm doing my best, but she's a pain in the royal ass, getting me to do this, and do that, like being pregnant makes her handicapped. I mean, in some countries in the world, women give birth in the fields and then carry on working. So why is she always griping?

I'm not particularly excited about a new brother or sister. My mom isn't exactly a huge success on that front, and now she's going to try again from scratch. Okay, so it makes me jealous, I admit. This kid is going to have an awesome dad like Clay, who doesn't wear leather pants that are too tight for him, doesn't drive a Harley and perv my friends' moms or older sisters. This kid is going to live permanently in a homey house – not in my weekend room, at least they've promised me that – and have Clay to drive them to school and check their homework. Neither of my parents ever even glance at my work. I taught myself to read by the time I was 4, and I've won the class prize for academics every year from Sub A. I don't need the help and they don't give it to me.

Clay's building a cot for the new baby in the workshop. He whistles as he works like a flipping dwarf, and if I go outside, he gets me to pass him this and that. At least then I can forget a bit about the fact I'm being ousted, and when I purposely scratch the wood with a screwdriver, Clay just takes me in his arms and says, "Come on kid – this is your brother or sister's cot. That's not very nice, is it? Now, how are you going to fix that?"

So I sand and buff and make the scratch go away. But I can't exactly get rid of the new arrival, who's planning to burst into our lives at the end of May.

Everybody says my mom looks radiant pregnant. I think she looks like a blimp with that big tummy and those swollen ankles. Her face has a tomato-ish colour and she's in the pool well into winter, trying to cool herself down. She's stopped taking tour groups on the weekends, and always finishes by 4 at the tourist board. This means she's around the house an awful lot, and Appa lets me go over more and more during the week. Before, they used to fight over who got me for a night, but that's not like it sounds: Appa was fighting for Mom to take me, and she was resisting it. She denied it, but I'm not stupid. I can see she wants to be alone with Clay.

In these pre-baby months I go on a bit of a campaign of self-destruction in the hopes that Mom might notice me. I nick Mom's cigarettes and chain-smoke in the garden. I have my ears pierced, my nose and my tongue. I walk straight out of school and hang out at Cavendish, spending money I "borrowed" from Asmita Ayaa's handbag. I buy black clothes, eyeliner, and nail polish the colour of blood. I get my friend Kerry to cut my hair. She cuts it with edgy slashes – very "daring and now". We touch tongues to see what it feels like – I kind of want her to kiss me properly. But I'm scared about what she'll think so I don't suggest it.

The school calls my parents. They sit opposite each other with me in the middle, while the exploits they know about are discussed right in front of me. I don't correct them on the facts. I actually left Herschel 4 times, not 3, I have 2 ear piercings they haven't yet discovered, and "forgetting" my homework was totally deliberate. I'm bored stiff in class – I feel like I'm sitting with a bunch of morons.

I watch Appa, his back tense and jaw clenching.

"The point is, Mrs Yates, my daughter is exceptionally bright, and it is quite clear to me the school is at fault. She needs to be challenged. Bright children like her can't just sit around being held back by a bunch of dimwits. What are we paying these exorbitant fees for?"

Mrs Yates's expression is priceless. "Your daughter, Mr Moonsamy, bunked out of school. That is an offence for which she can be expelled."

"You won't do that, though," Appa says, "since clearly the fact that she was able to leave the school three times indicates a severe lapse in security. If she can get out so easily, how easily can someone get in?"

"Obviously, sir, that is something we are attending to."

"I'm relieved to hear that."

My mother sits quietly patting her stomach.

"I see that you are expecting, Mrs Middleton. How has your daughter taken this news?"

Like I'm sitting right here. Why doesn't she just ask me?

"She's fine with it," Mom says. "Aren't you, Sanusha?"

I nod.

"Your behaviour, however, indicates otherwise."

"Now it's the baby's fault?" Mom pipes up. "Perhaps the school could learn some responsibility instead of blaming everything on an unborn –"

"Mrs Middleton, that isn't what I meant at all."

"Then why don't you just say what you mean? If you moved my daughter up three grades she'd probably still be brighter than every girl in the class, never mind the teacher. You're the *educator*, so why don't you just *educate*?"

I'm glowing. My parents have never put up such a united front for me before; this was the first time in my entire life I feel as though they are on my side. But Mrs Yates's hands are clasped tightly together on the table, the nail of her left thumb digging into her skin.

"I think, perhaps, we are missing the point. Your daughter is breaking the school rules. When she is out of the school, we cannot be expected to care for and protect her."

"So, she won't do it again, will you, Nush?" Appa says.

I nod, still mute.

"And I cannot allow her offences to go unpunished."

"So punish her," Appa says.

I grimace. *Now who's on my side?*

"She'll clean out the hamster cages, and take care of the tortoises for a month. Every afternoon, from three to four, she will check the animals. She needs to learn some responsibility; what it means to be responsible for others."

"Fine," Mom says. "But it goes two ways, Mrs Yates. You need to stimulate her better. For goodness sake, Sanusha is gifted. Our child could read and do multiplication tables before she was five. She remembers everything she reads. It's up to you to challenge her."

Yes, right. Like you do.

"I will talk to her teacher and come back with an education plan for her, but I am warning both of you, as her parents: Herschel will not allow this sort of behaviour to continue, however bright Sanusha may be." For the first time Mrs Yates looks directly at me. "Wipe that smirk off your face, young lady. This is not a joke. If I catch you off grounds without permission again, I am afraid I'll be forced to take further action."

I glare at her.

"What do you say, Nush?" Appa says.

"Yes, ma'am."

"And, for goodness sake," Mrs Yates says, losing her cool once again, "no more of that nail polish, those earrings or the weird hairstyles. Either you fit in, or you ship out. Do I make myself entirely clear?"

"Yes, ma'am."

"Detention starts promptly at three this afternoon. Don't be late, or I'll add another month without a second thought."

And that is how I get stuck at this stupid school with those stupid critters, with my hands reeking of rodent pee. And if that's how a hand-sized creature smells, I can just imagine how the baby poop is going to stink the place out.

At the first detention session, I'm told to put the hamster in a box while I clean out its cage. I shove it in, and then empty the straw and half-chewed corn onto the manure heap in the school garden. I get fresh water, new food and fresh straw. I wash off the wheel and reattach it to the side of the cage. Then I retrieve that little beast and drop it back in the cage near its little house.

With its nose snuffling against the metal it looks quite cute, but when I put my finger through the bars to pet it, the miserable furball bites me.

"Bugger," I say. "Fuck." Then, trying it out: "Fuck, fuck, fuck. You nasty little . . . shit."

The hamster looks at me, nose twitching, then turns, its almost-translucent tail skidding behind it. A whole month of this?

By the time Clay picks me up, I've had more than enough. What was that bitch thinking? I shove my book bag into the boot and slide into the front seat.

"I hate my life," I say to Clay.

"Hello," he replies.

"And why are you here anyway? Where's my mom?"

"She's not feeling so great; she's lying down."

"Typical."

"Nush?"

"Ja?"

"Give your mom a break. She's trying. And, as you'll find out one day, being pregnant is exhausting."

"Being related to Thea is exhausting."

"She loves you. They defended you this morning, and I'm not sure you really deserved defence."

"Well, you *would* say that. Nobody's *ever* on *my* side."

"I think you may just be imagining that. Want to get some cheese-cake?"

"I thought I was being punished." I eye Clay without turning my head, and notice a smile.

"And I thought you've just cleaned some hamster cages." Clay flicks the indicator, overtaking a yellow Range Rover loaded with jerrycans. "Don't make your problems my problems."

I start to laugh. "That piece of vermin bit my finger," I say, showing him the bite.

"Good word. You need a shot?"

"A shot of caffeine."

"You're *eleven*, Nush, how about a Baby Chino?"

"Oh, come on, Clay at least I'm not asking for beer."

"Thank goodness for small mercies," Clay said.

'Whatever."

Thea: Happy mother, happy baby?

"You feeling okay?" the doctor said.

Sitting in the gynae's office at thirty-two weeks, I was a bit surprised that Doctor Reynolds seemed less concerned about the foetus, and focused on me for a change. I have to say, it felt good: for once the *baby* wasn't the sole topic of conversation. I'd forgotten how I hated that with Sanusha: the moment people see you're knocked up, your body becomes public territory and you're just an incubator, your belly like a magnet to touchy-feely hands. And the only thing anyone's interested in is the sex of the baby, when it's due and what it's called. What's it to them, anyway?

"Your face is very flushed," the doctor observed.

Even Clay hadn't noticed. In the car on the way to the hospital, my head had been pounding. Clay'd talked non-stop, and I'd let him.

"Just a little headache," I said. "I'm fine."

"I'm not so sure about that. Can you lie down please," he said.

I wasn't all that worried. God, pregnancy involved *weeks* of discomfort; it wasn't like this was any worse than any other day. Nevertheless, Doctor Reynolds attached a blood-pressure monitor to my arm. He frowned.

"Your blood pressure is high, Thea. Much higher than it should be. We need to put you on a monitor upstairs and do a stress test on the baby."

"Do a stress test on Joe?" Clay asked.

"Is that his name? Don't panic now, Clay; it's just a precaution."

"Really, I feel fine. Is this really necessary?" I said.

"Just do what he says, angel. Please." Clay reached for my hand and squeezed it. And I cooperated because he asked me to.

Doctor Reynolds signed a few forms and sent us upstairs. Within minutes I was lying on the bed with a belt of sorts over my tummy. The baby shifted, and every now and then I could see the movement of a foot or hand under my skin.

"I see you, boy," Clay said, patting him. "But you need to stay in a bit longer, okay?"

The monitor dashed out some code, and the nurse nodded and told me to relax.

"Another twenty-five minutes," she said. "If Dad wants to pop downstairs to the café, that's fine. I know how long this waiting can feel."

To the dad?

"Thanks," said Clay, "but I'll stay with my wife."

I looked at Clay, trying to hide my rising anxiety. Clearly I wasn't doing a good job, because Clay reached for me, untwisting my fingers, which I'd plaited together.

I wanted a cigarette. Baby or no baby, I needed a smoke. It wasn't like Clay had had to give up anything: caffeine, or wine. Not that he hadn't offered. But, honestly, how completely pointless. If he could lug this baby around for twenty weeks, *then* I'd feel like he was actually helping.

I looked at the monitor, which was vomiting code onto a piece of paper. As the nurse handed it to Doctor Reynolds, I saw a look pass between them. She showed him a chart and he nodded, then indicated with his eyes that Clay should follow him.

Obviously Clay thought I hadn't seen it.

"I need to find a bathroom," he said. "You okay for five minutes?"

"Why don't you all just speak in front of me," I said. "I'm pregnant, not stupid."

"Of course," said the doctor. "So sorry. It's just that we need to keep calm now."

"We?" I said. "*I'm* the one who needs to keep calm, and that's not going to happen if you don't give me the information *I* need."

Doctor Reynolds smiled. "You, yes, of course. Firstly let me just say that it's under control, Thea, but we are going to have to monitor you.

At the moment, your blood pressure has reached a point where you're at risk. We're worried about preeclampsia."

I didn't say anything. I had no idea what preeclampsia was.

"What we need to do is bring your blood pressure down, and keep you on bed rest for as long as we can keep – Joe, is it? – inside. But I have to tell you at this point that it's highly likely we'll do a Caesar and it will probably be this week. We're going to try and get Joe's lungs ready using steroids, but ultimately –"

"If Thea's in trouble, then you'll need to do the delivery," said Clay.

"Exactly."

"Now, Thea," Doctor Reynolds said looking at me, "today is not the day to be a stress bunny."

I glanced at Clay, who actually looked more panicked than I felt.

"Thea, once your blood pressure's stabilised, we'll release you to be at home until the birth. But you are not, under any circumstances, to drive or do anything energetic. Quite frankly, I'd prefer it if the only time you got out of bed was to wash or go to the loo. And no steaming hot baths, and no locked doors."

I nodded. "Okay."

"If you don't have a blood-pressure monitor –"

"We do."

"Good. Then use it, please. And you have my pager if you need to get hold of me."

In the end they kept me overnight, and Sanusha, who would have been staying with us for the weekend, elected to remain with Rajit.

Clay drove me home the next day. I fidgeted while he chatted away.

I felt terrible. Weighed down. Black. Tunnelling into that foggy world that was both familiar and always a surprise. My head was hammering and I was so dizzy I felt like I wanted to puke. Every so often it seemed like I was going completely blind with just shooting stars bursting in my eyes. And I hadn't had a chance to steal a cigarette. Almost twenty-four hours with no nicotine. I heard Clay, but I didn't register everything he was saying: *Annie . . . dinner . . . worry . . . cooking . . . Sanusha . . . drop.*

"No," was all I could muster, in a whisper so soft that I could see Clay checking that he'd actually heard me.

"No dinner or no Sanusha?"

"No anything."

So when we got back to the house, Clay helped me in and out of the shower, and then opened the newly changed bedclothes for me to slip into.

"Hungry?"

"No."

Clay studied me. "Arm out," he said. "Your ankles are a little swollen. Let me just check how you're doing."

He tightened the blood-pressure monitor around my arm and took a reading.

"And?" I said.

"140/90." He bit his lip and loosened the monitor.

"Head feeling okay? No headaches?"

Acknowledging Clay was too much effort. I slid onto my side, shutting him out with my back.

"Okay," he said. "Well, I'll let you sleep – you'll feel better after a rest. I'll juice up some veggies and get you and Joe some vitamins."

What did he expect from me? I just wanted him to leave me in peace.

"I need to sleep," I said. "No juice. No vitamins. Just stop fussing, okay?" My voice was muffled but he heard me.

"Right. I'll go then. Okay." Shuffling. "Okay. I'll check on you later."

As soon as Clay had left the bedroom, I got up. I dug in my handbag, pulled out a cigarette and my lighter, and yanked open the sash windows. I leant out towards the garden, drawing nicotine into my lungs.

Whooooosh.

My hands were shaking and, balanced in the window alcove, I could feel the tightening and hardening of my belly in a Braxton Hicks contraction. With my one hand out the window and the other on my stomach, I wondered what would happen if I simply rolled myself out in one swift movement and beached myself in the garden below. I knew I was in trouble, like the time as a teenager when I'd taken the knife I was using to peel an apple and gauged it into my wrist, leaving my arm with a craquelure effect smelling of Appletiser and iron. Annie had found me that time, drawing on my exposed legs with my leaking blood, and shivering next to the tendrils of peel and browning flesh.

From the window now, I should have simply called out to Clay, who would have come running in a second, bundled me up, comforted me. Instead I puffed hard on the cigarette and tried to calm myself down, trying to ignore the pain building up in my shoulder and lower back.

I think being off the meds had been my decision – something about doing the best for our child – although I can't recall Clay ever suggesting I stay on them. But a happy mother is a happy baby, and all that. Some women are born breeders, carrying offspring with only a tiny bump and a knowing smile to show for it. I wasn't one of those women. I didn't sleep well. My back hurt. My legs swelled. Endless constipation and vomiting at least twice a day – well into the second trimester. The baby wasn't even born yet and I was already exhausted. I felt heavy, as though my whole body was weighted by a lead casing. Everything about my physical appearance was unfamiliar to me, and when I'd looked into the mirror beyond the fog, I barely recognised myself.

And the smoking was a necessity; the only thing keeping me vaguely on track, much as Clay didn't approve. I didn't care. I'd smoked with Sanusha too, and she was the cleverest child I knew. Unnervingly so.

I heard Clay making coffee. Then his footsteps and the muffled sound of the TV. I don't know how long I sat at the window, but I got through three Stuyvesants, before I realised the box was empty. I wanted to haul myself back down, but it was like my body had solidified, a feeling of impending doom almost overwhelming me. I flung the carton out the window – no point leaving evidence – thought about calling Clay, then tried to move.

*

I don't remember falling.

I might have blacked out, but when I woke up I was in an ambulance. I could vaguely hear Clay saying something about self-destruction. About me.

I moaned. My head hurt. And I was wet with what I thought was perspiration. Later Clay told me the sprinkler turned on seconds after I fell.

"It was a mistake," I said to Clay. And he looked at me with an expression that said, *I'm not quite sure if I believe you.* I'd never felt polarised from Clay before, not in this way, and that made me all the more aware of what I'd done. "I passed out," I added.

"From the window, Thea. You were at the window. *Then* you passed out. *If* you actually passed out."

"I needed some fresh air." This sounded weak, even to me. No doubt he'd found the cigarette carton in the garden.

"The baby?" Clay said to the paramedic. "Is he going to be okay?"

"Steady heartbeat, sir, but we'll need to get you to the hospital to know for sure. Your wife's symptoms aren't great. You've called your doctor?"

"He's on his way," Clay said.

I reached for his hand, urging him to look at me. "I'm sorry," I said.

"You can't just think about yourself any more. For Christ's sakes, you were *smoking* out the *window.*"

I'd never seen Clay that angry before – and his anger had never before been directed at me. I closed my eyes, focusing on Joe and the hand or foot that was pushing into my bladder.

I needed to pee. I needed to puke. I leant slightly to the side, as my body discharged the little I'd eaten just before I left the hospital. Then Clay was wiping my face with something cool, the sirens on the ambulance boring into my head like lasers.

"It's going to be okay," Clay said, his fingers through my fringe. "It's going to be fine."

And I wanted desperately to believe him, but all I could feel sweeping through me was pitch-black hopelessness and bile.

Sanusha (aged 11 and a half): Those who can't

School happens to be the most monumental waste of time ever conceived. I can do the work with my eyes closed, my hands tied behind my back and heavy metal playing in the background. Hockey is okay. I'm quite keen on clobbering the ball with my stick, but I've been sent off more than once for my "poor sportsmanship". If those girlies don't get out the way when I'm aiming at the ball, whose fault is it anyway?

My school is hopeless. They have no idea how to cope with me – it's like never-ending boredom. Most of the time I sit wondering when they'll finally work out that I'm sharper than the teachers and I could teach them a thing or 2. And what's that saying? Those who can't, teach. Something like that anyway. Then I have a loopy mother, a father who can't keep it in his pants – who knows how many half-siblings there are out there – and a grandmother who keeps telling me I would look a lot better wearing a dress and maybe – she always crunches in her shoulders when she says this – I might consider shaving my legs?

Hello, I'm 11?

Thank God for Clay, Kandasamy Ajah and Joe-baby. Clay doesn't give a toss about my homework. We watch sports, put our feet on the table and eat Karoo biltong – so much for my Hindu genes. My grandfather-of-few-words (a miracle in my life) spends most of his time under a car or looking into its bonnet, and I make extra cash helping him. I love fixing cars. They're, like, grease and logic.

And Joe – man, I love that kid. He thinks I'm the most divine thing on the planet – he has a smile to power the entire Eskom grid. Okay, so I'll admit that I wasn't all that thrilled when I heard he was coming, but now I absolutely dig him. When my mother finally stops wallowing, she and Clay can go out and I'll babysit. I'm not even bothered by nappies.

And my brother is about the only person in the world who doesn't expect me to be what I'm not.

The only bad thing about Joe is that he's brought out a side to Clay I haven't really seen before. He worries all the time – and I mean *constantly*. The first few weeks that Joe was home, the house was airless and unliveable since neither he nor Mom wanted to open the windows because of:

1. Germs

2. Draughts

3. Pollen

4. Bogeymen. (Okay, I added that one.)

But, thinking about it, Clay does have something to worry about. I know people think I'm not old enough to understand how adults think, but I've had my fair share of people in my life to study. For one thing, I can see he doesn't know what to do when Mom cries. No one else at school talks about their mother crying all the time. When I talk about my mom, the girls say she sounds weird and I've realised I'd better not mention her behaviour 'cos then I won't be able to invite friends home. Not that I've ever invited anyone, but I'd like to. The truth is that I don't have that many friends, and actually I have a feeling the girls at school think I'm weird too.

Clay has friends, but he doesn't get much of a chance to see them. He used to sometimes play squash with Tom, or cycle or run. Lately, he gets home as early as he can so he can take over from our new maid, Filda. He's stopped exercising so much, and these days I can see his clothes don't fit him well. He's always yawning and falling asleep in front of the TV and forgets to tell me to go to bed or brush my teeth. I haven't told Appa any of this because that would just be plain dumb. Then he'd say I can't visit – I still go every Wednesday and some weekends.

And then I wouldn't see Joe.

⋆

That's what I'm looking forward to when Appa drops me off after school: I can't wait to see Joe's cute little face and get one of his hugs. I open the gate and let myself in with the key I keep on a chain Mom bought me once, when she was a bit more normal.

"Hello, Nush," Filda greets me from the kitchen. "Are you hungry?"

"Nope. Where's Joe?"

"They're at the hospital."

"Again?"

Filda nods. I know she has a new weave because she's wearing a scarf tied over her head. I don't know why she does that – get a new hairstyle done all the way in Bellville and then cover it up? "Have you got homework, Nusha?" she asks me.

Most days I don't bother with all of that; I just go to school and do it in the 10 minutes before the bell rings.

"When are they coming back?" I answer instead.

"I don't know. But why don't you go greet your mother? She's not doing so good today."

So I walk into the lounge, where the curtains are closed and the windows are shut. I don't like the way it smells. Stale air and eggs. Mom's sitting on the couch like a mangy stuffed pet.

I march over to the windows and shove them open, pushing the folds of material back to let in some light. My mom jumps, the plate on her lap tumbling scrambled eggs onto her PJs.

"You need to get a life," I say. "To be honest, you're disgusting."

My mom looks at me blankly. For a moment it's like she doesn't recognise me. She scratches up and down her arms. "I'm not feeling so great," she tells me.

"Are you dying? Is that it? You think Clay or I want to come home to you like this? Maybe I just won't come round any more. Maybe I'll just stay with Appa."

"Don't say that," she says. "I've been waiting for you. Come sit." She pats the couch.

I'm reluctant. With Mom it's sometimes easier to keep your distance. No touching. No hurting. Mom pats the couch again. I want to feel sorry for her, but right now she makes me sick to my stomach. She has coffee and cigarettes on her breath, and no Stimorol to hide it. Her clothes stink of smoke, and she has stains on her sleeves, like she's dipped them in last night's gravy, or wiped away snot.

"You smell."

"Where's the baby?" she asks. "Is he okay?"

I sigh. "His name's Joe, Mom."

"I know that," she says vaguely. "He *is* my son."

"You have a funny way of showing it."

"Who taught you to be so mean? I'm not well, Sanusha."

"You never are," I reply without sympathy. "I'm going to take my bike and go see them at the hospital."

I actually want her to react. Maybe even come with me and sit with Clay as he waits for the eye doc to tell him some more news. Instead she nods, sinking back into the cushions like she's one of them.

It's almost dark. A normal mother would say it's too late to go out. A normal mother would check if I've eaten. A normal mother would say, *Wait, darling, let's take the car.* We'd go together. But I already know not to expect any of that.

I wheel my bike from the garage where it lives most of the time. To get to Vincent Pallotti, I'll have to go along the Common, under the highway and across to Pinelands. It's not far, but the cars go fast along Milner Road, barely slowing for the robots. I'm wearing dark jeans and a black T-shirt, and I hope the maniacs on the road will notice me.

I don't get very far, though, because when I get to Rondebosch Common, runners are streaming along, blocking the left-hand side of the road. I have to go around them, and they don't seem to notice that they're in the way. I'm so frustrated I want to scream. I mean, I'm actually just a kid, and for once in my life, it would be nice if the people around me didn't see straight through me. Eventually the joggers turn off to the left back onto the Common where I can see a stand set up with Energade and Bar-Ones. I cycle on, veering off down towards where Forest Drive begins, but this time there's yet another barrier. It's an Opel – you know, the Astra 1.6 Hatchback, not the Kadett – sitting half in the road, slowing the evening traffic passing it to a crawl. The young woman leaning over the bonnet looks like she doesn't have a clue. I wonder what the problem is. There's no smoke, which is a good start.

I hop off my bike as I get to her. "You waiting for the AA?" I ask.

She jumps like I've attached *her* to starter leads.

"For fuck's sake," she says, "you're not about to rob me, are you? I'm already having a shitty day and my day is getting shittier."

I like her style. What adult uses words like that to a girl my age?

"Do I look like I am?" I say. "So, the AA?"

"It's an I-told-you-so moment for my dad. I didn't join up."

"Parents don't know everything," I answer. "Anyway, I can help you." I lean my bike on its stand.

"Yes, sure. You're going to rebuild my engine, and I'm going to make it to my girlfriend's house before she tells me it's the last time she's prepared to wait for me and get the hell out of her life." She cracks a smile. "And now my knight in shining armour is a pint-sized teenager on a bike."

Strictly speaking, I'm not a teenager, but I let that go.

"I know a lot about cars," I tell her. "A *lot*. My grandfather and I fix them all the time. It's kind of my thing."

"Well, Pint, I'm –"

A car pulls up behind us, the door slamming hard a second later.

"Sanusha!" Annie says. "What on earth are you doing here at this time of night? I saw your bicycle, and then you. Are you in trouble?"

"I'm fine, as you can now see." I cross my arms over my chest. "I was going to see Joe at the hospital. And then I noticed –"

"Alicia," the woman says.

"Alicia was broken down and I offered to help."

"Does your mom even know you're here?" Annie says.

"I told *Thea*," I say, already tired of the questions. "It's not like she cares anyway."

"You *told* her? Really? And she *heard* you?" Silence. Then: "Of course she cares." Annie looks at the woman. "Funnily enough, Sanusha probably can fix your car, but I'll wait here till we know for sure."

I peer into the bonnet. "The symptoms?"

"What?"

"What was happening in the car before it conked in?" I say.

"I stalled in the queue and then the car wouldn't start again. The engine won't even turn at all."

"No clicks, nothing?"

"Nothing."

Alicia digs in the boot of the car, extracting a set of screwdrivers, a wrench and a few other items, most of which don't look used.

"From my dad," she says, handing them to me.

We lean over the bonnet. I dig around a bit, and watch the expression on her face change from disgruntled to impressed. The battery seems loose and I can see it needs tightening. Annie stands to one side, the streetlights turning her face and hair orange.

I finish the final screw. "Try the ignition," I say.

Alicia slips into the driver's seat, and Annie smiles and puts her arm around me as we wait. At first there's a subtle clicking sound, then a low hum. Then silence.

"Hang on, one more turn here," I say. "Okay, try again now."

The engine roars this time, and doesn't stop. Alicia's laughing and Annie grins at me. I slam the bonnet closed, and lean on the driver's door. "It should work fine now, but I think it's a good idea to get the battery checked just in case. Let it run for at least fifteen minutes. Check the water levels too. Or I could –"

"We'd better be going now, before visiting hours are done," says

Annie. "You okay, Alicia? Just don't let the car stall again. Come on, Nush, let's put your bike in the back."

"Well, thanks for saving me," Alicia says, then waves as she pulls away. She hoots as she turns the corner.

I get into the Volvo 850 sedan next to Annie. Her eyes flick briefly towards me, then back to the road. We drive silently to the hospital, my emotions all over the place. I'm feeling both indignant and gratified. Annie is so overprotective. Like a Jack Russell or a Spaniel or something.

"I didn't need you to pick me up," I say eventually. "I was managing just fine on my own."

"So I saw," Annie replies. "But you didn't know anything about that girl. She could have been dangerous."

"Fat chance. She seemed *nice*. Maybe she could even have been my friend. Anyway, why do you care so much? I don't need you watching over me or anything."

Annie raises her eyebrows. "So what if I like watching over you?"

She pulls into a parking bay.

"You're cramping my style. You're in my space. *And* you're not my mother, Annie."

"I'm sorry about that," she says, turning off the engine and sounding very unapologetic.

"That clunking noise from the driveline on the right?" I say.

"The what?"

"Your car. One of your CV joints is wearing out. You'd better replace it." I open my door. "So where were you going when you saw me?"

"Getting takeaways," says Annie.

"Chinese tonight? With John Wayne?"

"*Stagecoach*, actually." She smiles. "Do you want to go into the hospital on your own then? I can wait outside until I know you've found Clay."

"Clay's here. Look, his car's in that bay."

"I think I'll wait all the same," Annie says, touching my shoulder.

I slide out of the Volvo. "Suit yourself. Can you unlock the boot for my bike?"

She comes round to help me lift it out. "You know, Nush, it's not always going to be like this."

But I pull out of her attempt at a hug, and I shrug like I don't know what she's talking about. I don't want that kind of contact. I mean, what if I burst into tears? Instead, I put on my best Ringo Kid impersonation and tip my imaginary hat at Annie.

"Well, there are some things a man just can't run away from," I drawl.

She slams the boot, smiles at me and suddenly she's Hondo. "I don't guess people's hearts got anything to do with a calendar," she returns.

So I shape my finger into a gun, shoot and blow on the tip. Then I offer Annie my only admission: "All battles are fought by scared men who'd rather be some place else."

Thea: Floating away

Sometimes the skylights into my mind were open, and sometimes they weren't. I lost hours of time that I didn't remember, and when I thought it was only minutes since breakfast I would look out the window and see the sun setting. That's why I didn't understand why Clay was so angry with me. Sanusha was trailing behind him looking nervous – he'd never shouted like this before.

"*Jesus*, Thea! You don't even stop your own daughter from leaving the house when it's almost dark – on a *bicycle*, wearing *this*."

I flinched. "Don't hurt her," I said, as he pushed Sanusha towards me.

"Don't *hurt* her?" he repeated looking at me as though I was completely bonkers. "Don't *hurt* her? You're the one hurting her – do you even remember she was here earlier?"

I tried to shake out the wool, but all I could remember was something about my brother. A dream, I think, where he unzipped my body and climbed straight into my heart. I opened my mouth, but it was like it was glued together, or stuffed full of chewy pizza.

"Nothing to say, I suppose?" Clay ranted.

"Please leave her," my daughter said instead. "It doesn't matter, does it? I'm safe now."

But how safe was she really if I didn't even remember her being here earlier?

"Sorry," I said, but I didn't actually feel it – my head was so full of shadows there wasn't much space for other emotions. Sometimes I thought in the night that they'd been cut out of me, lobotomised.

"Stop it," Clay said, coming closer, as he pulled my hands roughly from my head. I realised I'd been pulling out my hair again. Tufts of it remained in my fist.

I looked at them and started to cry. My husband glanced at me, his face contorted, then he pulled Sanusha to the kitchen.

"You hungry, Nush?" he said.

I tried to follow them, but my legs felt like custard, solid on the surface, but unset on the inside. Their voices became a murmur. When Sanusha emerged, she was holding a tissue, and I felt her dabbing my eyes, wiping my nose like I was a child. Except she was the child, and she was wiping *my* face.

"He's losing patience with you, Mom. And what about Joe? He's in hospital and you didn't even notice he's not here."

"I thought he was sleeping," I protested. "And where's Filda?"

"'Mom, it's seven thirty. Filda left two hours ago. We phoned her. She told us she made you tea and said goodbye."

My daughter pointed to the cup on the coffee table. It lurked there like an algae pond, the milk leaving oily coils on the surface. A door slammed in the kitchen, a pot banged. I could hear Clay muttering, or maybe shouting – my head was so dull and dusty that everything seemed muted.

And my chest burned. It had been burning all day. That's why I'd tried to fade away – to get away from it. Away from the tremors in my hands and in my fingers, along my arms, fire-ants burning and biting all the way along my limbs. Sometimes I had to sit on my hands to stop myself from scratching and rubbing. I looked at Sanusha.

"I'm so bad; it all feels so bad," I said to her, and she touched my forehead, stroking me gently.

"You need to bath, Mom. I'm going to walk with you, and you are going to put on something clean. Something fresh."

She pulled me with more force than I was expecting, and I stood up and followed her meekly to the bathroom. Sanusha turned on the taps, and the steam rising up made me flicker back to a memory of Mother.

"Not too hot," I said. "Please, please, not too hot."

"I know," she said, "you've told me, like, a hundred times. Have a pee."

She was right – my bladder was distended from a day without movement and no release. I walked towards the toilet.

"What, you want me to hold your hand?" Sanusha looked at me, her arms folded. "I'm going to wait outside. Flush and I'll come back in to help you."

Even as I weed, I rubbed my skin, my arms across my chest like a straitjacket, as though if I held onto myself tightly enough I wouldn't float away.

The psychiatrist had said this couldn't last much longer, people always recovered from this. But I didn't believe him. And why it hadn't been the same with Sanusha, he just didn't know.

"Mom?"

"Thea?"

Clay. I hadn't heard him knocking. How long had it been? Then the door swung open and I was still on the toilet, my pyjamas curled on the floor. They were both standing there, studying me with those faces filled with twilight.

"Go downstairs, Sanusha. Put on a movie. I rented *Four Weddings and a Funeral* – it's supposed to be good. And don't wait for us. If you're hungry, the pasta's ready."

Sanusha nodded and the door closed. Clay stood in front of me, unbuttoning my pyjama top. Apparently I'd already lost seventeen kilograms. And when I stood there in front of the mirror it was obvious: my bones stuck out like a hyaena-picked kill.

"Where are you?" Clay said to me, his face a blank mask. "Where's my wife gone?"

I didn't know what to say to that, so I broke away from him, stepping gingerly into the water. Clay picked up the pyjamas, tossing them into the wash basket.

"You phoned me thirteen times today," he said. "Thirteen times that you reached me. And five messages."

"Did I?" I didn't remember that at all. "I'm not feeling right, Clay. It's like I can't contain myself, that if I don't weigh my body down, I'll fly away."

"You told me that."

"I'm afraid all the time. My chest hurts so much it feels like someone has poured petrol all over it and set it alight."

"I know."

"I can't stop shaking. It's difficult to lift a cup. And I don't need to eat. Time slips away from me."

"Yes." He picked up a sponge, soaped it and began to wash me. "They're going to operate on Joe tomorrow. You know Joe, your baby son? The one who's not here with us tonight?" Clay picked up the hand shower, rinsed my hair.

"What's wrong with him?" I said, trying to distance myself from my body. "Is it his eyes?"

"They're observing his reflux issues. And the retina of his left eye has partially detached. They may be able to repair it. They hope so."

"I hope they can," I said. I scratched my wrist. "I've got lava inside my veins, Clay." I lifted my arms, revealing my teenage scars, but he didn't even glance at them.

"You need to come and see your son in hospital tomorrow, Thea. I can't do this on my own." My husband's eyes began to fill with tears, and I felt my heart stop. "There isn't enough inside me to cope with all of this," he said. "I *need* you to come back to me. This is too hard. It's much too hard."

Thea: Nausea rising

Every mother has a birth story, and perhaps most dads. Joe's birth was frightening and early and happened within minutes after we'd arrived at the hospital. Although Joe was not yet in distress, the likelihood was that he would be before long. So Doctor Reynolds scheduled an emergency C-section. While Clay disappeared down a passageway to put on his scrubs, I lay on the hospital trolley waiting to be wheeled in. I looked at the ceiling and tried to make patterns from the cracks: Africa, a rhino and a Christmas stocking.

"Your first?" said a nurse as she lifted my head to put my hair into a net.

"Second, but I was only nineteen then. It's a while ago now. My daughter's eleven."

"A resident babysitter!" the nurse said cheerfully.

I doubted that actually. Sanusha had not been at all encouraging or supportive of the whole process.

"Right," I said, and then we were travelling down a corridor, a needle in my arm where I assumed the drip would go.

We stopped outside a delivery room. The door was closed, but I could hear murmurs and the mewl of a newborn. Then Clay was standing beside me.

"We're next," he said, smiling, his lips brushing my forehead. He moved his hand over my stomach, his focus switching to the moving bump. I'd shared Clay for almost eight months already, and I still wasn't used to it. I took his hand away from my belly, lacing my fingers through his.

Look at me.

The metal doors swung open; a mother was cradling a baby to her breast. She looked positively beatific. She smiled at me as her husband followed anxiously behind them to the recovery room.

"Are you ready?" the nurse said.

"Yes," said Clay, but she hadn't been talking to him.

"You sit outside, sir, just for a moment. We'll administer the epidural and then call you in."

The thing about environments like these is that of necessity they are sterile. Metal lights and white walls; people covered up so you can only see their eyes. Someone had put music on, something classical. At least it wasn't a talk show or a live cricket match or something. I thought longingly about my tapes at home: Nina Simone, Ella Fitzgerald, Ray Charles, then more upbeat tunes from Erasure, A-ha and Cyndi Lauper.

Perched on the edge of the bed, my head rushed as I leant forward. The anaesthetist who'd introduced himself, but whose name I'd instantly forgotten, peeled open a sterile wipe, cold and damp against my skin. A needle for the pain and then another, deeper injection a few moments later.

"Right," a male nurse said, "we're going to lift you. Move with us, okay? Half an hour and hopefully you'll have your precious little bundle in your arms."

I moved, grateful for the soft, warm blanket tucked around me. The theatre was icy. With my fingers twining and intertwining I wondered where Clay was.

"You're not going to start without my husband are you?" I said. "I need my husband."

"He's right outside, Thea. We'll call him in when we're ready."

Drip in my arm. Blood-pressure monitor. Other contraptions to measure me and the baby.

"Where's Dr Ferreira?" Dr Reynolds asked.

"I've paged him again," said the first nurse, who I now noticed had the most unusual turquoise eyes. "And look, Thea, here comes your hubby."

"You okay?" Clay asked, his lips on my forehead.

"Nervous," I replied.

"Me too."

It was then that the world started swirling.

"I feel funny," I said. "Really strange."

Doctor Reynolds looked at me. "Excited?"

"No. I really don't feel great. I need to vomit."

Then the turquoise nurse had a basin below the bed and everything collided in sharp lights and bitter tastes. I shook, hurled, watched the room move violently up and down. I realised I was crying, the tears gushing, my nose streaming. I'd bitten my tongue and I could taste the blood. I lifted my head, spitting blood and puke into the basin. I moved my head back onto the pillow.

"Where is Ferreira?" someone barked.

"I don't know."

"Page Dr O'Flaherty. We need to do this."

"Is everything okay here?" It was Clay. "This isn't normal, is it?"

"Hold your wife's hand, Clay, and just help her relax."

But his hand was so tightly gripped I wondered who was comforting whom. I lifted my head, the dizziness swirling and nausea rising again. While I retched, I could feel one of Clay's nails piercing my skin. I focused on that. But then Clay detached himself from me, and I noticed the slight shuffle as he retreated. The anaesthetist placed the mask over my face and told me to breathe.

"In, deeply in. This should calm you down."

I breathed, but I couldn't stop heaving.

"Another mask, please!" A clean one was inserted over my face.

"Can someone please tell me what's going on?" Clay said.

"She's going to be fine."

"That doesn't answer my question."

A face I didn't recognise – maybe a new doctor.

"Dr O'Flaherty," he announced himself to Clay. "Now, Mrs Middleton, we're going to have that little one out and as soon as that happens I'm going to be checking it, okay?"

"Him, checking *him*," said Clay, but the new doctor didn't respond.

*

How was that possible? They needed to cut me open first.

Then I smelt the singe of burning flesh, and a tugging and pulling below. The anaesthetist patted me gently on the shoulder, but his sympathy made me more concerned.

"What's happening?" I asked through the oxygen mask but nobody heard me. I didn't like the look of Clay's face; his startled eyes widening, a deep frown tunnelling through his forehead. He'd moved down the bed to watch his son emerge, but the sight was clearly not the bonding experience he'd wanted. For one thing, he'd let go of my hand, and I felt like I was leaving my life, hovering over the busy medical people next to my body.

"Okay, I've got him," I heard Dr O'Flaherty say as my baby was lifted and taken across the room to a scale on the examination table.

"Is he all right?" I asked through the mask, waiting for a cry, but nobody even acknowledged that it was me lying there, hacked open and harrowed. I yanked the mask off my face. "For Christ's sake, I'm the one lying here! Will somebody *please* tell me what the hell is going on?"

"It's okay, Thea, it's okay – they're checking Joe."

And then a soft yelp that sounded nothing like Sanusha's first bawl.

"He's not right. He's not fine!" Then I vomited over the side of the bed again with no special container to catch anything.

"Put the mask back on and breathe," the anaesthetist said. "Let the doctors take care of your son."

I may have lost consciousness, because when I was able to focus again, my baby and my husband were gone, and I was being wheeled into a recovery room, with no baby to show for it. I wept silently while a sturdy nurse with enormous breasts gently wiped my face, dabbing away my tears.

"Now, Mom," she said. "You're going to see your little one a bit later, so all you need to do now is sleep so you've got lots of energy to take care of him when he comes."

Was she joking? Sleep? Having not even *seen* the baby I'd carried around with me every moment of every day for the last thirty-two weeks? And wasn't this exactly what I'd feared? A baby taking my husband away from me?

"We're monitoring your blood pressure, and we're going to have to do a transfusion. You lost a lot of blood, my dear."

"I want my husband. I want my baby."

"I'm sorry, dear."

"I want my husband. I want my baby."

"Now, don't be difficult, Mom. We're going to do the best we can with this situation, aren't we?"

"I don't even know what the situation is, for God's sake."

"Well, we'll get Doctor Reynolds to come through in a moment and explain things to you, okay?"

"Okay," I said.

"A brave face, my dear, is what you need."

I turned my head away. If she wasn't going to tell me anything useful, why didn't she just shut the hell up?

Clay: Broken china

If I'd thought Thea looked fragile, Joe was like porcelain so fine you could see through it. He had wrinkled, old-man skin. So delicate you could trace the complex map of his blood vessels. And he was reddish-purple. Like a beetroot. His closed eyes had no eyelashes, but the rest of his body was soft and downy. Joe cried softly and strangely, like a kitten, but Doctor O'Flaherty said I should be thrilled. Not every baby born that early could even cry.

"A good sign," he said, nodding, and considering the birth we'd just experienced, I was prepared to accept just about *anything* as a good sign. "Nevertheless, his Apgar score is low. We'll check again in five minutes."

Twenty minutes earlier I hadn't even known what an Apgar score was. Now I was waiting for my son's results with bated breath.

I thought about Thea. People say they feel cut in two, caught between different responsibilities, different people. But I was seriously torn: my wife was lying bleeding on some slab, and my child was incapable of breathing on his own. Right then, his little lungs were being filled and emptied artificially. I wasn't sure who I should be with, who needed me more. Looking around me, though, I just hoped I was doing the right thing.

Standing in the NICU, nothing could have prepared me for this. There were weird wires and strange electronics. Lights flashing. Little babies attached to IVs, with machines keeping them alive. I heard words I didn't know, like: "surfactant", "drips", "ventilator".

Dr O'Flaherty made me stand back a bit. I didn't want to interfere with my boy's care, but I wanted to know what they were doing to him.

I watched as a needle was put into Joe's tiny arm. His wrist was so narrow my wedding band would have fitted it.

A nurse touched my arm, her coal-black eyes reassuring. "Antibiotics. He's tough, that little one. I can just see it," she said.

"You can?"

"I see a lot of little pumpkins like him. He's strong, trust me." She smiled and moved off, and I wished I'd asked her what the drip was for, what surfactant was, and when I'd be able to hold him. For now, his tissue-paper body was covered with wires and he didn't look like he was as sturdy as the nurse was telling me.

Next they attached a mainline IV to his belly button. I was told this was the equivalent of an umbilical cord. Then there was the temperature monitor on his chest. Joe was too small to breathe on his own, too small to adjust his own temperature and far too little to swallow.

My own helplessness was the worst part. While the doctors and medical staff crowded my son's little body, I could do nothing but wait. And it was then that Dr O'Flaherty turned to me.

"Why don't you give your wife an update? She must be terribly worried."

"What do I tell her?" I said.

"Tell her he's stable. We've administered the surfactant, which is like an oil to lubricate the lungs. Normally babies his age would take weeks to make it themselves, but because we've done it early, I estimate Joe will be off the ventilator within two days. Hopefully this will reduce the risk of any complications."

"And those?" I pointed at the drips and the wires.

"Joe doesn't have a sucking reflex yet, so he'll be fed intravenously. Not for long, though. We'll try to administer breast milk through a tube in a few days' time, as this helps babies mature quicker. Your wife will need to produce at least 10ml of breast milk an hour if he's going to thrive."

"I want to pick him up."

"Not yet, but you can touch his hand."

I approached my son, brought my finger to his left hand, which was free of attachments. And then I felt it. His firm grip around my finger.

Hello, Dad.

And I realised I was laughing.

*

So when I went back to see Thea, I was hopeful. Jubilant even.

"He's doing fine! He held my finger!" I told her, but I was surprised by her lack of enthusiasm.

He did? I expected to hear, but instead: "You left me alone here."

I'd never known Thea to be clingy – actually, I was often the more emotional one. The one needing physical reassurance. I realised that the birth had taken its toll on her. As it would.

"They know what they're doing here, darling," I answered, trying to be reassuring, sympathetic.

"Don't call me that," she snapped. "Nobody's come to see me, so I still have no idea what's wrong with me. *They* may know what they're doing, but *I* don't know what they're doing."

"I can update you on Joe until Doctor Reynolds comes."

"Right now, I want an update on *me*. I could have died, and you left me."

"I'm sorry. I thought you'd want me to check on Joe. He's just a foetus in an incubator instead of your womb, Thea – that's what I was told. We can't even think about him as a baby yet. But we can hope!"

"You left me. You made your choice. I could have *died*, Clay. I was frightened. I was by *myself.*"

I took her hand as I sat down next to her. "I'm sorry," I said. "Do you want me to go find Doctor Reynolds to see what's going on?"

"Don't leave me. I'm feeling terrible."

"Maybe you need to sleep. The nurse said they'll take you up to your room once you've been checked."

"Where is that bloody doctor?" she said to me. "I almost *died.*"

196

Thea looked helpless and her expression frightened me. Her left hand gouged crescents into her right palm. I separated her hands and ran my fingers over her cheek.

"You're okay now, Thea. You're okay. I'm here and everything is going to be fine. And despite what you've been through, we have the most beautiful son. How can I ever thank you?"

"Just don't leave me," she said, her hands interlaced with mine. "I feel like I'm bleeding away, bit by bit."

When Doctor Reynolds arrived at her bedside, his mood was sombre.

"We'll do the transfusion, and I think we've managed to save the uterus, but we'll know that in a few weeks. I highly suspect we'll do another D&C, perhaps two. There were some adhesions."

I didn't know what that meant, but I nodded, hoping everything would become clearer. Doctor Reynolds patted my shoulder.

"Look, Clay, I think you need to rally the troops. Your wife needs you, but Dr O'Flaherty and I also think that within the next two days, we'll need to try Kangaroo Care on Joe – it's a brand-new programme, but I think it will help. I'm not going to overload you with information, but you're going to need to be in the hospital rather a lot. It involves a lot of contact between you and the baby. Where is Thea's mother?"

"Let's just say she's not in this equation," I said.

"A sister then? Your mother? A friend?"

So I phoned Annie. She floated into the hospital half an hour later wearing a loose white thing that made her look like a ghost except for the chunky gold beads that jingled on her wrists and around her neck. When she kissed Thea, she left a crimson pucker on my wife's cheek – the only colour I'd seen on her face in twenty-four hours.

"You smell nice," said Thea.

"L'Eau d'Issey – you want some?" Annie dabbed a wand of perfume on Thea's wrists and neck. "Now, Clay," she said to me, "why don't you toddle off, and leave us girls alone?"

As I left I breathed a sigh of relief.

I wasn't really sure of this woman lying in the bed, but I knew that in the moment Joe had come into our lives, something between us had changed.

I hoped with all my heart that the change was temporary.

Thea: A mother when I met him

Five days after Joe was born I came home without him. On the drive back, Clay navigated the speed bumps and circles so slowly it felt like we weren't moving. I was stiff as a board, my hand over my stitches, my breasts already engorged. The nurses had helped me attach this pump to extract the foremilk, which they were going to give to Joe with a little dripper into some tube down the back of his throat.

In the eleven years since I'd had Sanusha, I'd changed – or else I'd forgotten an awful lot. Everything about the process was invasive: the way nurses jotted down my first "bowel movement", the casual inspection of my nipples, the catheter bag hovering above my head like a bright yellow headlight. And Clay's conversation became one-tracked, like a scratched record: Joe, Joe, Joe . . .

When Joe came off the respirator, just as Dr O'Flaherty had promised, they placed his little body in between my breasts, the contact of my skin on his, supposedly rubbing off any germs and keeping him warm. He was very odd-looking, with his skin now a jaundiced mustard, and rather than an overwhelming surge of love, I felt something akin to disinterest. As I lay with Joe, Clay took out his camera.

"Enough – you're photographing my boobs, for God's sake."

"Sorry," said Clay. "It's just that this is a special moment for both of you. Cuddling together. I want to record it."

"I'm tired," I said. "And sore. You hold him."

And that is what happened, until Clay had completely taken over the primary care of the infant who had bowled him over.

I was glad to see Sanusha, who'd only seen Joe from a window onto the neonate ward.

"Cute," she'd said on her one and only hospital visit. "You know what that means? Ugly but interesting." She placed a vase of flowers next to my bed. "From me and Appa. So when d'you get out of here?"

"A few days."

"Good, because Appa's got this new girlfriend who keeps patting my head like I'm a Labrador or something. She wants to fiddle with my hair *all* the time. I want to cut it, Mom, *short*! It's, like, just constantly in the way."

I looked at my daughter and wondered if I was as self-involved as a teenager. She hadn't once bothered to ask me how *I* felt.

"And Appa says you will have to talk to him about it," Sanusha continued.

"About what?" I said absently.

"My *hair*, Mom." I caught the roll of her eyes but I couldn't be bothered to scold her for it.

"It's *your* hair," I said, at that point caring little whether she shaved it all off or dyed it green.

"That's exactly what I said." Sanusha patted my hand. "You look awful. I think I'm going to skip babies and drive fast cars instead."

"Good idea."

"So, how much blood did you actually lose?" she asked, a confused look on her face.

"Litres or pints?" I retorted.

*

At home, Clay had hung a string of balloons and a welcome-home banner above the dining room table. I smiled weakly as he rushed to the bedroom to pull down the sheets. He helped me into my pyjamas, placed the crackly sheet protector on my side of the bed, plumped up the pillows. I put one arm around his neck and he lifted me up, gently placing me in bed. He'd put a few magazines on the bedside table, and a radio. As I rested my head, he dashed to the kitchen, returning with a cappuccino in which he'd made a little baby out of the froth.

"Sweet," I said, because that's what was required, and the grin he gave me made the effort worthwhile.

"So, I thought I could move a TV into the bedroom," he said. "Get a few videos for you. Maybe some old movies you've wanted to see."

"Sounds good," I said, thinking back to before Joe, when the bedroom was a playground lit by candles and smelling of vanilla incense.

"And then I think I'll go back to the hospital and let you sleep. Joe's doing better with the bodily contact. Maybe you could express a bit of milk before I go? We can put any extra in the freezer."

"I'm not a goddamn cow," I said, my whole body filling with resentment.

"No," he said, "but you *are* a mother."

"I was a mother when you met me."

Clay's eyes darkened, but then he stood up from where he'd been sitting on the edge of the bed. "So, darling, what would you like to eat?"

"Nothing. I'm not hungry." I expected him to cajole, to coax, but instead he kissed me on the cheek.

"Then it'll take me two ticks to get you set up."

And the sooner you can do it, the sooner you can go back to Joe.

*

I knew I was supposed to love Joe, to feel some amazing miracle bond between us. I knew I was supposed to melt as I gazed into his cobalt-blue eyes, watching the flicker of recognition as I put him on my chest. I should have felt pride that, though born at one point two kilograms, he'd put on two hundred grams in a week, so that his premie outfits didn't hang on him like a sleeping bag as they first did. Yet all I could feel was this sense of distance, as though I was observing him scientifically: male, Caucasian, good pulse, marginally jaundiced but improving. Though I dragged myself in and out of the hospital as soon as I could drive again, I left in the afternoons with a sense of relief. And as the weeks passed, even these journeys became difficult. Sitting behind the steering wheel I had to gird myself, sucking in the sobs that threatened to overwhelm me. Sometimes I drove through tears, mopping away the torrents at the traffic lights.

"Is this it?" I thought. "Am I back here again?"

Joe finally came home at thirty-nine weeks – to much fanfare, I must add, although I disappeared into my room and fell asleep while everybody sipped champagne and congratulated Clay, a celebration that I only heard but wasn't part of. I expected to get back to normality after that, or at least a semblance of it. I thought the return to home base would make me less wary, less afraid. Yet even as I stood in front of the freezer wondering what to make my husband for dinner, I couldn't even decide between chicken or beef. I left the freezer door open so long it began to sweat. Clay, finding me completely incapacitated in the kitchen, ordered takeaways. Sushi. So that was what I was supposed to make.

It wasn't just the cooking though – *every* task seemed insurmountable. I couldn't fold, couldn't iron, couldn't make a sandwich. A mop looked like a weapon and taking a shower was far too much to ask. My hair hung lank and limp; I stayed in my pyjamas all day. And I didn't care. If Clay went to the shops for food – I couldn't drive any longer, I just couldn't – I would walk up and down the driveway with Joe, waiting for him to come back. And if he was even a minute later than he'd said he would be, I'd be weeping on the front steps on his return, my baby unchanged, reeking of shit and thrown-up milk. And was I imagining that despite the warnings of retinal complications and possible hearing difficulties, he instantly recognised his father?

Doctor Reynolds put me on Eglonyl. It was supposed to help my moods, but mostly it just made my boobs pump out milk like a prize-winning Jersey. My shirt was continually wet, my child continually crying and my house a bombsite.

Clay brought in a domestic. Her name was Filda, and she was

Zimbabwean, cheerful, and zealous. When Joe was stronger and could support his head, she attached him to her back with a towel, and zipped through the house like a cleaning team of eight, singing all the time. She made *sadza*, which she forced me to eat. Sometimes she cooked sugar beans, or bream she'd purchased at church and de-scaled in the kitchen sink. Its opaque eyes reminded me of me.

Filda moved into the guest room for a short while, much to the horror of Clay's father who believed in apartheid separations, for why wasn't she living in the maid's quarters? Didn't we need our privacy?

We didn't. I didn't want to be alone. Filda was my mother, my friend, my lifeline. Clay was pleased to have her as I wasn't much company. The TV was on constantly, and sometimes when I saw my husband look at me, it wasn't love that I saw there, but fear. When he came home from work, he disappeared straight into the bathroom to bath our son, who gurgled with delight at the very sight of him. Clay did everything: the vaccinations, the birth registration (where he called Joe "Joseph" on the application, something we'd never even discussed), the weigh-ins at the clinic. When I looked at the baby with me, my only thought was to wonder how long it would be before I could go back to sleep.

Sometimes I slept twenty hours a day. After days of perspiration, I was marched into the shower by Filda, who stood outside the door saying she wouldn't let me out until I was clean. I didn't have the energy to disagree. I didn't even dress myself, but stood weakly while she pulled a nightdress over my head and clucked at me.

Sanusha visited, and Clay took over that responsibility too. While they ate Prego rolls on the stoep, Joe lay on the play mat, staring up at the soft toys hanging colourfully above him, the sounds of Mozart playing. At first, Sanusha tried to talk to me, sporting her new hairstyle, which reminded me of a scrubbing brush, but with strange tails that hung over her ears.

"What do you think, Mom?" she asked, preening.

I'm embarrassed to admit I hadn't noticed until she pointed it out. I wasn't heartless, you know – I was just . . . missing. I touched her hair and gave her the answer I thought she wanted: "You're like a model; the boys must be panting after you."

She rolled her eyes and said she didn't care about that. The Gucci queen at school called Erica had told her that she looked "grown-up" and "unique". Sanusha virtually swooned as she told me this.

"Wow," I said.

"God, Mom," she replied. "Could you at least *try* to mean it?"

When did my daughter become such a teenager – and at eleven?

"But I do," I said. "I do mean it."

"Mom, I think you need to see someone," she said, with wisdom beyond her years, albeit snarky teenage delivery. "You're acting really weird."

So I joined some sort of weekly women's group. We sat in the therapist's lounge and I focused on the table. It was divided into glass compartments with a large sheet of glass over the top. In each little glass box the therapist had placed something meaningful – or I assume they were meaningful to her. Babushka dolls. A thinking man from Indonesia ("Bali," she said, "to be specific.") A wooden hippo from the Victoria Falls. Some sort of fertility doll from Borneo. I sat in an unclaimed chair and watched from the outside looking in. The other women knew each other already, and I felt like a child at a birthday party who's only invited because her parents are friends.

"You're very quiet," said the therapist.

"What do you want me to say?"

"Why are you here, for instance?"

"I've lost myself, somewhere," I said, wondering how, in my state, I could be so accurate.

"Babies will do that to you," one of the women said, nodding. "I used to be financial director at Ubulele Telecoms and now I stay home and change nappies."

"My husband didn't want our child," said another. "And when I wouldn't have an abortion, he moved out. My daughter hasn't met him. Everything, I mean absolutely *everything* I do for my daughter, I do on my own."

"And I'm having an affair," a third woman said. "I want someone to look at me and not see tuck shops and school runs and finger-painting. He looks at me and sees a *woman*, the woman I used to be. The woman I *am*. And *that's* what I want."

I smiled at these women who'd put their lives under a microscope for me.

"I'm trying to love my new son," I told them. "But I'm not quite sure how to do it because I think my husband loves him more than he does me."

Clay: Just one damn time

After five months it felt like I was married to Filda, not Thea. Sometimes I'd come home and Thea would be sitting in the same position she'd been in when I left the house. Filda would be the one with dinner on the table, Joe in her arms or on her back, ready with an update on his progress. The house was spotless, the beds made. But Thea was lifeless, like a ragdoll. A magazine lying unread on her lap on the same page I'm sure she was looking at when I kissed her goodbye.

I loved my wife. Her vulnerability was partly what had attracted me to her in the first place. But when I met her, I'd felt like I could help her, make her life better. Now I realised that when she retreated into her head, it took absolutely everything to get her out again.

Medication. Talk therapy. Hired help. Patience. Understanding. Courage. And some of those things aren't exactly free. Trite as it sounds, I'm only human. If it hadn't been for Joe, and Sanusha to some extent, who needed me to bridge the gap, I think some nights I might not have come home at all.

Not that Thea would have even noticed.

And while my wife was hibernating somewhere in her head away from me, I was dealing with a premature baby, pretty much on my own. Like, six weeks after Joe was born, I went into the hospital knowing only that our little boy was in danger of developing something called ROP, "retinopathy of prematurity" as Dr O'Flaherty explained. Fatherhood was expanding my vocabulary every day. At first the doctor was reluctant to give too much detail, "Listen, Clay, let's just take this one step at a time, maybe it's nothing to worry about."

But then they knocked Joe out with a general and screened his eyes in the newborn ICU. They used some special new scanner to study his retina while I sat in the waiting room. I'd started biting my nails; they were in tatters, and my left jaw had developed a muscle spasm from grinding my teeth at night. When I chewed, my head echoed with a weird crunching noise like I was chewing my own bones.

But my worry was merited.

This time an ophthalmologist came to talk to me – all casual like he'd just stepped away from a date. White shirt. Tan trousers. Hair spiky like a toothbrush and wearing those Buddy Holly-style glasses, which made me worry further. If he was this super-hot eye doctor, then why the hell hadn't he got his own damn eyesight sorted out? Joe was still recovering from the investigation, overseen by some of the neonatal nurses, so this new guy Doctor Naidoo, asked me to come to his rooms. Showed me some models of the eye, and started explaining what was happening with my son.

"Mr Middleton," Dr Naidoo started.

"Clay."

"Clay. Let me first explain a little about how the eye works and forms. Simplistically put, the eye's a bit like a camera. The front of the eye is like a camera shutter letting in light. The inside of the eye contains a gel-like fluid, called vitreous. Then you get the retina, which acts a bit like camera film. Without film, you can't record an image. And without a retina –"

"Are you telling me my son has no retina? Is Joe blind?"

"Now, you're jumping to conclusions, Clay. What I'm trying to say is that because Joe was born prematurely, the process has not been completed in which the blood vessels provide nutrition to allow the retina to grow from the back of the eye to the front."

"So he's got a bit of growing to do," I said. "Like the rest of him."

"It's not that simple, I'm afraid. When a baby is born prematurely, its retina is only partially formed. Dr O'Flaherty may have mentioned ROP –"

"He didn't go into details."

"Unfortunately, Joe is exhibiting all the signs of the first stages of ROP. Essentially what this means is that his blood vessels seem to have stopped growing, and as such, a line separates the normal from the premature retina. Joe's situation is more advanced than this, as the separation seems to have been emphasised by a line of tissue."

He spoke like he was telling me Joe's toenails needed to grow a little straighter. It was a shitload more serious than that.

"Christ," I said, my head in my hands.

"Clay, I want you to know that at this point there is still a strong chance that the blood vessels will grow and the eyes will heal themselves spontaneously."

"Or?"

"Or, if your son's condition deteriorates into Stage Three or plus disease, we may need to operate. There are a few options available: cryotherapy, which involves a freezing technique, laser surgery – we've had some excellent results."

"What the worst-case scenario?" I said.

"We don't need to think about that."

"Trust me, we do."

"Well, the retina could detach from the eye. Then we'd need to do a vitrectomy, which involves removing the vitreous and placing a band of silicone around the eye. I would imagine, though, that in this case, perfect vision would be unlikely."

My jaw was clenching even as I sat there. "So, what do we do now?"

"Now, we wait," Dr Naidoo said. "We'll check again in a week."

And I knew that when I went home, I wouldn't even be able to discuss this with my wife. She was so out of it, even the slightest hint of bad news could push her over the edge.

Instead, I drove to Annie's. When she opened the door and saw my face, she led me inside and poured me a beer.

"I'm listening," she said, and gestured for the nanny to take Matt.

I knew then that I'd picked the right person to go to. Tom's my mate, but I couldn't have cried in front of him the way I cried then.

*

However, Tom still had his uses over those difficult months.

One day in August he rode up to the house in his Land Rover, hooting, then marched up to our front door. His third wife, Sybil, climbed out too, her newly enhanced breasts rounding the corner ahead of her.

Bleary-eyed from lack of sleep and worry, I have to say my heart sank a little seeing them. (Tom and Sybil, not the boobs.) I was not in the mood for entertaining. Much as I loved my friend, Tom's constant energy and endless successes were becoming draining.

"Hi," I said as I opened the door, Joe balanced against my chest.

"Hey, cutie!" cooed Sybil, and laughed at my expression. "Not you, silly. Your little chap. Here, let me take him."

I glanced at the empty chair in the lounge. There was a fire burning. Thea would have been totally mesmerised by it, but I doubted she'd even have heard the doorbell if she'd been there.

"Come on, Clay, hand over the baby," Sybil persisted. "Now."

And when I did, Tom turned me around. He picked up a bag I hadn't noticed next to the hall table and started to push me out the front door.

"We'll be back, when we're back," he told his wife, and she nodded.

"When's his next feed?" Sybil said. "Nappies in his room?"

"I can't –"

"Now, Clay," Sybil said, "say bye-bye to your baby."

In the car I sat next to Tom, feeling completely numb.

"Sybil will be fine with Joe, and Filda's coming in tomorrow to help if Sybil needs her," Tom said. "You need a break. Now just relax and let me drive."

Tom put on Rodriguez, bringing back a flood of memories of a campsite near Tulbagh, where I'd gone with Tom and my dad when I was a teenager. It'd been cold. There'd been snow on the Winterhoek Mountains, so when we went walking we'd peeled off layer after layer till we were down to our sweat-soaked T-shirts.

Like Thea, who had so many layers these days I sometimes hardly recognised her.

And boy, I'd done everything I could have. I'd seen Thea's therapist and I'd researched postnatal distress or depression. And the one thing that seemed to be true was that – eventually – this would pass. She'd surface again. Not, perhaps, I'd been told, as *exactly* the same person, but as a close approximation of her previous self. Being underground so long is bound to affect a person in fundamental ways.

I looked across at Tom.

"So, where we heading?" I said, trying – and failing – to sound upbeat.

"It's not a punishment, Middleton. We're going back to Tulbagh – why do you think I dredged up that old tape? And we're picking up your dad next."

"My dad?"

"Why not? We're reliving our youth! Except that this time we are *not* camping. My bones are far too fragile for hard floors."

"You're such a girl," I said.

"And you're such a misery!" Then Tom slapped me on the shoulder. "Sing along now, Middleton: *I wonder . . .*"

I wondered how Thea was doing. I missed her smile. I missed the way she talked about Cape Town like it was the greatest place on earth. I missed her body. These days she curled away from me, using her spine as a barrier. Her skin flinched away from me like a mimosa leaf. But every now and then she'd reach out to me, lacing her fingers through mine as though anchoring herself to the earth. And she needed to, because she mostly forgot to eat. Her beautiful cheekbones now looked gaunt, her mismatched eyes were hollow and almost too big for her face.

Before the events of last week, Thea had started to have a few good hours. I hadn't wanted her to waste them on chores, so we'd packed Joe in the pram and gone for walks in Kirstenbosch, around the new Waterfront construction or along the promenade. When she held our son, I could see her feelings about him were mixed. She didn't say anything but I knew she felt guilty: for not being the mother she should be, and for not feeling capable of changing. Perhaps I was being pushy, but I'd persisted. When she was lying in bed, clearly out of it, I'd try to cuddle Joe up to her.

"I can't," she said, several times. "I don't trust myself to hold him."

I'd say that I needed to clean the pool (or wash the car, or bring in the wood, or make a fire, or grind the coffee beans . . .).

"It's just for ten minutes. I can't take him outside – it's too cold." (Or too wet, or too dangerous, or too noisy.)

The first few times I did that I just stood on the other side of the door, peering through the gap next to the hinges, not quite sure if she *was* capable – even of holding him. If I did leave them, it was never for more than a few minutes. I couldn't concentrate long enough to think of any other task I had set myself. And when I returned they'd be eyeballing each other, or they'd both be crying – Joe bellowing, and Thea in helpless but silent tears. Thea couldn't hand Joe over soon enough.

But once when I was spying on them, I saw her smile. That same smile I remembered from our shopping trip when she was still married to Rajit, but was learning to trust me. She cooed softly, and then I heard the first few bars of a bluesy version of some Edith Piaf song she used to sing when she was happy.

I felt my heart thumping hard and loud. It had been *months* since I'd last heard my wife sing. I wondered then if she was finally coming back to us: resuscitated out of her cold and miserable sleep.

How wrong could I have been?

*

When we got to the cottage in Tulbagh, it was already late afternoon. The late winter weather was still chilly, but not as icy as it had been the last time. The biggest difference was in my dad, who wasn't as rugged as he'd once been. As teens we'd look up to him – the way he could light a fire with flint, or carve little creatures out of wood. Now, he seemed a little shaky.

Or maybe it was me who was shaky. Brittle even.

Tom got drinks out of a cooler box he'd obviously packed himself: enough booze and ice for twenty of us, but I accepted the first beer readily enough. We stood around my dad's fire, lit with matches these days, since he didn't have to prove himself any more. We watched the stars bursting out of the sky. And now that Tom was out of his slick suit and smart-lawyer persona he was more the guy I'd always known.

"Middleton," he said, clinking his bottle against mine.

"Tom," I said. I tried to be present but my mind was racing. At that existential moment I was actually considering what my life would be like if I hadn't put on the pressure about having a baby. If Joe hadn't come into our lives, would Thea still be singing in the bath? Making toile curtains, or whatever she goddamn called them? Cooking Cordon Bleu like her mother taught her when they were still speaking? Would I even be *here*? Would I be the lust-less, passion-less man I'd become? Would I study my wife like a father looks at his daughter, wondering how to protect her?

There was clearly something wrong with me. Even if she'd wanted it, sex with Thea was the last thing on my mind. But of course she didn't want sex – all she wanted to do was to tell me how her limbs were on fire, how mercury was coursing through her veins, sharp as silver.

Dad came out of the chalet kitchen. He was drinking a deep red Merlot, holding tongs.

"Steak's marinating and the *wors* is defrosted," he said. "Tom, how're those coals? I'm starving!"

"Ready in ten." Tom glanced at me. "Hey, Middleton, no thinking allowed. Tonight you're getting drunk, eating meat and pretending you're eighteen again. Although that might be difficult." He patted my stomach. "You've put on about fifteen k's since then."

"Screw you," I said, downing my beer.

"That's the spirit! Have another one."

Which I did.

"All right, son?" Dad asked a bit later, once we'd finished our meat braai, with not a salad leaf in sight.

"Sure," I said. "Why not?" Yet my hunching figure at the fire must have said otherwise. I stared into the flames, wondering what I could have done better.

Maybe another woman would have reacted to Joe's health troubles by kicking into an adrenaline-fuelled fight for her child. But Thea wasn't that woman. Thea seemed completely numb, like she was watching a TV soap that didn't affect her in the slightest.

On that frightening day, she'd actually come to the hospital, which made a change. She'd held Joe, touched his forehead, hummed and smiled. She was dressed perfectly, wearing make-up, looking good. The doctors had shaken our hands and had said she seemed well. She did, but I hadn't noticed until they'd pointed it out. In retrospect, I should have – the way Thea was those days, the effort was way beyond phenomenal.

The surgeon had then explained that that day's operation was Joe's best chance of *good* vision, though he could make no promise that it would be twenty-twenty.

Thea asked all the right questions and I was so elated to see the old Thea back that I started thinking about a celebratory dinner at Jake's that night, once we'd heard that our son was going to be fine.

But that's not what happened.

After the operation, which we spent staring at posters in the waiting room, Joe was settled in the ward. He was sleeping off the anaesthetic, so I suggested that Thea and I pop out for an hour while we waited for news. It was then she began to unbundle. She started holding on to her throat, touching her chest.

"I can't breathe," she said. "I think I'm choking."

She did look pale, but inwardly I hated myself for my first response: *Why can't she hold it together this one damn time?* Then I looked at her eyes, the way her eyelashes were fluttering. The fear on her face.

"I think it's my heart. My chest hurts." Her hands were shaking uncontrollably. I could hear the tension in her breathing. I sat her down in one of the hospital chairs in the corridor.

"You'll be okay," I told her. "I think you're just stressed."

But her face was getting redder and redder and she was opening her mouth like a suffocating fish. Then without any warning, she fell forward. She landed hard on the linoleum floor. The chair crashed on top of her ankle. Thea yelped, then began to caterpillar along the floor to a corner, as I watched, horrified. When she reached the wall, she slithered upwards, banging her head against the plaster.

"Stop it," I said, trying to lift her away.

But she kept on banging her head on the rough wall, like a tantruming toddler. Over and over again. She was already bleeding from her forehead, her nose. Even her ear lobe was scraped from the uneven wall. And all the time these otherworldly noises coming from her throat. Like a wolf baying . . .

Of course a crowd had begun to gather.

"What's wrong with her?" someone asked.

"Can you help me hold her?" I asked a nurse who was twice my width and looked strong.

In one movement, the nurse hooked down my wife's arms, holding her in a pseudo-Heimlich. I was sitting there on the floor, speaking to Thea softly. I doubted she could hear me over her howling. Then, without warning, she threw her head back and bashed the nurse on the nose. The nurse immediately let go and fell back in both pain and anger. She touched her bloody nostrils with her sleeve.

"Oh my God, I'm sorry," I said.

Thea was still wailing, and it didn't seem like she was going to let up. I tried to pull her away from the wall so at least she could stop thumping her head, but she turned and began to pummel me with her fists. I caught her wrists and tried to focus her eyes on mine, but her expression was wild and unreachable.

"Thea," I said. "Thea, it's me, Clay."

"Step away from her," someone said.

"She's my wife! I don't understand what's going on here."

"Move away from her, sir. Move!"

I suppose I didn't react, because I then felt myself being shoved, and a doctor stuck a syringe into her arm.

"Was that really necessary?" I asked feebly, though the carnage around us suggested it was.

"Her name?" the doctor asked me, holding her firmly, her body beset by tremors.

"Thea Middleton."

"Does she have a history of these types of episodes?"

"No, not like this and not before the baby."

"How old is she?"

"My wife?"

"No, the baby."

"*He* was premature by eight weeks. Joe was born five months ago."

"Thea," the doctor said, nodding at an orderly who had appeared with a hospital trolley. "On the count of three, we're going to lift you onto this bed. You are not going to fight us, because we are here to take care of you. Okay?"

"Thea," I said. "Can you hear him?"

She blinked. Then I could see the tears beginning to fall. All of a sudden she seemed to have gone limp; the fight was all out of her. Then she nodded.

"One. Two. Three." The orderly and the doctor lifted her as though she weighed nothing. "Move away, people, if you don't mind. This particular show is over," the doctor said. Then he turned to the nurse who had tried to help me. "Faeeda, is your nose broken?"

She shook her head. "*Nee, ek dink nie so nie.*"

"Then go and get it cleaned up and go home. Get Doctor Hing to prescribe something for the pain and swelling before you go."

I stood there shell-shocked and only realised later that I never thanked her. The doctor then touched my shoulder lightly.

"Come with us, sir. I think we need to admit your wife overnight. I'll also need to get a psychiatrist to come and see you."

"She has a psychiatrist here," I said. "You know, for the PND."

"Doctor Rosenkrantz?"

"Yes."

"I'll page her. And if I could give you some advice, sir: I would suggest you admit her for at least a week. Frankly, you look like you could do with a break. And she'll be safe here for a few days."

So that's how I ended up here at a campfire, wood burning into coals at my feet, whilst my wife was locked away in some loony bin, probably hating me for letting them take her away.

Sanusha (aged 12): Fried brains

I know what it's like to feel different from everybody around me. My peers, my parents, my teachers. Annie is the 1 person who gets me, and when I can't stand the others for 1 more minute, I get on my bike and ride to her house down the road. At least she doesn't question me. Instead, she just opens the door.

"Oh good, it's you, Nush," she says. "Come have a chat with me and Mattie – we're trying to work out these LEGO instructions. Deon's away at a seminar again. You know I'm useless at this."

Later we mooch on the couch and watch Westerns, usually the older ones with classic dudes like John Wayne, Roy Rogers and Gene Autry. But I like Clint Eastwood best – Blondie, the mysterious lone gunman who can sling a pistol like nobody's business. Just a few bars of the soundtrack of *The Good, the Bad & the Ugly* sends my spine into shivers. I want to learn to shoot, just like these cowboys. Things are going better on the home front, so sometimes I think I might chat to Mom about a pellet gun, so I can shoot cans in the garden. I don't want to kill birds or anything. Just hit targets.

Bang. Bang. Bang.

The whole thing about Mom going nuts in the hospital has been kept pretty hush-hush. I wasn't even supposed to know about it. At first Clay said something about her going on holiday to Hermanus for a few days, but I doubt he really thought he was fooling me. I mean, please. I'd seen the state she was in, and if a bit of time in there sorts her out, all the better. And she wasn't gone for a week like Clay said, but almost 3. Anyway, when there's a conversation like that going on, I just pick up the telephone super-carefully and listen in. It's not like it's none of my business or anything.

Appa doesn't know about the meltdown. He may be a crappy dad most of the time, but he wouldn't have wanted me hanging about my mom's house with only Clay there. Goodness knows why, since Clay was better with me than he was most of the time.

After Week 1, I told Clay he could cut the lies and tell me what was really happening because I knew my mom was loony tunes and was locked up somewhere with people frying her brains.

"Excuse me?" Clay said, his lip wobbling like instant pudding.

"I looked it up at the library. Electrodes, the works. They did it to Sylvia Plath."

"Who?"

"You know, that writer who axed herself. Head in the oven. But they zapped her first, trying to sort her out. Her husband was some sort of writer too. I think she was better than he was, but of course, he was like Appa – casing out women, even when they were married."

"How old are you?" Clay said, looking bemused. "Did you just step out of some time machine and simply grow up?"

"I'm 12. Yes, I know about sex. Blah. Blah. Blah. Just tell me if this Mom-thing is going to work, because having a mother like mine is not exactly a bonus."

"She loves you, Nush."

"I *know* that. I miss her. You know, the old Mom. The one who baked and sang and got cross with me for getting my fingers full of grease."

"She's still in there somewhere."

"Yes, but is she going to get better?"

"Let's put it this way: the psychologist said he'd never seen anyone suffering from postnatal distress who *didn't* get better."

"Well then," I replied, "those are pretty good odds."

*

When she comes home, she's fragile as a blown-glass swan. Her movements are tentative and she reminds me of the way she used to climb into

218

the swimming pool or the bath when she was testing the temperature. When I hugged her, I thought I might break her.

Her eyes flicker across the lounge as she orientates herself. I think she purposely avoids the sofa that trapped her for weeks on end – instead, she shuffles to the kitchen.

"You need a hairdresser," I say, ignoring Clay's frown.

"That bad?" She links her hand with mine.

"I don't want to be mean or anything, Mom, but you've got a few bald patches. You need a new look."

And then she laughs. Not a fake one, but a deep belly laugh. "What do you think, Clay? Should we sort this mop out?"

For the first time in months, I can see the tension wash out of his face.

"Let's make an outing of it," he says. "The four of us need to celebrate that you're home."

Part Four

Confinement

Thea: Playing catch-up

I'd lost the first eight months of Joe's life and there was nothing I could do to get them back. If I was trying to punish myself, I'd work out the days, the hours, the minutes I'd missed while I was in my black cloud. Holding him, his little body tucked against mine, I whispered to him that I was sorry. So sorry. That I would give anything to remember the day of his birth with joy, his first smile, his first laugh.

That if I'd been a real mother, a good mother, I would have been there for his eye operations and the investigations into his bowel to check why he couldn't keep anything down.

That if I'd been a bit less selfish, I would have been the one getting out of bed to get him a bottle or change his nappy or retrieve his dummy from the fold in the cot bumper.

I would have been the one making the decisions about his health, and whether or not he was old enough to move on to solids.

And I would have called him Joe, not Joseph.

But it was all a complete blur. I came home from the hospital. I went back in. Home. Then back to a clinic.

It hurt me so much to see that my son didn't quite trust me, and would wave his arms for Clay to pick him up when we were both there. Clay first. Always Clay. It seemed that despite my regret, my little boy was not going to forgive me. He didn't trust me and I didn't blame him. I didn't trust myself.

I felt like I'd missed everything: his first giggle, his first tooth, the first time he sat on his own without rolling over or falling onto his face. But that didn't stop me trying to play catch-up. For one thing, I was determined to take Joe to his first swimming lesson. And I did. Strapping him into the car seat, I drove to the Lucky Fish, changing him into his baby cozzie on the side of the pool. But the moment he was in the water he started screaming. And not just the average, *this is really not fun but I'll complain a bit and get over it* screaming, but an unholy shriek that sent the tears jetting down my cheeks.

Why can't I even get this right?

Watch off, shoes off, I was soon in the pool, cuddling my child against me, ignoring the strange look on the swimming teacher's face. I knew I'd done the right thing, because Joe stopped crying immediately, and gripped onto me like a baby koala.

We sloshed home together, the driver's seat a soggy mess and a new cassette in the car blaring "Wee Willie Winkie", which I was tired of, but Joe seemed to love – and that was enough for me.

When we pulled into the driveway, Clay was already home. When he came to find us we were stark naked in front of the washer as I chucked in my wet clothes.

"What the –?"

"We went swimming," I answered my husband with a smile. "And we had fun, didn't we, boy?"

And Joe just chuckled.

But it wasn't just Joe's life I'd missed. Sanusha was just over twelve and I realised we hadn't yet had "the *talk*", so I arranged to have it in a place where she was completely comfortable. Her zone, not mine: I raised the subject while we peered at the geyser in the roof, both of us covered in dust, and sweating. My daughter shifted, and put down her screwdriver.

"Mom, why are you up here with me? Is this going to be about sex or woman's stuff?" she said before I'd even begun.

"Well," I said, "A little bit of both."

"Mom, I've had my period for more than a year already. Annie helped me get what I needed."

"Annie," I said blankly, hating my friend for taking this moment from me and not even telling me. Hating myself for not being fit enough to be told.

"Yes. I told Appa I needed more pocket money for girl's stuff, and he didn't ask any questions – he just forked out the cash."

"A year already?" A stone sank into my gullet and settled there rather uncomfortably. It occurred to me that Rajit knew more about Sanusha's life at this point than I did, and I didn't like that at all. "That long, huh?"

She shrugged. "Listen, don't feel bad about it, Mom. It doesn't matter."

"But it *does* matter," I protested. "Of course it does. It matters to me. And why didn't you tell me? Why didn't Annie tell me?" My betrayal seemed absolute.

My daughter looked at me. "You can buy me a bra if you like."

And I couldn't believe the strange feeling of gratitude that came over me.

"Yes," I said, smiling at Sanusha, trying to pretend I liked her "look" – the jet-black eyeliner and the tight buckled boots that I would never have let her wear before this, because no matter what she thought, she was actually still a child. "I'd love to. I can't believe how fast you're growing up!"

We drove off to Cavendish that Saturday – just the two of us – but from the moment the morning began I had a feeling Sanusha was humouring me. She slunk through the mall checking her watch after only half an hour.

And she studied me. I don't know where she got it from, but Nush had this way of looking at me like she was reading my thoughts. And I'm sure she knew that I didn't really feel up to being there. The fluorescent lighting tired me quickly and my medication often gave me dizzy spells that forced me to stop and hold onto a banister while I collected myself.

I didn't remember ever having felt this strange before – it was like these lights were shining straight into my pupils, but I couldn't turn my head away.

"Let's get some breakfast," I said softly, trying to hide my unsteadiness.

After finding a table at a familiar coffee spot and ordering from the waitress, I looked at my daughter. She often wore dull colours like black or brown, but today her T-shirt was bright orange. It had a fish on it, with a speech bubble that said, "Going down for air". I didn't know where she'd got it, but it was cute and I said so.

"Annie," she said, her mouth half-full of almost masticated omelette. "She got it for me. We saw them at the Rondebosch Market. We thought they were pretty hilarious."

"Yes," I said, "very funny."

"There was another one with a hedgehog that said, 'And you think *your* mother's prickly?'"

Was that aimed at me?

"You can laugh, Mom. It's a *joke*."

"Oh." My laugh came out stunted and ridiculous.

"And then there was one for kids, with this, like, cartoon crocodile lying in the sun and it said, 'And you think *you* hate brushing your teeth?'"

"We could get one for Joe," I said, trying to get into the spirit. "You know how he screams about toothpaste at bedtime."

She looked at me. "Mmm," she said. "They do have them in pyjamas too. I like the blue ones the most."

Sanusha sipped her frulata. I could see the liquid battling up the straw. Any moment and she'd be slurping, and she knew how I hated that.

"So, what sort of bra do you want?"

"You're kidding, right? We're going to discuss bras in a *restaurant*?"

"Can we talk colour at least, so I know what I'm looking for?" I touched my head, which was now pounding solidly.

"Are you going to eat that?" she asked, picking the last of my bran muffin off my plate. "You look like you're finished."

And the bra hunting was even worse than the breakfast. Each time I picked something out, my daughter would roll her eyes like I had the worst taste in the world. And when had her breasts got so big? I hadn't noticed it before. God, I was a terrible mother. There I was checking the A-cups, only to find she was nearing a C. And that didn't seem to be enough, because she wanted a Wonderbra, and a balconette and a sports bra that reminded me of an old-fashioned swimming costume. I suggested beige; needless to say, she wanted black. Black lace, black satin, black cotton. She eyed me with a look of pure disdain.

Eventually I found myself sitting in the shoe department, my head in my hands, feeling close to tears. My brain was flipping incessantly and the lights around me penetrated my skull.

Sanusha brought armfuls of unsuitable underwear – *When did I agree to G-strings rather than nice simple bikini knickers?* – and I just nodded because I couldn't wait to get out of there.

When we finally got into the car, Sanusha threw her purchases into the boot, and turned on the radio loud enough to shatter glass. Jann Arden's *Insensitive*, and I was sensitive enough to resent it. With her heavy black boots on the dashboard, my daughter glanced over at me and told me she was going to Annie's later. She had to replace a bulb on the Volvo.

Thank God, I thought before I could stop myself. Maybe I could drop her off and then just keep on driving. But I'd done that before and I knew I could never do it again.

"I love you, Nush," I told her, very clearly, as though to convince myself.

Her eyes widened.

"I know it's been hard, but you don't have to put on an act for me. I'm going to love you anyway."

"What act?" She shrugged. "This is me, Mom. Take it or leave it."

"I'll take it," I said, hoping I sounded convinced as I thought I should. "I'll take it."

"Okay, fine," she said. "But maybe you should know: Annie and I went bra shopping months ago. And it was a hang of a lot more fun than this."

Clay: A leech . . . a dog?

When Joe was three years old, working out his adjusted age versus his actual age was no longer relevant. In fact, when he'd started reaching all his milestones by two, Thea and I had started to relax. We'd figured that everything was going to be okay.

There were quite a few things I'd learnt over the last few years, but the main one was not to take anything for granted. We'd come through it, and mostly Thea was her old self. For ten amazing days we went to Paris and planned a trip to the East. We took walks on the beach and in the Newlands forest. Took the cable car up Table Mountain, with Joe all bundled up against the elements. We went for a holiday to Knysna, took Joe to see wild animals in the bush (without Sanusha, who refused to come). And sometimes, while Filda babysat, Thea and I treated ourselves to some of the top-rated restaurants in Stellenbosch and Franschhoek.

Joe now wore glasses. One day, when he was closer to adulthood, we would do some more corrective surgery – but otherwise he really was quite normal. A little thin, perhaps, but he'd fatten up. I'd been the same as a kid: skin and bones, with my ribs showing. Unfortunately not any more, though – I didn't get to run or cycle much. Just didn't have the time. When I got home from Au Lait Au Lait, Thea would be checking her watch. I had my jobs – fixing the evening drinks, bathing our boy, reading the bedtime story – because Thea said she did enough of *that* during the day. Thea did the night wakes because I just didn't hear our son calling – and sleep was never Joe's forte. But having Filda also helped, of course.

Also, Thea was back to work. She'd developed quite a name for herself amongst the French tour operators and they'd been known to change their tour dates to fit around her. She did travel out of Cape Town sometimes, particularly down the Garden Route.

I really missed her during those times. So did Joe. When she came home, the jigsaw puzzle fitted back in place and I felt like my family was complete. The nights without Sanusha were usually better, I have to admit – that girl knew how to create drama. She was caught drinking on school property and was expelled. That was fun, trying to find another school to accept her. Luckily she's so damn clever. Then I found pot in her bedroom – removed it without even mentioning it to Thea to avoid another argument. Kid accused me of theft and making dagga cookies for my friends. If I hadn't been so pissed off, I think I might have laughed. Sanusha was fourteen going on twenty-one. The only thing I was grateful for was that she showed absolutely no interest in boys – in the romantic sense, I mean. She hung out with a crowd of blokes, but they spent their time tinkering with car engines. The older boys raced the cars – probably illegally. I put the fear of God into her about getting into one of those cars during a drag race, but the usual, rather trite answer was, "You're not my dad."

Tragedy is, Sanusha and I used to connect, but now it was like she had something to prove. Didn't need me, didn't need Thea. The only time I saw her soften was with Joe. He absolutely adored her. His Nusha was his Nusha. He didn't care about her revoltingly massive T-shirts, her studded boots, black nail polish. Joe didn't even notice her haughtiness or the way she sat slumped in front of the TV. *Thea and I* got the silent treatment, but she played cars with *him*, and built tracks for his wooden trains. Joe especially loved that she didn't give a toss about getting her fingers dirty in either mud or grease.

*

I won't lie. I'd thought about other children – kids a bit more like Joe than Sanusha. Another boy or girl running round the house, making us laugh. But when I raised the subject with Thea, she just looked at me.

"Are you out of your mind? Having Joe almost killed me. How can you be so selfish? If you really loved me you'd go for the snip and the subject would be closed."

And I don't know why I couldn't just accept that and let it drop.

"It won't necessarily happen again, what you went through, I mean," I persisted. "This time we'd be prepared."

Thea's eyes blazed. "I'm done with babies, Clay. Done. I'm done with night terrors, done with nappies, done with engorged boobs, and having to give up my life and my career for somebody else. I am making something of *my* life now. I'm happy. Why can't you be?"

"It's just –"

"Just nothing. I love you, Clay. Passionately. I'd do just about anything for you, but I'm sorry – I can't go down that road again. It's taken all this time for me to find myself. If you have more love to give, get a dog, go work in an orphanage. I don't care, but I'm not having another baby suck the life out of me like a leech."

"Wow," I said. "A leech . . . A dog?"

"Well, you know what I mean."

"A dog. Seriously?"

"Okay, so you're not a dog lover. Get a rabbit. A cat. Or volunteer at the Red Cross. Spend more time with Joe and Nush."

"Yes, Nush really wants to be with me. The last time we sat in the same room she uttered two words to me. I seem to recall they were 'fuck' and 'off'." (Which was also pretty much how I was feeling about Thea right then.)

"You shouldn't allow that," Thea said, trying to slip into my lap. She kissed my neck, tracing her lips along my jawline to my ear, where she nibbled gently. "You know, darling. It doesn't mean I don't want to have fun. And Joe's sleeping right now . . ."

Gently, but firmly, I pushed Thea's face away. "I think I'll go for a cycle. I haven't seen Tom for a bit." And without consciously wanting to be cruel, I enjoyed the crestfallen expression on her face.

For a moment I wanted to put my arms around her and tell her that I was sorry. I didn't do it, though.

"I'll pick up some fish and chips for dinner," I said, slightly conciliatory, "with those fish fingers Joe likes."

"Right," she replied. "I guess I've got some work to catch up on. And I want to wrap Nush's birthday presents."

"So what are we doing this year?" I said, lifting my helmet out of the cupboard near the front door. "Carting your daughter to some place she doesn't want to go, tripping over her lip while she tells us we shouldn't have and really means it?"

"Clay."

I knew that warning look, but I didn't care. I just wasn't in the mood.

"Sanusha doesn't like these things you organise, Thea. She doesn't want to go to smart dinners or bring her friends round for pizza. Let *her* choose her own way this time, and save us all a lot of heartache."

"I thought we could go for a picnic like we used to do when she was little."

"Ask her this time, for Christ's sake. No more dramas. If she'd rather have some strange gadget, let her have it. Listen to *her* for a change, Thea."

"Right," she said.

It was only when I walked out the door that I realised that although I was holding my cycling helmet, I wasn't wearing suitable cycling gear. But there was no way I was going back inside. Tom could kit me out. If he was there – now that his face was in the papers 24/7, he was usually at the office. Sybil was pretty frustrated by it.

Is there ever such a thing as a completely happy marriage?

At the end of the road, I waved at a couple walking a pram. My heart hurt. No more babies. No more *babies*. I guess every relationship is about compromise. Did this have to be mine?

231

Thea: Closer to terrified

Staring at the pregnancy test with my knickers still round my ankles, I felt like throwing up.

No, not from the nausea. From knowing something terrible has happened and you can't turn back the clock.

How often had I thought that Rajit had taught me all the lessons I needed to know about life: that unexpected babies turn into little people who carry feelings of abandonment their whole lives? And that those feelings make them do crazy things. Like Nusha's wild motorbike ride had sent her tumbling down an embankment, resulting in bruised ribs, a broken arm and a jagged wound down the side of her face that we were hoping would fade away eventually. Or me, falling pregnant because I couldn't keep my legs closed, as every boy I met was going to take me away from my adopted mother.

Sanusha and I. Neither of us were good girls, and I'm all too certain that comes from knowing rejection.

And even if I explained all of this to Clay, he wouldn't get it, because hadn't he been the one who'd saved me? And didn't I feel fulfilled now that we had Joe, and a house in Rondebosch, a boat and holidays to new places at least once a year?

I shook the test, wondering about a false positive. I'd been so careful. But clearly not careful enough. How had I managed to get caught with this twice in my life? Was I just particularly stupid or particularly fertile?

I pulled up my pants and flushed the loo, tossing the test in the dustbin. I'd have to try again in a few days. Deal with my anxiety until then.

Annie, with her perfectly ordered family and good humour, wasn't one to beat about the bush. Warming her hands on her cup of tea, she looked at me.

"God, who was in the bathroom, Thea? You look like you've seen a ghost."

A bit weird that I'd chosen to do the test while Annie was having tea at my house, but I'd somehow needed Annie to be there as backup, a safety net. And the not-knowing was killing me.

She took her last sip, then put down her cup, and reached her hand out to me. "You're shaking Thea. What's wrong? Are you ill?"

"No," I said. "But I think I'm pregnant."

"Oh."

"That's it? No words of advice for the newly knocked up?"

"This is not a good idea, T. You know that."

"Clay will think it's an excellent idea, and you know *that*, Annie. But I can't do this again, I just can't."

We both fell silent as the emotion of my new discovery washed over me.

How had this happened anyway? If Clay'd had the damn vasectomy like I'd asked him to, I wouldn't be in this mess. I bit into my carrot cake, then pushed the plate away as the bile rose in my throat. The reason of course that he'd refused to agree to the op was exactly for the dilemma that I was now facing – one slipping past the goalposts as I could hear him calling it.

"You're going to have to go straight to the shrink, T," Annie said. "What about all the meds you're still on?"

"I guess I'll have to go off them. Unless they're okay for the baby."

"But what about *you*?"

"What *about* me? This is it, Annie. I can't make this unhappen."

Annie looked meaningfully at me, her blue eyes penetrating. She didn't say anything but I'd known her long enough to know what she meant.

"No," I said, very firmly. "Absolutely not. If my birth mother had done that, I wouldn't be here."

"Clay doesn't know, and what he doesn't know can't hurt him."

"Secrets kill marriages, Annie."

"So does major depression and electroshock therapy. You're not healthy, T. This would be a medical decision, not a moral one. And what happens if this baby is premature like Joe?"

"I won't do it. I'll do anything but that." I started clearing away the tray.

"You're running away again, T," Annie said with a small smile. "You can't get away from me that easily."

"I need to do another test," I said. "I'll go get one now. Maybe that one was wrong."

"Sure," she replied. "I hope so." Annie pushed back her chair. "I can come with you, if you like."

I shook my head. "I'll call you later."

I left the house at the same time as Annie. By the time I'd got home and taken the next test – which confirmed everything I wished wasn't true – I was already starting to feel calmer. And it's amazing how time can block out past pain, past misery. All I could think was how Clay and I had handled a lot together and we'd made it through.

When he came home, I was sitting in the lounge with Joe. I'd lit a fire, which was no mean feat with a three year old trying to help. Each time I'd tried to put in a log, he'd insisted on carrying it, which took double the time. But my son's enthusiasm was infectious. One of Joe's most endearing qualities was his way of making me laugh for almost no reason at all. He just expected people to like him, and they did, and his friends had been known to box anyone who'd tried to tease him about his glasses.

Now he was sitting in front of the fire, wearing his Spiderman pyjamas and looking very pleased with himself. His specs were slightly misted from his proximity to the fire and I gestured for him to move back a little. We were drinking hot chocolate with marshmallows *before* dinner – so he must have known something was up. His mother wasn't known to break rules like that.

"I love you, Mommy," Joe said, smiling at me. "This is fun."

"I love you too, Joey."

As the front door slammed and Clay's footsteps echoed on the wooden floor, we both laughed.

"Daddy's home!" I said.

"So what's all this about?" Clay asked as he poked his head round the door.

"We made a fire!" Joe replied.

"So I see. You guys did this on your own without me?"

"I helped Mommy."

"Good boy." Clay ruffled Joe's hair and came to sit next to me on the couch. He kissed me lightly, and slipped his fingers through mine. "Nice day? Or not-so-nice day?" he said, testing the waters.

"I'm not sure, really," I said. "I'm trying to work it out."

"Cryptic," he replied. "Want to talk about it?"

I nodded towards Joe. "Later."

"Right." Clay flopped onto the carpet and wriggled on his belly towards Joe. "So, mister. You're all grown up now, making your own fires? I guess I'm going to have to teach you how to braai."

"*Boerewors*?" asked Joe.

"Of course *boerewors*."

We ate our dinner on our laps around the fire – another deviation from my usual routine, so Joe was in his element.

"Can we do this every night?" he asked, his face covered with tomato sauce.

"Every night and it wouldn't be special," I said to him. "That's why we have treats."

"But it's bedtime now, buddy," Clay said. "You've got nursery school tomorrow."

By the time Clay came back to the lounge, I'd cleaned up the pots, stacked the dishes, wiped the surfaces.

He slipped his arms around my waist. "Man down," he said. "But it took a while – sorry. Listen, Thea, is everything okay? You didn't eat much and you're acting a little –"

"Strange?"

"Out of character."

"I'm pregnant," I said to him. "So I think I'm working out how to deal with this little bit of unexpected news."

"Oh my God!" Clay said, his face lighting up like a string of fairy lights. "Wow! But how?"

"The usual way, I assume," I said, watching the array of emotions crossing his face: excitement, joy, anticipation and perhaps even a touch of relief. I wished I felt the same way, but seeing his happiness made me realise how much he'd wanted this.

My husband put his arms around me.

"I know this is hard for you," he said. "I know you're not happy about a baby, but I promise you, Thea, we can survive this. We'll go to doctors straight away, monitor your thyroid, discuss medications you can take safely."

"I missed so much of Joe's early months," I said a little tearfully.

"And you can make up for that now with this little one. We know what to expect this time; we can be prepared."

"I'm frightened," I told him. "Actually, I think I'm closer to terrified."

"It's going to be fine."

"'And what if I lose my mind completely this time?" I said.

"I've got you."

"You think you do, but when I go in there, sometimes I don't know if I can come out."

Clay lifted my chin and kissed me softly on the lips. "I'll be waiting for you," he said to me. "And if you don't come out, I'll come inside and get you."

Sanusha (aged 15): Rhino hide

It's so gross. My mom's too old to be pregnant. *Again.* She's, like, nearly 40. Positively ancient. When the baby's jumping around in her stomach and she's wearing a tight T-shirt, you can literally see her belly undulating, like she's been taken over by some alien. She tries to get me to put my hand on her stomach so I can bond with the foetus, but I think the whole thing is just totally repulsive. Babies actually wee inside your uterus. It makes me sick even thinking about it. Yuck. And the 2 of them – Clay and my mom, I mean – are like a pair of lovebirds cooing at each other. Actually, it's nauseating. Clay sits with his mouth to Mom's stomach and says things like, "This is your daddy speaking." He sounds like a complete twit.

I'm never going to have kids. I'll be travelling the world and having an actual life – no little ankle biters cramping my style.

At least it's drawn attention away from me. At school they've done some of those IQ and aptitude tests on me, and the problem is I don't lean in any particular direction. I could pretty much study anything I want. So I've been thinking a lot about it, because I'm already a year ahead and I'll finish school at 17. Just 2 more years of this crap.

Appa wants me to go into his sphere – actuarial science – but it looks so incredibly dull. I did some job shadowing at his office, not that I got paid a single cent for my time. I mean, why I did it, I don't know. I had to get up early, *and* it was in the holidays. But I guess I was curious about what makes my father tick (other than the usual, of course). I wasn't any the wiser having spent 2 weeks there. He looks impressive in meetings, and people respect him and stuff, but mostly he seems to be sitting on the sidelines, while the real action happens elsewhere.

Anyway, I like to touch things. I love the way a car responds when I adjust a bolt or replace a valve. It seems to me that inanimate things are just more interesting to be around. Joe's fun though, of course – he follows me around like a little puppy. To him, anything I do is godlike. I believe, truly, that he is the only person in the world who thinks I'm totally awesome. Even Annie gives me lectures about being irresponsible, rude or insensitive. With a family like mine, you need a rhino hide, and that's what I have. Thank God. I mean, even when Asmita Ayaa kicked the bucket, I didn't let myself cry. I mean, what's the point?

Okay, so it was a shock. An aneurism and, whoops, there you go: no more roti and Rogan Josh. No more home-made Diwali treats.

My grandfather was beside himself. Instead of retreating into the workshop like he always used to do the moment a crisis hit, it seemed to me like he just hung up his tools. Then he started leaving the house. It was only after a few months of mourning that I realised he was actually playing poker with a group of buddies, and smoking as much as my mother.

The baby – the new one – seems to be a lot tougher than Joe, because Mom hasn't had any physical issues this pregnancy at all. But she told me she literally begged the gynae the other day to take the kid out because she's sick of feeling like a bloated whale. (Fishing for compliments, I tell you – from the back, you can't even tell she's 37 weeks pregnant. Not that I'd tell her that.)

Personally, I think it'd be better if the new kid stayed inside. My mom clearly doesn't cope with pressure. This time, Clay's taking some extra time off to help with the baby, and Filda's all hands on deck. Everyone knows that for the first year of Joe's life Filda practically raised him herself, so if I was her, I would've run for the hills. I like Filda, even though sometimes I ignore her when she tells me not to do something or checks up on me when I'm lying on the bed listening to music. It's more than my mom does.

Even Appa seems to have vaguely settled down. He's found a nice Indian girl, Venita, and bought an overly ostentatious mansion in Noordhoek. I had the choice of moving in with him or staying here with Mom, so I worked out a way of scoring them:

Table 1.1: Numerical analysis of Rondebosch/Noordhoek homes

	Mom's house	Score/10	Appa's house	Score/10
Food	Biltong! (+5) Meat (+3)	8	Vegetarian (−2) Too much temptation (sweet stuff) (−2)	6
Bedroom	Most of my stuff is there. (6) Don't have to move anything. (4) Doesn't have a lock. (−1)	9	Can redecorate if I want. (10) Big effort (−4)	6
Noise	New baby!!! (−5)	5	Appa shagging!!! (−5)	5
Freedom	Mom and Clay distracted. (5) Can cycle/bunk. (5) Do they actually even care? (−1)	9	Far from everything. (−3) Have to get lifts. (−3) Appa interferes with my homework and my clothes. (−3)	1
Company	Joe (4) Petrol heads (2) Filda (2) Annie (2) Mom (−2)	8	Appa? (−2) Barely know Venita and why bother? She won't last. (−3)	5
View	Overlooks telephone wires (−2) Tree blocks my window (−2)	6	Mountains and sea (8) Close to beach (2) Not close enough to walk (−2)	8
House	Basic family house (−2)	8	Full-on luxury. The works. (10) Appa won't let me use some of the kit without being there (−1)	9
Bathroom	Have to share. (−2) Joe won't let me go in on my own. (−3)	5	Private (5) Jacuzzi jets (5) Appa says long baths waste water. Ruins it. (−2)	8
Commute	None (10)	10	Sucks (−6)	4
Entertainment	Clay's/Kandasamy Ajah's workshops (3) Drag racing (3) Westerns with Annie (2) Formula One (2) Can't play music loud (−1)	9	Boring (−3) Computer (1) Can't work on engines in the garage 'cos leaves grease. (−3)	5
TOTAL/100		77		57

Not really much of a choice, but I'm here at Mom's most of the time, which is fine with me. Venita is sweet enough, but she thinks she'll win me over by feeding me – every time I spend the weekend, I put on about 3kgs. Not that I really care any more. I've got that scar from the motorbike accident as well, so I've lost the battle to look like my mom anyway.

Actually, all I care about right now is saving for a gap year just as soon as I finish matric. I'll travel for a year and figure out what I want to do with myself. When I get to university – *if* I go to varsity (debatable) – I'll be able to reinvent myself.

Nobody will know me and I can be whoever the hell I like.

Clay: Clean slate

Caitlin was born at 10:09 on the morning of April first, 1999. April Fool's Day, although I didn't realise that at the time. She was delivered by scheduled Caesarean section. Thirty-eight weeks. 2.91kg. Her Apgar score was 9, and 10 after three minutes. She was almost hairless, with pink skin and long eyelashes. Her fingernails had grown so long and pointy that when she latched onto Thea, she left spidery criss-crosses across her swollen breasts. When the doctors positioned our daughter so Thea could see her, Thea began to cry. But this time she was smiling.

"She's absolutely gorgeous! Isn't she, Clay?"

"Beautiful."

I gave Caitie her first bath while Thea was asleep. Annie brought Sanusha and Joe to come meet their sister just hours after she was born. Joe, just four, looked bemused, especially since Caitie had been thoughtful enough to bring him a LEGO set he'd been after straight from the womb.

"But she's a girl," he said, somewhat perturbed. We'd decided to keep that a surprise, but maybe this hadn't been the best idea. He thought for a bit, then said, "What are we going to do with her?"

Sanusha picked Caitie up. She looked her in the eyes, then passed her back.

"Babies all look the same to me," she said all offhand. Then, rather facetiously: "Caitlin, why didn't you bring me anything? I wanted a cellphone."

"Actually, Sanusha," I said, "I think this may be the first time you've actually addressed her."

"Whatever. Annie, can we go now?"

Annie kissed Thea on the cheek and rolled her eyes dramatically at me. "Sure."

I laughed. This was so different from the last time round, and I was filled with hope. Thea seemed calm, almost tranquil. Her touch against our baby's cheek was both confident and gentle – a good sign.

When the children were gone, she brought her mouth close to my ear and said my name softly. Then: "I don't remember any of this with Joe. None of it. I'm racking my brain but there's absolutely no happiness I can remember about that moment."

"You lost a lot of blood. You lost consciousness."

"I'm better this time then, right? I *am* better?"

"You're perfect," I said.

"But what kind of mother doesn't remember all of this? What am I going to say to Joe when he grows up and asks me about his first day?"

"You're going to tell him that he was so eager to come out that he arrived early and that we were worried but happy to meet him face to face."

"And when we did –"

"We loved him instantly."

Thea's eyes clouded. A breeze must have stirred up the pollen from the newly delivered flowers. I sneezed and our baby turned towards me, her face wrinkled in confusion as though she was wondering whether or not to cry. She didn't, but her expression made us laugh.

"It doesn't matter, Thea. What's done is done. Here we are now. Clean slate."

"I don't want to stay here three nights," Thea said. "I want to go home as soon as I can."

"Okay."

"Hospitals make me nervous."

"Okay."

With the catheter still attached and her lower half still lame from the epidural, Thea had no hope of leaving soon, and I knew it. But she smiled at me and held out her hand.

"I think I'm happy," she said.

"Good."

"I hope to God this time it lasts," she said, almost as an afterthought.

Thea: Bird-filled lungs

I came home. By the second day back, I began to recognise the strange fluttering deep in my chest: a trapped bird, sometimes a little *mossie*, sometimes a wide-wing-spanned albatross fighting to get out, leaving me breathless, my diaphragm stretched to its limit.

I didn't say anything about the way the panic sometimes built inside me like a volcano. I tried to keep busy, which was easy enough with a new baby, a preschooler and a teenager. But they kept my hands busy, not my mind.

And Caitlin was not an easy baby.

Not trusting my own instincts, I began to wonder if there was something wrong with her. I couldn't remember much about Joe's first days at home – had he also screamed like this? Sanusha I did remember, but again only vaguely. I'd had Asmita shadowing my every move, and at the time I'd been slightly irritated but secretly relieved that she wouldn't let me mess up. And Sanusha, even as a little girl, had had this way of making me feel like I was extraneous, barely tolerated. Until, of course, my attention wandered – then she'd do something to get it back, and drop me again as soon as I responded. She'd draw me in and fling me out like a fly at the end of a fishing line.

Caitlin was completely different. She'd only go to sleep lying directly on me, stomach to stomach. It was not that she was heavy – she'd actually lost a few hundred grams at hospital – but after a few hours her body would start to feel like a dead weight. I'd keep waking up, worried I'd pulled down the blanket and suffocated her. So even if she was asleep, I was half awake. More than once, Clay leant over, picked up our daughter and placed her in the bassinet. She would wake up immediately and scream unbearably, so we'd put her back on my chest.

We tried other things. Swaddling. A polar bear you could heat in the microwave. We thought we could fool her into thinking the hot toy was me, but Caitlin wasn't fooled. Clay was an acceptable alternative, but he just couldn't sleep with her wriggling all over him.

"I've got to work in the morning," he'd say groggily.

I knew he did. But really, lying there with my daughter on my heart, I remembered this was all his idea. As he snored gently next to me, sometimes I hated him. He'd got me into this mess. As I padded into Caitlin's room – which hadn't actually been used except for nappy changes and feeding – I wished we had a heater that was on all night. The room was freezing. And it was lonely in the dark. My toes almost blue. My breasts exposed one by one to the snuffle-snuffle of a lapping, hungry mouth. I wanted to put on a radio and find some company in the darkness, but everybody said you should feed in silence. To get the baby back to sleep.

Oh God.

The burping. The lack of burping. How could it take so long to untrap a few air bubbles out of such a little body?

"Clay." I shoved him awake as our daughter howled.

"What? What?"

"You've got to burp this baby. I can't do it."

It took a few seconds for him to register what I was telling him.

"Take your daughter."

Take her, because right at this moment, in the middle of the night, I don't want her. Like I didn't want her on the day I found out I was pregnant.

Clay rolled out of bed, pulled on a dressing gown over his pyjamas.

"Go back to bed," Clay said to me. "Get some sleep." He took Caitlin and looked into her teary blue eyes, the angry frown crossing her puce face. "Come, beautiful. Let's go watch some sport."

Only a dad, I thought as I lay back on the bed, relieved to have the responsibility taken away from me. I fell into the depths of sleep, only to find another creature nuzzling me only minutes later.

"I can't sleep, Mommy. Caitlin is naughty. She woke me up, *again*."

"Climb in next to me," I said to Joe. I wrapped my arms around him.

"I've met her now," Joe said softly. "When can we send her back?"

⋆

Another night. More feeding. More musical beds, but without the music.

I woke up in Joe's bed. Joe was in ours. Caitlin was on Clay in the lounge. The only bed virtually unused was Caitlin's bassinet. We drank coffee in the morning unable to speak four words to each other. Joe said it was time to go to school and I drove him virtually silently, except for the basic checks:

"Lunch? Check. Hat? Check. Juice? Check. Bag? Bugger."

"You said a bad word, Mommy."

I hadn't even realised I'd spoken aloud. I walked him into the nursery school, relieved to have one responsibility off my shoulders. But even having dropped him off, I felt the familiar expansion of my bird-filled lungs. *Breathe, breathe.* It wasn't easy.

I'd told myself I'd feed this baby myself for at least three months, but I didn't know how long I was going to last like this, unmedicated. I think I was making up for barely feeding Joe at all. Yet my hands were trembling dreadfully.

Back at the house, Caitlin attached herself to me. I'd thought I would hate the breastfeeding, but it was true what they said about the connections created by skin-to-skin contact. I hadn't experienced it with Joe, but I could see the way my second daughter fitted to me like we were matching nuts and bolts. My heart surged, but despite this I was shaking.

My mind mists were returning. When I rediscovered myself hours later, my daughter was wet through, the urine soaked into my shirt. I gave her to Filda, ran a bath for myself, thinking I needed help.

I forgot about Joe. His pick-up time vanished into my fuzzy brain, and resurfaced only when Clay arrived looking harried. I had left my child at school in exactly the same way that my mother had left me, except Joe has been looked after by his teacher, and hopefully was young enough not to have noticed that something was amiss.

"What happened, Thea? You left Joe there?"

I shrugged. It was all the communication I could manage.

"They fell asleep on the feeding chair," Filda said. "It was my fault. I should have woken her up. I'm sorry."

Clay looked at me, then kissed me lightly on the forehead. "No harm done, I suppose."

"I suppose," I said as Caitlin began to scream.

And scream.

*

A baby's shriek is like a chainsaw to the head. You can't escape it, even from the other end of the house with a pillow over your head. Caitlin started at five thirty. If we were lucky, she finished by midnight. And nothing soothed her. We were told she had colic, the catch-all for shrieking babies between the ages of a few weeks and about six months. With her fist in and out her mouth, and her little legs pulled up to her body, Caitlin's face was almost entirely wrinkled.

"Tension at home?" the paed asked.

"I'll say," said Clay, "with screaming like that!"

"I can't even have a shower without her howling. She doesn't stop," I added.

"The good thing," the doctor said, "is that this ends. It's one of life's mysteries, colic. And you're unlucky. Boys are much more likely to get it than girls are."

"Great," we said simultaneously, as the paed wrote out a script for homeopathic powders he thought might help.

This was a typical evening: after Joe was bathed and dressed in his pyjamas, we'd put him in the lounge with some toys – LEGO or a train set. Sanusha would be nowhere in sight. She'd usually only appear when dinner was actually on the table, unless I forced her to come into the kitchen and help. Her sullen face was more than I could handle. It was easier to just ignore her.

Clay would take Caitlin and bath her on her own. I would feed her just before the bath, and again straight afterwards. The aim was to put her down, get her to sleep so we could have even just a half hour of peace. At bath time Caitlin was probably at her best. The warm water seemed to soothe her and her face relaxed into cute-baby chubbiness.

I could sometimes hear Clay singing to her while I cooked the evening meal. Pasta. A stew from the hotpot. Rice. Soup. Something simple. Sanusha had always been fussy about her food, especially because she didn't like tomatoes. If I hid them by liquidising them, she didn't notice. I'd grown used to doing this over her fifteen years, but now, with a thousand other things to think of, liquidising tomatoes was the last thing on my mind – she'd have to like it or lump it.

But then I imagined the thick lip, the moroseness over dinner. I fetched the machine out of the cupboard, resenting it thoroughly.

When I was a little girl I'd been expected to help my mother. She'd had a sick child to attend to, and sometimes I'd had to cook the whole meal myself. Yet now I allowed Sanusha to hide herself away. The truth is, with Sanusha's resentment and bad humour, it was often simply easier to do it myself. Another thing that made me a bad mother, I suppose: we're supposed to enforce boundaries, create discipline, but the only discipline I was enforcing was my own self-discipline.

Get up in the morning. Survive. Go to bed. Wake up all night.

Contain my flapping birds. Hoover up the mists.

Survive.

I lifted the fettucine into the pot, stirred the bolognaise. I could hear splashing, gurgling. Perhaps Clay had the best job with Caitlin, but I swear by the end of a day of howling, I hated the very sight of her. These moments without her demands were vital.

Despite his bad start, Joe was a ray of sunshine. He so rarely gave us any hassles that I feared sometimes that Caitlin, and Nush to a lesser extent, would eclipse him completely. And that when he really needed us, we wouldn't be looking in his direction.

My few minutes of respite already over, I could hear Clay taking Caitlin out the bath; her howls of protest.

"Thea!" Clay called, and I took the food off the stove.

Top open. Latching her carefully, I sat down on an armchair in the lounge. Clay smiled as he went to the stereo.

"Mellow? Upbeat?" he asked.

"Calming," I answered. "As calming as possible!"

The sounds of Coltrane soon blew softly out the speakers. Caitlin lifted her head for a moment, snorted, then reattached herself.

Sitting there, I watched my fingers trembling again. Sometimes I literally had to sit on my hands to stop the tremors. Though that was impossible when holding a child.

And when Clay came towards me, the look on his face said everything. "It's back, isn't it?"

"Really, I'm fine."

"Thea, you're not fine. Look how you're shaking."

"A few more weeks and we'll wean her. I can manage for a few more weeks."

"You sure?"

"I would tell you." (I wouldn't, but he didn't need to know that.)

It wasn't long before Caitlin started shrieking again, so the subject was closed before it had properly started.

"She's supposed to sleep so we can eat," said Clay. "What now?"

"Shift work," I muttered. "But we need to burp her first."

Up and down the passage.

Clay first. And I found I didn't want to eat on my own.

Up and down.

Then me.

Pacing, bouncing, the howling in my ear, I watched Clay for a bit, my mind clouding. I wanted to sit, to just melt into a chair.

I wanted to dissolve.

"What's the freaking racket?" – Sanusha – "I can hear her through my freaking headphones!"

"Colic," Clay answered tiredly from the couch where he sat staring blankly at his plate.

"I'm never having one of these. They're a pain in the bum."

"Caitlin is your sister," said Clay.

"Ja, well, I didn't ask for her. I'm starving. Where's the grub?"

"Jesus, Nush, have some heart."

"Why? Is that what's for dinner?"

"Ha! Ha!"

"Sorry, I can't hear you. Can she turn down the volume?"

"Here," Clay said suddenly, "you take her." And with one quick movement, he was off the couch, scooping Caitlin out of my arms and handing her to Sanusha. Instantly, Caitie quietened, eyeing Nush with a wary glare. "Great, you've got the touch."

"I'm not keeping her."

"Just rock her. She likes you."

"The feeling is *so* not mutual."

But Clay winked at me because Sanusha was clearly bursting with pride.

I sat down. Head in my hands, I leant forward.

Blood rushing through my ears, a muffled roar.

Then I fell forward, hitting my head on the coffee table. It wasn't a bad gash, but the blood seeped all over the carpet.

"Jesus, Thea, what's going on?"

"I don't know. Maybe I'm just hungry."

Sanusha jiggled her sister, peering at me over the back of the couch. "I think you should eat then, Mom. I'll watch the terrorist."

"Really?"

"Just don't make a habit of it, okay?"

Clay: Black noise

Sanusha was right – Caitlin was a terrorist and this was guerrilla warfare.

I'd never heard screaming like that. Not in my whole life. Sometimes it was all I could do to dose her with colic meds, ensure she was fed, changed and burped, and then close the door while she howled herself to sleep. If I didn't leave her, I wasn't always sure I could control myself.

Sometimes I retreated to my car. I put the music on loud and pretended I was driving somewhere. Anywhere away from the noise. So I didn't notice immediately that my wife was beginning to disappear. Her looks of suspicion, I supposed, were looks of pure exhaustion and desperation. The sort of exhaustion and desperation I was experiencing myself.

I should have noticed. But I didn't.

Sanusha (aged 16): Cottage pie

I've been doing a lot of thinking about happiness. I've even measured it:

Figure 1.1: Middleton-Moonsamy happiness quotient

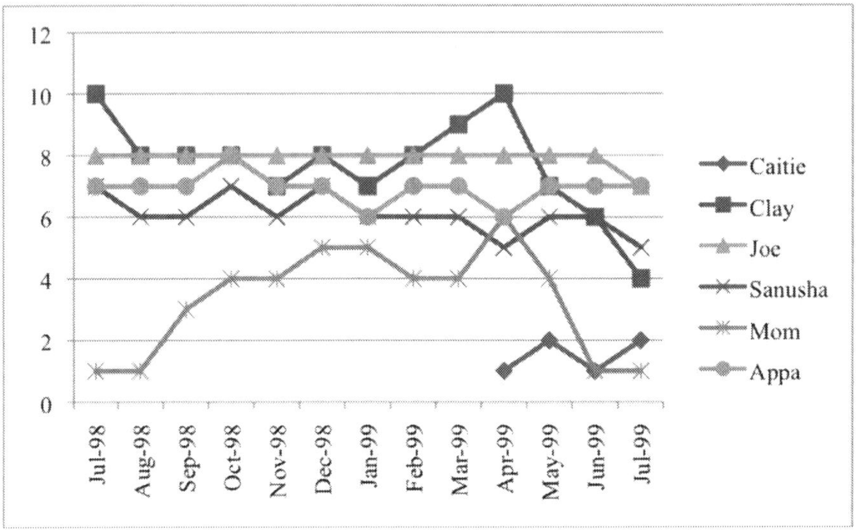

Source: My Brain

So when I fling my school bag next to the door, I am even more perceptive about the mood in the house than normal. And it doesn't feel all that kosher.

"Mom?"

She's sitting in the kitchen, peeling potatoes. But she isn't using a peeler. Stacked in front of her is a selection of knives, the likes of which I never knew we had in the house.

"Who let you in?" Mom asks immediately. "Was the door unlocked?"

I shake the keys under her nose, making her flinch. "Keys, Mom, heard of these? We having mash?"

"I'm peeling potatoes," my mom says.

"Yes," I reply, "I can see that." I watch the peels forming ringlets on the wooden board. "Where are the kids?"

"Who?"

"Joe and Caitie."

"Filda took them to the park. Why are you asking me so many questions? Do you know something?"

"What?"

"Did Clay ask you to interrogate me?"

"Chill, Mom. Just making light conversation. We're done now."

My mom nods and continues peeling. "I thought we might have mashed potato tonight. Cottage pie, maybe."

"Okay," I say. I don't really care – I'm not planning on eating much anyway. Sitting at the dinner table is a bit of a chore. The longer it takes, the worse for me.

My mom looks at me blankly. Without knowing why, I pick up the knives strewn across the kitchen counter. "Why are all these out?" I ask.

"I want to sharpen them," Mom says. "You could do it."

"I could," I say.

We have one of those old-fashioned sharpeners shaped like a spear. I run the first knife along the edge, watching the tiny shavings collecting on the metal. My mom's lips are moving as though she's talking, but no sound is coming from her mouth. All I can hear is the scrape of steel against the sharpener. I pick up a cloth, wipe the blade clean. I like this sort of physical work. And conversations with my mom these days are beginning to frighten me. I found her in the bedroom speaking softly to someone who wasn't there. We all talk to ourselves now and then, but it wasn't like that. I swear, I thought Annie was in the room with her. When I asked Annie about it, she shook her head.

"When she's struggling, she talks to her brother," she told me.

"Robbie's dead."

"Not to her. Remember when you had that car accident when you were little? She told me she saw him in the hospital several times. Listen, don't worry about it, Nush. He's her guardian angel, that's all. Sometimes she needs him so she can be stronger."

"She's nuts," I said.

"Aren't we all a little crazy in our own way?"

"Not me. I'm as sane as you can get. That's my tragedy in this family."

Now, my mom shifts. The potatoes are all chopped and peeled. I swear, if I measure them, each potato cube will be exactly the same size. It's freaky – like they've gone through some sort of chopping machine.

"The children must come inside now," Mom says. "I don't think it's safe out."

"But they're with Filda, you told me that yourself."

"It's late. I want them home *right* now."

"Mom," I say, "you said the kids were at the park."

"'That's silly. I never said that. Those kids need to be inside right now. It's time for Caitlin's bath."

Mom stands up. I notice that she's barefoot. For somebody usually so body conscious, she looks unkempt – her toenails are half-painted, and her heels are cracked and dry. She got strange bald patches on the side of her head.

She opens the back door and calls and calls. Except it sounds more like the bark of a hadeda.

"I'll go look for them," I say, watching the anxiety building in my mother.

Her arms are shaking but she's holding them across her body like a waistcoat, trying to keep them still. "I'll go get them. You stay inside, Mom," I say.

"Where are they? Where are my kids?"

"I said I would look for them." I put my arm around my mother, who still towers above me, and usher her towards the lounge. "Why don't you get the bath ready and the clothes? I'll go down to the park and bring them back to you."

"I'm making cottage pie," Mom tells me. "Do you think that's all right?"

"It's fine. It's all fine." I realise that she isn't talking to me. Her face has this blackboard look, like something needs to be written on it. I wish she'd just walk herself down the passage.

It's not very long before I bring the kids and Filda home. Maybe 30 minutes, tops. We come in through the kitchen door, which is unlocked even though I took a key. Almost every single knife that has been sharpened is now speared into the kitchen door, like my mom's been doing a circus act. A few of the knives have snapped and are lying on the floor. Some are upended and have pierced the linoleum.

There's blood on the floor.

"Mom," I call, nervously. "Mom?"

Caitie is still strapped to Filda's back. Filda's charcoal eyes, as she looks about, are the size of dartboards.

"Stay here for a moment with Filda, Joe."

I go down the passage, feeling increasingly agitated. The house is silent, except for the sounds of water flowing. And then I find her.

My mother is lying on the bed. In her bathroom, the bath is overflowing, the kids' clothes floating in neat piles in the water. Already the bedroom carpet is a sodden mess where the water has streamed out over the tiles and beyond the door.

In that minute, I know my mother is dead.

"Filda," I call, my voice a high squeak.

I hear her quick footsteps as she comes into the bedroom, still holding Joe's hand, with Caitie tied to her back. Filda looks at me, then at the scene in the bedroom, her normally calm façade briefly cracked. Then she quickly steers Joe into the en suite and turns off the taps, whisking him out the bedroom again before he sees anything.

"I'll phone your father," she says loudly. "Check your mother. Be brave now, Sanusha."

"But what –?"

"You can do it."

"Is Mommy sleeping?" I hear Joe ask. "Why is it raining all over the floor?"

I run to Mom; the bedclothes are up to her chin. There are spots of blood all over the normally pure-white sheets, but nothing of the quantity we saw in the kitchen.

She's breathing, the pillowcase is wet from tears and snot.

"She's breathing!" I call.

"Good, now check her arms," comes Filda's voice.

I lean over, digging beneath the bedclothes. Her hand is cut – gaping like a wet fish mouth. She's tried to bandage it, but the bandage has soaked through and unwound itself. It's died on the bed. Her hand, however, looks like it needs stitches.

Filda comes back into the room – without the children this time.

"Get the First Aid kit." She shakes my mother. "Thea! Thea, what happened?"

My mom stirs, touching her sore hand and wincing. "What?"

"I said what happened to your hand?"

"Cut it, s'ppose. It's sore."

"Sit up."

My mom shuffles upwards.

"Come on. We're going to have to clean it out, and get you to the hospital for stitches."

"What happened here?" my mother mumbles. "Did I do this?"

Filda nods. "Clay's on his way. I'm going to call my daughter and tell her I'm staying tonight." Then she goes to the bedside table and picks up the phone. As she speaks in rapid Shona, I can hear her voice rising and falling. And then: "Can you smell something, Nush? Something in the oven?"

"I made cottage pie," my mother offers, her eyes meekly following Filda around the room. "Do you think that's all right?"

Filda looks at me, gesturing with her head to the door. "Go sort that out, please, Sanusha. You're a good girl."

I'm not a good girl. Actually, I'm pretty messed up. And most of the time my actions speak louder than my words. But this time I put my arms around Filda and start to cry.

Mom turns her head, a confused look on her face. "I don't understand, Filda. What's she crying about? What did I do wrong?"

Thea: Just us here

They sewed up my hand with stitches so neat and precise that even Mother would have been impressed. I looked at Clay, wondering why my husband was so wound up.

It was just a mistake. Everybody makes mistakes.

"He's going to ask you about it again," said Robbie. "Don't mention me or you'll get me into trouble."

"Okay," I said, "but it *was* your idea."

"*My* idea?" Clay said, aghast, his normally tanned skin washed out as though completely drained of blood. "Just tell me this, Thea: were you trying to kill yourself?"

"Accident."

"Well, maybe somebody should just come and chat to you. You know we need to take care of you, darling."

I heard Robbie clicking his tongue and I was comforted. He'd been around more often over the last few weeks. Since Caitie, I needed him more than ever. He whistled a bad rendition of "Home on the range" and I giggled.

"You're laughing?" Clay said. "Thea, this is not a joke. There were knives in the goddamn door."

"I'll go if you want, sis," Robbie said. "Just say it, and I'll go."

"No!" I shouted. "Don't go now."

Clay came and sat closer, then nodded at the nurse. "I'm not going, Thea. I'm right here. Here, feel my hand. I'm right here. And don't worry about the kids. Annie has them."

The kids?

I squeezed his hand, but I was looking for Robbie. Then Doctor Rosenkrantz came into the ward.

"It's the good doctor," Robbie said. "She won't want me here."

"But I do," I replied.

"Hello, Thea," Doctor Rosenkrantz said. "What do you do?"

"Private conversation," I mumbled.

Doctor Rosenkrantz nodded at my husband. "Clay."

"I'll be downstairs in the coffee shop," he said.

"They fixed my hand, doc. I think I want to go home now."

She sat down next to me on the bed. "You've got those tremors again, dear. And you haven't come to see me?"

"A baby needs her mother's milk."

"A baby needs a healthy mother. What happened, love?"

"At the house? Honestly, doc. I don't really remember. It's all a bit of a blur."

"You like her?" Robbie asked me. "I think there's something a bit fishy about her."

"There is not," I replied, looking away quickly.

"Thea?" Doctor Rosenkrantz said. "Are we alone?"

"That's all it comes to when we die."

"Oh? And is death something you've been thinking about? Were you unhappy tonight?"

I shifted. "Why do you always ask me that? I was happy once."

"Only once?"

"A few times. You know."

"And now?"

"Caitie has colic. I want some sleep. I'd sell Joe for some sleep. She's a screamer. I love her. But the screaming?"

"And is Clay helping you?"

"He's the perfect husband," I said, biting on my tongue. "But he doesn't have boobs."

"You know, bottle feeding isn't all that bad."

"We'll try it. Can I go now? I'm knackered."

"You could. But I think you're not being upfront with me. Let's talk a little more. Anything specific going on at home I should know about?"

"What's there to say? We have a baby, a little boy, a troubled teenager. I feel like crap, but that's pretty normal on no sleep."

"What does crap mean to you?"

"The same as it means for everybody, I assume."

"Are you suicidal?"

"I wouldn't *do* anything. Doesn't everybody want out, every now and again?"

"Listen, Thea, look at me. Look at me." She took my face and made my eyes meet hers.

Robbie sighed melodramatically. "Don't trust her; I told you, there's something not quite right about her."

I shook my head at Robbie, warning him off.

"Thea, I repeat, are we alone?"

"What do you mean?"

"I think you know perfectly well what I'm asking. Is there someone here, talking to you?"

"Look around you, doc, do you see anyone?"

"Good girl," cheered Robbie.

"No," she said, enunciating this very clearly. "I don't see anyone at all. It's just us here."

I started to stand, but Doctor Rosenkrantz said sharply: "We haven't finished, Thea. You don't stand up until I discharge you."

"What, now I'm a prisoner? I cut my hand, for Christ's sake. I had a lapse. Give me the drugs and let's get this over with."

Doctor Rosenkrantz didn't even blink. "Thea," she said, "have you ever considered hurting your children?"

"Every child needs a good smack every now and then. You think the naughty corner works for everyone?"

"Stop being flippant. Are you or your children in any danger?"

"Give me the drugs. I'll take them when I'm ready. The kids will be fine. I want to go home." This time I stood up and I wouldn't let her gesture me down again. "Clay!" I called. "Clay! Clay! Clay! Clay!" I screamed, my voice echoing down the hollow corridor. "Clay! Clay! Clay!"

"You're making a scene, Thea," Doctor Rosenkrantz said. "Let's wait calmly for your husband."

"I'm not calm," I said to her. "I'm really not calm. I'm trapped here and I don't like it. Clay! Clay!" I started to walk down the corridor, my handbag clutched under my arm, my footsteps resounding on the floor. I couldn't see Robbie, but I pictured him running behind me. "Clay!"

"Can I help, ma'am?" a male nurse said, coming up next to me. "Who are you looking for?"

"I want my husband!" I shouted, the tears coursing down my face. "I want to go home."

The nurse tried to grab my arm, and I forced him away. Momentarily taken aback, he lost his balance, then righted himself. Clay was sprinting up the passage. "Now what?" he said, his eyes glimmering.

"I want to go home and the doctor won't let me."

"Thea," she said.

My eyes filled with tears. "I'm tired, Clay. I want to be with my family. I cut my hand. That's it."

"That is *not* it," said Doctor Rosenkrantz. "You need to be medicated, my dear. Caitlin will do just fine on formula. She really will."

"We're talking about this here in the *passage*?" my husband said. "Is this at all professional?"

"Then let's go back inside the ward and chat. We can switch you over safely."

"I said," Clay repeated, the lines between his eyes becoming increasingly pronounced, "this is a *passage*. I'm going to take my wife home now and we will make a proper appointment. Thea is tired. It's late. This is not the time or the place to make this decision."

As Clay charged to my defence I felt like crumpling into him. I could hear the doctor's disapproving tut-tut. She shook her head.

"Frankly, Mr Middleton," she said, "I think that's a mistake. I'm here now and the earliest I would be able to see Thea is next Tuesday, as I have a conference in Barcelona. It's only Wednesday today."

"I am perfectly aware what day it is as, I'm sure, is my wife."

"Wednesday," I said defiantly.

Robbie chuckled.

"She needs constant care."

"We'll manage." My husband put his arms around me. "Did they tell you when we need to come in to take out the stitches?" he asked.

"Seven to ten days," I said.

"Fine. We'll phone your rooms tomorrow and book for Tuesday. We can get the stitches out afterwards," said Clay.

The doctor hesitated. "I'm not happy, Clay. I won't sign off on this."

"I don't think you have to," he said. "I can take care of my own wife."

"She's hallucinating. She may be suffering delusions."

"Don't be ridiculous. She's not."

"Can we go now, Clay?" I said softly, my hand in his.

"Clay, I'm warning you: this is not the right decision. She needs to be medicated right now."

"Thea," Clay said looking at me, "do you need the meds?"

"I'm tired. I just want to sleep."

"I'm sorry, Doctor Rosenkrantz. I know you feel slighted, but Thea's always better at home. And we can get our nanny to stay in."

"The knives?"

"Packed away."

"And you think your children are safe?"

"Of course. She's their *mother*."

"Goodbye, doc," I said pointedly, nursing my hand against my chest.

She frowned. "Don't forget that appointment. And start switching Caitlyn over to the bottle. You need to take over some of the night feeds, Clay."

"Fine," said Clay. "We'll start tonight."

The doctor sighed, a worried – and I thought condescending – smile lingered on her lips. She clearly had more to say, but she nodded and started walking away from us. Then she turned, opened her mouth once more, then shut it.

Like a goldfish in a bowl.

"Don't worry so much, doctor," Clay said. "Thea will be fine."

Famous last words.

Clay: Thawing the mannequin

I was awake all night with the baby. And then Thea starting shouting at me: "I hurt, I hurt. Christ, we should have done this slowly."

We got the pump out. All I could hear between the baby's howls was the milking machine – it sounded like my wife was being sucked in by the Kreepy Krauly. I couldn't believe it, but then I was doing it, pulling cabbage leaves out the fridge and layering them over my wife's breasts like she was a bloody salad. Joe, miraculously, slept on.

I was just wearing a pair of shorts, because that's all I'd managed to pull on before all hell broke had broken loose. Cuddling Caitlin, I tried to burp her. Usually I had the touch. This time, she opened her mouth and spewed all over me. The sickly vomit clung to my chest hair like lice. I wiped myself down. Then I had to change Caitie since her little babygro was all soaked through. Just as I finished, she puked again. Over me, the bedclothes, herself. The stuff was projectile. Hit the opposite wall, dripping down like hot wax.

Thea was lying on the bed, stinking of sulphur, and muttering to herself. She didn't react to the crisis. In fact, I don't think she even noticed it. I cooed over Caitie, changing her again. Just as I was about to close up, she farted loudly, then shat all over the changing table. I started again. Wiping, powdering, creaming. Caitie opened her eyes, studying me, and then –

"She smiled!" I said triumphantly. "See, Mommy. Caitlin's first smile was for her dad! And fucking hell, I deserve it, excuse the French."

Thea didn't react. She was curled up again like a foetal ball, the blankets lifted over her head. I got the message and took my daughter to her room. Lay on the floor next to the cot and thought about morning. It would come soon enough. Everything always looked better again in the morning.

When I woke up later, Thea was already in the kitchen. Pots were banging, bacon frying. Relief surged through me. This was once our ritual. If things were looking good, I'd soon go into the kitchen to find a plunger of coffee on the table, mugs placed neatly on a tray – always matching because Thea didn't like disorder. When she was well, Thea was the sort of person who'd go round the house straightening towels and paintings, lining everything up perfectly.

I sat up, feeling the crick in my neck. God, sleeping on the floor wasn't what it used to be when I went camping as a lightie. I peered into the cot. Our little angel was fast asleep and, oh man, the silence was blissful. I stood up, shivering – I'd only had a pile of baby blankets covering me. And I honed of last night's toxic escapades.

In the shower, I whistled. I was happy. Life was going to be fine. Joe was going to have his op one day so he wouldn't have to wear those thick glasses that kids who didn't know him teased him about. Sanusha was going to grow up and set up her own home, and we'd worry less about what she'd be up to next. Caitie was going to smile, smile, smile at me. I was going to be the best father and husband in the universe. And as for my wife, she was going to get better. Especially once I'd told her I'd booked myself in for a vasectomy.

I dressed in jeans, a white T-shirt and a V-necked jumper that Tom used to rib me about. I liked it because Thea had bought it for me as a surprise. I gelled my hair – a rare occurrence – but Joe liked to touch the spikes when they dried.

I could hear Joe was awake – he was chatting to Thea in the kitchen. I listened to the rise and fall of her voice, a soft laugh; his infectious giggle. Filda wasn't in yet. She usually only arrived at eight. By that time I would have dropped Joe at nursery school and Sanusha would already be at school after leaving home on her bike (though I did wonder if she always actually arrived). I bumped into Nush in the passage.

"Good morning!" I said heartily.

"God, I saw you sleeping on the floor," Sanusha replied. "If this is what it does to you, I should try it."

"Any time you want to clean vomit and rock babies, just let me know. There'll be an opening for you, I promise."

She snorted but then flashed a rare, unguarded smile and I felt like singing. Life was *good*.

In the kitchen, I put my arms around Thea's waist. I kissed her on the cheek, but she pulled away as though I'd hurt her.

"Nush!" she said. "You're already up. I was just going to bring you some coffee."

"No need. I'm here. I'm motivated. It's not pissing down today. Yet."

"Language," Thea and I said simultaneously.

"What? Even Annie says that."

"Well, if *Auntie* Annie says it, it must be all right," said Thea.

"She is not my auntie, *Mother*."

"Don't call me that," Thea said quickly, her face darkening. "I'm Mom." She looked to the side, then shook her head quickly, marching to the sink as though something was after her. "No," she whispered. "I don't want to."

Sanusha's eyebrows rose, then she shrugged theatrically. "I'm going to see Annie later. I'm helping Matt with his science project on electricity. We're building a circuit."

"Is that okay with your mom?" I said. "Thea?"

"Mmm?" she said, smiling slightly.

"That okay?"

"Is what okay?"

"Sanusha and Annie."

I could tell she had no idea what I was talking about but she said, "Sure." Then she dished out the bacon and eggs.

Joe, it seemed, had already eaten, and was building a tower with his toast crusts – actually, I was quite impressed and nearly donated mine but didn't want to piss Thea off. Anyway, it didn't take long before Joe tired of the exercise and slipped out of his seat to the playroom.

"Caitie's fast asleep still," I said to Thea. "Last night wore her out."

"I like her more asleep." So Thea had heard me this time. "She's not quite so intimidating."

"She's a baby, *Mom*," Sanusha said pointedly.

"Yes, and she screams *a lot*."

"Was I intimidating?"

I tried to make the conversation lighter: "Sanusha, my girl, you still are."

She stuck out her tongue. "I'm outta here. Got to do my homework still."

"You told me *last night* you did it *last night*," Thea said.

Nush shrugged. "So I lied. Ciao for now." The back door banged behind her.

"So, there you have it: further proof that I am a terrible mother is now cycling down our driveway," Thea said, looking out the window.

"It's just a stage," I replied.

"Like Caitie?"

"Yup. Do you want me to set up the breast pump for you? Are you feeling a little better?"

"The pain woke me up. I pumped already. God, this is what we are reduced to: discussing my milk production over bacon and eggs."

I didn't like the agitation in her tone so I forced a grin. But nothing much would have put me off my breakfast – I was starving.

"I'm going to come home a little later than usual today," I said. "I have a meeting with the coffee supplier, Francesca. She's flying in at four. I said I'd pick her up at the airport, then drop her off at the Vineyard."

Thea was standing next to the sink, but it was clear she wasn't listening to me.

"Thea?" I said. "Did you hear me?"

"What?" she said, rather sharply.

"I'm going to drop her at the Vineyard and then come home."

Silence.

"Thea?"

It was finally the sound of the telephone ringing that startled her. Her eyes widened. Without looking at me, Thea left the kitchen, her feet soundless as she walked to the phone in the entrance hall. I followed.

"Hello. Oh, Filda, really? Shame! That's awful. All night? Yes, we'll be okay. Now you take care of her. Yes. Bye." Thea put down the phone. She turned to me with a blank look on her face. "Filda's daughter has food poisoning or a bug or something. She's too weak to move."

"Are you serious? She's not coming in?"

"Well, what do you expect her to do? Leave Ruda in a pile of puke?"

"That isn't –"

"So our family is important, but hers isn't?"

"Did I *just say* that? I don't remember saying anything of the sort."

Thea glanced to her left, tipped her head like she was listening. "Yes," she said softly, then she turned to me with a penetrating glare from her unmatched eyes. For a moment, I thought I saw something close to distaste, or as though someone else was staring at me. Someone who didn't like me at all. But perhaps I was being paranoid. I tried to break the eye-lock with a smile.

"You can go and get changed," I suggested. "Enjoy a nice relaxing shower? I'll wait with Joe and Caitie – I've got a few minutes and Joe can be late."

Still she didn't move. God, this was beginning to freak me out. I walked over to her, put my arm around her and walked her to the bedroom.

"Bath or shower?" I said.

No response, although she did allow me to move her forward.

"Shower," I said, unbuttoning her. There was nothing sexy about it though.

She complied but it was weird, like she wasn't really in that mannequin-body. I turned up the spray, slightly cooler than how I liked it. Then I prodded her gently in. Even under the torrent, I could see that she was crying. She crossed her arms across her breasts and I wondered if the water was hurting her.

"You okay, love? Are you hurting?"

She nodded and I pulled her out the cubicle, wetting my shirt all the way up to the shoulder. I wrapped a bath sheet around her, dried her hair with the hand towel. All the time, my mind running wild:

I shouldn't leave her here alone. She isn't okay. Caitie will wake up and then what?

But I had meetings lined up – a potential franchise opportunity I'd been working on for months. My good spirits of only half an hour before had faded.

For fuck's sake. How much longer can this go on? This neediness. This really freaking weird behaviour?

It's not like Thea had ever thanked me, not that I wanted her to grovel. A simple thank you would suffice! Right then, I just needed a change of scenery. I needed to be away from this house, this space. She wasn't the only one stifling in it!

I breathed in, trying to realign myself.

What I needed didn't matter. I'd have to cancel. I'd made that promise all those months ago that I would help her through this. Idiot that I am, what was it that I'd said then? *I'll come and get you out.* Like I was even capable of doing that! Thea's mind was often so impenetrable I wondered if even Dr Rosenkrantz could bash a hole through it. Still, I needed to work. I needed to earn a living. Maybe Annie could do a stint this afternoon while I went to the airport. Or Tom (fat chance). Or maybe my dad?

All this time, I was putting my wife's shrunken arms through her sleeves, her legs into knickers, her body into warmth. I sat her down, dried her hair with the blowdryer, thinking as she sat under the singeing heat.

When Thea was dressed, I led her back into the bedroom. She'd thawed slightly and sat on the bed as I changed out of my drenched shirt. And every moment, I felt Thea's eyes on me, enormous, almost predatory, but not in the sexual sense – as though she was sizing me up. Hard to describe it, really, but my heart was beating in my ears, my fingers tingling. I wanted to laugh it away. But I think what I felt was nervous. Around my own wife.

"Let me help you clear up the breakfast things," I said.

She nodded, uncurling her legs, and went ahead of me to the kitchen.

I quickly checked on Caitie and Joe. One was asleep, the other entranced in front of a Disney movie, and when I got to the kitchen, Thea was sitting down at the breakfast nook, having made *no* attempt to start cleaning up. Ignoring my irritation, I began to wash the frying pan. *How difficult*, I thought, *would it have been for her to pick up a damn cloth, or even put the bread back in the bread bin?* I needed to get going and she knew it. The toast crumbs, scattered all over the kitchen counter remained where Thea had left them. I grabbed a cloth next, cupped my hand and wiped. Some shrapnel floated to the floor. I bent down, scooping up the bits between my fingers. Then I used the cloth to dab away some butter that was also on the floor. Any other day I would have got a lecture about hygiene: *Clay, that's a cloth for the counters, not the floors.*

I stood up again, walked over to Thea and touched her hand. "We should have moved over to the bottle earlier, my love. You were clearly exhausted."

"That's motherhood for you," she said.

"And fatherhood, it seems," I said, a little irritated. There may well have been some dads who hadn't seen the shit-side of a nappy, but I had. I'd done the vomit, the blood, the tears, the crap and the piss. I'd done the nights. I'd done the late-night drive to the twenty-four-hour chemist in Wynberg, and the early morning wails for juice: *Not the apple one, Dad! No – not in the yellow cup! Give-it-give-it-give-it!*

"Yes, well," Thea said. "You asked for it."

I shoved the bread in its plastic bag. "Sure," I said. "If you say so."

270

"I do say so," Thea said. "I *say* so." Each word was enunciated so carefully and bitterly, it sounded like a curse.

"Great," I said. "You say so. Now what?"

Thea sighed. She no longer looked cowed and defeated, but seemed to have taken on a belligerence, a level of defiance I didn't recognise. "Now I'm going to see Mother. I need to see her today."

My jaw dropped. "You're joking, right?"

"Actually," she said rather primly, "I am not."

"But you haven't driven for weeks," I burst out, although I was thinking so many things I was rather surprised that that's what I came up with.

"Don't be ridiculous. You don't forget how to drive."

"Yes, well, Thea. That. Is. *Not*. A. Good. Idea. Not now. You're not –"

"Stable?"

"I was going to say ready, but, yes, if you like."

"I do not *like*. Don't be so damn condescending. I need Mother," she said. "I miss her. Being a mother makes you need your mother more. Not that I have to explain it to you, but I just think it's time to mend fences."

"That may well be true, but hers is made of barbed wire, with electricity running through the top."

"God, Clay. How can you even say that? You haven't even met her."

"Well, I've heard enough stories to hate her. From *you*. When you disappeared, she didn't even care. Rajit told me –" I studied my wife. My voice had started to rise in pitch. Sounded like I was whining.

I bit my cheek, trying to calm myself down. This was outrageous. *Her mother* was a bitch. *Her mother* would unbalance her completely. And then what? What would happen to *my* family. *Our* family? I looked at Thea. Her arms were crossed firmly across her chest like a spoilt brat not getting her way.

"You don't own me," she said. "Just because you married me. As far as I can remember, we dispensed with the love and obey."

"We dispensed with the *obey*, Thea. Not the love. Never the love."

Even this didn't soften her. "I want to see her. I want to see my mother!" She sounded like Sanusha that time we hadn't let her go to a Springbok Nude Girls concert in the middle of a school week.

Thea's frown creased between her eyes and for a moment I pictured her as a much older woman – a vision that scared me. I walked over to her and patted her shoulder, but her reaction was horrifying: she cowered, crunching herself up in a half-ball against the kitchen wall.

"Thea," I said softly. "I would never, never hurt you. Let's just talk about this. If you want to see you mother, let me come with you. But not today. I can't do today."

She lifted her head. "I need to see her. *Today*. And what's with this Francesca woman anyway? Why do you need to meet her? What's wrong with a damn taxi?"

I was surprised she'd even remembered Francesca's name – I hadn't thought she was listening.

"She's my supplier, Thea. But, really, I'm just paying her back for her hospitality when I was in Costa Rica. You know how it is."

"Her *hospitality*?"

The word was loaded, prompting me to think back to my time in Arenal in that year before I'd reconnected with Thea. Cocktails in the hot springs. One thing led to another; a one-night-only event. It was a long time since I'd thought of Francesca in *that* way and I blushed.

"Oh," said Thea, her expression darkening. "Clearly she was a *superior* hostess."

"You and I weren't even together then, Thea. Francesca is just a friend now."

"I thought she was just your *supplier*."

"Friend, supplier. Why can't she be both?"

"Why can't she get a taxi?"

"She could, but now she's expecting me."

"So you go to the airport to fetch an ex-lover and I'm not allowed to see my own mother?"

Okay. We were back to that. I tried to sit down next to Thea on the kitchen bench but, disconcertingly, she refused to move up. I didn't like towering over her it so I bent down, trying to get her to look at me. Even with my hand cupped at her chin, she didn't budge.

"Please, darling. Can we just wait a few weeks? Until the meds are adjusted and you've seen Doctor Rosenkrantz a few times? We have to get you right for the family you have, not the family that abandoned you when you needed help."

"You're keeping me away from my mother! What is your problem, Clay? Why do you feel so threatened?"

"I'm trying to protect *you*."

Thea looked past me. Her eyes locked on something behind me. Slowly she nodded, twirling her finger in her hair. Then she stood up. "Protect me? I don't think so, Clay. I can see when I'm being manipulated. I'm not stupid, you know."

"Manipulated?" I asked, completely confused. "How am I doing that?"

"You're just going to put it off over and over again, until I'm completely trapped in this house, with you directing my every move."

"You're kidding me, right? Your every move?"

"Stop repeating everything I say. I know what you're doing and I don't like it!"

"Thea," I said, "you're unwell. Your mother –"

"It was all my fault. I was sleeping around when I was still at school. I got knocked up. I *humiliated* her."

I couldn't believe what I was hearing. "Kids make mistakes. We all make mistakes. She should have been there for you."

"But she was right, wasn't she? Raj was a cad. I was too young for a baby. Imagine if I'd followed her advice – I'd be in a completely different place now. I might have a degree, a real career . . . maybe I'd even be happy!"

Without willing it, I found my fist on the kitchen table. "So now your entire existence is a mistake? What about Sanusha – your beautiful daughter? What about Joe and Caitie? For God's sake, Thea, what about me?"

She smiled with a cloying sweetness that made me want to choke. "This isn't about you, Clay. It's about me; where I start. Where I end."

"You start and end in this family, where you belong, not the family that chose you once, then let you go." And then I made the crucial error: "I forbid you, Thea Middleton. I forbid you to see that witch now. Perhaps in a few months, we can go together. But until then, I cannot have you upset by *that woman*."

Silence. Then: "You forbid me?" Frosty. She stood up and began to clear the last plates from the table. "How very atavistic of you."

I didn't even know what the word meant, but her meaning was clear. "I love you, Thea," I said. "When you are hurting, it hurts me."

"Don't talk such psychobabble bullshit; it doesn't suit you one bit." She smashed a plate into the sink so hard that it cracked in half. She glanced at it, tossed it straight in the bin. She chipped the next one on the tap, and it followed the first plate. "Yes, yes," she said without turning to look at me. "I get it."

"What do you get? What?" I said.

"Back off, Clay. Leave me alone."

I don't know why it took this simple sentence to push me over the edge, but it did. "Leave you alone? I've done nothing but leave you alone for the last few months. I've been patient. Understanding. Supportive. I can barely touch you without you flinching and I haven't complained. Barely a response ever. Not a kiss. Not a hug. Never a thank you. Every day I wake up and I put a fat smile on my face and try to be what you need. But, God help me, I just don't know what that is. And what about me? What about *my* feelings? How *I* am coping? What about *my* needs?"

I walked over to Thea, and gripped her wrist so hard I probably bruised her. I was just trying to turn her around so she would just meet my eyes, but she rammed hard against me, flailing her arms so I had to let her go. That made me even more incensed.

"Look at me, damn it. Look at me!"

For a few microseconds Thea was completely still. Then she turned abruptly. "Is that what this is all about. Fucking? Fine, let's just do it and get it over with. You want to take me on the counter? On the breakfast nook? What's going to make you feel manly enough? You want me to suck you off, or shall we just get down to business?"

"Jesus, Thea, that's not –"

"Oh, come on, Clay, you can't have it both ways. Do you or do you not want me to attend to *your* needs?"

Thea unbuttoned her jeans, pulled them down roughly, kicking them away. She yanked her panties so hard they ripped, and I couldn't help it: it turned me on. She lifted her shirt above her head, tossing it aside.

"What's wrong with you, Clay? Don't you want it?" Even the taunting note in her voice made me hard. "Well, don't you?"

I shouldn't. I did.

I didn't. I did.

And then my body took over. I pushed her back against the pantry door, lifted her up, hastily freed my cock and plunged into her. I didn't listen to her voice now. My brain rushed like a river in flood. Thea's head hit once against the wood but I was almost oblivious. I banged into her again, and again.

It had been months and it was over in what could have been seconds. I don't know. Time was jelly.

Thea retreated from me. She wiped herself roughly between her legs with a dishcloth from one of the drawers.

"Do you feel like a real man now, Clay?" she said, pulling her shirt back on and wincing as she touched where the cupboard must have hit her. "Are you all fixed up?" The expression on her face was filled with disdain. Disdain, and hurt. The moment was anything but cathartic.

What is happening here? What is happening to us?

I stood there silently trying to muster up something appropriate to say.

"Why don't you just go now?" Thea said. "Just leave! You've got what you asked for!"

"Thea –"

"Get out!"

I zipped up, picked up my wallet and keys from the counter. "I'll –"

"Just go, damn it, and leave me in peace."

"Fine. I'd be glad to." I glared at her, then slipped into Caitie's room, kissed her quickly on the cheek, high-fived Joe where he was playing.

"What's all the shouting, Daddy?"

"Nothing to worry about, buddy."

"You shouldn't fight, you know. You'll end up in the naughty corner."

I smiled, ruffled his soft hair. "See you later, alligator."

*

The last thing I heard as I closed the front door was Thea sobbing violently in the kitchen. After all my promises to put her back together, to make her whole again, I'd broken her completely.

And I didn't know how I would ever undo the damage.

Thea: The baldness of the head

I heard Clay's car going down the road.

"You'll need to get the kids away from that man," I heard my brother say. I flinched, not expecting him.

I wiped away a stray tear. "He's their father," I replied mutinously. "It was just a fight."

"Well, he certainly brings out the big guns," Robbie said, then started to scream with mirth. His laughter made me shiver.

"God, Robbie, you can be juvenile at times," I said. I tilted my head, as though to shake out the sound of his voice.

It didn't work.

"Right," he said. "Now *he's* gone, we can go too."

"Go?" I asked.

"I want to see Mom," Robbie said. "Like we agreed."

"I don't know, Robbie. Clay said –"

"You are *not* serious? You're going to let yourself be bossed around by *him*? He isn't all good, you know. That husband. He's trying to trap you in this house, like he owns you. Why do you always choose men like this?"

Half-dressed, I was shivering. "I don't know. I don't feel so good. I'm all confused."

"What's the confusion? You want to see Mom. Get the kids, get the car, drive. Simple."

"I don't think we should," I said, looking at the shadows under the curtains, pointing their fingers across the carpet. "Clay will be –"

"Angry? Furious? Incensed? So what? Anyway, he doesn't have to know. Get dressed. Start with that."

From the bedroom, I heard Caitie waking. At first she mewled softly, then began to yell. When I picked her up she eyed me, then quietened, sniffing at my breast. Nuzzling me, she looked like a newborn guinea pig. Sitting in the tub chair in the corner of the room, I started to unbutton my crumpled shirt and then remembered there'd be no more of that. But my daughter's hungry screech told me this delay – any delay – was an outrage. I prepared the bottle one-handed, trying to pat Caitie to calm her, while at the same time pouring milk powder into the half-prepared bottle on the compactum. My hands trembling so I could hardly grip the milk tin. Caitie's cries drilled into my head until I finally clamped her mouth shut with the teat.

Silence.

I gasped, shaking.

"Let's go," said Robbie, his voice taking on an anxious whine. "I want to go *now*."

"Can't you see I'm feeding the baby?"

There was silence for a moment. Then I heard the sound of tapping, impatient fingers against wood, starting to drive me crazy.

Then Joe trailed into the bedroom demanding juice. "I'm thirsty," he said. "Fruit cocktail."

"Fruit cocktail, *please*," I said.

"Fruit cocktail, *please*."

"Okay, I'll get it in a moment. Let Caitie just finish up."

Robbie snorted rudely. "And you chose this? Being a mother? It's nothing but work, work, work."

*

When Caitie was finished feeding, the burping done, I changed her quickly. Unlike how Joe had been as a baby, she was pliant, and hardly wriggled. It was an unusually sunny winter's day, but still chilly, so I dressed her in a pink babygro and furry rabbit jacket, with white bunny ears. Though she wasn't moving much, she started to cry and I dug in my pocket for her dummy. I popped it into her mouth, noticed the confused frown, and then the suck-suck-suck that was so familiar.

Joe was standing sorting LEGO on the table in the playroom. Yellow. Orange. Red. Blue.

"We're going out, Joe," I said. "Here's your juice."

"Am I going to school?" he said. "We're making penguins out of toilet rolls."

"You can make those tomorrow. Today, we're going on an adventure."

"Are we going on a plane?" he asked hopefully.

"No," I said. "But we can pretend."

"I want to go on a plane and see a *huge* waterfall."

"Okay," I said. "We can do that."

"Not for pretend. For *real*."

"Some day, but not today, all right?"

"I want to go to school then. I want to make penguins out of toilet rolls."

"Joe, you're coming with Caitie and me today."

"I don't want to go with you. I want to go to school and make *penguins*."

"You will get in the bloody car if I tell you to."

Joe looked horrified. "Mommy, you said a bad word."

"Get in the car, Joe."

"You said bloody! That's a bad word. Daddy said I mustn't say that word."

"Don't speak to me like that. I am your mother. I will say what I want!"

Joe looked at me hard then spat a globule right in my face. "Then I want to make some *bloody* penguins!"

I slapped him. I didn't want to but I did it. He started to bawl. Caitie's face twisted in shock and then she was howling too.

"Get in the car!" I shouted.

"No!"

"*Now!*"

"No!"

With one arm around Caitie, I picked up Joe by the elastic of his trousers. He flailed and wriggled. Caitlin screamed piercingly.

"Christ," I muttered.

"Being here infects them," said Robbie over the din. "Infects them with a dark shadow. The darkest shadow you can imagine. It's getting darker by the minute."

I moved forward, stumbling on the step going into the garage, righting myself and cursing.

"Quiet!" Robbie yelled. "Quiet – you're hurting my ears!"

I put Joe on the ground, and he rolled onto his back on the tiles, hitting his head as his stomach lifted, his back arched like a caterpillar in reverse. "Shhhh," I said. "You're frightening your sister, for God's sake."

"Shut them up!" Robbie yelled. "Shut them up!"

"I'm trying! I *am* trying."

I manoeuvred Caitie into her car seat. Once she was clipped, and her dummy was back in, she seemed calm, or calm*er*, at least. She looked at Joe, who was still crying but no longer screaming. Instead he was sucking in air, his little chest heaving. I bent down, patted him. This really was Clay's domain, soothing kids. Joe glared at me with the purest hatred.

"Look at the kid," Robbie said. "He's already touched by darkness. Look at that miserable face, Thea."

"Come on, Joe," I tried to croon, but my voice came out croaking, like I'd just woken up. "Come on, sweetie." I put my arms out and then, mercurial, he reached out to me, putting his arms up trustingly. He put his head against my chest and I could feel the weight of him on my hip. I opened the car door on the other side and placed him in his booster seat. The fight had oozed out of him, and now he was looking at me, his little face full of questions.

"Today," I said to him, "we are going to do something amazing. Today we are going to go and meet your other granny. My mother."

"Daddy says you don't have a mommy."

"Daddy was wrong. My mommy lives down the road. We had a big fight and now I want to be friends again."

"Are we friends, Mommy?" Joe asked.

"Of course."

"I still want to make penguins," he said.

"Not today."

"Maybe tomorrow," he said hopefully.

"Jeez," said Robbie, "does he ever flipping shut up?"

*

When Nush was a baby and I was desperate to get her to sleep, I used to drift by my childhood home, hoping my mother would be outside with her secateurs at the roses near the front lawns, and that maybe I would catch her eye. I thought then that if she saw me, she might relent. She might be alone in that big old house – no Robbie, no Dad – thinking that what I'd done wasn't nearly as bad as she'd believed. She might even let me stop the car, then poke her head through the window to glimpse her granddaughter, who, asleep, would be positively cherubic.

But she was never outside. Never. Not once. And in a city as small as Cape Town, I couldn't fathom how we'd never bumped into each other.

This time, I was going to do things differently. I was going to park outside, ring the buzzer next to the gate, with my son by my side, and my daughter in my arms. I was going to stand there and smile, and look like I wanted nothing, but had everything to give. I would have liked Nush to be with us, but this was a start, and if things went well we could come back, next time, with her. Perhaps at another moment in my life I might have questioned what I had intended by coming here, but I was following Robbie's lead, like I had as a child.

It seemed right; I was always safe with Robbie. Robbie knew best.

Yet driving the short distance to my mother's house felt like crossing Siberia by train.

Slow.

Endless.

The odd interesting house to look at out the window, but then the undeniable sameness of it all combined with a hope that the journey would be worth it. (And, of course, the murmur of other passengers. There is no such thing as total silence on a train.)

Unlike many houses on the less privileged side of Newlands Avenue, my mother's house in Bishopscourt had a long driveway. So long, that as children Robbie and I never had to go to the park to ride our bikes. We were self-sufficient behind our big wall, safe and contained. Of course, that hadn't helped Robbie, even though he'd come back to me.

The front gate had always impressed me. I loved the lion face in the centre, twisted out of wrought iron. When the gate opened its face was split in two, so sometimes when we drove inside I imagined we were being swallowed up whole. Now I had the same sort of feeling.

As I drove, I studied my fingers on the steering wheel and noticed their random tapping on the leather. I tried to silence them, but it was as though my hands were acting beyond me. I could feel a headache coming on and I wondered if perhaps I had chosen the wrong day for this. I lifted one hand off the steering wheel and massaged my temple.

"You're just making excuses," Robbie said – loud enough to make me jump. "Drive. It's time. Drive!"

I hated the way he read me, but I drove, just like he said.

When we got there, the gate was closed. I stopped the car and sat there for a few moments. A little way down the road a guard stood in a hut erected for security, his bicycle chained to a wooden post outside. After a few minutes he sauntered over.

"Hello ma'am," he greeted me as I climbed out of the car.

"Hello," I said. "Is she there?"

"The old *missus*?"

Is that who she is now?

When I'd left, it was just before her fortieth birthday. Not much older than I was, in fact.

"I suppose," I said.

He nodded. "She drove in about an hour ago. Like always."

"Like always" meant very little to me. Always was a long time ago, and then she'd have been returning from private tennis lessons, or ballroom dancing, or the historical society. My mother had developed a method of coping with her losses, filling her time.

"You ring the bell, *sisi*," the guard said encouragingly.

"I know," I said, glancing back at my kids in the car. Caitie was looking sleepy and Joe's face was scrunched up against the window. He'd left traces where he'd licked the glass – silvery, like slug slime.

"It's here," the man said, clearly wondering if I'd completely lost my mind.

"I'm nervous," I told the man. "I haven't seen her in a long, long time."

He was silent for a moment. Then he said, "We say in my language: *Inkqayi ingena ngenlontlo*. The baldness of the head begins at here." The man touched his temples.

Now I was the one who was confused.

"Big thing come from small beginning," the guard explained, and with that, he smiled and pressed his finger on the button. He nodded at me and began to walk away. The decision had been made; the action actioned.

"Hello?" I heard my mother say. "Who is it?"

"It's Thea, Mother," I said. "It's your daughter and your grandchildren."

And then Caitie opened her mouth as wide as it would go and began to screech.

Part Five

Miscarriage

Sanusha (aged 16): Still the most beautiful woman in the room

Outside the Wynberg court, I feel my temperature rise. There's a flipping long queue and the grey building is really intimidating. I follow my father inside. Appa has this thing about pushing his way through, and though there are crowds snaking up this cement passageway, he marches straight up the stairs as if he owns them. I'm wearing a head-scarf, and Appa makes me hold it so it partly covers my face. I can't miss every day of school, but I insisted that I want to look my mother in the eye, and today she is going to plead.

I haven't told Appa this, but maybe he knows: I need to know what she'd intended for me; what she'd thought about me when she did it.

I glance at my father. He isn't the same man my mother married. Then, he'd looked schoolboyish, with narrow hips, a wide smile and his hair neatly cut and plastered to his skull like a beanie. Now he's wearing a leather jacket, his hair's in a ponytail, his chin edged with last night's beard. He even wears a gold stud in his left ear. And of course he drives a completely ridiculous BMW convertible that makes my friends swoon. They say he's "hot" or "cute" but I just wish he'd buy himself a nice sedan – a Honda or something unflashy like a Toyota – cut his hair and wear normal clothes, like jeans and T-shirts, not the sleeveless ones that show off his biceps but also leak armpit sweat. My father is completely embarrassing, and my mother is in jail. With stats like that, what chance do I stand?

In the lift, a man jostles me, brushing his arm accidently against my breast. Appa looks at him, then pushes him forcibly, his hand on his chest.

"Keep back," he says. "Don't come near my daughter."

"It was just a mistake, Appa," I say, and my father glares at me.

"I know men, Sanusha," he replies as if this actually means something to me. The guy shuffles as far from us as he could possibly get so that when more people climb into the lift, there's a human buffer between us.

I'm nervous. I'd never been in a place like this and we're late. The prosecutor called Appa 2 days ago and said that we should get in at 9 and be prepared to wait.

"I don't like waiting," Appa muttered when he put the phone down.

Like, who does?

"You could drop me off," I said. "I could go in on my own."

"And yes, that's really going to happen," Appa said, trying to sound like a teenager. His afterthought: "The scum of the earth are traipsing around that building, and I'm not just talking about the defence lawyers." (Smirk, ha, ha.)

This morning, of course, he couldn't find his keys, and needed a proper breakfast, and thought we should fill up because he'd heard the petrol price was hiking again. Then we had to drive all the way over Ou Kaapse Weg from Noordhoek behind a truck with smoke grossing out the place, and Appa had insisted on having the top down.

Now that we're here, I'm biting my cuticles and wondering if the trousers and court shoes I picked out are appropriate. (And this outfit took it out of me; I'd prefer a pair of jeans any day.) But for once Appa didn't say anything, or send me back to my room to wear something that didn't make me look tomboyish.

We get to the right floor and I watch my father step out in front of me. Despite his peculiarities, I'm glad he's here with me. Though I'm not the sort of girl to shrink into the shadows, today I feel vulnerable and exposed – like a flayed arm open to a possible bacteria invasion.

When we get to the court, the door is already closed. Of course. It's after 9:30 and I'm so anxious my skin is itching. I rip my nails along my triceps and wonder what to do next. There are crowds sitting on benches outside, and without being a snob (although, I am one), the people here are not exactly the sort of folk I'm used to being around.

Gold-capped or missing teeth vs. private-school braces and orthodontics

+

Fourth-hand jackets and sagging jeans vs. expensive brand names from Cavendish

+

Vowel drags and mixed languages vs. Mostly white middle-class snootiness

=

Totally out of my comfort zone

Listening to the voices around me, I remember how Mom always defends the purity of Afrikaans. But this isn't Breyten Breytenbach's kind of *taal*. And there's a smell of staleness: day-old BO and food I'm not used to. I can't keep my eyes off the hair either – lank or frizzy, as though some of the women have recently made contact with an illegal power connection.

Appa doesn't seem to be taking any of this in. Instead he walks straight up to an old woman and asks her why she's not inside.

"Witness," she says. "My case in there."

So Appa grabs my hand, and pulls me to the door. "Let's go," he says.

My heart sinks. Is everyone going to turn and stare at us? I lift my chin and put on my I-don't-give-a-stuff look.

We enter the courtroom and I take everything in. The South African flag, still so new, dominates the room. The coat of arms, the strip lighting, the low murmur ahead of us. In front, the magistrate (I assume), then a whole lot of other people behind the wooden barriers. And then Clay, sitting in the front spectator bench with Annie, his coat flung over her.

"Over there," I say. Although Appa tries to jerk me into a different seat, I plonk myself next to Annie, who immediately puts her arms around me.

"Late," I mutter, then roll my eyes in a way that used to make Annie laugh. "Appa's fault. Where's Mom?"

My father sits down next to me, nodding at Annie and Clay. Since Clay married Mom, my father has had little to do with him, but for the most part they are civil to each other. The only time I ever saw them riled was when Appa spoke to Mom in a way Clay didn't like. I was much younger then, but I got the gist of it.

I don't remember Appa ever doing it again.

After another 15 interminable minutes of people shuffling before the magistrate, and this woman not much older than me bumbling through their defence (I know she's messing up because the big cheese up top keeps correcting her, and saying *that's not strictly true Miss de Jager, perhaps you would be better to phrase it this way*), I hear my mother's name being called by the bailiff.

"Thea Middleton!" (Except he says "Tea Middleton", as in rooibos or jasmine.) "Thea Middleton!"

The magistrate, who looks a bit like Mr Potato Head, glances up, a frown carving just above his eyebrows. "Where's the accused, people? We don't have time to waste; we're breaking for tea in half an hour."

One of the cops in fancy yellow epaulettes and a navy-blue studded jacket checks his papers. "She's in the cells, Your Worship."

"Well, take her out of there. It isn't doing anyone any good having her in there *now*."

One of the cops nudges another, who stands up quickly, a set of keys on his belt. When he lumbers downwards, I realise that the cops've been standing at the top of some stairs, which lead through the floor. I've always associated the sound of a gate closing as one of safety, because usually we're behind it. But today the sound reminds me of *Shawshank Redemption* or the documentaries I've seen about Mandela on Robben Island. My heart thuds, and I find myself leaning in to my father. Behind us, journalists are jostling for a good view of my mother, their story, dehumanised into a headline.

When she finally emerges, there are 2 policemen behind her and 1 in front, and her wrists are handcuffed behind her back. With my eyes glued to the shell that is my mother, I haven't noticed that Clay has stood up. Then I see his hands reaching out to touch Mom as she passes.

"Keep away from the prisoner," the bailiff says.

"Sit down, sir," says the magistrate.

"My wife –" Clay says.

"In my court you can follow my rules or you can get out and touch whomever you like."

Clay slides back into his seat. And since he's no longer blocking my view, I have a chance to see my mother properly.

Her cheeks are as hollow as a zombie's, her hair screwed into a bun. Her skin is this greyish colour, like my friend's mother during chemo. Yet, even with all that, I am amazed that I have a mother who can still be the most beautiful woman in the room.

But then she looks at me, and her eyes are glazed as though she can't focus properly. To be honest, it feels like she has absolutely no idea who I am.

Clay: Everything I've lost

"Mr Middleton! Mr Middleton!"

"Clay!"

"Mr Middleton!"

Walking out my dad's house I tried to get into the car without meeting their eyes. Impossible. There were too many of them. Sometimes I saw pity. Sometimes I saw bloodlust. Scarily, sometimes I saw boredom.

"Don't say anything to them," Tom had told me. "And don't react to *anything* they say. They're going to try and rile you. They want a comment and if you rise to the bait you're going to give them one – and it'll probably be the wrong one."

This time, I slammed the door behind me and gunned my engine. The journalists scattered. As I drove, I wished – and not for the first time – that Dad had a walk-in garage. One like we had.

My stomach. Round the corner, I stopped the car to vomit in the bushes. I wiped my mouth on a tissue. That was dinner gone. No breakfast. Over the last few weeks I'd lost six kilograms.

And of course that wasn't all I'd lost.

Our house was sold. I couldn't even go back inside to say goodbye. Tom had arranged it all.

"You absolutely sure, Clay? Golden Mile. Excellent condition after all the work you and Thea have done on it. It's going to sell in a week. You might want it later."

"Sell it."

"Maybe it's not a good time to make a decision like this?"

"Sell it!" I said.

He didn't need to tell me that our house was now notorious. The first show day they had to call the police – viewers were helping themselves to mementos. Taking our photographs. Cuttings from the curtains in Joe's room.

I'm not joking.

One woman grabbed a handful of Thea's costume jewellery out the top drawer of the dressing table. Photos of our home made it onto the Internet, and some into *You* magazine.

I was not quite dead yet and they were already picking at my carcass.

The day after the show day, Annie went to the house with a team of movers. Packed everything up and put it in storage. When I have the courage I'll go through the boxes myself. Maybe one day Thea will help me. Probably not.

Annie said they labelled each box by room: *Caitie's room. Kitchen. Playroom* . . . Sanusha went with her and took her stuff and whatever else she wanted.

Sixteen years old and braver than I am.

I don't know how Annie did it. When I spoke to her, her eyes were swollen. She hugged me and told me she had to go home. She was exhausted. Spent. The day in our house had broken her.

You'd think that the house would have sold at a rock-bottom low. Not so. It was more like an auction. Bids came in more outrageous than the last. Seems we'd made a good investment.

I didn't give a toss.

In the car then I could feel the sweat down my back. I was wearing a suit, which was a little tight at my shoulders. When I parked across the road from the court, the scavengers were waiting for me.

"For God's sake," I muttered, scratching at my collar.

They seemed to know an awful lot about me – maybe their cameras were telescopic. They probably knew that I'd drunk a double shot of coffee, no milk and three spoons of sugar the moment I'd woken (just before four), and that I'd showered last night and again this morning because I sweated so much from my nightmares. They probably even knew that my suit wasn't the one I'd originally picked out with Annie, which made me look like a gravedigger, which in this context, I suppose, was completely appropriate.

I ignored the questions shouted at me through the window.

How the hell do they think I feel attending my wife's trial?

I strode forward. Where the fuck was Tom? Where was Annie?

Oh God, I'm so terrified.

This was worse than the first day of school, worse than realising I'd sunk every cent into my restaurant with no guarantee of success. But it'd all always worked out for me. Not this time, though, whatever happened.

A man tapped me on the shoulder. He was wearing a suit, a red tie and a slick smile that bothered me.

"Sir?"

"No comment," I said roughly, jerking his hand off me.

"Mr Harper sent me to get you inside," he said.

"Let's do it then," I said, feinting left and dodging the scrum. He got me in the building holding my elbow. I put my bag in to be scanned, stepped through the metal detector. By the time I looked around I'd already lost him.

Great job.

I studied the crowd milling around outside the lifts; so many people that I couldn't even see where I was supposed to go.

"Court D?" I eventually asked a security guard.

"Fourth floor." She nodded towards the lifts.

Outside the courtroom was yet another throng and a huge poster explaining our legal rights. But I wasn't drawn to that. I was drawn instead to the innocuous piece of white paper tagged outside the door. On it were the various appearances set for the day.

Klaas Booysens, Justin Pieters. Kidnapping, rape.

Chris van Heerden. Assault.

Frederick Baloyi, Leon Zulu, Karien Pretorius, John Ngema. Armed robbery, attempted murder.

Thea Middleton . . .

Each had a case number and a lawyer's name next to it. My mate, Tom, once again up in lights. With a little help from my wife.

"God, Clay," Annie was behind me, "what on earth are you wearing?"

Annie looked strained. More strained than before. Her eyes seemed huge, black rings under them, emphasising how blue they were. "Look, I'm really sorry I didn't meet you outside, but those bloody journos –"

"It's okay," I said. "Thanks for coming."

"You look awful."

"I know."

Annie looked around, took in the crowd. I liked the way she'd grown her hair – made her seem softer. When she pulled me into a hug, I sank into her like a piece of moulding clay, a sob rising. I gulped it down.

"It's going to get a lot worse, I suppose," Annie said into my ear. "This is just the start of it."

Tom came up behind me. "Clay"

"Where the hell've you been?" I said, disengaging myself from Annie.

Tom smiled, didn't quite manage to hide his irritation. "With *my client*. They've just brought her in from Valkenberg. I gave her some clothes to change into. Or did you want me to hang out here talking about rugby?"

"I'm sorry," I said.

He nodded.

"How does she look?"

"Awful. Who knows when she last washed her hair. She's on suicide watch still, and given half a chance I think she'd do it again if she could."

"Tom!" Annie said.

"Listen, Annie. I don't know you very well but let's just get this out while we're here, the three of us together. I'm not going to beat about the bush. I don't have the patience, and I've seen enough people over the years to make a judgement. Hell, you don't need a psychologist to guess what Thea's thinking. She can barely speak. Her lips are almost bitten through, and if it's quiet enough you can hear her teeth grinding."

That made sense to me. How many times over the years had I woken to hear that sound of enamel on enamel?

"Did she ask about me?" I hadn't realised that's what I was thinking.

A hesitation. "Of course," Tom said, and I knew then why Tom didn't like to lie. He was crap at it. "Well, Thea's not up for at least an hour or so. If you want we can go and get a coffee, but otherwise it might be worth it just to sit in there and learn the ropes."

I nodded. Coffee was the last thing on my mind. What happened if they weren't watching my wife and she actually did it – hurt herself? Where would that leave me?

"I want to sit in the court," I said.

"Fine." Tom pushed through the door, and gestured for us to go inside.

"Hey, Mr Harper," one of the cops said. "Now you're defending that freak of nature? Could you stoop any lower?"

"She's sick!" I growled back at the policeman.

"She must be," the cop replied. "She must be *fokkin' mal*."

"You jerk," I shouted at him and the magistrate looked up from where he was writing. He was wearing a black gown with red trimmings. Light shining on his bald patch.

"Come forward, sir. Closer where I can see you," he said. "Yes, you. You with the silver hair."

I stood closer, as he'd instructed.

"Now what's the commotion here?" he said. "This is a court of law in session. You understand that, don't you?"

I looked at him blankly.

"Engels of Afrikaans, *meneer. Verstaan jy my*?"

"Apologies, Your Worship," Tom said for me. "This man's wife –"

"Mr Harper, I don't seem to remember addressing you, sir. If this gentleman belongs to you, kindly keep him in check, or I'm going to have to ask you to wait outside. We're behind schedule as it is. Now has that translator arrived yet or am I going to have to put on record that he's vanished yet again?"

"He's still not here, Your Worship," the bailiff said.

The magistrate looked towards the guy in the docks and sighed heavily. "I do not want to postpone again for lack of a translator. Does Mr Mabuya understand any English at all?"

"Permission to speak to the accused, Your Worship?"

"Come along then."

Case after case was postponed and I began to wonder how the legal process ever ran its course. I couldn't hear much anyway – this was no impressive courtroom drama, no *LA Law*. It was a lot of writing. Not much debate. Most of the time it looked like nothing was happening, except people being let off when witnesses didn't arrive. Rapists and murderers let loose on the streets because their accusers didn't pitch in court.

My butt grew numb on the hard wooden seat. Annie had a book balanced in her lap but didn't seem to be turning the pages. She glanced at me briefly. Then reached out and squeezed my hand.

"We had a big fight, a really big fight," I said softly as if I hadn't told her a hundred times. "I left her there. I shouldn't have left."

The magistrate looked up, eyebrows raised in a glare.

Tom had moved into a huddle of defence attorneys on the right. He was shuffling through papers but he saw the magistrate's look and he turned to me, his finger firmly to his lips. It was like being back at school, except now *he* was the one keeping *me* in check. Back then, he'd been the guy borrowing my notes and scoring an A+ while I struggled to get a C. He'd be the one smoking dagga behind the bike racks and I'd be the one on guard. He dyed the school pool red just for the hell of it, and I made sure he didn't get caught. And at varsity, he'd sailed through with his photographic memory of cases and facts, while I scraped through my B.Com.

There'd been many times I'd been jealous, but right then I couldn't have been more grateful. I recalled a colleague of Thea's telling me at a braai, "I saw your mate, Tom, doing his thing. Let me tell you something now, my friend. If I was ever in trouble, I would sell my house to get that guy to defend me. Hell, I might even sell my wife."

But it was Thea in trouble, not me. And perhaps if it were me I would have had a better handle on this. Maybe I would have *understood*.

Sitting there with Annie's hand still in mine, I noticed how different it felt from Thea's. Thea's fingers were long, her nails uneven and not particularly cared for, especially most recently. Sometimes I'd found myself picking at her rough cuticles, suggesting a hand massage with oils. *Leave it, leave it,* she'd say, but I knew she meant I must leave *her*. But Thea's hands had always been warm, while right then Annie's felt like a slab of meat from the freezer.

Letting it go, I took off my jacket and draped it over her chest because I'd noticed she had goosebumps on her arms.

"Thanks," she said. "I'll remember for next time."

Next time.

The waiting was interminable. As names were called, people sitting next to and behind us moved to the dock and faced the court. Normally I wouldn't have felt intimidated by these youths, in their slanted caps, their tracksuits, their Nike tackies. Most of them weren't older than twenty-five. If I'd passed them in the street, I wouldn't have looked twice. They were slim, insubstantial, yet up for murder, assault, rape, kidnapping . . . If my perception of crime hadn't already been toppled by Thea's actions, this might also have done it. How could such insignificance cause such damage?

But then, Thea was proof enough that damage can come from the most unexpected of sources.

Sanusha (aged 16): Exactly what happened

I hadn't ever set foot in a courtroom before all of this. And here I am talking from the stand about my mother, the mother who once again didn't love me enough to try to take me with her.

Tom puts his hands on the table in front of him and leans forward. I find that I'm counting nervously – the way I used to do as a little kid.

His jacket has 2 buttons. The piece of paper in front of him, hand-written, has 32 lines. My heart: 85 beats per minute.

"Hello, Sanusha," Tom says.

"Hello," I say, feeling shrunken, diminutive in my seat.

7 stripes on his tie. 3 policemen to the left. 46 minutes of waiting before I was called. The clocking ticking, second by second.

"I'm going to ask you a lot of hard questions today. You're very brave and we really appreciate it. Your mother appreciates it."

My mother? Thea Middleton, who looked right through me on the first day she saw me here. Is he joking? My mother barely remembers who I am.

I look across at Appa. He nods, slowly, encouraging me. Even that's weird. Appa sitting next to Clay as if they are friends or something. Clay nods too. This is bizarre. Maybe if I shake myself hard enough I'll wake up.

"S'okay," I say, pulling my earlobe between my fingers.

3 piercings, 1 hole closed up.

"Let's go through that day. I'm going to ask you a few questions, get you comfortable, before we continue on to the hard stuff. All right?"

I nod.

5 buttons on Tom's shirt.

"Sorry, Sanusha, but we can't accept nods in the court. We need you to speak aloud. Is that all right?"

"Yes." My voice bounces off the walls. "That's fine."

"Where were you on August fifteenth?"

I hesitate. Not because I have anything to hide but because my time with Annie that day was kind of awesome. We have a special friendship, a special understanding. Sometimes we can sit together without speaking and still get each other. I don't care that Annie's so much older than me, that she's Mom's friend. I keep her separate – when I'm with Annie, it's like my mother doesn't exist.

"Sanusha?" says Tom, coaxing.

"I went to school. Then I went to Annie's."

Tom looks at his notepad with its 32 blue lines. "Andrea Calitz?"

Like he doesn't know who she is. What a prat.

"Yes, but I call her Annie."

"How did you get there?"

"On my bike."

"Right, so you rode your bike to Annie's. Then what did you do there?"

"I was building an electric circuit with Matthew. Matthew is her son. There was something wrong with the way he'd done the wiring. It took some time, but I worked it out."

I think I must have smiled under Tom's scrutiny, because he flashes one of those fake smiles from a toothpaste ad. "You had fun there?" Tom asks, but the question's obviously rhetorical as he doesn't wait for an answer. "Good," he says. "So where does Annie live?"

"In Rondebosch. Just near Bishops."

"How long were you there?"

"I got to her house around three. I stayed about three hours or so. Then Annie put my bike in her boot and drove me home. It was raining, and getting dark already."

"That's very sensible," says Tom. "She got out the car, saw you inside?"

"Of course not."

Tom scratches his head in a show of confusion. "Why not?"

I look down, unwilling to vocalise it.

*

"Mom's gone batty again," I told Annie that afternoon. "She's, like, zombie city or something."

Annie didn't say anything.

"I wish I could live with you," I said. "Sometimes I think I hate her."

"Sometimes you probably do hate her," Annie commented. "And sometimes you probably love her too."

"She isn't all that lovable these days. Even Caitie knows she's wacko. What normal baby prefers to go to Daddy?"

"Babies have their stages, just like us."

"Why do you keep defending her?" I asked. "My mother isn't normal!"

"Because she's my oldest friend and she *needs* me to defend her."

*

"Sanusha? Why didn't Annie walk you inside, see you were safe?"

I hadn't realised, but I've answered with my hand over my mouth.

"I didn't want her to," I whisper.

"I'm sorry," Tom says. "Would you repeat that for the court?"

"I didn't want her to," I say, louder this time. "My mother was acting weird again. I wanted Annie to know I could deal with her myself."

I'm silent for a moment, and Tom leans forward, his hands in front of him on the table. For once he doesn't question me. He's waiting me out. Finally I say it.

"When we were alone, Annie cared about *me*, not *her*! I didn't want my mother to spoil it."

"So your mother, Thea Middleton, spoilt things a lot for you?" Tom says.

301

The other lawyer guy, the one wanting to put my mother away, stands up.

"Objection. What's that got to do with it? The witness is a teenager, parents are supposed to –"

But we are talking over each other –

"I just wanted a normal mother. Most of the time I had to mother *her*."

"You recognised your mother had psychological issues?" says Tom.

"Your Worship, this is ridiculous. The girl is sixteen years of age; how on earth would she know that?"

"True enough, Mr Harper. Let's keep this tidy, shall we?"

"I apologise, Your Worship. Let's do it this way instead. Sanusha, tell me *exactly* what happened when you got home."

*

It was bucketing.

I thought about Joe, who was afraid of the rain. He didn't like storms. He said they were like monsters fighting. Joe didn't like noise, but I used to tell him that trains were noisy, boats were noisy, planes were noisy. He wasn't afraid of *them*. Usually he would look at me as though I just didn't get it. Rain wasn't a plane, boat, or train. Rain was completely different.

And this was the kind of storm that bothered him most. It wasn't one of those days of gentle non-stop rain – the kind you see on TV when Wimbledon is on. It was wild. Annie had to drive around a huge branch that had broken in the wind. It had crushed the wall under it, so the entire structure was a web of cracks and you could see the rich brown centre of the wood, the leaves skittering up and billowing across the road in the headlights.

"God, it's miserable," said Annie. "We should have waited this out. I could have brought you home after dinner."

"Now you tell me," I said. "I'll be home just in time for the scream fest."

Annie raised her eyebrows.

"Bath time."

"Ah," she said. "Here we are then. You want me to walk you inside, help you with the bike? Check on Mom?"

"Don't bother."

"You seem awfully sure about that."

"I am. No need for you to get wet too. Thanks, though," I said, yanking my bike out of the boot, then slamming it hard. I was already drenched and I hadn't been in the rain even 2 minutes.

"Run, Nush!" Annie said, as she pulled into the road.

I slipped in through the gate, and dumped my bike under the shelter at the front door. Clay was going to give me hell about it; he hated clutter under his feet. Too bad, too sad.

I jiggled the lock. We always had trouble with this door when the wood swelled in winter. It really needed to be sorted out, but Clay preferred more interesting projects, like the cot he'd built for Joe. Above my head the wind chime we'd bought once at Greenmarket Square jingled.

But inside it was insanely quiet. All I could hear was the hum of a motor. I closed the front door, put my keys on the rack.

"Mom? Joe?" I called. "Where *is* everybody?"

I looked round into the kitchen. Unwashed dishes lay next to the sink, the dishwasher hung open like a cave. Cereal boxes lay on the breakfast nook and used eggshells next to the stove. How many times had my mother told me never to leave the house with the kitchen in a state? And where were they anyway?

Suddenly, I had this feeling. It was like a quivering on the surface of my arms, my back. Pinpricks of awareness pierced all over my skin.

Then I listened more carefully; the humming motor was coming from the garage, when originally it had sounded like it was coming from the street.

303

The downpour had muffled it, but from the kitchen it was louder.

I tried to open the door from the kitchen into the garage, but it was locked, the key nowhere to be seen. What on earth was going on? I moved around the kitchen, opening drawers, wondering where my mother would've put the key. And why was it out of the lock anyway? We never moved that key.

And oh, my heart, fluttering like a leaflet trapped in a windscreen wiper. How can you know in just an instant that things have been irrevocably changed?

I began to count, to calm myself. Without knowing why, I walked back to the entrance hall and checked the telephone.

12 footsteps.

I was sweating. The telephone handset was lying neatly on the table off the hook – it couldn't have looked more purposeful. I picked it up, checking for a dial tone, and when there was none, saw that even the chord had been pulled from the wall socket. Reconnecting the phone, I hesitated.

I could have done things better. Differently. But I actually hesitated.

1, 2, 3, 4, 5, 6 . . .

Then I picked up the telephone and called Clay.

"You need to come home," I told Clay, without preamble. "There's something very wrong here at home."

"What is it, Sanusha? I'm at the airport."

"Why? Oh never mind, whatever. Clay. The. Car. Is. On. In. The. Garage."

"What?" There were sounds of people in the background. Someone shouting "Taxi!" Laughter. "Did I hear you right about the car?"

"Clay, it was on when I got home. I can't get in, the garage door is locked. I can't find the key. The phone was unplugged. I can't find anybody."

And then I heard the deep intake of breath.

"Oh, Christ. You're going to be brave, okay? Get the spare remote from the top drawer of my desk, and then go around to the front, and try to open the garage from the driveway."

"And then what?" I asked.

"I'm going to call an ambulance and Annie. And I'm on my way."

"What am I going to find, Clay? What's going to happen now?"

"I don't know, Nush. I really don't. But you're going to do the best you can until Annie or I reach you. Switch off the car. You can do that?"

"Yes, of course."

"Put something over your face. A wet dish towel or something. Do that before you go into the garage. And don't put yourself in any danger, okay? I'm coming. Run now. Be brave."

I disconnected, then sprinted to Clay's desk. Of course the zapper wasn't in the top drawer, or the middle one. It was right at the back of the bottom one, but I found it. I found it and ran to the front door, too frantic to see the weird pipes running along the side of the house.

Or perhaps I did see them. It's difficult to remember the order of things.

The car was on, as I'd thought, but there was nobody inside. I yanked the door open and turned off the engine, choking on the acrid air.

What had my mother done? Why was the car backed in when she usually drove in forwards?

I went round to the back of the car. The pipe attached to the exhaust was plastic of some kind. Though she may have wrapped some sort of tape around it, now the pipe had melted around the exhaust, and I couldn't detach it. But I could see where it was going – down along the floor, up the wall, through the window.

I felt truly sick then. Sick at the professionalism of this contraption, and I remembered my mother under the sink once when the pipes blocked: *Well, at least I can appreciate my father was a plumber. There's nothing more useful than being able to sort out your own pipes.* She'd giggled, but I hadn't thought that smell was funny at all. Gag-worthy.

Unable to remove the plastic tube, I left the garage but followed its crazy route along the outside wall of the house. It didn't go far: past the kitchen, and through the window of the kids' bathroom. My bathroom. It was too high for me to see through, so I ran back inside.

Another locked door.

I knocked hard. Harder.

1, 2, 3

1, 2, 3

"Mom, Joe, Caitie? Mom, Joe, Caitie?" I was screaming by then. "MOM! JOE! CAITIE!"

The silence roared in my ears. I started to cry.

I couldn't get in. I couldn't get in.

"Mom, Mom, MOM, answer me, damn it!" Then I stepped back, rushing at the door with all the force of my weight.

It didn't budge and I didn't feel any pain. I rushed at it again.

Bang. Bang. Bang.

I tried again, this time carrying a chair from the dining room. My first success was the crack running down the door.

"MOM! JOE! CAITIE!" I was still beating against the wood, when someone appeared next to me.

"Okay," he said, almost tenderly. "Why don't you let me have a go?"

"They're in there," I said. "The gas."

"Let me try," he said, taking the chair from me. "Andile," he said behind him. "Get an axe. Stand back, girl."

The man moved fast, the chair dashed against the door. Another crack. A small hole.

The same smell of the garage, but so much more bitter. Stronger.

The axe. The splinters, and the heartache.

"Take this girl outside and treat her for shock," the man said.

"No!" I screamed. "No! No! NO!"

My mother was leaning unmoving against the bathroom wall, the hems of her jeans wet from bath-time puddles.

And the kids.

Oh my God, the kids, floating in the bath. Surrounded by plastic toys.

Yellow ducks. Purple whales. Orange fish. And prism bubbles.

Caitie floating forward, her face invisible. But Joe, on his back. His little naked body half exposed by the bubbles and on his face the slightest glimmer of a smile.

Clay: Breathing under the blue lights

Tom and I rushed to Groote Schuur behind the ambulance. I'd called him immediately. I don't remember doing it. But before I could turn around, he was there, holding me in a bear-hug while I sobbed. I left snot on his designer suit.

"Don't say anything until we know more," Tom advised. Sharp lawyer mode, but also my friend.

Tom pushed his way inside the house, pulling me behind him. "Andile," he said, nodding at one of the policemen. "We'll need access to the bedroom. She'll need clothes."

The policeman followed. "Don't go anywhere where I can't see what you're doing."

Tom showed him his hands. "Look, I've even got gloves on. Okay? Don't touch anything, Clay. Just sit on the bed."

The cop and I watched Tom walk to my cupboard. He pulled out a jersey for me and threw it in my direction.

"You're in shock. Put that on."

Then he packed a few essentials for Thea. Did it so fast I didn't notice what he had until he'd handed it over to the cops at the hospital.

Pyjamas. Tooth brush. Panties. T-shirt. Hairbrush.

Outside the garage Annie was holding Sanusha, both crying uncontrollably, sounds like I've never heard in my life. Annie had always kept us together, kept us sane. But she didn't have it in her then – keening, rocking Sanusha against her. When I'd phoned her she'd literally just dropped Sanusha off.

She'd been at the house in minutes. A crowd had already gathered. Hoards of live-in domestics. A few cyclists. Security guards from opposing firms. Everyone shocked, and grimly fascinated. And this despite the rain.

It was just a patter now, but still present. The wind chime jangled on my nerves. I'd never listen to a wind chime again – it made my blood ice.

Police vans circled blue lights on the wet pavements. I thought of Joe as a toddler: "Noise!" he used to shout each time a cop car passed, because that's all they were to him. And now –

"This isn't happening. This isn't happening to us." Grief so strong I couldn't stand. Lean over; lean forward. Then I banged my head against the wrought iron bedstead, as though to knock out the memory.

Shards of wood. Puddles on the floor. Wet towels rolled up length-ways like sausage-dogs laid across the floor where the door closed. Thea in the clothes I'd dressed her in. Thea with vomit down her shirt, being lifted onto an ambulance trolley.

My kids. Little bodies like bright red cherries, oxygen masks clamped over their noses and mouths. Paramedics, professional but unable to disguise their panic and distress.

"Let me in!" I'd shouted. "Let me closer. I want to see my family!"

"You're in the way, sir. You're not helping them by standing there." A hand yanking me back, pulling me outside to where Sanusha was cowering with Annie, her skin almost white. I'd put my arm around her. We were so caught up in our own private grief that we couldn't help each other.

In my bedroom, Tom looked at me, saying nothing. Then he nodded towards the door.

"Let's go," he said. "You need to protect your wife."

"She gassed my kids, Tom. Our kids."

"And if Nush had got here any later . . . Thanks, Andile." He nodded at the cop. "It's going to be a long night."

*

Being married to Thea had got me used to hospitals. But not a hospital like Groote Schuur. Hulking concrete, layer upon layer separated by windows. It looked like a prison.

We drove through the entrance. Tom pulled up in his Porsche to one of the guarded entrances.

The rain had stopped. There was an unearthly glow over the statue high above the old entrance. Gave me the creeps.

We checked our keys as we walked through the metal detector, picked them up as we reached the other side. A sign: *Visitors until 8 p.m. only.* Admissions was almost deserted; just a few people lined up along the rows of beige plastic chairs.

Along the passage, once we turned left, there were signs for Organ Donor Month. Hearts. Livers. Eyes.

I felt ill. Was this a decision I was going to have to make? Or was it too late for that?

Tom pulled my arm. "Just walk, Middleton."

He seemed to know where he was going and I was grateful. We passed a snack shop. In my old life – the one with two beautiful children and a sexy, normal wife – we'd have eaten dinner by now. Yet I wasn't hungry.

It was like this passage was the heart of the hospital. Everything happening in slow motion; my eyes panned like a camera lens.

People: medical students with clipboards and UCT tags; doctors; nurses in uniform; cleaners trundling mops and brooms and huge containers of bleach. Three coloured women shuffled slowly past: one on crutches, one limping, one wearing a plastic shower cap. Two women on a bench sharing a packet of crisps. An old man wearing a dusty hat holding a sleeping baby. A golf cart passing us; some sort of taxi service. Tom flagged the driver.

"C14? We need to get to the trauma unit urgently."

The man nodded. He smelt like he'd been working all day. We slid into the vehicle, holding on as the driver put foot.

Paintings on walls done by young hospital patients, patients of about Joe's age.

Joe. Joe . . . And little Caitie.

Breath like I'd been running. Pounding blood. Spinning head. I gaped to drink in oxygen, hands at my throat I felt like I was suffocating.

Tom's face registering a rare emotion. Fear.

"Okay, okay, Clay. Look at me, now. Look at me. You're going to be okay."

I hadn't noticed the woman on the cart with us. Now I felt the vehicle stop sharply under her instruction.

"What's his name?" I heard her say.

"Clay," Tom replied.

"Heart problems?"

"No, not him. His wife's very ill. His two children have just been admitted."

Like it's some sort of accident.

She climbed off the cart, came round to where I was sitting. Tom stepped aside. A strongly accented voice. "Clay. My name is Nathalie. I'm a doctor. I want you to copy me. Okay?"

She was holding my hands between hers, and then she breathed in slowly. One. Two. Three. Then out. One. Two. Three.

Again.

Again.

I copied her.

"It's like yoga breathing. You done yoga before, Clay?"

I shook my head.

"No matter. Just breathe. Breathe. Watch me. Then do it. Breathe out. Breathe in. Look at my face, Clay."

I looked. A nice face. Friendly. Oriental eyes. Red hair clipped at the nape. Freckles.

"You're having a panic attack, Clay. It's going to go away, all right? You just need to breathe."

I focused on her face. My God, I was frightened, but her calm made me feel . . . safer.

She breathed. I breathed.

My throbbing heart normalising. She was still holding my hands, looking at me. As I began to settle, she let me go. My hands were warm where she'd comforted me.

"There now," she said. "Better?"

I nodded.

"You were on your way to C14?"

"Yes," said Tom.

"I can take you there if you like."

"Thanks," I said.

We walked to a lift. A huge metallic one, with iron grills at the ceiling. To keep people climbing out, or in? On the side, a word scratched into the steel: *Hope.*

My kids . . . my God, I had no hope.

The lift clunked down, the door opened. The passage was painted burgundy-brown. Signs pointed us down and right.

To something like a transit lounge. Same beige plastic chairs as upstairs. Then the outside doors swinging open to a loading area and the ambulance.

And there, with bright yellow legs like a hornet, was a stretcher, with my wife on oxygen.

Next to the ambulance stood the cops who hadn't let me travel with her. She was, after all, *under arrest.*

Nathalie saw my look and cautioned me. "Breathe, Clay."

"Keep it together, my friend," Tom said.

"I'm together. I'm together, for fuck's sake," I said.

"Do you want me to find out what's going on?" Nathalie asked.

"Please," said Tom, usually so confident, was out of his comfort zone. His arm around me, trying to keep me steady.

Nathalie moved through the doors, flashing her card at the security

guard in the blue uniform with a walkie-talkie, fielding hospital traffic. One of the policemen approached Nathalie – the same guy who'd
spoken mostly in Xhosa at my house. The one with the healing scar on
his face just under his eye. Who'd kept me away from Thea. He looked
over at me, and nodded. I nodded back.

We couldn't hear what they were saying. The ambulance was still
running, the lights flashing in the parking area. I tried to move through
the doors too, but the guard stepped in front.

"*Net dokters hier,*" he said.

"That's my wife."

His expression of pity. "*Ag,* sorry, man. Just doctors."

Nathalie came back. "They'll move her to C24. She's alive. They're not
sure if she'll regain consciousness. They have to keep her on oxygen. Do
some tests. We don't know how long she was in there. There's a danger
of damage."

"To the brain?" Tom asked.

"Yeah."

"Can I be with her?" I said.

"Yes, but only under supervision. The cops are staying in the hospital.
They'll need to speak to her and you."

"If Thea wakes up."

"Yes."

"My kids?"

"They've gone to the pathologist. I'm sorry, Clay." Nathalie's eyes
clouded. I was going to have to get used to that look. Emotion was overtaking me like a wave filling me from my heart outwards. Tom caught
me by the arm before I fell.

"Sit," he said, pulling me into the waiting room. "I'll get you a Coke."

"You hold him," Nathalie said to Tom. "I'll get it. And we might need
to tranquillise him."

"No meds," I said. "I'm going to need to make decisions."

"No meds," Nathalie repeated. "You eaten tonight?"

"No."

"Leave it to me," Nathalie said, as I watched them wheel my wife in from the icy-cold parking lot.

Thea: Dead

When I woke up I was in a hospital. My head felt like a block of wood.

There was a man standing outside the room; from his posture, I could see he was there to keep me in. I was supposed to be dead, but my arm was attached to a blood-pressure monitor, squeezing me like a python, the beep-beep telling me I was alive. I didn't want to be there, in that room, breathing in the oxygen that was being forced into my lungs through a mask so tight it hurt my mouth. I yanked it off, then pulled at the drip, ripping it out of my arm. It was bruised and bleeding. I winced, hating the pain, because it meant I could still *feel*. "Robbie?"

"What are you doing?" a woman said, walking in.

"I killed myself," I said. "I killed myself."

"No, madam," the woman said. "You killed *your children*. And now I'm going to do everything in my power to keep you alive so you can live with the consequences."

I felt dizzy. My head was pounding. "We were going together," I said. "The three of us. Robbie said –"

"Mrs Middleton, I am going to say this only once," the woman said. "I am not your friend, your confidante or anybody who gives a damn about your explanations. Tell it to somebody else or I will repeat absolutely everything you say to the cops." She pushed the mask back on. "Right now, I'm getting the carbon monoxide from the haemoglobin in your blood so your oxygen levels get back to normal. If you take that mask off one more time, I will get the staff to restrain you."

But as she approached me, I bucked, and without so much as a hesitation she slapped me across the face. Surprised, I touched my face. It stung. "You can't –"

"What are you going to do about it? You're a child-killer. You're not worth the oxygen I'm pumping into you. You think anyone is going to believe anything you say? Now lie still."

As she pulled the mask back on, I wept. Robbie had promised me it was going to get better. But if this woman was to be believed, I'd murdered my own children. Joe. Caitie.

My babies.

But I was making them safe, taking them from the shadows. No one in the world should have shadows like mine. They were menacing, razor sharp. I was *saving* us. Had I even failed at that? Were they all alone without me, while I was here, in this bed, manacled by machinery?

I lay back, trying to figure out what to do. Fumes or shadows clouded my thinking; everything was fuzzy. My head pounded like someone was hammering into it, bit by bit. First skin, then bone, then brain.

I'd killed my children.

From blankness, my mind flickered to heavy metal gates, my mother walking down the driveway in clipped steps. She'd aged so much, I was shocked. Her face, once firm, rounded, was now scrawny; Botox keeping her forehead and the crow's feet unnaturally smooth and her whole face stiff, as though covered in latex. Her back, which used to be so straight it seemed braced, had started to curve. She was shorter. Or was I taller? But I'd always been taller than her. She was just stronger.

Her expression had narrowed.

"I suppose I'd better let you in," she'd said, her voice glacial. "Let's not give the street something to talk about. Drive in, but don't get too comfortable."

"She'll mellow," Robbie said casually. "Won't you, Mom?" he added to her retreating back.

"To you, maybe," I said. "Or maybe to the kids." Hopeful.

At the end of the driveway, I parked under the carport like I used to when I lived there. I saw my mother's face and knew at once what she was thinking: presumptuous. Could one presume on one's parent?

As I unclipped Joe, I tried to smile at Mother.

Her face was grim. Tight-lipped. The smile on my own mouth died.

"This is your grandmother, Joe," I said to him.

"She looks scary. Is she cross?" he whispered loudly. She must have heard him.

"A little, maybe. But not with you." Nevertheless, he clung to my leg and refused to move, even when I tried to lift Caitie out of her seat. I held her little body against my chest. She wasn't crying, but she eyed my mother pensively.

"So, Thea June, you come crawling back," my mother said. "No brown babies? Where's Rajit's child?"

I looked at her aghast, my stomach clenching angrily.

"Sanusha's at school," I said, glad my daughter hadn't been around to hear *that*. "Top of her class. She's so clever she skipped a grade." I sounded pathetic, fawning.

"Well, well," Mother said. "I certainly doubt she got that from you. You were always rather an average student."

I blanched, but fitted into my role perfectly. Better she was attacking me than my children.

"You'd better come inside, I suppose. Hello, boy," she said, not bothering to ask Joe's name. She smiled though, and he smiled back. "Maria, bring some tea. And some chocolate biscuits for the child."

A little woman poked her head around the corner. I didn't recognise her, but I could see she knew something interesting was happening.

"Boy, you go with Maria now and choose a biscuit."

"Yes ma'am," Maria said, and held out her hand.

Surprisingly, Joe took it.

"So, you're here," Mother said as she gestured to me to sit down. "You lasted longer than I thought you would."

The lounge had changed. Although it had always been neutral, the room was now almost entirely without colour. Pallid. My father's burgundy leather chair with brass studs was gone. Instead there was an L-shaped white suede couch, two wingbacks in cream and a glass table a child was bound to split his head on.

The vase on the coffee table had white flowers. Roses. The scatter cushions, so exactly in line they looked as though they'd been pinned, were the only deviation: a soft lemon yellow. On the wall was a depressing landscape, the clouds tinted with the same yellow as though just before a cloudburst.

I didn't like the changes, and I wondered what had happened to the rest of the house. My bedroom. Robbie's. My dad's workshop, with its pipes and tools all neatly displayed.

"Why are you here?" Mother asked, leaning forward.

I looked at her hands. Nestled in her lap, they were trembling. I noticed the same flickering of her chin. For a moment, I softened; with age, my mother no longer seemed invincible. Time was ravaging her, just as my shadows were ravaging me.

"I wanted you to meet my children," I said.

"Whatever for? We've lived apart successfully for the last sixteen years."

"You counted them, though," I pointed out. "So you must have noticed the time passing."

"It tells on your face, dear," she said. "Not such an easy life out of the nest."

Stung, I sat back, but the sudden movement set Caitie off again. As she bawled, my mother stared at her, unblinking. I stood up, shush-shushing my daughter. My head began to pound.

"Clay said I shouldn't come back to you," I said. "But I wanted to give you the benefit of the doubt."

"You should have listened to Clay," my mother said. Then, after a long pause, "Whoever he is."

And then I didn't want to explain. Clay was the one thing in my life she wasn't going to taint, whatever had happened that morning. Instead, I patted my baby, feeling heaviness come over me. The silence was thick as syrup, but not as sweet.

"Why did you always hate me so much?" I asked.

"I loved your father," she said. "More than was good for me."

"That's not an answer, Mother. You loved Robbie too," I said. "More than was good for you."

"Hey," Robbie piped up. "Don't bring *me* into this."

"Maybe," she said, considering.

"So why couldn't you just love me too?"

I looked at my mother's hands, quivering in her lap, almost as separate entities from the rest of her body.

"I was forced to bring you into *my* home. *My* home. *My* family. *My* life. That, Thea June, was enough."

"Not enough for me," I said.

"Yes," she nodded. "You always were a needy child. Unhinged half the time. I blame that slut who gave birth to you."

My heart congealed. "You told me you never knew her," I said.

"Ah," she said, "that was your father's choice. But we did. We knew her, your father and I. Your father much better than I. You might as well know it."

Maria came back into the room carrying a tea tray from my childhood. The one with the lavender-blue floral patterns, the one Mother had once upended when I didn't fetch the sugar from the kitchen when she asked me to. I remembered the hot tea seeping onto the carpet, the skim milk pale, almost diaphanous, drip-dripping onto the floor. Shards of porcelain like mica on my skin, sharp but not cutting.

My mother nodded at Maria. "Put it down," she said. "Then take the boy into the garden. He can play in the tree house."

"You still have the tree house?" I asked.

"Why wouldn't I? Though it's probably covered in spiders' webs. The swallows made a nest in it. I left them to it. He'll be fine. As long as he doesn't do anything stupid."

The thought hadn't occurred to me that he might not be. A silence descended between us.

"What was she like? My mother?"

"*I* was your mother, Thea. I didn't want to be, but I was. All in all, it was rather a disappointing exercise."

"You're so restrained," I said. "So proper. Disappointing? Is that really the right word?"

"It fits," said Mother. "Sugar?"

"Nothing fits. Nothing! I can't even fit into my own life!" I knocked the sugar spoon out of her hand. The white granules scattered, white sugar on the white carpet in the white room.

"See?" My mother said primly. "That's exactly what I was talking about. Maria! Maria! Bring something to brush up this mess!"

"I don't understand you," I said. "Don't you want to know *anything*? Aren't you even remotely interested in anything about me? I was your daughter for eighteen years! These are your grandchildren."

My mother sipped her tea. "There is no room in my life for you, Thea. And frankly, they are not my grandchildren." She stopped, her head slightly cocked. "Although the boy is cute. He reminds me a tiny bit of Robbie."

"You're right," I said. "He *is* like Robbie. If you gave us a chance, you could get to know him."

"I can't do it," said Mother. "I won't do that again. It is too . . ."

Her voice faded. For the first time in my life, I saw my mother vulnerable. Though she blinked it back fast, I could have sworn there was a tear there.

"Mother?"

"For God's sake, Thea. Why did you come? What do you want from me?"

"Who was she? Who was she really?"

"I don't want to talk about it."

"I don't care what you want, Mother. I need to know. For fuck's sake, get over yourself and tell me the truth."

She baulked. "Don't talk to me like that!"

"Why not? It's not like being nice has any effect. Was she a druggie?

A whore? A rape victim? A schoolgirl? The minister's daughter? What? I need to know."

"You need to know?" Mother said. "You need to know that your father had an affair with a virtual teenager? Promised her all sorts of things except marriage. She didn't believe him."

I sat back. I was my father's daughter after all.

"She thought she could trap him. Steal him from me. But she wasn't the first and she certainly wasn't the last to try. He wanted me in the end, always me."

"And me? Did he want me?"

"Honestly, Thea. Why is that so important?"

"Did he ask you to bring me home?"

"Of course not. You think a man like him really wants shame like that in his house? You were his punishment. His reminder."

I went cold. I had loved my father, admired him. Now everything was felled by my mother's chainsaw tongue.

"Now," said Mother, "doesn't that just prove that knowing the truth isn't always for the best?"

"He loved me," I said, pulling my baby to me.

"You can think whatever you want."

"He loved me," but even as I said it, the doubt had begun to buzz in my too-full head. "I'm going now," I said, stumbling as I lifted myself out the chair. "Joe," I shouted. "Joe! Come inside."

"Ahhh, Mommy, not yet. I'm in your tree house!"

But it wasn't my tree house any more.

Clay: Warnings

If we *had* been allowed to bring Thea home before the case started, I wondered if I would have been able to do it.

It didn't matter anyway. My dad wouldn't have allowed Thea on his property. Never mind through his front door. That's why I didn't fight it like I could have. She'd be taken for further observation. First back to Valkenberg. If she was imprisoned on psychological grounds, she'd eventually be moved to Lentegeur. I wondered, not for the first time, how Tom could do his job.

Watching him at work revealed sides of him that I'd never appreciated. That used to downright annoy me. He could compartmentalise, separating his career completely from his emotions. It didn't seem to matter to him that he was defending his goddaughter's murderer. Or that when he comforted me, it was for something his client had done.

I didn't know what else to do. Thea needed help; I'd obviously let her down. But I wasn't sure I could actually stand to be alone in a room with her.

Tom could also pick at the facts, like a child in a scratch patch finding the best stones. He knew what should be thrown back – like the predictable tiger's eye, however pretty. Tom also knew which facts made the best pattern. Despite his being my best friend, I'd never really fancied his sense of morality. He didn't ask me if I wanted Thea punished or saved – actually, he didn't want to know. The case was a sensation. His face (and Thea's) was on the front of every newspaper. Hell, she was a career boost – not that he needed one. He'd never been busier. Where he was sometimes cold and distanced about "the *case*", Sybil reminded Tom that he was talking about my wife and my dead children. He rarely even apologised. As we walked out the courthouse, Tom looked at me.

"You've lost weight, Middleton, but you need to tone up," he said. "You're coming to play squash with me. Where's your stuff?"

Annie looked at Tom. "Come on, Tom, I'm sure that's the last thing Clay needs right now."

"Oh?" said Tom. "So you recommend incessant wallowing and vomiting as a cure? How long do you prescribe that for?"

"Until he doesn't need to any more," said Annie.

"Bullshit," said Tom. "He needs to get a life."

"Fuck off," I said, wanting to punch him.

"That's the spirit. You can borrow some of my things."

"Actually, I don't think I'm up for it. I think I'll take my off-road bike to Tokai."

"Great," he said. "I'll join you."

"No," I replied. "You won't."

So why was it that I was battling Constantiaberg with my overachieving friend ahead of me setting the pace? I was shooting beads. Later I realised that those hours of physical hell were the only mental rest I'd had. By the time we got back to Tom's car, I could hardly stand on my jelly-legs.

"You're going to have to go back to work," Tom said to me as I attached my bike to the rack.

"Why don't you just shut up for a tiny fucking second?" I said. "I've got you jabber-jabbering in my ear twenty-four seven. I've lost my children, for Christ's sake. I've lost my *whole family*."

"Yes, and if you carry on like this, you'll lose your business as well. You think I like doing this? I have to. I am your friend and I'm protecting you."

"Well, I don't like it."

"You think I care about that? Maybe you want me to come and *chat* to you like that little nursey from Groote Schuur? You want me to bring you some home-made rusks and tea?"

"Nathalie's a doctor, not a nurse."

"I don't give a damn if she's the chief of surgery. You think you need her – before long she's going to welcome you with open legs and you'll find yourself screwing her brains out, while she thinks she can *fix* you."

"Christ," I said, feeling the blood drain from my face.

"Oh, come on, Clay – you can't tell me you haven't pictured it? You and a bit of mousey *doctor*, a bit of escapism? Hey, you even get to punish Thea while you're doing Nathalie."

"Of course I haven't!"

Of course I have.

"I'm just telling you to focus on your work, and keep away from those complications. You don't need them right now."

"Says the man who makes extra-marital affairs a preferred sport."

"I'm not talking about morality, Clay. I'm talking about sense. What happens if I get Thea off and you decide you want her back? I know you, my friend. You won't be able to resist the urge to confess. Then *your wife* will be unbalanced yet again and this time it *will* be *your* fault."

"But this *is* my fault. This is *all* my fault. You wouldn't understand what –"

"Oh, come on, Clay. Maybe you shouldn't have married her, but you did. Maybe you should have learnt your lesson after Joe, but you didn't. Maybe you shouldn't have fought with her, but you did. Maybe you shouldn't have gone to work that day, but you did. Now you're in a horrible situation, and you need to survive. What you don't need is any more guilt."

I looked at my friend and felt an urge to hug him, but I didn't.

"Want to get a beer?" I said.

"Sure, but only one; I've got a pile of prep to do tonight. Then I'm going to walk you through what I'm thinking about for Thea's defence."

"Can you win it?" I said as I climbed into his car.

"If I can't, no one can," Tom said, and for once I was glad for his arrogance.

*

When I got back to my dad's, there was still the odd journalist lodged outside. Tom wound up his tinted window.

"I'll say goodbye now, my friend. Can't talk to the news folk – I'm not looking my best." He wasn't joking.

"Sure, we wouldn't want your sweaty face on TV. Give me a minute, okay?"

I slammed the door after me, glancing at the approaching reporters. I decided to try a different tack.

"Listen," I said. "I know you're just doing your jobs. I'm just really not up to it."

One woman, in her mid-twenties, moved towards me anyway. "So then I won't ask you any questions today, other than this one: Are you okay?"

"No," I said simply, "I'm not."

"I've been doing the crime beat a while," she said. "It never gets easier seeing people in pain."

I pulled my bike off Tom's car. "Then why do it?"

"I don't know," she said. "I guess I have this feeling that if I report right on something, then maybe I can prevent it happening again in the future. I don't want to believe in pure malice in this world. Your wife, for instance, was very ill, wasn't she?"

"Look, Ms –"

"I'm Gia Karelse, from Cape Talk."

"Well, Gia, you got your one question in, wasn't that the deal?"

Gia touched her ponytail and smiled. "You got me. But if you ever want to give your story to someone you can trust, I'm your girl." She handed me a card, and I kind of liked her charm. "That Tom Harper in the car?" she asked.

"One question, Gia," I reminded her and she grinned again.

"Right. A warning, Mr Middleton –"

"Clay."

"Your stepdaughter's inside. She brought a bag. I think you may have a house guest for a few days at least."

Sanusha (aged 16): Too much

I sit with my bag in front of me, wondering why I've chosen Clay over Annie, or my grandfather for that matter. Clay's dad shifts uncomfortably, his eyes on the clock.

"He's cycling," Mr Middleton Sr says.

"So you said."

Even though we haven't seen each other much, I've always liked Clay's dad. But when it comes to words, he bumbles.

"How's school?" he says after another pause.

"I've decided I'm leaving school. I'm going to be a mechanic." And, just like my father, he almost spits into his drink.

"You don't mean that. A great brain like yours?"

"School is boring; I'm not learning anything new."

"Well," he answers, "you won't be the first person to think that."

"Yes," I say. "And virtually nobody *actually* leaves."

"That predictable?" he said.

"Yes."

"Well, you can't blame an old man for trying."

"I'm going to ask Clay to buy me some tools. I've fixed thousands of cars with my grandpa and I don't see why I have to do what I've been doing when I could be earning my own money."

Clay startles both of us as he comes through the front door. "And why d'you need your own money?" he says.

"You weren't supposed to hear that," I said. "I was going to give you my business plan."

"Your *business* plan?"

"Isn't that what I need to get finance? I just want you to stand surety for the garage."

"Garage?"

"Aren't you listening? I don't want to stay at school."

"Is this about court today?" Clay says.

"Clay, it's about every day of my life. Today was just another horrible day."

"To be fair –"

"Jesus, Clay, there's nothing fair about this. They're going to lock her away! I'm not going to wait 2 more years at a private school, sponging off my weird nympho dad, waiting for her to get out. I need to support myself. I've done the numbers."

"For crying out loud, Sanusha, when did you get the time to do that?"

"While you were wallowing in your own body odour – which, by the way, is fairly repellent – I was using my brain. It's not like I haven't thought of this before. I want to get my own place."

"But you're sixteen."

"I am well aware of that. 16 years, 4 months, 3 days and almost 20 hours."

"You really freak me out when you do that."

"Is it cool, that word?"

"What word?"

"Freak. Bit out of your age range, don't you think?"

Clay looks at his father. I know that look: it says "Save me". Both my parents use it fairly often. No wonder I want out.

"It's not like I won't pay you back, Clay. I should be able to reimburse you with 8% interest within 6 months. The surety will stand, of course, but I could offer you a 10% share as a thank you, though you won't get anything until I start turning a profit. And then I'll need a salary so my living expenses can be covered. I'd like to reserve the right to buy the 10% back in 5 years."

"Sanusha –"

"Yeah, yeah. I know I'm driving you crazy. I get it, especially after a day like today. But it's made things clear for me – I need to look after myself. I just want you to think about it, okay? And your dad said I could crash here for a few nights."

"Does your father know about this?"

"Oh, Rajit's happy with the sleeping arrangements. He and Venita broke up again. By now he's probably found some bird at Woolies – and I'm not talking about a roast chicken."

This makes Clay smile, which makes me smile. I'm not used to his misery face – he's usually the one saying "buck up" and "nothing is impossible", like some character out of Enid Blyton. It used to seriously piss me off, but after weeks of tears and anger, I need to laugh.

"You're too much, Sanusha," Clay says.

"You think that's too much, wait till you see this!" I whip up my top to reveal the tattoo on my stomach. It's a beautiful king cobra, twisted around my belly button, its fanned head arching as it prepares to spit.

"What the hell?"

"You like?" I turn around. Across the small of my back are a J and C, intertwined.

"Jesus Christ!" he says, then slaps his hand over his mouth.

"No, Joe and Caitie," I say, and his face twists as he slumps into the lounge chair, his fingers running through his hair.

"It's just too much," he says. "Too much, too much, too much."

I think he's talking about my body art, but when he doesn't lift his head, I realise it's more than that. His father walks to the cupboard, pours him a whiskey and me a glass of wine.

"Well, Sanusha, if you can choose to desecrate your body like that, I don't suppose a glass of red will matter."

Like I haven't cycled to a shebeen in the middle of the night and bought quarts. This is even in a glass.

"Desecrate?" I say. "Nice word, Grandpa, but I think the word is *decorate*. I look good! And it wasn't nearly as sore as I thought it would be. Actually, I kind of liked it."

Clay's dad's eyes widen further. "What kind of tattoo parlour lets you do this without consent from your parents?"

"I told them my mother was in jail and I showed them her picture.

And I made sure they used new needles, so don't stress. I know all about Aids and HIV."

By now, Clay's already knocked back his drink. He looks at me with eyes I don't recognise, then stands up.

"Dad, I'm sorry, but I'm not up to dealing with this. This tattoo stuff should upset me, but I actually don't give a fuck."

"Clay!" says his dad.

"Tattoo your whole body for all I care, Sanusha; I have enough problems to deal with. You're always welcome here, but I can't be your father – if you're wanting me to jump up and down about this, I just can't."

"That's not what I want," I say quietly.

"Well, whatever it is you want from me, I can't bloody do it."

"I can take care of myself, Clay. I can take care of *myself*!" My face is stinging.

"Then why are you *here*?"

"I already *told* you." I don't want to show Clay how much he has hurt me, so I look him in the eyes. "I just need the cash, a place to crash for a week or so, and then I'm out of this flipping place."

I guess I'm not that great at hiding my feelings because he tries to hug me.

"Listen –"

"Get away from me! You're not the only person who's lost a family. I've lost Joe and Caitie too. And your dad is sitting here missing his grandkids."

"I know," he says quietly, removing his hands from my shoulders. "I know."

"Let's have a braai!" Clay's dad attempts brightness. "We have to eat."

"A *braai*?" says Clay as though his father's just suggested dinner at La Colombe.

But I get it.

"Yes," I say, "let's light a fire and burn stuff, starting with today's newspaper. Not a good photo of you, Clay. You don't suit the suit."

Clay considers me, and I wonder if this is the moment when he's going to fall apart. Instead, he takes a deep, steadying breath.

"I don't, do I?" He walks resignedly towards the patio. "And just so you know, that cobra tattoo looks good on you. Just don't tell Raj I said that." He pauses at the door.

I smile. "You're going to shower first, right? Because I don't think I could eat anywhere near you right now."

"Just one question, Nusha. Why the snake?"

"Because I'm spitting mad," I say.

Clay: Finding happiness

The divorce wasn't my idea. When the trial was over I accepted my marriage as just another form of punishment. So when I walked in that day at visiting hours in Worcester and I found Tom outside the prison, I was surprised.

He was dressed in one of his tailor-made suits. Sweat at his temple. He didn't look at me directly. I didn't realise I was being ambushed until later.

"What you doing here?" I asked.

"Work."

"Are you coming in?" I asked, but he shook his head.

"No. I'm waiting for a call."

He wasn't lying; he just didn't explain what the call was. And that it was at Thea's request.

Inside, Thea was sitting to one side of the room – a "private space" in a place where there was no privacy. Which, although I didn't know it, had been organised by my friend.

Despite myself I still loved my wife.

But I didn't like her. I couldn't meet her gaze or touch her face. From the tugging in my heart, I knew I wanted to be able to forgive her, and forgiveness did not seem completely impossible – it just couldn't happen yet. Especially not while I carried my grief like a laden backpack, the load almost breaking me. My wife was very sick.

How many times would I recall the size of those coffins, Caitie's blanky in one, Joe's favourite train in the other?

Thea had been moved from Pollsmoor immediately. *Ship 'em in, ship 'em out.* Fielding all those media calls was a pain. Once the verdict was in, they were shot of her.

When Thea saw me, she stood up. Her hair was tied in a ponytail high on her head like a palm tree. It made her look younger, innocent.

She had on a trace of lipstick. Surprising – I didn't know that sort of thing was allowed.

"Hello, Clay," she said.

I tried to smile but I couldn't. She pointed to the chair opposite her. Plastic. Scratched and slightly jagged at the edges.

"Come and sit."

I sat down, my arms shielding my chest.

Silence. I racked my brain for something to say. It was like trying to have a conversation in a nightclub. Background noise so overwhelming, talking almost seemed pointless.

"I can't remember very well any more," Thea said after a while. "The gas has curdled my memory. Like, for instance, I have no idea how I got here."

A feeling of nausea, which she must have seen.

"Oh no, Clay, no. I don't mean I don't remember what I've done. I remember *that*. I wish to God I didn't. I just don't know how I got here physically. My mind's a blank."

We sat awhile further. Not a companionable silence, but it was as close to silence as one could get in a place like this.

"What I'm trying to say, really," Thea continued, "is I'm not the same person. You're not either, probably. We can never go back."

Her eyes began to fill, and I could feel my chest tightening – in it, a premonition that I'd want her to unsay the words she was about to say.

"Hush," I said. "Let's not say things we're going to regret."

Thea leant forward, reached out. Traced the contours of my face with both hands. She kissed me gently on my forehead.

"As of this moment," she said, "I'm cutting you free. I've already signed the papers. Tom has them. This is the last time you'll come here, Clay."

I felt like she'd stabbed me.

"You don't get to make those sorts of decisions on your own, Thea.

You've already done more than enough. So I won't listen to you." My voice rose and a prison guard began to walk over.

"You will," she said quietly. "Because after today, I am not going to receive your visits. I won't answer your letters. And I won't take your calls. After today, we are dead to each other."

"'You can't mean that. You don't know what you're saying!'"

"I know exactly what I am saying. Exactly. Don't come back, Clay. This is goodbye. Try to find some happiness."

When she stood up, I remembered the first day I saw her, walking across the restaurant, and my heart ripped with rage.

"Happiness? Are you out of your mind?" I shouted, standing up too.

She gave an ironic smile. "Apparently not enough to be let out of prison, despite Tom's best efforts. Not for the next twenty years at least." She looked at her chewed-down nails. "A bit of jail humour for you."

"'This is *not funny*."

"It hasn't been funny for a long, long time."

"I'm sorry!" I broke. "I'm just so, so sorry."

"What do you have to be sorry for?"

"That morning, what happened. It shouldn't have. I shouldn't have left you."

"It wasn't your fault."

"We should have listened to Doctor Rosenkrantz."

"Yes, perhaps. And now we are stuck with this."

I looked at my wife, so composed. Her eyes opaque, almost without emotion. And heavily medicated, I realised.

"Please go now, Clay," she said. "Go and live your life."

"Live my life? *Live* my *life*?"

"Go," she repeated. "And maybe one day you can forgive me."

As Thea started to turn away, I grabbed her shoulder.

"You don't get to dismiss me like that. This is a marriage!"

"This *was* a marriage." She began to walk towards the exit.

"No! Stop! Look me in the eye and tell me you don't need me in your life. Tell me!"

Thea turned and walked the small distance back to me. I could feel her soft breath on my face, when she spoke to me for that last time.

"Let. Me. Go. I. Don't. Love. You. Any. More."

Part Six

Stillbirth

Sanusha (aged 27): Trying to get free

Almost 12 years since the trial and I am my mother's I.C.E. – her person to contact In Case of Emergency. And there have been some, emergencies, namely:

1. Appendicitis
2. Acute depression
3. Severe headaches
4. Recurrent memory loss from the carbon monoxide
5. Anger-management problems
6. Issues with victimisation
7. Agitation
8. A broken arm where the bone could be seen poking through.

I'm 27 and despite what my mother did to me and my family, I have been trying ever since to claw my way back. The problem is, I can never free myself from her. Ironic, considering *she's* the one in the chink. I left South Africa 3 years after starting my business – without a Matric, something to be proud of – but I have never escaped her clutches.

Why is it that as a woman, I can't avoid seeing life through my mother's eyes? I have pieced together the fragments of my childhood so many times, but they never quite fit together.

I didn't leave permanently. I was gone for 6 years, the first 4 working on boats. The Caribbean. The Med. Some of the Pacific Islands. I started on the big cruise ships, but moved to smaller vessels because I liked being involved in the details: the cogs and wheels of a luxury floating palace. I kept my mouth shut and I could fix things – the celebs loved that. I loved a celeb for a while – got photographed in a steamy clinch with her on the deck. My moments of fame in *People* magazine, until my mother, Joe and Caitie were resurrected by some over-zealous paparazzo and my lover couldn't look me in the face without flinching, their dead bodies floating between us.

I left. I found another boat, another job. Saw some more islands. Fixed some more motors. Built a bigger wall around myself.

Annie was the only person who knew who I really was. Annie and Clay. I saw him once or twice in Aus, when the boats docked. He married that chick he met in the hospital the night our babies died. Rebound, I'm guessing. Shortly after that he moved with her to Sydney.

The last time, Clay and I sat across from each other, a seagull settling on the window to check us out. I remember the cyan sky, the taste of the mussels. Salt and garlic and wine. Fake laughter. The pics of his replacement kids, Dana and Scarlett, stuck awkwardly in his wallet like he had something to prove.

"You're looking more like her as you get older," he told me.

"Don't tell me that," I said.

"You used to hate looking like Asmita."

"I know."

He put his hand out, and I measured mine out to meet it. Our fingertips touched. No more. No less.

Later, we walked along the beach. I lifted my face and we kissed, like he might have kissed my mom once. We siphoned her between our lips, our tongues. It was surreal. Thea in our saliva, our breathing. He sighed, then sat me down in the sand in front of him, my back, my head against his chest. And I felt safe; his legs along the outside of my thighs, his arms around my waist as I leant into him. We didn't speak for ages, sitting there, as the waves pulled to the rising moon. I may even have fallen asleep, dreaming in his heartbeat.

Eventually, pins and needles forced us to stand, to separate. Clay's phone buzzed and I could hear the irritation in his wife's voice. The ebb and flow of worry washing its way into their conversation.

"You need to go, Clay," I said, squeezing his hand.

"Yes."

"I'll come see you again," I said.

He nodded. "And about –"

I let his hand go. "It was nice. Gentle."

"I don't think I love her," he said.

"Mom?"

"My wife. Nathalie. I'm still so lost, Nush."

"Me too," I replied. "Sometimes I think it's all completely hopeless."

Then he straightened up, his shoulders back. "Oh, God. Don't *you* say that – I couldn't bear it."

*

After the boats, the diving, the dive mastering (2 years at Ban's Diving, a "PADI 5-Star Instructor Development Center" in Koh Tao), I was back in Cape Town. Unable to keep away, I visited my mother 3 days after I arrived. Driving through the Huguenot Tunnel as it sliced through the Du Toitskloof mountains I held my breath like I used to do as a kid with my mom on holiday – if you could do it the whole way through a tunnel, you got to make a wish.

I wish, I wish, I wish.

We never managed then, and I still didn't.

And there would be many visits like this. The queue. Shuffle-shuffle. The blunt faces, the slabs of second-hand shoes, the dusty jeans – all of us winnowed out from society by something someone we cared about had done. Later, when we'd left the prison, re-found our cars, waiting taxis and pathways, we became just like everybody else who had a secret.

Except we had bigger secrets than most.

But before each visit, we submitted ourselves to searches and gun checks. Judgement. There was no privacy. It wasn't how it was on TV. My mother, unthreatening now that she had no babies left to kill, wasn't kept out of touching distance.

I could hold her hand if I wanted to.

I didn't.

Half the time, I didn't even know what I was doing there. How much is there to say about prison food, or the early wake-up calls, the hours of sweeping the cells and corridors, because there was not much else to do?

"You could eat off the floors," my mother would say to me. "*Literally* eat off the floors! *That's* how clean it is."

But who would want to eat off the floors of a prison?

The first time, my mother looked at me. "You've been in the sun," she said.

"I've been in Thailand, Mom. I told you that."

"I forgot," she said. "I can't remember much these days, Nush. And you know what? I don't really care . . . Where did you go? Did you tell me that already?"

"Thailand," I said again.

"I always wanted to travel. Clay and I went to Paris once," she said. "I guess that'll never happen again now."

I didn't contradict her – what country would grant a visa to a convicted felon? – so I tried to paint pictures for her instead. I did this, I said to myself, because she was interested. Honestly, though, it was so much easier to talk about places than about feelings, abstractions. So I told her about the smell of the longboats, their engine throttles on full. I described the taste of phad thai: coriander and coconut milk. Swims in the soft rain, the sea like a warm bath. The feel of neoprene; soaking vats of used gear. And I especially liked to talk in numbers: 30°C; 150km/h; 400m; 30ml.

"Photos," my mother said. "Can you bring me some to stick on the walls of my cell? There's a woman here – she's from Argentina. She's got her own cell and the whole wall is decorated in pictures. Virgin Marys and crucifixes, and sirens with pouting purple lips. Her family snapshots. It's homely."

I didn't comment on the irony of this. "Do they visit?"

"No. Perhaps they've disowned her. She's difficult to talk to, anyway, although I sometimes try my French. It makes her smile, like she thinks I don't know it's a different language."

My mother's smile was too subtle to be electric, but still it jolted me to a time when I was very little and we were in Asmita Ayaa's kitchen, dancing to Wham! on the radio. Our hands clasped together, jiggling, and shouting the words to *Wake me up before you GO-GO*. So long ago – before George Michael became the toilet perv and my mother the murderess.

"I've got to go," I said, ignoring the look of disappointment on her face. "I've–" Even in this, I stumbled. What excuse did I have for cutting the visit short, except that I couldn't stand to look at her any longer? I was there, wasn't I?

Wasn't that enough?

"I'll post you some photos," I said. "I'll get them printed as soon as I get back."

I paid the toll, I drove too fast.

After that first time, I thought I'd never visit her again, wipe her out of my life for good. Any sane person would understand my need to do that. But I could only ever last 6 months, 4 months before my guilt would abrade me to breaking point. Then I forced myself back through the mountain pass, into the queue for yet another look at what had been ripped from me, the jagged edges of loss visible in every line of her face.

And probably on my face too.

Year after year.

After year.

Thea: Snapping back

We sit at a table that's dented from years of use. We're making laundro-mat hangers out of wire.

It toughens your hands. I have calluses now.

Calluses and grey tips in my hair, needing professional attention, not the nasty dyes the prison supplies for women learning the craft of hair-dressing for when they got out.

My skin is almost as grey as my hair. Not enough fresh fruit. Sunlight. Decent exercise.

On work detail, we spend a lot of time with the same people. Hell, in *prison* we spend a lot of time with the same people. I often look at the others through my medication mists, my recurring black curtain, and wonder what has brought them here. In the absence of anybody else, these are my companions, my company.

Thando has this thing she does with her hands – this constant scratching that makes a noise like pantyhose between fat thighs. Usually her hands are at her face; her caramel skin covered with glaring red gashes where she's ripped through it. Her nails are long and also sharp. She gouges up and down her arms. Sometimes they bandage her hands – big white mitten-hands that can't write, can't point, can't scratch. When the meds are working, like today, she's calmer. Folding, bending, contorting the wire so it can hold a jacket.

Thando jumped from a bridge onto a car below her on the highway. The couple inside died. She bounced and somehow survived. That's a miracle, right? Except that she didn't want to live and she ended up here. Any other woman, a middle-class woman with money and decent-enough legal representation, would have got out after a psychiatric evaluation and treatment. Out and back home years ago. Yet here she still is, here with me. Caught in limbo. In purgatory.

Fatima doesn't talk much. She wants to wear her headscarves but they're worried what she'll do with them. She stabbed her mother after fighting over the use of the family car. She talks about that car as though she's in love: a dream machine, a fantasy vehicle. (A beaten-up mustard-coloured Mazda with two broken windows and ripped seats.) Her mother she hardly mentions except vaguely, in passing. *Tik* had something to do with it. She doesn't remember the murder at all but Elizabeth, one of the counsellors, says she's blocking. Elizabeth doesn't know that Fatima's still high most of the time. It's not difficult to get drugs here if you want them. And I'm not sure that it's true what Elizabeth said: that to get better you have to remember.

I may not remember much of the present. But I remember my past all the time, and I'm not sure how this helps me.

Rabia lived near a river once. She drowned her baby in it. She has this way of looking at you as though she sees through you with her dark, unflinching eyes. In all the seven years I've known her, she hasn't expressed a moment of regret. They found her baby in a dustbin, on top of some used sanitary towels, rotting fruit and piles of beer bottles. Quarts. I don't want to be like her, but I guess I must be. Rabia without the drugs and the HIV. Does that make me better or worse?

When I allow myself to, I think of that other time. When I was a tour guide, a translator. A mother. A wife. Now I'm doing hard labour with pliers, aspiring to get on the cleaning detail. Everybody wants to get on the cleaning detail, because then we get to leave the ward. I've watched those women leave, with their mops and their buckets, and can't believe how much I long to be them. It's a long waiting list, with so many lifers wanting the privilege. Every time I get near the top of the list I lose my temper over some trifle, cause a scene and get bounced back down. I can't help sabotaging myself.

But I suppose I'm luckier than most.

Clay – oh, Clay, I can barely think of him without feeling my body seize. He married somebody else, had some new babies, replaced me; sends me money sometimes from Aus. I don't think his wife knows.

In my cell at night, I close my eyes and think about him, the ache of him like a kick in the stomach. His absence is my penance. How many times did he try to call? How many letters did I force myself to return, wishing I could just open them, read them once and imprint them on my body like Sanusha's tattoos?

I take the money, though. I have to. The house was half-mine.

Our life, half-lived.

Here in the prison, I'm learning to balance my own budget because, ironically, this is the first time in my entire life I'm making my own financial decisions. First there was Mother, then Rajit, then Clay, counting away our money and dealing with our pensions and insurance. Now I have to care for myself. I'm not good at it and that's why the prison is not at all what I expected: it's a safe, comfortable womb. Everything is provided for me via the Correctional umbilical cord. My timetable. My food. My uniform. My medication.

And sometimes even my daughter.

Sanusha looks different since coming back to South Africa. She's weary. World-weary. I can see it in her eyes. The sight of me repulses her, but she visits me. It's a shock each time I see it; each time she sees me. Sanusha knows her duty, but I think it's more than that. The elastic mother-daughter bond, it always snaps back. Despite this, the moment she arrives she can't wait to get away. She pulls like a dog on a leash. I think about untying her but I can't bring myself to. Maybe one day, we could be friends again. And if not friends, talking at the very least.

Yesterday, I took out the photos from the pre-slit envelope she once sent me – the slitting happened here, of course. Ten photos, exactly. No note, except on the back of each one there's a place and a date.

Koh Samui – Full moon party, 2004

The Katherine's engine – Kyle at work – June 2009

Boat crew – Penang cable car (2003)

Cannes – getting ready for the Film Festival (2008?)

Steep cliffs and dense woodland, our approach to Dubrovnik (July 2005)

Barcelona – Sagrada Família, Gaudí's unfinished masterpiece (mid-2005)
Pacific Diamond docks during a storm in Sydney Harbour – 2007
Repeating Captain Cook's landing at Oholei Beach and Hina's Cave, Tongatapu Island – Jan 2008
Ouzo and seafood mezedes, Kastella Hill. View of the Saronic Gulf behind (2008?)
Murano glass blowing, just outside Venice (2009, spring)

And not one photo of her in all of them. It's as though Sanusha's tantalising me, offering a brief entry into her life without actually revealing anything about herself. Who's Kyle? Why were the boat crew on the cable car? Who was at the party? What was the Australian storm like? She may as well have bought postcards. I've been studying the pictures, trying to decipher why she chose these specific places or these rare people shots. Perhaps they're the only photos she had that *didn't* include her.

Yet if I know Sanusha – and perhaps I can't even claim that – there's a subtle message in the pics. I just don't understand it. And despite my original idea to put the photos up in my cell, I don't think I will. They don't make me happy.

Sanusha's seen Clay, I know, so where's a photo of him? It's like she's offering something with one hand, and taking it back with the other. If I had the nerve, I'd ask her. But when I've seen her, Sanusha's body language has said it all: *I'll take care of me if you take care of you.*

*

And yet, that's not how it turned out.

The head of the prison called us in, one by one. It was rare to get so close to the entrance, so close to freedom, but he waved me into his office.

For a prison official, he was rather a small man, with a pug nose, a ruddy complexion and an accent so thick you could have stood a spoon in it. His skin fitted him badly, as though he'd once been not just fat, but obese. We'd heard once that his friends called him "*Oogbal*", on account of his bulbous eyes. But I'd never minded the man – he'd always shown his humanity, which was more than I could say for most of the people I encountered. I was a child killer, after all. That made me lower than pond scum. Yet somehow not to him.

"Sit," he said, then poured me a glass of water. "So, *hoe gaan dit*?"

"I'm fine," I said. It was true, because on the days when the shadows weren't colonising my brain, I *was* fine.

He smiled. "I haff good news for you." Then he pushed the order across the table. "*Goeie nuus, jong.*"

I picked up the paper, and he slid his BIC across the table. "I'm happy to borrow you my pen today, Middleton."

"But why?" I said as I took in the words on the paper.

"Mr Zuma's feeling generous. For Freedom Day, we give you freedom, hey?"

He went on to sum it up succinctly: Full prisons. Space needed for the *real* killers. The hijackers, rapists, armed robbers. (He emphasised this with a finger across his throat followed by miming of a gunslinger.) Parole, and with only one misdeed I'd be back in here, in Worcester, in a second.

With this, Oogbal snapped his fingers, the click of skin on skin re-sounding.

"One second, you hear me, Middleton? But I trust you. I've thought sometimes you shouldn't be here. I've seen how you are suffering your sins. Suffering your sins every day."

"But what will I do?" I said.

"*Ekskuus?*"

"What will I do out there? In the world?"

This time, Oogbal did look flummoxed. "In the world?" he said then, as though I'd uttered a profanity. He sat there a moment, with a fixed expression of consternation. Then after a long silence, it came to him: "You'll be free!" he said, then smiled, having worked out how to answer my absurd question. As if his answer was My Answer.

"Free?"

"Free to live, to move, to put your feet in the sea!"

"But where will I live? How will I earn a living?"

"*Ag, toe maar*, Middleton. It sorts itself out. You lived before? You earned before? Anyways, there is programmes to help you." His face had grown increasingly puce, and I realised my troubles were already weighing on him.

I was supposed to be thrilled. I was meant to be charmed. Excited. Enthusiastic.

"I'm not ready," I said, then. "I don't deserve this." Was I crying? My face seemed wet, and I wiped it with the back of my hand.

"You're feeling all *deurmekaar*, I understand, but you are leaving this place, Middleton. Now pull yourself together. Your –" he checked a piece of paper "– daughter, Sanusha, *ja*? She will be contacted, unless you want to ask for a telephone call?"

"No, that's fine."

Oogbal reached out and patted my hand. It was a simple gesture, but in prison comfort was hard to come by. I braced myself to stand up.

"Be happy, hey?" Oogbal said. "You can start again."

I nodded, already overwhelmed by panic. Oogbal pushed the paper and pen towards me again. I signed.

My babies were dead and I was going to be free.

But how could I possibly live with myself?

Thank you

To Mike Nicol, who has mentored me and shared his invaluable writing experience and knowledge.

To Janita Holtzhausen and the team at Human & Rousseau for giving me the wonderful gift of an audience.

To my editor Nicola Rijsdijk, for her thoughtful insights and attention to the details I missed.

To William Booth, South African criminal lawyer extraordinaire, for considering my questions seriously and giving a knockout show in court, while still managing to explain the trial as it progressed.

To Martin Truter for his police procedural and forensic experience and for not incarcerating me when I asked about the best way to kill people.

To Sean Kaliski and Claudia de Klercq at Valkenberg Hospital for their insight on psychiatry and filicide.

To Warrant Officer Avron Trautman for organising for me to get into Pollsmoor – not an easy feat!

To the staff at Pollsmoor Prison, who asked not to be named, for the tour and information on life in prison.

To Nerisee Marais for sharing her wonderful culture and always giving thought to my somewhat strange questions.

To Regina Marais for her knowledge about premature birth and its complications.

To Linda Lewis, psychologist and author, for first interesting me in postnatal distress and psychosis.

To the various friends in my life who offered me both appropriate (and inappropriate!) vocabulary for my characters.

To Common Ground for much-needed coffee, encouragement and a place to write.

To my Master's class at UCT for sharing.

To my writer friends and fellow Bread Loafers all over the US, for the inspiration and encouragement.

And last but not least, to my family, especially Dave, Jed and Cole, for understanding that if I do not have time to write, I am not a whole person.

Information on Postnatal Depression and Psychosis

Post Natal Depression Support Association, South Africa (PNDSA)
  National help-line: 082 882 0072
  Sms 'help' and your name to 082 882 0072
  Email: help@pndsa.org.za
  HEAD OFFICE
  33 Bishoplea Road, Claremont, Cape Town
  Office no: 021 823 7333
  Fax no: 086 645 2536
  Email: info@pndsa.org.za
  Website: www.pndsa.org.za

Cylc, L., 2005, Classifications and Descriptions of Parents Who Commit Filicide, in *Concepts*, viewed 10 April 2011, from http://concept.journals. villanova.edu/article/view/256.

Lewis, L. & Marais, P., 2011, *When Your blessings Don't Count – A Guide to Recognising and Overcoming Postnatal Distress*, Metz Press, Welgemoed, South Africa.

McKee, R., 2006, *Why Mothers Kill – A Forensic Psychologist's Casebook*, Oxford University Press, New York, US.

Pregnancy Info, 2011, *Postpartum Psychosis*, viewed 17 March 2011 on http://www.pregnancy-info.net/postpartum_psychosis.html.

Sichel, D. & Driscoll, J.W., 1999, *Women's Moods, Women's Minds: What Every Woman Must Know About Hormones, the Brain, and Emotional Health*, William Morrow & Company, New York, NY.

Spinelli, M.G., 2005, *Infanticide – Psychosocial and Legal Perspectives on Mothers who Kill*, American Psychiatric Publishing, Washington, US & London, UK.

Made in the USA
Coppell, TX
29 April 2020

23496614R00206